THE TRIKON DECEPTION

Praised by the critics

'Fast and furious.' *Booklist*

'Thrilling . . . relentlessly believable . . . one hell of a story. I didn't want *The Trikon Deception* to end.' *Keith Ferrell, Omni Magazine*

fellow writers

'The combined efforts of Ben Bova, a master of science fiction, and Bill Pogue, experienced astronaut who worked with Skylab, have produced a thrilling account. It is a book soundly based on accurate scientific probabilities. The result is exciting.' *James A. Michener*

'Pulse-pounding . . . has velcro hooks to pull you from one page to the next . . . Bova's and Pogue's talents match perfectly.' *Walter Boyne*

'I believe that the science fiction author who will have the greatest effect on the world is Ben Bova' *Ray Bradbury*

and an expert

'Frighteningly real . . . Will startle and surprise the reader.' *Alan Bean, Commander of Skylab II*

Also by Ben Bova

Mars
Death Dream

About the authors:

Ben Bova holds degrees from the State University of New York and Temple University, Philadelphia. He has taught writing at Harvard University and at the Hayden Planetarium in New York, and lectures regularly on topics dealing with high technology and the future.

An award-winning editor, president Emeritus of the National Space Society and a Fellow of the British Interplanetary Society, Ben Bova is also the author of more than eighty futuristic novels and non-fiction books. *Mars* and *Death Dream* are the most recent. He and his wife live in Florida and Connecticut.

Bill Pogue, astronaut and pilot of Skylab, has clocked thousands of hours in space. He flew for the United States Air Force Thunderbirds and was a test pilot for both the USAF and the Royal Air Force before his selection as an astronaut in 1966. He served in the support crew of the Apollo 7 and Apollo 11 missions, and was the pilot for Skylab 4, the final Skylab mission. He is the author of *How Do You Go to the Bathroom in Space?*

The Trikon Deception

Ben Bova
and
Bill Pogue

NEW ENGLISH LIBRARY

First published in 1992 as a Tor Book, published by
Tom Doherty Associates, Inc.
First published in Great Britain in 1994 by Hodder and Stoughton
a division of Hodder Headline PLC

A New English Library paperback

10 9 8 7 6 5 4 3 2 1

A CIP catalogue record for this title is available from
the British Library.

ISBN 0 450 58882 3

Printed and bound in Great Britain by
Cox & Wyman Ltd, Reading, Berkshire

Hodder and Stoughton Ltd
A Division of Hodder Headline PLC
338 Euston Road
London NW1 3BH

**TO BARBARA AND JEAN,
AND ESPECIALLY TO KEVIN.**

ACKNOWLEDGMENT

PERMISSION TO QUOTE from the *Science* magazine issue of 28 September 1990 (vol. 249, p. 1503) was graciously given by the American Association for the Advancement of Science and by the author of the article, Leslie Roberts.

The lyrics quoted are from "Space Oddity," words and music by David Bowie, copyright © 1969 by Westminster Music Ltd. London; TRO-Essex Music International Inc., New York, owns all publication rights for the USA and Canada. Used by permission.

"Ashes to Ashes," by David Bowie, permission granted by Isolar, New York.

"Rocket Man," by Elton John and Bernie Taupin, copyright © 1972 Songs of PolyGram International, Inc.

AUTHOR'S NOTE

DIMENSIONS ABOARD Trikon Station are frequently expressed in the metric system. For those not familiar with this European system of measurement:

One millimeter is about twice the width of the lead in a mechanical pencil.

One centimeter is roughly the thickness of a piece of sliced bread.

One meter is about three inches longer than a yard.

One kilometer is almost two-thirds of a mile.

One kilogram equals 2.205 pounds.

4 SEPTEMBER 1998
TRIKON STATION

TO THE HUMAN eye, space is serene. From three hundred miles above its surface, our Earth appears as a vast, smoothly curved panorama of deep blue oceans and brown wrinkled landmasses decked with parades of gleaming white clouds, ever changing, eternally beckoning. Our world shines with warmth, with beauty, with life.

Floating in the emptiness of space three hundred miles above the luminous curving glory of Earth is a glittering jewel, a diamond set against the infinite darkness of the cold void.

From a distance, hanging against that black infinity, it seems delicate, fragile, a child's toy construction of gossamer and dreams. It is not until you approach that you realize how large it really is.

Nearly three football fields across, its skeleton is a giant diamond of gleaming alloy girders. Ten sparkling white aluminum cylinders form a raft fixed to its central truss; three of them bear the painted flags of nations: on one cylinder are the twenty-two flags of United Europe; on another is the rising sun of Japan; a third displays the Stars and Stripes of the United States and the Maple Leaf emblem of Canada.

At two corners of the huge diamond are attached two bulbous, blimplike structures, burnt orange in color and far larger than the white cylinders. Once they were external tanks for space shuttles; now they are extensions of this island in space, moored to the diamond-shaped structure like giant balloons. The gently tapering nose of one of the ETs points directly forward, the other directly aft, as the diamond knifes through the calm emptiness of orbital space. The trailing ET bears the curious circle-and-arrow symbol of the planet Mars.

Robots slide back and forth across the station's main truss, silent in the airless vacuum, their metal wheels clasping the special guide rails, their spindly arms ending in gripping pincers strong enough to hold hardware that would weigh tons back on Earth. From the topmost corner of the diamond, bristling batteries of instruments aim outward at the stars while others, at the nadir corner, peer down at the dazzling blue sphere of Earth with its white swirls of clouds. On the station's trailing edge, broad wings of deep-violet solar panels drink in sunlight while smaller, darker companions radiate away the heat generated within the station.

For there are men and women living and working at this outpost in space. This is Trikon Station, the first industrial research laboratory to be built in orbit.

Trikon.

To the human eye, space should be serene. Trikon station floated in its orbit on the sunlit side of the Earth, passing across the radiantly intense blue of the wide Pacific, adorned with clouds of brilliant, purest white.

The station shuddered. Like a giant sail suddenly caught in a crosswind. Like a man startled by danger.

Alarms screeched in every laboratory and living module, Klaxons hooted along the lengths of its passageways, and a computer-synthesized woman's voice called from every intercom speaker in the station with maddening mechanical calm:

"Emergency. Emergency. Major malfunction. All personnel to CERV stations. All personnel to CERV stations. Prepare to abandon the station."

No one cared. No one heeded the alarms. No one moved toward the Crew Emergency Reentry Vehicles.

From the astronomical observatory at the uppermost corner of Trikon Station two space-suited figures emerged, one of them encased in the "armchair" rig of a manned maneuvering unit, MMU.

Dan Tighe, commander of Trikon Station, fought back murderous fury and a terrible fear that clawed at his chest as he watched the space station begin to wobble and sway. Through the heavily tinted visor of his helmet he saw the bulbous burnt-orange structure of the Mars module detach itself from the station and begin to drift away, like a rudderless ship caught by an evil tide. The broad wings of the solar panels were swaying, undulating visibly. Dan knew they would break up within minutes.

We're all going to die, said a voice inside his head. We're going to die and it's my fault. All my own goddamned stupid fault.

15 AUGUST 1998
TRIKON STATION

Names are important. When we hammered together this consortium of major industrial corporations I insisted upon a name that would reflect its spirit of international cooperation, a name that would not offend any of the sensitive egos among the various boards of directors, or in the governments to whom they paid taxes. The corporations were based in Europe, North America, and Japan. Three continents: Trikon.

The original spelling proposed was Tricon; however, my public relations consultants suggested that this might cause confusion over the hard or soft pronunciation of the letter c. The letter k connotes strength and provides an echo of classical Greece.

So they said.

—From the diary of Fabio Bianco,
CEO, Trikon International

THE STATION HAD been in operation for more than a year on the day when the trouble began.

David Nutt still encountered that moment of vertigo, that feeling that his insides were adrift and he was falling into a strange pastel-colored abyss. Everything was shifting, swirling like a kaleidoscope.

Clutching at the metal edge of the entry hatch, Dave took a deep breath and lined himself up with the strip of black tape stuck onto the bottom of its lip.

"This side down, stupid," he muttered to himself.

The pastels tumbled into perspective. A long cylinder with a pale blue-floor and yellow ceiling. Silver and white equipment in racks along the walls. Ovens, centrifuge, microscopes all where they should be, and right-side-up. But it didn't help that the damned technician was floating almost on his head at the far end of the lab.

The American scientific laboratory module had been nicknamed The Bakery by an earlier rotation of researchers. The pastel colors were the brainchildren of a team of psychologists who had never left the ground. Nutt was grateful for their help. After six months aboard Trikon Station, he still had trouble orienting himself whenever he moved from one module to another. In the microgravity world of the space station, with everything weightless, he had trouble telling up from down without help. If he pulled himself through the hatch at any angle except true vertical The Bakery became a distorted alien world and his guts would start churning. Nutt was a confirmed "flatlander." He felt queasy unless he had his feet on a solid floor, even in the almost-zero gravity of the space station.

Fifteen meters away, at the far end of the cylinder, Stu Roberts was loading tempered glassware into the two huge microwave ovens that had inspired the lab's nickname. His thick mop of brick-red hair was puffed up into a wild, waving nest of weightless microgravity snakes. The mesh hairnet he was supposed to be wearing was nowhere in sight. His white coveralls looked grimy and spattered. Thin-faced, lean, and loose-jointed as a scarecrow, Roberts was making this rotation the longest six months of Nutt's life.

Roberts fancied himself a creative soul. Simple tasks such as sterilizing glassware and monitoring experiments were too easy for him, so he constantly poked himself into Nutt's research. He invented shortcuts, misused organic material, and analyzed data in ways that only he could interpret, all with an irrepressible cheerfulness that irritated Nutt beyond measure.

Roberts closed the oven door, then floated upside down over to the keyboard that controlled the ovens and other equipment and deftly tapped out a combination. He clamped a pair of earphones over his wild hair and immediately started to convulse, feet kicking wildly and arms flailing at tiny spheres of color that bubbled up around his head. A stranger might have thought that Roberts was being electrocuted or zapped by lethal microwaves. Dave knew better.

Heaving a sigh, Nutt pulled himself through the hatch. Properly oriented, he could maneuver through the narrow confines of The Bakery fairly well. It was almost like swimming in air instead of water. The microscope and centrifuge workstations slid quickly past before he grabbed a handhold and steadied himself at the refrigeration section. Roberts's convulsions had slowed down. He was moving in time to rock music from a portable compact-disc player Velcroed to the ceiling between the strips of fluorescent lights. Nutt could hear its thin wail and the thump of a heavy bass beat. The kid must have the earphones up to max, he thought. He'll be deaf before he's thirty.

The colored spheres floating around Roberts's red mane were globules of water shot through with dyes used for experiments, the kid's version of psychedelic lighting effects.

Roberts's back was still to him, twitching in time to the music. Nutt pushed himself past the module's computer terminal, reached the CD player, and cut off the music.

"Circus time is over," he said.

Roberts abruptly turned his head. His body automatically twisted in the opposite direction; his flailing arms made the colored spheres scatter. He caught himself and for a moment hung in midair, a lean youthful scarecrow in dirty white laboratory coveralls hovering a scant few inches in front of the bearded, puffy-faced "old man" of nearly forty who was his boss. Nutt was slightly pudgy and potbellied back on Earth; in the weightlessness of the station his body fluids had shifted to make him look even rounder.

"Aw, Dave," Roberts whined as he yanked off the earphones, "you never let me have any fun."

"Fun is for the ex/rec room. Find your hairnet and do something about those spheres. If one of them gets into a specimen you'll have ruined six months' work."

Roberts hung up the earphones and then shepherded the spheres into a group and pressed them against the door of a small freezer. They adhered to the cold surface and formed perfect hemispheres. Soon they would evaporate and leave smudges of food coloring that could be wiped off with a damp cloth.

"Did you unzip the wrong end of your sleep restraint?" asked Roberts. One of the most annoying things about the kid was that he constantly tried to adapt Earthbound clichés to the realities of life on a space station. Few translated well. "I thought you were happy about going home."

"I'm damn happy about going home. But there's this little matter of a report I have to write in order to justify all the money we're being paid."

Nutt shoved himself backwards to the computer terminal and slipped his stockinged feet into a pair of loops attached to the floor. Chairs were useless in microgravity; it took more work to force the body into a sitting position than to stay on one's feet. All the work surfaces were breast high because under the weightless conditions one's arms tended to float up almost to shoulder level.

Standing at the chest-high desk, his body hunched

slightly in a zero-gee crouch, Nutt began pecking at the computer keyboard. After the obligatory beeps and grunts, the display screen lit up in bright blue and spelled out in cheery yellow letters: GOOD MORNING! TODAY IS THE FIRST DAY OF THE REST OF YOUR LIFE!

Another of Roberts's little cutenesses. Nutt cast the technician a sour look.

He entered his password, received clearance, and typed in the preliminary set of instructions he had written with the help of a programmer back on Earth. The computer responded with the date and the time that each file had last been accessed.

Nutt felt his heart spasm in his chest.

"Were you in here last night?"

"When?" asked Roberts.

"Two A.M."

"You're kidding, right?"

"What about Wilson and the other techs?"

"Beats me," said Roberts.

"The computer says my files were last accessed at two A.M.," said Nutt. He typed in another command; the computer responded with another message. "Holy shit! There's been a download!"

"What?"

"A download." Nutt typed furiously, his stomach wrenching with each response that played across the monitor screen. "The genetic files. Goddammit! Some sonofabitch copied all my genetic files!"

"Dave, there's no problem."

"No problem? Six fucking months of work stolen and you say no problem?"

"If you'll let me explain . . ."

"Explain what? The computer's already explained everything. Somebody slipped in here at two this morning and downloaded all the genetic files!"

"There's nothing to worry about," said Roberts.

"Nothing to worry about!" Nutt shouted. "I'm not talking about a glitch in an experiment! I'm talking about a career at stake. My career!"

Nutt unlooped his feet and pushed away from the computer and its terrible string of messages so hard that he sailed across the width of the lab and banged his head against a cabinet on the opposite wall. The pain stunned him momentarily. He tumbled slowly, running his fingers through his hair and checking for blood. Roberts grabbed his arm to steady his movement, but the touch only angered him.

"I've got to tell Tighe." Nutt yanked away from Roberts's grip, spinning himself halfway toward the hatch.

"Dave, don't!"

But Nutt swam away toward the hatch, his shouted curses fading to echoes.

"Well, if you want to make an asshole of yourself, be my guest," said Roberts to the empty lab. He patted the hip pocket of his coveralls.

Mission control for Trikon Station was at Houston. Many of the consortium's European members had objected, but it made more sense to lease time and equipment from NASA's existing Manned Space Center than to build an entirely new complex somewhere else.

So it was at 0753 hours central daylight time that Commander Dan Tighe closed the light-blue plastic accordion-fold door of the cramped cubbyhole that served as his office. It was no larger than a telephone booth wedged into a forward corner of the command module.

His regular morning call to Mission Control was scheduled for 0800, as usual. And after that he was supposed to see the station doctor for his weekly exam. Like most fliers, Dan Tighe did not trust doctors, not even attractive female doctors. He rummaged through the small cabinet built into the corner of his office where the curving shell of the module met the forward bulkhead. His face, red and chafed, was set in a grim scowl of determination.

It was a face built of contradictions: finely sculpted cheekbones and a hawk's nose that had been broken long ago when he had crash-landed a crippled jet fighter. Strong stubborn jaw with a mouth that seemed almost too small for it, lips as thin and sensitive as a poet's. He kept his dark brown hair short enough to meet the old military regulations, but combed it forward to conceal his receding hairline. The gray at his temples bothered him, even though women called it distinguished.

And the eyes: electric blue, vital, brilliant. The eyes of an eagle, a flier, probing incessantly, never still, never satisfied. But now they were wary, guarded, the eyes of a man who had been defeated and banished. The eyes of a man who wanted to be alone in the cockpit of a nimble supersonic jet, but found himself smothered in the responsibilities of commanding a glorified schoolhouse that plodded along a fixed and calculated orbit—and in danger of losing even that.

A small bonsai bush trimmed into the shape of a bird floated at the end of a tether attached to the wall of his cramped office. Tighe whispered to it, "Sorry, no time for you this morning," and gently pushed it out of his way as he searched through the Velcro-lined shelves of the narrow cabinet.

At last he found what he was looking for: the blood-pressure cuff. With a grunt of satisfaction he rolled up the left sleeve of his coveralls and wrapped the plastic around his biceps. Taking a deep breath that was supposed to calm him, he inflated the cuff and then read off the glowing digital numbers on its tiny electronic display: 163 over 101. The readout was adjusted for the effects of microgravity. Not bad, he thought. But not good enough.

The command module was the smallest of all the sections that made up the Trikon space station, and the most densely packed. While the laboratory and habitat modules were each fifteen meters long, the command module's cylinder was half that length. It was jammed with computer systems that tracked everything and everyone aboard the station, communications gear that kept Tighe and his crew in constant touch with Earth, and a command and control center that maintained the station's life-support systems and external equipment. Dan's office and the infirmary were wedged into opposite ends of the cramped module. Next to the cubbyhole infirmary was the sick bay: three sleep restraints fastened against the only bare spot on any of the walls. As if to compensate for the crowding, it was the only module with a view: a trio of small fused-silica viewing ports were built into the bulkhead at the command and control station.

Tighe anchored his slippered feet in the loops at the base of the chest-high desk that held his personal computer and tapped out the instructions that patched it into the station's communications network. He plugged in the headset and clamped it on, adjusting the pin-sized microphone in front of his mouth. Make it fast, he told himself. Give yourself a few minutes to trim the bonsai and relax before you let *her* take your blood pressure.

The daily transmission from Earth began precisely on time.

"Houston to Trikon Station," scratched a voice. The display screen unscrambled to reveal the bullet head of Tom Henderson, ceiling lights gleaming on his bald dome.

"This is Trikon. I read you, Houston," replied Tighe.

"Hello, Dan. How you doin', boy? You look redder'n a beet."

"I ran out of razor blades and had to use the wind-up. Beats the hell out of your face."

"Looks like you'll have to make do without blades

for a few days more. Hurricane Caroline is stalled in the Atlantic, so the shuttle's being delayed."

"How long?"

"Three days, maybe five. Depends on when Caroline clears out."

"Christ," said Tighe. "I have a frazzled crew, a bunch of immature scientists, and now this."

"Can't do anything about Mother Nature," said Henderson. "And you forgot the Martians."

"I'm trying to forget about them."

The two men ran through their daily housekeeping chores—analyzing the amount of food, water, air, and fuel remaining on board, plotting the orbital path, coordinating the photographs that would be taken by the camera array on the station's nadir platform. Meteorologists were especially anxious to get all the photos of Caroline that they could provide. One task originally scheduled for today's communication—fixing the rendezvous with the shuttle—would have to wait.

"One more thing," said Henderson. "Trikon has added another scientist to the next rotation. His name is Hugh O'Donnell. American biochemist. I don't have his file yet, but I see that he has standing orders to report to your medical officer on a daily basis."

"Health risk?"

"Looks it." Henderson arched his eyebrows. "I'll shoot you his file as soon as I receive it."

"Keep me posted on the shuttle."

"Roger that," said Henderson. "Out."

Tighe removed the headset and clipped it to its receptacle on the wall. It was important to fasten down everything in microgravity. Otherwise they somehow floated away, lost until they turned up stuck to an intake ventilator grid. Tighe remembered waking up in the middle of the night on his first shuttle flight to find a green snake gliding toward him. It took him a couple of panicked heartbeats to realize that it was the garden hose that one of the mission specialists had brought aboard for a botany experiment. The jerk hadn't tied it down properly and it was undulating like a cobra across the middeck section where the crew slept.

Then he remembered his last shuttle flight, and felt his pulse quickening with anger. The bonsai bird hovered near his shoulder. He nuzzled its beak. Calm me down, pal, he said to the green bird. Calm me down before they throw me out of this job, too.

Somebody rapped on the bulkhead. Before Tighe could answer, the accordion door squealed back and Dave Nutt pushed through. He was gasping for air. His T-shirt had come untucked from his nylon pants and rode up over his paunchy stomach.

"What's wrong, Dave?" Tighe liked Nutt; otherwise he would have snapped at him for barging into his office. Nutt was dedicated and sober, not at all like the other cases of arrested development Trikon called scientists. But now he was wild-eyed, panting, his hair and beard beaded with perspiration.

"My computer!" heaved Nutt. "Someone's tampered with it!"

"What? How?"

"Downloaded my research files."

The scientists were always complaining to Tighe about people tampering with their work. Although the corporations that made up the Trikon consortium were supposed to be working cooperatively, industrial espionage seemed to be the major industry aboard the station. Most of the accusations were false alarms bred by overactive imaginations or personal animosities among the scientists. Or at least they could not be proved to Tighe's satisfaction.

"How do you know?" Tighe asked.

"I have a subprogram that logs every use. Somebody went into our module at two A.M. and downloaded my goddamned files!"

"I'd better take a look," said Tighe, mentally post-poning his date with the doctor.

Stu Roberts was still in The Bakery when Tighe and Nutt arrived. Now that Nutt had taken the extreme step of actively involving the station commander, Roberts decided to lie low and let the scientist embarrass himself. He hovered on the edge of audibility as Nutt gave Tighe a fevered explanation of the messages appearing on the computer monitor.

Tighe had only a general idea of the work being conducted in the three Trikon laboratory modules. He knew that the project involved microbial genetics: the scientists were trying to engineer a bug that would eat pollutants or toxic wastes or something like that. His interest in the bug was purely practical. As station commander, he constantly worried about containment of all the potentially toxic agents used by the scientists in their research. Accidental release of bacteria, caustic chemicals, or pollutants could wreak havoc in the delicately controlled environment of the station. In space you cannot open a window for fresh air. One mistake with chemical or biological materials could kill everyone aboard very swiftly.

Tighe had worked with many scientists during his years in the Air Force and with NASA. He was accustomed to competing philosophies because scientists and the military usually were at odds. But on Trikon Station there were cliques within cliques. The Americans stayed with the Americans. The Japanese stayed with the Japanese. And the Europeans, true to their history, fought among themselves as well as with all the others. While the corporations that employed them trumpeted the benefits of cooperative research in slick brochures and television specials, the scientists were more competitive than Olympic athletes. They never traded information willingly and regarded each other with the warmth of professional assassins.

The situation was particularly tense just prior to a rotation. Every ninety days a third of the scientific staff was replaced by new people from Earth. That was when a successful industrial spy could take his loot back home.

"That's what happened," said Nutt, winding up his explanation.

Tighe leaned close to the keyboard as if scrutinizing it for fingerprints. He realized how ridiculous he must have looked and pushed himself away.

"What do you want me to do about it?" he asked.

"Search everybody on the station! Force whoever downloaded the files to turn them over."

"I'm not a policeman."

"This is very sensitive material! It's . . ."

"And I'm in a very sensitive position. I'm not just dealing with an international contingent of scientists. There's a couple of dozen governments who view these scientists as diplomats. If I start strong-arming people without good cause, the shit will fall on my head, nobody else's."

"You're saying I should work for six months, have my results stolen, and do absolutely nothing about it?"

"The files are still in your computer, right?" said Tighe. "They've been copied, not stolen."

Nutt reluctantly nodded.

"Then consider yourself a benefactor of mankind."

"The hell I will!"

"You're supposed to be working cooperatively with all the others, aren't you? Why the panic?"

"*I want the credit!*" Nutt snarled through gritted teeth. "I did the work and I want the credit for it. The work's got to be published in *my* name. A scientist's reputation depends on his publications, his discoveries. Don't you understand that?"

Roberts decided it had gone far enough. Gliding over toward his flustered boss and the tight-lipped station commander, he interrupted, "Hey, there's really no problem."

Tighe looked at Roberts, then cocked his head toward Nutt. The scientist's bearded, puffy face twisted into a grimace of exasperation.

"Explain yourself," Tighe said to Roberts.

"Dave put that security subprogram into his PC because he was worried about theft. I had a suspicion that the subprogram could be fooled, so I played around with it. Sure enough, I was able to hack into the files and download them."

Roberts produced a diskette from a pouch pocket of his pants.

"*You* did it!" screamed Nutt. He pushed himself at Roberts and knocked the diskette out of his hand. The diskette skittered crazily in midair while the two men tumbled in a confusion of arms and legs. Tighe pried them apart.

"Explain yourself," Tighe said again to Roberts. "Fast."

"That wasn't Dave's files," said Roberts, rubbing his forehead gingerly. "It was another subprogram I wrote to protect the files. Whoever downloaded them will never be able to access them, not without jamming his own computer."

Tighe shot a look at Nutt, who was glaring at the technician.

"Say that again," Tighe commanded Roberts.

"I wrote in a bug that's programmed to be triggered by an unauthorized download. When somebody tries to access the stolen files, his monitor will fill with I AM A THIEF in big yellow characters and the bug will replicate itself in his computer."

Tighe suddenly grabbed Roberts by the front of his coveralls.

"Can you delete that program?"

"I think so."

"Don't tell me what you think." Tighe wedged one

foot into a floor loop and shook Roberts as if he were made of straw. "Yes or no? Can you delete it without starting the bug?"

"Yeah. . . . Yes!"

"Do it. Top priority. And when you're finished, find that disk and break it into little pieces. If we're fast enough and lucky enough, we just might get through this alive."

Tighe pulled himself into a tuck and shot like a torpedo through the hatchway.

"Am I missing something?" said Roberts.

"You fucking idiot!" screamed Nutt. "The computer terminals are all tied into the station's mainframe! If whoever downloaded the file tries to access them here, that bug will worm its way into life support and kill us all!"

15 AUGUST 1998
FLORIDA

The Earth is dying. The human race is rushing head-long toward extinction.

The problem is not for our grandchildren, or our children. The problem is ours. It is happening now. The dying has already begun.

We are killing ourselves. Smog chokes our cities. Farmlands are becoming barren while megatons of chemical fertilizers poison groundwater. Deserts are expanding, and rain forests are rapidly being destroyed. The ozone layer is being eaten away by pollution. Global temperatures are rising toward the greenhouse level.

Worst of all, the oceans—the great embracing mother seas that are the foundation of all life on our planet—the oceans are being fouled so thoroughly that all life will die off in a few short years.

We do not have a century to clean up the environment. We do not even have decades. The oceans are already beginning to die. We are in a race against our own extinction.

And while the Earth dies, most people go about their daily lives as if nothing is happening. Unthinking, uncaring, they are helping to kill the Earth, murdering their own world, committing mass suicide.

A few persons are aware of the danger. Very few. Some try to get their fellow humans to pay attention, to stop fouling the Earth. Some even blame our modern technology for polluting our air and water to the point where the entire environment is beginning to collapse around us.

They are almost right.

The basic problem is that human habits change slowly, so slowly. A hundred thousand years ago, what did it matter to a Stone Age hunter that his campfire sent smoke into the air, or that he urinated into a clear mountain brook? But today, with six billion humans burning and urinating, life on Earth cannot survive much longer.

There are those who say we must stop all technology and return to a simpler way of life. How can that be done without killing most of the people on Earth? We depend on our technology to produce food for us, to give us heat and light, to protect us against disease. To stop our technology would mean allowing billions to starve and freeze and die.

Instead of stopping technology, we must invent new technologies, clean and efficient ways to do all that our old technologies have done for us—without polluting our world to death.

And we must invent a means to clean up the filth that is choking our air and our water, destroying the atmosphere and the oceans. We need that now, if we are to survive the next few years.

That is why I created Trikon. To save the world. To save the human race.

But salvation means change, and most people fear change more than anything else. To save the Earth means that we must engage in genetic research. There is no other way. Only by developing new forms of life, creating microbes that can eat up our pollutants and convert them into harmless biodegradable waste matter, can we hope to cleanse the Earth quickly enough to avert our own destruction.

Yet to the great masses of people all around the Earth, genetic research is new, and what is new to them is terrifying.

So I decided that the genetic research would have to be done in orbit, entirely off the Earth. Too many important people are frightened of having something go wrong, causing a man-made plague or some other disaster. It is a foolish fear, but it is very real.

In the U.S. and many other nations, it is impossible to do the research that we need. The U.S. Supreme Court, no less, decided against field testing of genetically altered plants and bacteria, stating that "damage to the environment from testing cannot be ruled out to a scientific certainty," even though there have been no recorded incidents of accidental release of genetically altered organisms into the environment.

This proved to me that the pressures against genetic experiments are getting worse. We want to save the world, but the world does not trust us!

There is literally nowhere on Earth that scientists can do the research that needs to be done. That is why we needed a research laboratory in space. No national government would do it. No single corporation could afford to risk the necessary investment capital. That is why Trikon Station had to be a multinational effort by the multinational corporations.

To save the world. To keep the human race from going the way of the dinosaurs.

> —From a speech by Fabio Bianco,
> CEO, Trikon International, to the
> United Nations Committee on the
> Global Environmental Crisis, 22
> April 1997 (Earth Day)

HUGH O'DONNELL TREMBLED, soaked with sweat.

"Don't worry, O'Donnell, my main man. No jury in this state will convict you."

Pancho Weinstein, Esq., directed O'Donnell's attention to the jury box. One juror drooled, another played solitaire, a third had his hand stuffed into his shirt à la Napoleon. All were cross-eyed.

O'Donnell turned back to the gallery where Stacey, his live-in girlfriend, sat in the first row. She wore black stockings and a miniskirt short enough to reveal the garters crossing her thighs.

"I'm cold," she said with a pout.

Weinstein plucked O'Donnell's motorcycle jacket from the back of his chair and tossed it to Stacey. She smiled and drew her tongue across her lips.

"Order!" The judge banged a ball peen hammer, then affixed a surgeon's lamp to his forehead. "I'm as ready as I'll ever be."

A bailiff wearing polka-dot suspenders danced into the center of the courtroom.

"Foundation for Thus 'n Such versus Agri Bio Futuro Tech Something or Other," he announced through a megaphone. "Aw hell, read the program."

"Oh, that one," said the judge. "The defendant is directed to rise so we all can take a look at his mug."

Weinstein elbowed O'Donnell in the ribs, then blew Stacey a kiss. O'Donnell struggled to his feet. The people in the gallery hissed. At the opposite table, the foundation's attorney floated on a perfect cumulus cloud. He was dressed in a long white robe; a halo circled his head.

"What'll it be?" said the judge. "Testimony evaluated by an impartial jury, or would you two rather just duke it out?"

"Duke it out," said O'Donnell.

"That's what I say," said the judge. "Let's hear the evidence."

A young boy materialized on the witness stand. He looked like a normal teenager except for the tomato plant growing out of his shoulder. The tomatoes were ripe enough to pick.

"I grew up next to a field sprayed with SuperGro Microbial Frost Retardant produced by that man." The boy leveled a leafy finger at O'Donnell. "The tomatoes were very juicy."

He pulled one from the plant and offered it to the judge.

"Not on your life, baby," said the judge. "Next."

The boy dissolved and re-formed as a pretty woman with vines for hair. A watermelon hung from each ear.

"I worked on a farm that used GroFast Microbial Fertilizer," she said. "We grew watermelons in five weeks. But as you can see, progress had its price." She tossed her head and one of the watermelons slapped the judge in the face.

"I think we've heard enough," the judge said as he readjusted his surgeon's lamp. "Has the jury reached a verdict?"

"Shouldn't they deliberate?" O'Donnell asked. But Weinstein did not answer. Stacey sat on his lap with her tongue in his mouth.

The foreman stood and tapped the jury rail with a conducting wand. The rest of the jurors began to chant: "O'Donnell, O'Donnell, O'Donnell . . ."

"We the members of the jury," said the foreman, "being duly constituted in the State of Grace, and otherwise perfectly fit to determine the issues presented here, find the defendant guilty of playing with nature and otherwise trying to make the world a better place."

"Couldn't have said it better myself." The judge looked at his watch. "Might as well sentence now. Has the jury a recommendation?"

"Sentence?" cried O'Donnell. "This isn't a criminal trial. You can't send me to jail. I'm a scientist. I've committed no crimes."

But everyone ignored him. The jury, whose chanting had reached a crescendo, suddenly lowered its collective voice to a whisper. Slowly a new chant rose in volume: "OD, OD, OD . . ."

"What a clever idea," said the judge. "Saves the state a ton of cash."

A black suitcase appeared at O'Donnell's feet. It began to shake, as if something insider were trying to escape, then burst open. A storm of white powder filled the courtroom, swirling, drifting, chasing people out the door. All except for O'Donnell and the disembodied chanting of the jury. He couldn't move. The powder rose to his waist, his chest, his neck. And then it plugged his nose.

Hugh O'Donnell bolted upright. His heart thumped wildly and his hands shook. He unwound himself from the bed sheets. Gray light leaked around the edges of the thick dusty drapes. The wind was still howling outside; it felt as if the motel walls were shaking. He reached up to flick on the bed lamp. Nothing happened. He looked over at the radio/alarm clock on the nightstand. That was out, too.

Stumbling into the bathroom, he splashed cold water on his face. Another wanger of a dream. No two were alike, yet all were strangely the same: sanity and reason turned on their heads, enemies cloaked in righteousness, friends selling out to friends, and the misinformed sitting in judgment. Just like real life. He pinched water into his nostrils and shot several staccato breaths out his nose. His sinuses were clear.

O'Donnell passed a wet comb through his hair. It was quickly turning from the sandy color of his misspent youth to a scattered and premature gray. Life begins at forty, he told himself. I sure hope so. He fit his wire-rimmed glasses on his face and looped two wings of slicked hair behind his ears. He stepped into a pair of gym shorts and went out to the balcony.

The wind was gusting so hard he had to lean against

it, but it was warm, like the hand driers in cheap restrooms. Clouds boiled across a gunmetal sky. The palm trees were white, their fronds turned inside out by the buffeting gale. On the parking lot below he saw a newspaper plastered against the side of a car. The full-color picture of the space shuttle *Constellation* bled into the pavement.

"Yo, O'Donnell."

Freddy Aviles, dressed in an abbreviated jumpsuit, hand-walked down the balcony rail. For an absurd instant O'Donnell thought he was still dreaming. Then Aviles stopped in front of him and deftly sat on the rail; one of his pinned-up jumpsuit legs showed only a stump inside it, the other not even that. He had mocha-colored skin and a tuft of wispy black hair on his jawline that he was trying to cultivate into a beard. His muscular arms and chest bulged the metallic suit fabric as he smiled lazily at O'Donnell. A gold canine flashed briefly.

"Tree knocked down a power line," he said. "Me and Lance, we're gonna take a walk to find someplace that can cook us some food. Wanna come?"

"In this?"

"We dodge the branches. Be fun, eh?"

O'Donnell looked at the sky and scowled.

"C'mon, man." Freddy flipped up into a handstand and began a set of vertical push-ups. A huge gold crucifix fell from the collar of his jumpsuit. It dangled from his neck and clicked against the rail with each repetition. "What you gonna do, sit in your room all day and count the walls, eh? They is only four."

"Give me a minute so I can shave," said O'Donnell. He paused at the door. "Hey, Freddy, do people dream in space?"

Dan Tighe raced down the passageways and through the hatches toward Trikon Station's command module, grabbing handholds and literally flying weightlessly past startled technicians and crewmen, his feet never touching the deck.

All of the station's energy and environment control systems were regulated by the life-support program in the station's mainframe computer. The life-support program monitored air quality in every one of the ten pressurized modules and regulated the circulation fans and carbon-dioxide absorbers on a second-by-second basis. Heat, electrical power, air, water—every breath taken by every man and woman aboard Trikon Station depended on the uninterrupted operation of the life-support program.

If whoever copied Nutt's files tried to upload the stolen data, Stu Roberts's bug would cripple the thief's computer and spread to the mainframe. The life-support program would be stopped along with everything else. They could all die within minutes.

Tighe pulled himself into the command module, banging his knee on the entry hatch and tumbling toward the floor.

"Ouch!" said Dr. Lorraine Renoir. Her infirmary was adjacent to the hatch. Her accordion door was open, and she was floating freely inside the cubbyhole making notes on a clipboard.

Tighe ignored both the comment and the pain in his knee. Before his body hit the floor he pushed with his palms and redirected his momentum down the length of the module like a swimmer barreling off the bottom of a pool.

The command and control center was located in the aft end of the module, adjacent to the space shuttle docking port. It contained the main computer terminal, manual controls for all systems, and the viewing ports.

Tighe curled his feet into the loops at the base of the computer and hurriedly typed in his password. The computer beeped. Tighe breathed a sigh and entered the emergency code. A series of options played across the screen.

WHICH ONE, COMMANDER TIGHE? asked the last line. The cursor blinked.

"What's going on, Dan?"

Dr. Renoir steadied herself in the doorway to the command section. A French braid of chestnut hair floated from the back of her head.

"We have a real problem, Lorraine. I'll explain in a minute."

Tighe selected the option that read: AUX COMPUTER/ AUX POWER/ESSENTIAL UTIL ONLY. The lights in the command module went out. He heard a gasp of surprise from Lorraine, behind him. Then the emergency lamps came on, substantially dimmer than the normal cabin lights.

Tighe flicked on the station intercom.

"This is Commander Tighe. A situation has arisen that requires a transfer to the station's auxiliary power supply. All essential utilities such as life support will continue to operate at normal levels. However, nonessential utilities will remain inoperable until the situation is rectified. I am ordering everyone to remain where you are until full power is restored. The only exceptions are crew members Jeffries and Stanley. They are to report to the command module immediately."

Tighe clicked off the intercom.

Lorraine was staring at him, eyes wide with either surprise or fear. Or both.

"Some idiot scientist stole files from the computer terminal in The Bakery. Turns out that a bigger idiot's infected the files with a bug that'll jam the computer of anyone trying to access those files." Tighe patted the computer terminal. "If it gets in here and starts to replicate, then we're in deep yogurt."

"Can you keep it out?"

Nodding, Tighe forced a grin. The old command philosophy: Instill confidence in the crew. Maintain their morale and you'll automatically maintain their respect. It occurred to him that he wanted Lorraine's respect. She was an intelligent, level-headed woman whom he could depend on. Even though she was the physician who could permanently ground him.

She smiled back at him. She looked much better in micro-gee than she had on Earth. Back on the ground her face had been handsome, strong features and dark brows, her figure slim, almost boyish. The fluid shift that microgravity caused had served her well. Her brown eyes had an almost oriental cast to them now; her face was rounder, more feminine. Even her body seemed to have filled out better beneath the royal-blue jumpsuit she wore.

Abruptly, Jeffries and Stanley slid through the hatch. Jeffries, a rangy, long-limbed black from Virginia Polytech, was Tighe's most experienced crewman, with more than a year in space, the last six months on Trikon Station. He would be rotating back to Earth when the shuttle finally arrived, and Tighe would be sorry to lose him. Stanley was the station's only Aussie: sandy hair, lazy grin, the powerful build of a swimmer. Neither man had ever experienced an emergency power-down. They both looked worried.

Lorraine backed away from the doorway so the two crewmen could enter. Tighe quickly explained the situation, unconsciously spicing this version with more jargon than the account he had given Lorraine.

"Okay," he said, taking a breath. "Stanley, you stay here with Dr. Renoir. I want nobody, and I mean *nobody,* to enter the command module except for me. Jeff, you and I are going to conduct a complete search of the station."

Jeffries shoved off. As Tighe followed toward the hatch, Lorraine floated back to the infirmary and started to unlock a pharmaceutical compartment.

Tighe stopped his momentum and cocked his head.

"Preparing tranquilizers," she said in response to his unstated question.

"Good thinking," said Tighe, and dove after Jeffries.

Wordlessly Lorraine watched him disappear down the passageway.

Hugh O'Donnell cast a dubious eye at the roadhouse. Its windows were boarded with plywood and its cratered gravel parking lot was empty except for a single pickup truck.

"Looks like it's closed," shouted Lance Muncie over the growl of the relentless wind.

Freddy bounced off the skateboard he used for long-distance treks and clambered up an awning post to an uncovered section of window.

"Somebody inside," he said as he cupped a hand against the glass.

Muncie was young and big, varsity-football big, with heavily muscled arms and powerful hands. Yet he looked almost baby-fat soft: short-cropped blond hair and pinkly cherubic face. He frowned at the tattered sign clinging to the doorjamb, advertising topless dancing, and at the photos, censored with black squares across each woman's chest.

"Let's try another place," he said, pulling himself away from the peeling poster.

A cardboard box smacked against O'Donnell's legs, then flew across the parking lot. "There isn't any other place," he snapped, already regretting that he had accepted Freddy's invitation.

Freddy slid down the post until he was eye level with Lance.

" 'Scuse us a second, eh, O'Donnell?" he said.

O'Donnell moved out of earshot, which was only a few feet away in the thundering gale. Apparently Freddy knew how to handle this Muncie kid. Freddy spoke earnestly, and some of the hardness drained from Lance's face. Lance shrugged. Freddy shot a stage wink at O'Donnell and bounced onto his skateboard. Lance held the door as Freddy rolled through.

The bartender was an amiable sort, fat and bearded and looking like he would be more comfortable in the cab of an eighteen-wheeler than behind a bar on Cape Canaveral. The storm had interrupted food delivery, he explained, but he might rustle up some tuna on toast if that suited their fancy. Everyone agreed that would be just fine.

"Where ya'll stayin' at?"

Freddy was gawking at the uncensored photos of the dancers taped to the mirror and Lance was staring at his fingernails, so O'Donnell answered, "The New Ramada."

"That's where they put up shuttle passengers." The bartender looked at Freddy. "Say, I know you. You're that legless guy they're sending up."

"Astronaut Fernando Aviles at your service." Freddy vaulted onto the bar and spun himself on one hand.

"Goddamn," said the bartender. "You don't need no micro-gee to be an acrobat."

Freddy returned to his stool.

"Goin' to Space Station Freedom, huh?"

"Not Freedom. Trikon." Freddy mussed Lance Muncie's hair. "Lance and me, we're part of the crew."

"Trikon, huh? That's the industrial one, ain't it?" The bartender looked at O'Donnell. "You a scientist or something?"

"Something," said O'Donnell.

The bartender served tuna sandwiches and poured three glasses of grapefruit juice. Freddy accepted a shot of rum in his; Lance and O'Donnell refused. As the men ate, the bartender made small talk and professed a deep interest in all matters extraterrestrial. As if to prove his dedication, he switched the television to the "Good Morning, World" show. The screen showed a man wearing a crimson flight suit and bobbing effortlessly in what appeared to be a padded room. Nearby, a lanky blond wearing an identical flight suit pedaled a cycle attached to the floor.

"Ever watch this?" asked the bartender. "They do a segment every week, live from Trikon Station. That guy there, he's Kurt Jaeckle. He's that scientist writes all them books about Mars."

Freddy and Lance grunted in recognition. O'Donnell gnawed on a burnt section of his toast. Seeing that his patrons were less than talkative, the bartender retreated to a well-cushioned stool set up next to the cash register.

Kurt Jaeckle was smiling earnestly into the camera. His face was thin, pallid except for heavy dark eyebrows that shadowed his eyes.

"One of the problems of extended space missions," said Jaeckle, "is the effect of weightlessness on the muscular system of the human body. In microgravity, objects retain their mass but not their weight. Tasks that require the exertion of muscle power on Earth require virtually no effort in space. Hence, without a planned exercise regimen, a person's muscles will atrophy."

The camera pulled back as Jaeckle floated effortlessly toward the blond puffing away on the exercise cycle.

"Ms. Gamble here is demonstrating our stationary cycle, which exercises the leg muscles and, more importantly, the heart as well. The heart, remember, is nothing more than a muscle. On Earth it pumps blood against the force of gravity, but here in space there is no such resistance. Therefore, the heart can atrophy just like any other muscle."

At a nod from Jaeckle the blond stopped pedaling and tried to smile prettily into the camera.

"I require each member of the Mars training mission to spend a minimum of eight hours on the cycle each week. The station commander has a separate set of exercise requirements for his crew, and the teams of research scientists on board are advised by the station's medical officer to exercise on a regular basis."

"Ho boy, I'm in trouble," said Freddy.

"You can pedal with your hands," said Lance.

"Where do I sit?"

"You don't need to sit."

"Tha's right," said Freddy. "Maybe we can pedal with her, eh?"

"She's a local girl," the bartender piped up. "First name's Carla Sue. She was a beauty queen at the University of Florida a few years back, though you wouldn't know it to look at her on that cycle. Space travel don't agree with her. Professor Jaeckle talked about it last week. Somethin' about the body fluids rising from the legs to the chest and face in micro-gee. Carla Sue was prettier'n a movie star down here. But up there her face kinda looks like one of them big all-day lollipops, don't it? Not that I still wouldn't give her a lick."

Freddy giggled; Lance's face reddened. O'Donnell didn't know whether the kid was embarrassed or angry.

"Don't none of you guys get any ideas about Carla Sue," said the bartender. "She's Jaeckle's."

"She hasn't met us yet," said Freddy.

"I oughtta know," the bartender went on. "The two of them were in here makin' kissy-face enough before goin' up."

No one picked up on this morsel of gossip, so he folded his arms across his gut and swiveled his head back to the television. Jaeckle was in the midst of explaining that the stationary cycle, for all its virtues, did not provide enough exercise for the calf muscles.

To demonstrate, Carla Sue unzipped the bottom of her pants leg. Her calf was as straight as a rail and so thin that Jaeckle was nearly able to encircle it with one hand.

"And, as you can see, it is quite flabby, too." Jaeckle rubbed his hand up Carla Sue's calf. A ripple of flesh preceded his fingers toward her knee.

"In order to exercise these muscles, we have a treadmill," continued Jaeckle. "Now Ms. Gamble apparently has not been spending the required amount of time on the treadmill." He smacked her calf sharply. "Better work on these."

Lance tapped O'Donnell's wrist.

"Did I ever show you the picture of my girl?"

O'Donnell grunted noncommittally. He had tried talking to Lance Muncie during preflight instruction and had received nothing but a hard stare in return. His initial impression was that Muncie somehow knew of his past and disapproved on a deeply moral level. Later, from talking to Freddy, he learned that Lance came from a Pentecostal community in the Oklahoma panhandle. Just what we need, he had thought, a fundamentalist aboard the space station.

Yet the kid didn't seem too bad. Uptight, of course, but not a fanatic. O'Donnell thought of his own father, sneaking booze even into the hospital room where they tried to save him from cirrhosis. There are all kinds of fanatics in the world; maybe the son of a Bible-thumper will work out better up there than the son of an alcoholic.

O'Donnell did not want to see the picture, but Lance opened his wallet and flipped through its plastic folders until he finally came to a photo that looked like a high school graduation picture.

"Here she is," he said, wiping away a stray piece of thread stuck to the plastic cover. The girl had blond hair in a conservative midwestern-style flip and a smile full of milk-white teeth.

"Her name is Becky. That's short for Rebecca. What do you think?"

"She's nice, Lance," said O'Donnell, although his own taste ran to women with a hint of the lowlife about them.

"Do you have a girl back home?"

"I'm in between girlfriends right now."

Lance's mouth dropped open for a moment; then he guffawed like a donkey. "Is that anything like being in between jobs?"

"Exactly like it," said O'Donnell. "Excuse me."

He crossed a sorry-looking dance floor and found the men's room. The tiles smelled of urine and stale disinfectant. The walls were etched with graffiti. The wind whistled through a crack in the frosted glass of a window.

He chose the cleaner of the two urinals. As he pissed, he thought he saw a spider dangling near his shoulder. But when he turned, the spider became a small swastika cut into the wall with a knife. The creepy-crawlies had found him.

All the members of the club were haunted by these creatures that hovered at the periphery of their vision. Some creepy-crawlies resembled insects; others resembled rodents. A few belonged to phyla no biologist would ever dream existed. O'Donnell seemed to have a penchant for spiders.

The creepy-crawlies were a bad sign. They meant that the protective shell he had built up during the past three years was in danger of cracking. With Hurricane Caroline delaying the launch for as long as five days, O'Donnell faced an eternity with no work to keep him occupied and uptight Lance Muncie bent on male bonding. In between girlfriends. Shit. A girl-friend was the least of his problems.

O'Donnell took a long look at the swastika before leaving the men's room. He thought he saw the ends wiggle, but he couldn't be sure. If the phones are back in operation tonight, I'll call in at the motorcycle club meeting. A chat with my bike buddies will do me some good.

Back at the bar, the television screen was blank.

"Show over?" asked O'Donnell.

"Don't know," said the bartender. "We lost the picture. Jaeckle yelled and Carla Sue screamed. And then we lost the sound."

15 AUGUST
TRIKON STATION

When placed in orbit, a long skinny object exhibits a peculiar property due to the basic physics of orbital mechanics. Once aligned so that its long axis points toward the center of the Earth, it tends to maintain this attitude. The bottom end (nadir) remains at the bottom and the top end (zenith) remains at the top as the object orbits around the Earth. The forces that cause this phenomenon are called gravity-gradient torques and the object is said to be gravity-gradient stabilized.

As applied to Trikon Station, this means that the modules will always be oriented so that the Earth is "down," or "below" the station in relation to its internal architecture.

Trikon Station orbits about 480 kilometers (300 miles) above the Earth's surface. Space is not entirely a vacuum at this altitude; there is a faint, thin atmosphere composed principally of atomic oxygen. This highly reactive gas can erode the station's components. To minimize this erosion and the orbital decay resulting from the slight but real aerodynamic drag, the station's normal orbital orientation is to fly "edge on," like the blade of a broad knife flying edge-first.

However, Trikon Station's natural tendency to remain gravity gradient stabilized is not enough to keep it properly functioning. The solar panels must always be oriented toward the sun to collect energy. The radiators must be aimed away from the sun to discharge waste heat. As the station orbits the Earth, the positions of the solar panels and radiators must be constantly adjusted for the most efficient orientations.

The station's computerized inertial measurement unit (IMU) constantly monitors orientation and the attitude control system (ACS) automatically corrects any instability. Although the station carries gas jet thrusters to make gross changes in its position and to reboost itself to higher orbit when necessary, thrusters are an imprecise and costly method of "fine tuning" attitude.

Trikon Station therefore employs a sophisticated system of control moment gyroscopes (CMGs) to correct and maintain proper orientation. These gyroscopes are mounted in the external truss of the station's skeleton.

               —*Trikon Space Station Orientation Manual*

"WE'LL START WITH the European module," Tighe said to Jeffries. They were in the connecting tunnel, a slender tube that ran within the station's central truss and between the rows of modules. The tunnel looked eerie in the half-light of the emergency lamps. Normally bright green and shadowless, the tunnel was now murky and splotched with dark recesses created by rows of storage lockers. Tighe felt like a crab scuttling along the bottom of the ocean.

Under normal conditions, the station gathered its energy with huge "sails" of solar cells while it flew on the sun side of the Earth. Half of the energy was delivered to the power distribution system for immediate use and half was stored in nickel-cadmium batteries to support the station when it slipped into the Earth's shadow. The auxiliary power configuration employed by Tighe disconnected all the individual computer terminals from the mainframe, but also had the undesired side effect of disengaging the station's utilities from the solar arrays. The nicad batteries were capable of providing full power for one complete orbit. The emergency configuration lowered the demand to one-sixteenth of full power, which theoretically allowed the crew sixteen orbits—barely a day—to correct whatever problem existed. Tighe hoped the search would not take that long.

The Trikon laboratory section of the station was composed of The Bakery, the European Lab Module (ELM), and the Japanese Applications and Science Module ("Jasmine"). The three modules were situated adjacent to each other, with ELM in the center. Viewed from space, they were identical except for the markings painted on their white skins. Their internal designs and color schemes were adapted to suit the tastes of the individual nationalities.

Tighe and Jeffries arrived at ELM to find a technician floating near the entry hatch and shouting in German at someone in Habitation Module 2, at the other end of the connecting tunnel. The tech fell silent at the sight of the commander, but a babel of voices quickly rose within Hab 2. Some demanded to be informed of the problem; others shouted advice for whatever that problem might be. Tighe acknowledged none of them. He pulled himself into ELM.

The lab was even murkier than the connecting tunnel. The gray floor and salmon ceiling blended into a single, dismal blah. Tighe moved through the shadows cast by the equipment. He passed two technicians, a stocky blonde Swede and a silent dark Spaniard. Each nodded solemnly. Tighe floated toward the end of the module, heading for the bulky figure waiting for him there.

"What is the meaning of this, Commander Tighe?" The reedy tenor voice floated clearly in the thin air.

Tighe stopped himself with a handhold. Looming in

front of him, in fact blotting out several of the emergency lamps, was the corpulent figure of the chief scientist of the European contingent: Dr. Chakra Ramsanjawi. Unlike the others, who wore regulation coveralls and lab smocks, Ramsanjawi insisted upon wearing a saffron-colored *kurta* that billowed out from his body, making him resemble a hot-air balloon.

"Good morning, Doctor," Tighe said tightly.

"I repeat, what is the meaning of this power-down, Commander?" said Ramsanjawi. He spoke with an upper-class British accent and just a faint hint of Hindu singsong. His skin was the dead-gray color of ashes. At first it had seemed odd to Tighe that an Indian had been placed in charge of the European lab, but Ramsanjawi was an employee of a Swiss firm, one of the corporations that made up Trikon's European arm. And despite his personal appearance, Ramsanjawi was more English than Big Ben. Or tried to be.

"The power-down is necessary," said Tighe.

"For whom?"

Ramsanjawi pulled himself toward a cabinet so that he no longer blocked the light from Tighe. Unconsciously Tighe backed away slightly. The Indian exuded a faintly acrid body odor, subtle but unpleasant, that he tried to cover up with cloying cologne. Tighe mentally pictured a cloud of mingled vapors hovering weightlessly around Ramsanjawi's bloated body and thought, If only he'd stay in one place long enough he might strangle on his own stink.

"Someone downloaded files from the terminal in the American module," Tighe said.

"Is that a problem with the Americans?" said Ramsanjawi. "For shame! I thought we all were dedicated to the common good."

"I don't care what you do among yourselves. I don't care if you kill each other, just as long as you do it off company property."

"Pray tell then, Commander, why are these American files so important?"

"Because they contain a bug. Whoever tries to upload those files will crash his computer. If that bug gets into the mainframe, this power-down will look like the Fourth of July in comparison."

A laugh bubbled in Ramsanjawi's throat, but Tighe sensed there was precious little humor in it.

"Commander Tighe, if your power-down had not been so ill-timed your explanation would be merely pathetic. My staff and I have worked for one month"—Ramsanjawi held a stubby finger aloft—"one entire month to produce a microbe with a genetic structure capable of neutralizing seven toxic substances. Not one, not two. Seven! Just before eight o'clock this morning, we began testing the microbe in that pressure tank behind your left shoulder. Don't bother to look, Commander. This particular microbe can survive only under prescribed conditions of temperature and pressure. Your power-down has caused one month's work to, how shall we say—evaporate?"

His dark eyes were glittering now, betraying the fury that his smile was trying to mask.

"And now you tell me that this bold move was occasioned by a theft of some American computer files." Ramsanjawi laughed again, and it sounded even thinner than before. "Are you intimating that I would covet the work of the American microbiologists?"

"Cut the crap, Doctor," Tighe snapped. "I don't give a damn what's in those files except for that bug. I want to know whether anyone in your group stole those files. Because until I find them, the power-down will continue."

Ramsanjawi exhaled deeply; again, Tighe backed away.

"I will question my staff," said Ramsanjawi, "I assure you that if any one of them is responsible, he—or she—will turn over the files."

"You know where to find me," said Tighe. He started to move toward the hatch.

"And Commander," said Ramsanjawi. "I would wager that anyone clever enough to download those files would be too smart to attempt to access them here."

"I don't have the luxury of being a betting man," said Tighe.

The next stop was Jasmine. As Tighe and Jeffries traversed the five meters of connecting tunnel between the two entry hatches, they noticed a slight figure speeding toward them in the shadows. They pulled up to a stop. The red-suited figure floated through a band of light. Kurt Jaeckle.

It always surprised Tighe to realize how physically small Jaeckle really was. Tighe himself had the compact build of the typical fighter pilot. Jaeckle was tiny in comparison, skinny and big-domed, almost like a child. But his voice was powerful and he knew how to use it.

"Dan, what the hell is going on?" demanded Jaeckle.

"I ordered everyone to remain where they were," Tighe said.

"I didn't think that applied to me," said Jaeckle. In the weak light his eyes, set deeply in his skull, were totally black pools, like a mask.

"It does."

"Wait a second, Dan. I'm not one of Trikon's employees."

"You'll be briefed when I deem it necessary," said Tighe.

"That's not fair. I'm responsible for eleven other people. I have a right to know the nature of this emergency and I demand to take an active role in whatever decision you intend to make."

"Everything is under control," said Tighe. He turned to Jeffries. "Escort Professor Jaeckle back to the Mars module."

"I wasn't in the Mars module. I was in the rumpus room, broadcasting a show."

"All right, Jeff, take him to the rumpus room."

Jeffries placed his hand on Jaeckle's shoulder. The professor glared at Tighe but did not resist.

That's why Jaeckle's sore, thought Tighe as he watched the two figures fade in the tunnel. His almighty TV show was interrupted.

The Japanese contingent waited together just inside the entryway to their module. Each wore a short lab smock neatly belted at the waist and nylon pants with many pouches. The chief scientist, Hisashi Oyamo, greeted Tighe with a bow. Oyamo resembled a downsized sumo wrestler, stubby but wide in every dimension, practically no neck at all. He had a pockmarked complexion and large watery eyes that complemented the opal ring he wore on one pinkie. Ripples of fat ran up the back of his severely crewcut head.

"We are concerned about your emergency," he said. "How may we help?"

"Well, Doctor, it seems we've had a theft," said Tighe. Whenever he talked to any of the Japanese, he found himself exaggerating his natural drawl. He assumed it was an unconscious reaction to their clipped, formal manner of speech. "Seems some enterprising person downloaded a set of files from the computer in the American module. I'm not myself concerned about the guilt or innocence of any particular party. I am concerned about those files because there was a bug written into them that will jam any computer used to access it. If that bug gets into the mainframe from any of the terminals, it'll shut the whole station down."

"So you disconnected the terminals from the mainframe as a precautionary measure," said Oyamo. "I understand."

Tighe waited for more, but Oyamo floated impassively before him.

"Well, Doctor, you're the first person who's grasped the situation without sticking it back in my ear."

"You have been to the European module?"

"I have."

"Dr. Ramsanjawi was uncooperative?"

"Dr. Ramsanjawi was Dr. Ramsanjawi," Tighe said. "He promised to let me know if anyone on his staff was responsible."

"I will consult with my staff and inform you immediately," said Oyamo. "If you will excuse me."

Jeffries rejoined Tighe as the six Japanese huddled in the center of the module. "Jaeckle's pissed, sir," said the crewman. "He didn't appreciate being escorted."

"I don't care what he did or did not appreciate."

"He wants to lodge a formal complaint."

"With who?"

"Beats me. Maybe you, sir. He wants to see you after the power is restored."

"I guess I'll see him," said Tighe. How the hell can you avoid anyone on a space station, he added to himself.

They watched the meeting of the Japanese. Oyamo seemed to do all of the talking. The others simply listened.

"What do you think, sir?" asked Jeffries.

"I think we're in the wrong module, if you ask me."

Oyamo floated back toward them, his face as impassive as a blank wall. But he was unconsciously rubbing one hand across the chest of his crisp white smock.

The Japanese director deftly slipped his feet into the nearest floor loops and made a slight bow to Tighe.

"I regret," said Oyamo, "that I am unable to help you. None of my technicians seems to have the offending computer disk in his possession."

Tighe thought that Oyamo was choosing his words as carefully as a lawyer speaking into a tape recorder.

"The power-down will have to remain in force until I am certain that the bug will not infect our life-support program," he replied, equally stiffly.

Oyamo bowed again, nothing more than a dip of his chin, actually. "I understand your concern. However, it would not be advisable to continue the power-down indefinitely, would it?"

"No," said Tighe, "Certainly not."

"Therefore, perhaps the best that can be hoped for is the assurance that whoever copied the American files will learn of the virus implanted in them and will refrain from attempting to read the files."

He's telling me to go stuff myself, Tighe realized. Very politely, but the message is loud and clear.

"Furthermore," continued Oyamo, "even if someone should hand you the offending disk, it would be impossible to know if it actually was the one with the copied data on it. Any attempt to read it would cause precisely the disaster you are trying to forestall, would it not?"

He's got me there, Tighe admitted to himself. "Yes," he replied aloud. "It would."

Oyamo's face betrayed no hint of emotion, not the slightest flicker of triumph or even satisfaction. "Indeed, even if someone did hand you such a disk, there would be no way to know if he had made another copy of it."

Tighe smiled grimly. "It can't be copied without activating the bug."

"Ah so. Of course."

Out of the corner of his eye Tighe saw Jeffries watching like a spectator at a particularly intense chess game. Behind Oyamo's thick frame the Japanese technicians huddled together like a bunch of school kids, not daring to move.

After long moments of silence, Tighe finally said, "I guess you're right. The best we can hope for is that whoever copied the files won't be foolish enough to try to download them."

"I will do my best to make certain that everyone is made aware of that fact," said Oyamo.

"Thank you." Unconsciously, Tighe made a stiff little bow.

"It is my pleasure to help you, Commander." Oyamo bowed in return.

"What the hell was that all about?" Jeffries asked once they were back in the connecting tunnel.

Tighe huffed a humorless laugh. "Oyamo just as much as told me that one of his people swiped Nutt's file, but now that he knows there's a bug in it, he won't download the file. At least, not here aboard the station."

"You're sure?"

"Nothing's sure, Jeff." Tighe could feel a sullen anger welling up inside him as they floated back toward the command module. "Except that we can't keep the power-down going forever. The bastard's got me there."

"Then whoever stole the files is going to carry them home, after all."

"Right. I hope he chokes on them," Tighe said with real fervor.

Hisashi Oyamo ran his right hand across his burly chest as he watched the two Americans duck through the hatch and leave Jasmine. His fingers pressed against the computer disk in the breast pocket of his smock.

Typical American impetuousness, he thought.

Power-down the entire station! Does the commander truly believe that someone clever enough to break into another scientist's files would be so stupid as to attempt to access the stolen material while still aboard the station, where anyone might catch him simply by monitoring the computers?

Still, Oyamo had not expected the files to be bugged. It was kind of the commander to inform me of that fact, he said to himself. It would have caused great unhappiness in Tokyo if one of our mainframes were ruined by the Yankee virus.

Turning back to his technicians, he barked an order. They sprang into instant activity.

Oyamo nodded to himself. It is well. What we cannot buy from the money-mad Americans or the bickering Europeans we can steal. The warrior uses whatever means come to hand; there is no shame in seizing opportunity. Japan's destiny is to lead the world out of the morass these Westerners have created. It is the duty of every Japanese to use every atom of his strength and intelligence toward that goal.

Dan Tighe shut down his communications console after completing his official report to Tom Henderson at ground control in Houston. The time was 1130 hours, CDT. Three hours of emergency power-down and twenty minutes of explanation to the Earthside brass. He hoped the rest of the day would be less eventful.

Henderson had been just as unhappy as Tighe about the situation.

"You mean whoever stole the data still has the disk? With the bug in it?"

Tighe had nodded sourly. "Not much more I can do about it, Tom. Can't keep the station powered down forever."

"Yeah, I know, but . . ."

"Whoever's got the disk knows that if he tries to run it he's going to jam the mainframe."

Henderson had been silent for a moment. Then, "Better pop an unscheduled CERV test."

"Right. Good idea." But Tighe pictured in his mind the bitching the scientists would do if he called a surprise emergency evacuation drill on top of the power-down.

Tighe let his feet slide out of the restraining loops and floated toward the ceiling of his cubbyhole office. The bonsai bird circled on its tether in an eddy of air. Tighe noticed a twig springing out from the bird's belly. He pulled the bird to the floor, secured himself, and carefully snipped the offending twig with a pair of shears from his toiletry compartment. He had requisitioned tiny scissors, the kind suitable for trimming a mustache or beard. But the cretin in the Trikon supply depot groundside had sent him heavy-duty shears. His bonsai bird hadn't suffered from an errant snip. Not yet, anyway.

There was a knock on the bulkhead.

"Just a minute," said Tighe. He inspected the bird carefully, then nudged it back toward the ceiling.

Kurt Jaeckle slid the folding door back. The office was not big enough for two people to fit comfortably, so he hovered in the doorway.

"I want to apologize for my behavior in the connecting tunnel," he said.

"Sure you do. That's exactly what Jeffries told me you intended."

"I was angry."

"A lot of people were angry," said Tighe. "I would have been angry if I'd had time to think about it. Bugs on a space station, as dependent as we are on computers. Some people are crazy."

"That's part of the reason I'm here. I think we need a set of ground rules for emergencies."

"We have 'em. I followed them."

"Then we should rethink them. Abruptly shutting down power to the science modules has its consequences."

"I know all about them," said Tighe. "Unfortunately, the only way to cut off the computer terminals from the mainframe was to go to auxiliary power."

"That is entirely my point," Jaeckle said slowly, carefully. He seemed to be planning each word as he spoke. "Your only move was to disconnect the terminals which, through no fault of your own, necessarily cut off power to the science modules. That being the case, you should have warned us."

"There was no time for any warnings."

"Dr. Ramsanjawi informed me that the download occurred at two A.M. and was discovered at eight. That's six hours, Dan," said Jaeckle.

"Dr. Ramsanjawi, huh?" said Tighe. It wasn't the first time that Jaeckle had proposed a novel way of running the station after consulting with the Indian scientist.

"We both decided that an extra few minutes would not have been critical. It would have saved a month's work in his case and my television broadcast."

"Your goddamn show," muttered Tighe.

Jaeckle put on a diplomatic smile. It made his gaunt, high-domed face look almost like a death's skull. "Look, Dan. I know you were dead set against the Mars module becoming a part of the station. And I know you hate the idea of my TV broadcasts."

"I think that this station could accomplish much more in the way of terrestrial research if we didn't have to coordinate our orbits for TBC."

"But we are accomplishing things," said Jaeckle. "Trikon, the Mars Project. Just the fact that the first commercial industrial space station exists at all is a blessing. It is a toehold in the heavens for every man, woman, and child on Earth."

Tighe rubbed wearily at his eyes. On Earth, Jaeckle's stentorian voice and skill at popularizing science commanded thousands of dollars in lecture fees and enthralled millions. On the station, he had lost none of his penchant for making speeches.

"But it is not enough," continued Jaeckle. "If we are to establish bases on the moon, if we are to travel to Mars, we need the backing of the people. We must beat them into a frenzy of scientific interest, the way it was in the sixties. We can't have them asking why billions of dollars are being shot into the sky rather than spent on Earth. You and I know the reality. But they don't. That is why the power-down was so critical."

"How the hell did we get from our toehold in the heavens to this morning's incident?" asked Tighe.

"There were millions of people tuned to their sets this morning when Carla Sue and I were explaining the importance of exercise," said Jaeckle. "Halfway through the script, the screen cut to black. The vice-president in charge of programming has been trying to reach me like mad. I don't know what the hell I'm going to tell him. They were caught completely unaware in New York."

"'Good Morning, World' will survive," said Tighe.

"Sure it will. But will the Mars program? Millions of people thought the show was cut because of ineptitude."

"Close. It was pure stupidity," said Tighe. "Are you now about to tell me I should have waited until your broadcast was over?"

"Of course not. But the warning would have made a difference," said Jaeckle. "I could have informed the studio, then put our situation into perspective for the audience. The dedicated scientists, the brave crew, the station commander faced with a critical decision. It would have been great drama."

"We've got enough drama up here," Tighe grumbled. "Whoever stole those files still has the damned bugged disk."

"Drama sells," said Jaeckle, unperturbed. "All it would have taken was a warning and a two-minute delay of the power-down. Who knows how many millions of dollars it would have generated for the space program?"

"You sound like a television producer."

"Unfortunately, it's what I have to be. I hope you understand that."

Jaeckle pushed himself away from Tighe's office and headed for the hatch. As he passed the infirmary he peeked in at Dr. Renoir with his telegenic charm on full beam. Tighe grimaced sourly. Nothing in his conversation with Kurt Jaeckle bothered Tighe as much as the sight of him talking to Lorraine Renoir.

He waited until Jaeckle pushed himself through the hatchway before he started for the doctor's office. Why does my weekly blood-pressure check have to come on a morning like this? Damned pressure must be high enough to pop my eyeballs.

Dr. Renoir saw him approaching and waved an upstretched finger at him. "I'm rather busy right now, Dan," she said. "Can we make it this afternoon? Say, two P.M.?"

A wave of relief and gratitude washed over him. He nodded, trying to keep his emotions from showing on his face. "Fourteen hundred hours," he said.

Lorraine smiled at him. "Right. Fourteen hundred hours."

Not trusting himself to say anything more, Tighe turned back toward his office. You've got two hours and some to get your pressure down to where it ought to be, he told himself. A part of his mind noticed that Dr. Renoir did not seem particularly busy; there was no one in her infirmary; she was not working on her computer or on the phone.

But he ignored the observation. She's a doctor, he reminded himself. She can ground you for good.

15 AUGUST 1998
THE MARS MODULE

The concept of using biological techniques to repair ecological damage is called bioremediation. Bioremediation was first tried in a major way in the late 1980s, when bacteria were used to help clean up crude oil spilled into the ocean by tankers.

After the Exxon Valdez spilled 10.1 million gallons of crude oil over 368 miles of Alaskan shoreline in 1989, Exxon researchers sprayed some seventy miles of beaches around Prince William Sound with a fertilizer called Inipol that had been developed by the French petroleum company Elf Aquitaine. The aim of the $10-million experiment was to stimulate the growth of bacteria that already existed naturally in the environment and were known to consume hydrocarbons. The beaches sprayed showed dramatic improvement over areas not sprayed, often within fifteen days.

In June 1990 the supertanker Mega Borg caught fire and released nearly four million gallons of crude oil into the Gulf of Mexico. Microbial strains specially developed at the University of Texas to eat a wide variety of crude oils helped to clean up the spill. The microbes were engineered to die off once the oil that served as their food was consumed.

In the aftermath of the environmentally horrendous Middle East war of 1991, genetically engineered microbes helped to digest the hundreds of thousands of barrels of oil deliberately pumped into the

Persian Gulf by the Iraqi army. The microbes con-
verted millions of gallons of crude oil into relatively
harmless methane and carbon dioxide.

Researchers have suggested using genetically engi-
neered microbes to break down a wide variety of
toxic and even radioactive wastes.

Trikon's goal is to develop bioremediation tech-
niques, using genetically engineered microorga-
nisms, to help reverse the environmental damage
done to our planet by generations of air, water, and
soil pollution.

—Trikon International media release

AFTER LEAVING TIGHE and Lorraine in the command
module, Kurt Jaeckle made his way down the station's
central tunnel until he passed through the double
hatch marking the boundary between Trikon Station
proper and the Mars module.

The Mars Project was a joint effort between NASA
and the European Space Agency to test humans for a
planned flight to Mars. Twelve men and women had
been selected to spend two full years in space. The
original purpose of the project was to simulate the
rigors of an actual flight to Mars. This gradually
metamorphosed into a study of the subtle stressed
microgravity places on the human body and the
not-so-subtle conflicts that can arise when people live
in close quarters for extended periods of time. Finally,
it degenerated into a hodgepodge of conflicting and
overlapping experiments as different factions within
the two space agencies overlaid their pet projects onto
the original scheme.

The greatest conflict centered on the role of the
Martians within the Trikon Station community. "Pur-
ists" contended that the Mars facility should be a
self-sufficient module and the Martians completely
segregated from the other people on the station.

"Realists" believed that total separation was logistically impossible. Besides, they argued, interaction with outsiders would not invalidate the results because the actual Martian travelers would be able to communicate with Earth, albeit electronically.

The philosophical argument raged for months, and in the end both sides won—and lost. The Martians were divided into two groups of six persons each. One group was allowed to interact with the general station population. They slept in the habitation modules, ate their meals in the wardroom, and spent their leisure time in the exercise and recreation area. The other group never left the Mars module and were shielded from any visitors. In the first six months of the project, no serious differences between the two groups had emerged.

The Mars module was a shuttle external propellant tank adapted for scientific use by a technique known as the "wet workshop." Unlike the station's lab and hab modules, which had been completely outfitted on the ground and transported to the station on heavy-lift boosters, only the major structural elements of the eventual Mars module—flooring, workstation wells, bulkheads, internal tunnel—were built into the tank's two internal sections. The tank was then filled with liquid oxygen and liquid hydrogen; these powered the *Constellation*'s engines as the shuttle flew into orbit. Since safety considerations required the shuttle engines to shut down before the fuel was completely expended, small amounts of these propellants remained floating weightlessly inside the tank after it achieved orbit.

The liquid hydrogen was removed by a clever pumping device conceived by a former Apollo astronaut working for Trikon as a consultant. The liquid oxygen was simply heated by sunlight until it turned into its gaseous, breathable state.

On subsequent shuttle flights, teams of mission

specialists brought up the office facilities, compartments, galleys, and workstation equipment; they installed them in the larger of the ET's two sections, the huge volume that had contained liquid hydrogen fuel. The former liquid oxygen volume, located at the tapered front end of the tank, was converted into an observation blister. The ET was then attached to the trailing edge of Trikon Station's skeleton, its own internal tunnel an extension of the connecting tunnel that ran the length of the station's main horizontal truss.

The Martians themselves were payload specialists from several different scientific disciplines. Their workdays were devoted to Mars-related experiments. A meteorologist studied Martian weather patterns using data gathered by satellites orbiting the red planet. Two biochemists searched for signs of life in soil returned from Mars in the US-USSR robot probes landed on the Martian surface a few years earlier. A geologist examined rocks for clues to Mars's distant past. All the while, the participants were tested, probed, and analyzed by physicians and psychologists on the ground.

Kurt Jaeckle was the leader of the Mars Project. An internationally renowned astronomer on permanent leave from a professorship at Johns Hopkins University, he had defeated an equally famous French exobiologist in the contest for project leader. Then, through shrewd negotiating, he had arranged for the Mars module to be attached to the privately owned Trikon Station rather than to Freedom, the United States' space station. The main reason for the switch was that Jaeckle had secretly cooked up a live-television contract with TBC and the Canadian Broadcasting Company.

Jaeckle swam down the Mars module's internal tunnel, heading for his own office. The tunnel had been a hasty design addition, its purpose to provide all station personnel with direct access to the module's elaborate observation blister without chance encounters with the segregated Martians. The tunnel was two meters in diameter, its flat gray walls a dim contrast to the brighter Trikon connecting tunnel. Several doors along its length opened into the module's working and living areas.

Jaeckle entered through the first access door and directed himself across the spacious open expanse of the module's laboratory section toward his office, located in the fore starboard corner. All of the Martians were busily at work and only one, Russell Cramer, noticed Jaeckle's entry. Cramer stared at Jaeckle from his workstation five meters away. His jowly face was expressionless, but seemed to demand an acknowledgment. Jaeckle obliged with a wave. Cramer, without responding, returned his attention to his microscope.

I must have a word with him, thought Jaeckle. He stopped at his office door and consulted the blister reservation list attached to the bulkhead. Carla Sue Gamble was in the observation blister now. As usual, none of the other Martians had reserved the following hour. Jaeckle wrote his name into the next slot.

Inside his office, Jaeckle powered up his communications console and called TBC headquarters in New York City. As Mars Project head, he was exempt from Trikon's restrictions on secured communications and had a selection of voice encryption chips at his disposal. The chips broke up the voice transmission into meaningless signals that would be reassembled by another chip at the receiving station. Eavesdropping ham-radio operators would hear nothing but Chinese violins. Jaeckle didn't often use encryption when talking to TBC, but today the language could become dicey. He pressed a chip into its slot.

The link was shunted from receptionist to secretary to executive secretary and finally to Jared Lewis, the vice president in charge of "Good Morning, World."

Lewis was angry, his fleshy face blotchy red. Jaeckle was exactly one sentence into his explanation of the morning's event when Lewis launched into a tirade. He railed about confusion in the control room and about the co-anchor who had taken a break from the set during the live broadcast from space and then could not be located when the transmission abruptly ended.

"You think we like showing an empty chair!" shrieked Lewis. He started ranting about advertising dollars and market share.

Eventually Lewis slowed down and Jaeckle had a chance to talk. He used all of his narrative skills to paint a picture of confusion and horror on the stricken space station.

"Jesus," said the chastened Lewis. "Hey, maybe we can start the next broadcast with a reenactment. I'll get one of the segment directors to contact you about it pronto. How is Carla Sue doing?"

"Actually," said Jaeckle, shifting narrative gears, "I think the mission is beginning to wear on her."

"You know, it's funny," Lewis said. "I was thinking the exact same thing this morning. Those legs. I mean, come on. We're talking anorexic."

"I've explained the fluid shift several times on the air."

"Words are words. Pictures are what counts," said Lewis. "We don't want people coming away with images of anorexic astronauts."

"Unfortunately, it cannot be avoided."

"Maybe if you had someone else," Lewis suggested. "Someone with a little more heft or a little less fluid shift. Paint a prettier picture for our viewers."

"There is someone," Jaeckle said slowly, as if the idea had just entered his mind. "But she isn't a part of the Mars Project."

"Hey, there's nothing in the contract that says your

assistant has to be a part of the Mars Project. She could be a Venusian for all I care."

"I don't know how Carla Sue would react to being replaced."

"It's a rough business, Kurt."

"This other one may not even want to be on television."

"Everybody wants to be on television," said Lewis. "Who is she?"

"Lorraine Renoir."

"I like it," Lewis said. "French?"

"French Canadian, actually. She is the station medical officer."

"Nice tie-in. She could interest the Canadian audiences. Ratings have been low there. Attractive?"

"Well," said Jaeckle. "Not anorexic."

"Talk to her and let me know. Have to run."

The telelink broke. Jaeckle snapped off his communications console. He felt encouraged, expansive. Talking to TBC always was entertaining, especially since Jared Lewis was so malleable.

Jaeckle propelled himself toward the observation blister up at the tip of the module, a dome of strong and perfectly transparent Lexan. The outer surface of the dome was covered by an aluminum clamshell shield that could be closed to prevent damage from meteoroids or debris. Retracting the shield in different ways offered stunning views of the Earth, the night sky, or both.

Everyone on the station was allowed to use the blister for personal R and R on a reservation basis. In the context of the Mars Project, the blister was more than just a place for quiet solitude or spectacular scenery. Since transit to Mars would entail long stretches of time out of Earth view, project coordinators assigned specific viewing privileges to the two groups. The segregated group was allowed to view only the empty night sky; they never saw the Earth.

The other group had no restrictions. Psychologists on the ground were eager to see if the two groups differed in long-term adaptation. Carla Sue Gamble was part of the "free" group.

Jaeckle rapped on the metal hatch of the blister. After a long moment, the bolt slid back and the door opened. There was the Earth, immense, breathtaking, sparkling blue and brilliant white, gliding past beyond the Lexan windows. But Jaeckle barely noticed the spectacular panorama. He focused on Carla Sue, long, lean, and angry. He could tell from the tightness of her lips and the knit in her brow that the delay in unlocking the blister hatch had been carefully calculated.

Jaeckle closed the door softly, carefully. Carla Sue waited until she heard the click of its latch. Then:

"If you don't think I'm beautiful anymore, I'd be obliged if you would tell *me* before you tell the rest of the world."

Her voice was deadly calm. Carla Sue was never strident, never out of control. Even when she was angry. Even in the heat of lovemaking. Her mind always ruled her body.

Jaeckle summoned his most sheepish grin.

"Don't try to mollify me, Kurt. Flabby legs. I know what you were driving at."

"I was stressing a point, Carla. I told you when I first asked you to be my assistant that I would make comments you might construe as critical. You can't take them personally."

"So you think I'm still beautiful."

"I think you are brilliant and beautiful."

Carla Sue's expression changed from an angry frown to a grudging smile. Jaeckle moved forward to kiss her, but his knee struck her hip before his lips reached hers and she tumbled away. He caught up with her and squeezed her lips into a pucker. Those lips. Microgravity had improved them, if nothing else.

They were redder, thicker, poutier. They made him want to unzip his fly on sight, and many times he had. He kissed her deeply, then spun her around so that they both faced the Earth.

"I never know where we are," said Carla Sue.

"The North Atlantic. We'll cross the Azores soon."

He felt warm toward her, warmer than he had felt in days. It wasn't a sign that their relationship was on the rebound. His conversation with Jared Lewis had solidified that decision. He recognized it as the last flourish of ardor before he pulled one of his patented disappearing acts.

"Did I ever tell you what people did in the Azores?" he said, nestling against her from behind.

"Mmmmm," said Carla Sue.

As head of the North American research team aboard Trikon Station, Thora Skillen should have been respected and admired. Instead, she counted herself the loneliest person on the station.

She walked the treadmill in the ex/rec room, setting herself a blistering pace, working out her fury and contempt for those around her with tireless long-legged strides. David Nutt, she seethed to herself. A good name for him. The perfect name. And Commander Tighe, Mr. Machismo himself. Warning me about Roberts bugging Nutt's files. As if I didn't know how irresponsible Roberts can be.

There were five other men and women in the ex/rec room, working the bicycle, the rowing machine, throwing darts in the strangely flat trajectories of weightlessness. No one spoke to Thora Skillen. No one even looked in her direction.

She was a tall, athletically lean woman in her late thirties with severe, chiseled features and prematurely graying hair. Almost a classic face, strong and serious, like a sculpture from ancient Athens. She seldom smiled. She knew that they called her "Stone Face" behind her back. That, and worse.

She was in the prime of life: a brilliantly successful molecular geneticist who already had taken on heavier responsibilities than women ten years her senior. Everyone predicted a splendid career for her, but Skillen knew better. Her career was already finished. Her life was finished. She was merely going through the motions.

Thora Skillen was dying. No one on Trikon Station knew that except the medical officer. But the males who dominated the worlds of scientific research and corporate politics knew it. They knew it full well.

The only reason they had selected her for Trikon Station, she realized, was to make an experiment of her. They wanted to see what effect microgravity might have on the corruption that was eating away her lungs. Her work, her brilliance, her drive and dedication all meant next to nothing to them. She was a laboratory animal, that's all. Naming her head of the North American segment was a sop, a meaningless bone thrown to a dying lab specimen.

What they did not know was that she had lost all faith in her own work. The achievements of her science meant nothing to her now. She felt as if she had spent her life working for the enemy. It had taken the death of her sister to awaken her to the awful reality of the world. The death of her sister, and her own impending death.

They're killing us, she knew. Their factories and automobiles and supermarket foods are killing all of us. Even the scientists are part of it, probing into the secrets of life, releasing all kinds of poisons without even thinking about it. I was part of that. I was one of the guilty ones. It took Melissa's death to make me see the truth.

So what I'm doing isn't wrong, she told herself. Of all the people on this station, I'm the only one who does see the truth. The only one willing to act on it.

I'm going to die anyway, so what does it matter?

The men aboard the station hardly spoke to her, except when their work required it. Once she had trounced a few of the overconfident oafs at micro-gee handball they steered clear of her and made crude jokes about testicles. The women seemed afraid to strike up an acquaintance with her, as if they thought she would try to seduce them. Skillen had never announced her sexual preferences; her personnel record certainly contained no hint of it. But they knew. As if they could smell it on her. They all knew and they all shunned her.

Lorraine Renoir was the only one on the station she could confide in, and even there Skillen was careful not to reveal the entire truth. Dr. Renoir was sympathetic and discreet, but she also kept her distance.

Dave Nutt was leaving as soon as the shuttle could get to the station and take him away. Good! she told herself as she paced the tireless treadmill. He had accomplished far too much during his six-month stint. Now he could spend the next six months on Earth writing reports instead of making progress.

Skillen watched the others as she strode nowhere. Inwardly she snarled at them. You think you know all my secrets, she silently said to them. You think you can avoid me and crack jokes about me behind my back. Go right ahead! Your day will come. I promise you. And it will come sooner than you think.

16 AUGUST 1998
BATH, ENGLAND

I should have been wise enough to see the trouble brewing, but I was not.

With perfect hindsight, of course, it is all so clear. Even as far back as 1994 when the foreign ministers of the European Community voted to allow the Eastern European nations to join them.

The emergency meeting in Brussels was filled with angry voices for many days. It had been called by the French foreign minister, Pierre Belroi, in order to resolve this thorny issue of permitting the impoverished former communist nations to join the far wealthier EC.

Since the European Community had officially begun, in 1992, there had been growing tension over the question. France and Germany wanted all of Europe—including, eventually, even Russia—to become part of a single, integrated economic group. Britain, traditionally suspicious of the continental powers, feared that by admitting the poor nations of the former communist bloc the Western Europeans would be placing undue strains on their own economic future.

At the meeting in Brussels the vote went 11-1 in favor of the French and Germans, with Britain the sole dissenter. The British foreign minister, Sir Derek Brock-Smythe, pleaded with his fellow ministers to nullify the vote, saying that he feared Britain would

*pull out of the European Community altogether if the
decision was not reversed.*

*The vote stood. Furious, Brock-Smythe returned to
London. Although he represented his nation's position as strongly as he could, it was clear that Brock-
Smythe was at odds with the xenophobes in his own
government. While he was not especially fond of
having the Eastern European nations join the EC, he
was clever enough to realize that Britain's economy
would stagnate if she were not part of the Community.*

*As Brock-Smythe predicted, Parliament reacted vi-
olently and Britain quickly cut all ties to the European
Community. Brock-Smythe publicly damned the decision; he said it would be ruinous for Great Britain.*

Privately he took other actions.

—From the diary of Fabio Bianco,
CEO, Trikon International

THE MIST WAS heavy enough to drive the tourists into
the shops and pubs, but not so heavy that walking was
unpleasant for a man accustomed to English summers. Sir Derek Brock-Smythe crossed Pulteney
Bridge, his patent-leather elevator shoes tapping
smartly on the stone pavement, his double-breasted
chalk-stripe suit maintaining its razor creases despite
the humid air. Bath had been the city for natty
dressers ever since Beau Nash established it as the
capital of polite society in the seventeenth century.
Sir Derek, the nattiest of all despite his diminutive
stature, was perfectly at home in his weekend retreat.

Harry Meade, not so dapper, lumbered ten paces
behind. He was sweating beneath his black turtleneck
and tweed sports coat, and his shoulder holster dug
into the sheath of burly muscle curving under his
armpit. His feet were swollen in his rubber-soled
Clarks; he had been walking most of the day.

Sir Derek descended the stairway on the east side of the bridge, gallantly tipping his bowler to a pair of elderly ladies making their way up the stone steps. Meade passed the stairs, lingered momentarily at the head of Argyle Street as if wondering whether to continue away from the city center, then turned back and followed Sir Derek's path. If anyone had noted the pair of them they would have thought of a husky prizefighter trailing after a dapper tap dancer.

Sir Derek stood with one hand balled into a tiny fist and the other drumming its manicured nails on the top of the stone parapet. The Avon was swollen from several days of rain and skimmed across Pulteney Weir without breaking into foam, so silently that he could hear the soft strains of the waltz being played by the band in the gazebo on the green across from the cricket field. Meade took up a position five feet away and studiously avoided looking at Sir Derek. Across the river, the market shops were crowded. A sightseeing boat moved south with the current. It would be forty minutes before the queue for the next departure began to form.

Meade pulled a bag of stale bread from his jacket pocket. He nervously tore a slice and tossed the pieces into the water.

"I understand there was an incident aboard Trikon Station yesterday," said Sir Derek, his eyes following the bobbing tufts of bread.

"A theft of American computer files, apparently by one of the Japs. All for naught, Sir Derek. The files were protected by a bug, and the American station commander cut power to prevent the bug from entering the computer system. They never found the thief, but at least it's been made clear that he can't access the data without wiping out the whole station."

Meade stole a sidelong glance at Sir Derek and searched for some hint of a reaction. There was none.

"What else?" Sir Derek snapped.

"Well, uh . . ." Meade always thought he was sufficiently prepared for these meetings. He would pace his hotel room and rehearse buzz words to jog his memory. But Sir Derek's brusque manner always struck him speechless. His reports, as neat and as clean as one of Sir Derek's suits, became rumpled tangles of stuttered sentences.

"There was a bit of a row," Meade said, seizing upon an innocuous tidbit of gossip. "The American scientist and a Japanese tech in the station wardroom."

"I am not interested in barbaric behavior," said Sir Derek. "What about Dr. Ramsanjawi?"

"The loss of power ruined an experiment," Meade reported, his memory jogged. "He made a great howl about having worked a month to create a microbe that could neutralize seven different toxic-waste molecules. It was completely destroyed."

Sir Derek permitted himself a smile. This incident could not have occurred at a more propitious time. Fabio Bianco was due to address the directorate of the European arm of Trikon International at its annual meeting in Lausanne within the week. Bianco was prepared to boast of Trikon's success. He was prepared to predict that Trikon International, with its ability to coordinate the new technologies of North America, United Europe, and Japan, could rid the world of the pollution spawned by centuries of misguided old technology. In short, he was prepared to drive the last nail into Great Britain's economic coffin.

Now Bianco had, in the Yank vernacular, egg on his face. The incident aboard Trikon Station was worthy of headlines in tabloids from Fleet Street clear around the world to Tokyo and New York. The Nips and the Yanks were taking pokes at each other. It would be months, perhaps years before they cooperated again, if indeed they ever had since the beginning of Trikon.

And to top it all, Chakra Ramsanjawi had convinced everyone that the most complex toxin-devouring microbe ever engineered by man had vanished in a power outage ordered by a Yank astronaut.

Meanwhile, a team of scientists in a Lancashire laboratory, using data gleaned by Ramsanjawi and transmitted in code directly to Sir Derek, were already testing a microbe capable of neutralizing fourteen distinct toxic-waste molecules. Britain would beat the foreigners at their own game.

No, not Britain. England. Not the Welsh nor the Gaels nor the damnable Irish nor any of the mongrels that had been allowed onto this blessed isle. England would triumph over them all.

Sir Derek excitedly patted the damp stone of the parapet. Common men, preoccupied with banal concerns, saw events as merely happening willy-nilly. The visionary could sense the stirring of distant events long before they crossed the horizon. This evening, in the soft summer mist, Sir Derek positively heard a rumble. England would no longer be the outsider, the also-ran.

"There is one more item," said Meade. "About the shuttle."

"Delayed by Hurricane Caroline, I know," said Sir Derek.

"Trikon has added another scientist. An American."

Sir Derek looked at Meade for the first time. "Who?"

"Name of Hugh O'Donnell."

"Well, who is he, man? Out with it."

"We don't exactly know, Sir Derek. We haven't had the time to investigate him thoroughly."

"Is he there to work on the toxic-waste microbe?"

"We assume so," said Meade. "We understand he is employed as a staff scientist for Simi Bioengineering, in California."

"What makes this O'Donnell gentleman important? His employer is hardly on the cutting edge of genetic engineering."

"We don't know, Sir Derek." Meade noticed that his boss seemed to be staring through the brown surface of the Avon. "Simi is a member corporation of the American arm of Trikon."

"I am fully aware of that," said Sir Derek. "Are you attempting to portray this new scientist as some sort of mystery man?"

"We don't know enough about him to be certain of anything," said Meade. "We are following your orders to keep you apprised of all developments on Trikon Station. We wanted you to be aware of O'Donnell."

"Dr. Ramsanjawi should be advised and kept informed of anything you uncover about this man."

"I'll see to it."

"Is there anything else?"

Meade shook his head, then realized that Sir Derek was not looking at him. He dropped the last pieces of bread into the water. "No."

The bread caught the current and dipped quickly down the shallow steps of the weir. A young couple swaddled in yellow slickers walked past and stood at the dock for the sightseeing boat. They paid no attention to the two men.

Sir Derek watched the bread swirl into the distance. He watched it long after it disappeared from view, long after Meade's presence faded into the misty evening air, long after the sightseeing boat appeared under the Parade Bridge. The Avon drained the lands where, more than eleven hundred years earlier, a young King Alfred rallied a band of Saxon warriors and defeated the Danes at Ethandune. Without that victory, there would never have been an England, and Sir Derek—if he had been born at all—would have been speaking Danish. The peril facing this last fragment of the Empire was no less great. Economic power had been squandered by a xenophobic government. But he, with a band smaller than Alfred's, would restore England to its preeminent position. And make millions of pounds for himself in the process.

Sir Derek left his place on the river and retraced his steps across Pulteney Bridge. A freshening breeze lifted the shops' awnings and the lowering sun edged through a seam in the cloud cover. A pale yellow glow seeped into every corner of the city. Bath seemed alive.

Five years earlier, when it became apparent that Great Britain would separate from the European Community, Sir Derek had invited Chakra Ramsanjawi to his weekend estate in the Mendip Hills. The two men had not seen each other in several years, and Sir Derek was both surprised and gratified to see how paunchy Chakra had become. Chakra was dressed in a rumpled gray pinstripe suit that Sir Derek noted had been inexpertly pressed. The vest was stretched across his belly. His slick black hair was parted in the middle in a caricature of a style in vogue among the fashion trendsetters of Savile Row.

Sir Derek was barely able to keep his distaste of Ramsanjawi from showing on his patrician face. This Indian fakir, this would-be Englishman with his ash-gray skin and his pretenses of gentility. This would-be brother whom his misguided parents had foisted on him.

The two men had cocktails on an enclosed veranda in virtual silence, dined at opposite ends of the long table in the main dining room, then retired to the firelit parlor for brandy and cigars. They stood before the fireplace and stared at the flames licking the blackened mouth of the chimney—the true English aristocrat and the dumpy Indian hopeful. Chakra held his brandy snifter with his pinkie aloft. His other hand was half dipped into his jacket pocket, thumb exposed.

"How is it you are supporting yourself and Elaine now?" asked Sir Derek. His nose pinched at the cologne vapors swarming around his guest.

"Research."

"I see," Sir Derek said. "For whom are you conducting this research?"

Chakra mumbled something unintelligible. It did not matter. Sir Derek already knew the answer.

"I have a proposition for you," said Sir Derek.

"I need none of your propositions."

"Chakra, let us speak frankly. More than anything in the entire world, you want to return to Oxford."

Ramsanjawi took a quick sip of his brandy. There was no need to respond. The truth of Sir Derek's comment was obvious.

"My proposition is that you resign your present post, whatever it might be, and apply for the position of chief research coordinator at Ciba-Geigy's laboratories outside of Basel."

"They already refused to hire me after—"

"Apply, Chakra. I assure you, the position will be yours. There are ways for these things to happen."

"I know," said Chakra. He leveled a hard stare at Sir Derek. His eyes were two black dots in narrow yellow slits. "I know the way things can be done—when you want them to be done."

Sir Derek let the comment pass.

"Ciba-Geigy is not Oxford," Chakra said.

"It is your first step back," said Sir Derek. "Allow me to explain. If you have been reading the newspapers . . . sorry, that's right. You no longer read newspapers. If you have been paying attention to the telly, you undoubtedly realize that the United Kingdom is threatening to pull out of the EC. I think this is a foolish course, and I have labored long and hard to convince the Prime Minister and Parliament that participation is in our best interests. But none of the dolts has the wit to listen to me. I predict that by the year 2000 our economy will be in a shambles and our once preeminent place among nations will have been lost."

"So what?" said Chakra, almost vehemently.

"I know you don't feel that way," said Sir Derek. "You love England as much as I, almost."

"You think that?"

"Almost."

"What is your proposition, Derek? I want to be reinstated to my professorship at Oxford. You tell me to work in Switzerland."

"Simply this. I trust you are familiar with Fabio Bianco."

"He is a microbiologist of great reputation," said Chakra. "And he has the soul of a crusader."

"His crusader's soul is currently ascendant," Sir Derek said. "He is attempting, with a significant chance of success, to create a consortium of multinational corporations that will pool their research capabilities in order to solve various environmental problems facing the world through the use of genetic engineering. The work will be so sensitive and so potentially hazardous that it will be performed on a space station."

Ramsanjawi's eyes widened slightly.

"The Ciba-Geigy board of directors fully intend to vote in favor of joining the consortium," Sir Derek continued. "If you are chief research coordinator of the Basel lab, you will most likely be assigned to this project."

"What do you want, Derek?"

"What I want is to be the father of a new empire. Since that cannot be, I will settle for saving us all from going to hell in a hack."

Chakra smirked. "And you propose to do that by sending me to Switzerland to work for a research lab that may become part of a research project that has not yet begun."

"Will participate in a project that will begin," corrected Sir Derek. "It will be a coordinated effort to create a supermicrobe. I want that microbe."

"For Britain?" asked Chakra.

"For England," said Sir Derek.

"For yourself, you mean."

Sir Derek's nostrils flared slightly. "I am already a very wealthy man, Chakra. This will make me even wealthier, it is true. But I do this for England, believe me. I want to save my country despite the obstinate idiots in charge of its government."

Chakra knocked back his brandy. Instantly, a servant appeared and whisked the snifter out of his hand.

"And my cooperation will lead to my reinstatement at Oxford?"

"If at all possible."

"Now it is merely possible," said Chakra. "My banishment was not merely possible."

"You brought that on yourself."

"Bah!" said Chakra.

"What other options do you have? Seriously."

Chakra turned on his heel and walked toward the doorway. Sir Derek noted that the years had added a rockiness to his smooth gait.

"You know," Sir Derek called, "Mumsy—that is, Lady Elizabeth—encouraged me to become an economist."

Chakra froze at the doorway.

"It was after you declared your intention to become a scientist. Her reasoning was that economics was far enough removed from science that our egos would not clash. Wouldn't she be gratified to see us cooperating so swimmingly."

Chakra walked out the door without turning around. Sir Derek knew the words had stung.

"I'll wait to hear from you, Chakra," he muttered.

17 AUGUST 1998
FLORIDA

DRUG SWEEP NETS 1,000 ARRESTS

A task force consisting of Drug Enforcement Administration agents and the Los Angeles police conducted massive sweeps in three drug-infested Los Angeles neighborhoods early this morning.

"It looked like D-Day," said one witness to the operation.

The three sweeps were coordinated to occur simultaneously. Police and DEA agents arrested virtually everyone they found on the streets and hustled them off to school buses waiting at strategically positioned staging areas. People found exiting tenements and houses during the commotion were arrested as well.

The school buses, each manned by six armed guards in addition to a driver and equipped with reinforced metal screens covering the windows, transported the suspects to the Los Angeles Coliseum. There, in the eerie glow of the stadium's floodlights, the suspects were arraigned in six open-air courtrooms hastily constructed on the playing field.

The sweeps, the largest in the history of Los Angeles in terms of arrests, followed a blueprint established in similar operations in New York and Washington, D.C. The American Civil Liberties Union, which has challenged the outdoor detention centers in New York and Washington on constitutional

grounds, has filed suit against Los Angeles County on behalf of the detainees.
—*Los Angeles Times*, 14 July 1995

THE DAY FELT and looked exactly like the aftermath of a storm. The sky was a brilliant clean blue, the highway was littered with debris left by Caroline—branches, palm fronds, Spanish moss, even a mailbox still attached to its post. The rented Rover sped south, its balloon tires whining on the macadam. The thick palm and mangrove forest that swept past in a blur plunged the highway into complete shadow. The air was cool, almost frigid.

Aaron Weiss gripped the dashboard with one hand and pressed his Donegal walking hat to his head with the other. He hated open cars, hated convertibles of any sort. If he ruled the world, or at least that portion of the world responsible for overland travel, every motor vehicle would have a roof reinforced with a roll bar and a governor to prevent it from exceeding fifty-five miles an hour. But there was a story beyond that mangrove forest, and he knew that speed was essential.

"Can't you go any faster?" he screamed over the rush of wind.

Zeke Tucker glanced at him, then looked back at the littered highway. He said nothing, but nudged the accelerator slightly. He smiled enough to reveal the gap in his front teeth. He was amused by Weiss's consternation.

Tucker and Weiss had worked as a team for seventeen years, since the Reagan assassination attempt. He had seen the reporter annoy thousands of people, from headwaiters to heads of state. When it came to aggravation, Aaron Weiss was a true egalitarian. And Zeke Tucker was the ideal cameraman to team with him: lanky, slow-drawling, absolutely unflappable.

Tucker slowed and squinted at the hand-drawn map Weiss had taped to the dashboard. He swerved off the highway and punched the Rover through a screen of brush and young palmetto, engine growling, camera gear jouncing on the back seat. Beyond the brush, two slender trails of sand curved through the trees. The makeshift roadway was not exactly wide enough for the Rover; Weiss was stuck several times by overhanging palmetto spines. He grumbled curses each time. Eventually the trees and bushes thinned enough to reveal the glare of the sun reflecting off the ocean. The Rover broke out onto a beach. Tucker let it roll to a stop on the white sand.

"Great," Weiss snapped. "Now where the hell are we?" All he could see was a ridge of sand and, beyond that, the glittering water stretching to the horizon.

"Not far now," said Tucker, a long bony finger tapping the map. "If you want to, Aaron, we can sit here and watch the shuttle launch." The gap-toothed grin came back to his long-jawed face.

"Fuck the shuttle. Nobody wants to hear about shuttles anymore, only when they blow up. The big news is right here." Weiss pounded the dashboard to signify the surface of Planet Earth.

Nodding, Tucker released the clutch and the Rover churned through the loose sand. Weiss leaned over the windshield and shaded his eyes against the sun. As the Rover crested the ridge, he saw them. They were about half a mile to the north, several huge gray slabs lying in pools left by the outgoing tide.

"There they are," said Weiss, pointing.

"My God," Tucker whispered. "My God."

"I count twelve," Weiss said.

"Yeah," said Tucker. "Looks like nine adults and three calves."

The Rover descended the ridge, then sped along the hardpan close to the water. No one except the police seemed to be there. A group of sheriff's deputies were pounding stakes and stringing bright orange tape between them.

"They're treating this like a crime scene," said Tucker.

Weiss noticed a van marked Sea World of Orlando approaching from the opposite direction.

"Maybe it is," he said.

They stopped the Rover at the police line. Weiss and Tucker showed their press badges to a deputy and swung under the tape.

"Christ, you boys are here before the gawkers," said the deputy.

"It pays to pay your sources," Weiss answered. He signaled for Tucker to follow.

"Damn," said Tucker, fanning his free hand in front of his face. The other held a Minicam.

"Here."

"Suntan lotion?"

"Smear it on your nose. Shit, Zeke, after all this time I still have to mother you. The ozone layer's shot to hell. Remember? We did a story on it last year."

The first carcass they inspected was a calf. It lay on its side, its one visible eye the color of milk, its skin sunk between its ribs in deep troughs. Seaweed clogged the strips of baleen in its open mouth.

Weiss paced it off, ignoring the ankle-deep water that sloshed over his Hush Puppies. Eight paces, plus. Twenty-five feet.

"Make sure I'm in the frame for perspective," he said.

"Yeah, yeah," said Tucker. Weiss constantly harped at him, but rarely about something as elementary as perspective. This whale beaching bothered him.

"These are the same kind we saw in San Diego last week," said Weiss. "Right whales. You can tell by the curving mouth and the callosities on the adults' faces. The old Nantucket whalers used to call them right whales because they didn't sink when you harpooned them; they were the right whales to go after."

"Since when did you become an expert on whales?"

"Since last week."

Weiss waved Tucker over to a full-grown bull. This one was fifty feet long and, flat on its belly, was twice as tall as Weiss. Its baleen plates splayed out from its mouth like the bristles of a worn-out broom. Weiss pressed between two ribs. The rubbery skin yielded easily and did not bounce back when he released his hand.

"I'll be a sonofabitch," said Weiss. He grabbed Tucker by the shoulder. "You shoot every one of these babies. I want to look around."

Weiss slogged from carcass to carcass, borne by a sense of unreality. The dead white eyes, the sunken flesh, the tattered baleen, even the symmetry with which the ocean had coughed up its victims smacked of a dream. But it was real; something strange was happening. He had felt it a week earlier when he and Tucker chanced upon the pod of right whales stranded on a beach north of San Diego. He felt it again that morning when word of a drunken beachcomber's find reached the motel. Now, seeing huge carcasses for the second time in eight days, he was convinced. Animals as large as whales did not die en masse without there being something very wrong with the world.

The Sea World van had multiplied into four. A swarm of employees, all young enough to be summer help, were unloading gear and fanning out among the carcasses. Weiss approached the only employee who was not moving at double-time, a young woman securing her long red hair with a pin.

"Do you have a boss?"

"Professor Adamski."

"Ted Adamski?" asked Weiss.

The woman nodded. She had a pert little nose sprinkled with freckles. Photogenic. She pointed toward a man leaning into the back of one of the vans. As Weiss moved closer, he recognized the bald spot and the leathery skin set off by the scraggly white beard. He called the professor's name. Adamski straightened up as if his back ached.

"Weiss," he said. "You are like a bad dream."

"I guess that's better than being a bad penny." Weiss reached for Adamski's hand but the marine biologist did not reciprocate.

"Are you following me?"

"Pure coincidence, Professor. I'm actually covering the human-interest story of the first legless man being hurled into space."

"And in San Diego you allegedly were covering the senatorial primary," said Adamski. "You don't stick to your assignments very well."

Weiss laughed. "Lemme tell you how this business works, Professor. If a flying saucer landed on this beach, do you think I'd still be interested in the whales?"

Adamski was not amused. "Is this more important than your legless astronaut?"

"I would say that twelve whales washing up dead in Florida one week after eight washed up dead in San Diego is news."

"But not exactly a scandal." Adamski leaned back into the van and fiddled with the hasps of a metal box.

"Scandals used to put a lot of bread and butter on my table."

"And when they didn't occur spontaneously, you invented them."

"That was a long time ago."

"Some of us have longer memories than others." Adamski opened the box, revealing a set of glittering surgical tools. He selected an assortment of scalpels, scissors, and tubes and placed them carefully on a towel.

"Are you preparing to perform an autopsy?" Weiss asked.

"Maybe."

"What would you say killed them?"

"It would be inappropriate to venture a guess."

"Don't guess, Professor. Hypothesize, theorize. Take a look at that adult there. What do you think killed it?"

"Weiss, I don't give a damn about your new legitimate journalistic career. I'm not telling you a goddamned thing."

"Pretend you're not talking to me."

Adamski looked at the whale lying in a tidal pool twenty feet past the front of the van, big as a cross-country bus or a tractor-trailer rig. A wrinkle crossed his brow, then faded.

"The storm," he said.

"Bullshit the storm," said Weiss. "I inspected each one of these whales and they look emaciated, just like the ones in San Diego."

"Thank you for your observation, Mr. Weiss. You have just cut my workday in half." Adamski rolled the instruments in the towel and stuck it under his arm.

"Not so fast, Professor. You performed an autopsy last week on those San Diego whales. You must have the results by now."

Adamski turned away and slogged into the tidal pool. Weiss was right at his heels.

"Is that a yes? Is that a yes, Professor Adamski? Or are you going to tell me that a storm killed those whales, too?"

Adamski put his nose an inch from Weiss's.

"I have been quoted by you for the last time," he said, baring his teeth and enunciating each word very carefully. "Now you either leave me to my work or I'll ask one of those police officers to eject you."

Weiss backed off. As soon as Adamski disappeared behind the first carcass, he set out looking for the young redhead he had spoken to earlier. He found her scraping green gunk from an adult's baleen into a plastic container.

"Hi, remember me?" he said.

"You were looking for Professor Adamski," she said. "Did you find him?"

"Yes, thank you. Nice guy. Do you work with him often?"

"First time. He flew in from San Diego to review our marine mammal protection project. Then this happened."

"He didn't exactly have the time to talk to me, but he did say all of you fine young people would cooperate. I wonder if I could ask you some questions."

"Who are you?"

"Sorry. I'm Aaron Weiss. The Aaron Weiss TV Tabloid. Remember?"

"Oh God, you're right!" The young woman's sudden smile crossed the line from charmingly cute to downright goofy. She said her name was Sandy. Weiss immediately knew that he had an ally.

"Do you know much about whales?" he asked.

"Not really. I'm an English major at Florida State and I'm working at Sea World for the summer. But I did write a bio paper last semester on the diets of several species of baleen whales."

"Great," said Weiss. "Are you familiar with the whales that were found off San Diego?"

"Sure am. That's all we talked about this week."

"Isn't it true that they were thousands of miles from where they should have been?"

"That's right," said Sandy. "Right whales ordinarily spend their summers off the Alaskan coast."

"What about these whales?"

"They're far from home, too. I can't say exactly, but

generally the right whales of the North Atlantic should be up around the mouth of the St. Lawrence this time of year."

"What are they doing here?"

"They could have been sick and the sickness disoriented them."

"What about the hurricane?"

"I don't know. I guess it could have killed them." Sandy scraped more gunk into a separate container.

"What're you doing there?" Weiss asked.

"Different species of whales eat different types of food," said Sandy. "Grays prefer small, schooling fish. Blues prefer small crustaceans. Right whales and bowheads feed on phytoplankton and zooplankton. They siphon water through their mouths and their baleen plates catch the plankton. This green stuff looks like seaweed. They can't eat that."

"Why are you interested?"

"It's Professor Adamski's orders."

"Why is he interested?"

"Could have something to do with the autopsies of the San Diego whales."

"The autopsies." Weiss drew out the words in a knowing tone. "What were the results again?"

"I'm not exactly sure of the technical conclusion," said Sandy. "But everyone around here is pretty sure those whales starved to death."

"In the ocean?" Weiss couldn't contain his surprise. "Those whales starved to death in the Pacific Ocean?"

"That's the rumor."

"And Adamski wants to see if these did, too," said Weiss.

"I guess so," Sandy said.

Weiss looked down at his feet. Wavelets lapped against his jeans. A single minnow darted around his shoes. Something big was happening. Something bigger than politics, bigger than war, bigger than any scandal he ever had uncovered. He thanked Sandy for her help and rushed around the carcasses until he found Tucker.

"Come on," he said, grabbing the cameraman by the collar.

"I'm not finished."

"Fuck 'em. We've learned all we can from here for now." He started back toward the Rover.

"Where're we going?" asked Zeke. He had to run to keep up.

"Remember a few years ago," said Weiss, ignoring the question because he had no real answer, "NASA had all those wigged-out ideas for manufacturing oxygen for long duration space flights. Remember what they were going to use?"

"Plants."

"Not exactly plants. Plankton. Phytoplankton. Microscopic bugs that're the most efficient oxygen-producing organisms on the planet. Better than trees."

"So?"

"These whales eat plankton. They also look like they died of starvation, along with the ones in San Diego."

"What's that add up to?"

"Damned if I know," Weiss said, puffing now, sweating as he scurried across the hot sand toward the waiting Rover. "But it's something big. I can feel it in my bones."

Tucker made no reply. He knew that an Aaron Weiss hunch meant there was a story waiting to be uncovered. Besides, Zeke had that same quivering feeling along his spine.

17 AUGUST 1998
SPACE SHUTTLE
CONSTELLATION

It is important to realize that space workers are not astronauts in the original sense of the term. Their function is not to pilot spacecraft or explore other bodies of the solar system. They are not trained pilots or former military officers.

Space workers live and work in orbiting facilities such as the Trikon Station for extended periods of time, much as oil-rig workers go to remote sites such as the Alaskan North Slope or platforms far out in the North Sea. They perform construction and maintenance tasks or conduct scientific research under conditions that cannot be duplicated on Earth. They live in isolation and with the constant knowledge that there is less than half a centimeter of aluminum separating them from the extremely hostile environment of space.

There is no predicting how a particular person will react to life in an orbiting facility. Test pilots seemingly immune to motion sickness have been stricken by severe nausea during the early portions of their time in space. Calm, seemingly well-adjusted scientists and technicians have developed whole constellations of personality dysfunction symptoms that the psychologists have dubbed Orbital Dementia.

Apparently, Orbital Dementia is similar to the psychological malady found among certain members of Antarctic "winterover" teams, but is overlaid with the physical stresses unique to the microgravity envi-

ronment of outer space. Studies have revealed three general phases. In the first, the person will be cranky and/or angry. In the second, the person will become reclusive. In the third, the person will become violently aggressive, even murderous or suicidal.

Transdermal motion-sickness pads have been developed to counteract nausea until the person adjusts to weightlessness. But so far, no such "quick-fix" remedy has been developed for Orbital Dementia. Psychologists and psychiatrists have studied the experiences of the Skylab, Salyut, and Mir missions, as well as Antarctic "winterover" teams, but have failed to devise a test that will accurately predict a person's behavior in space. One psychologist likened the task to predicting the weather. I think it more akin to trying to predict an earthquake.

> —The diary of Fabio Bianco,
> CEO, Trikon International

HUGH O'DONNELL FELT his teeth loosening, his spine coming apart, the breath leaving his chest in a rush of involuntary grunts. God, don't let me piss myself. Don't let me . . .

The thunder of *Constellation*'s lift-off obliterated his thoughts. He fought to raise his eyes toward the digital clock on the bulkhead above the middeck storage lockers. His neck slapped back against the headrest after a single, stroboscopic glance. Mission time was T plus forty seconds. Eight minutes of this. That was what the instructor had said. Eight minutes of sheer hell before serenity.

The thunder suddenly stopped. Shit goddammit engine failure. We're falling I'm gonna die. Still he felt as if a gang of giants were pressing down on him. He wrenched his head to the right. Next to him, Lance Muncie still bucked crazily in his seat, hands plastered to the armrests, his face twisted as if he were peering into the mouth of hell. O'Donnell managed another glance at the clock. T plus fifty seconds. That's right. That's why the silence. The shuttle had gone past Mach 1.

"Main engines at sixty-five percent." The voice of Commander Williams crackled over the loudspeaker as flat and calm as a scorekeeper's at a tennis match. O'Donnell and the other eleven passengers bound for posts on Trikon Station were stacked in the middeck of the converted old NASA orbiter. *Constellation* had completed more than thirty missions before being purchased by Trikon International in 1994. It was an ungainly-looking vehicle compared to the Europeans' spiffy little *Hermes,* or the six sleek aerospace planes developed jointly by NASA, Rockwell, and Boeing. But the space shuttle could haul more payload than the space plane, and *Hermes* was just beginning its flight test program. Reliable old *Constellation*'s generous cargo capacity was essential to the maintenance of Trikon Station.

"Roger," said the ground. By popular vote, the passengers had requested a feed of the voice transmission between the flight deck and mission control.

Calmer now, O'Donnell imagined a picture he had seen countless times on television screens: *Constellation* arcing over the Atlantic Ocean in its "heads down" attitude, the burns of the two SRBs and the three SSMEs spewing out a combined pillar of fire, shrinking to a dollop of orange, and finally disappearing in the darkening blue of the sky. He was on top of that flame, his hands gripping armrests and a three-hundred-pound cinder block pressing squarely on his chest and those giants still shaking and pummeling him.

He turned his head enough to see the portside monitor. The shuttle was some thirty miles above the Atlantic. The bright Florida sky had deepened to a fuzzy blue-black.

Looks like I'm going to Trikon Station, O'Donnell thought optimistically. From sunny Cal to a metal booby hatch in low Earth orbit. He trembled inwardly, whether from anxiety or anticipation he could not tell.

The g-forces abated appreciably. Williams spoke directly to the passengers on the middeck: "We are now in a low elliptical orbit. In approximately thirty-three minutes, we will have a second OMS burn to boost us into the same orbit as Trikon Station."

"Whoooweee!" Freddy Aviles howled.

O'Donnell realized that his hands were floating free. He forced them back to his lap and curled his fingers under the strap of his safety harness. His head felt funny, stuffed, as if his sinuses were jammed full of cotton wadding.

"Hey, Lance, this is something, ain't it?" called Freddy. He sat immediately to O'Donnell's left, but his voice sounded muffled through the congestion in O'Donnell's head.

Muncie groaned in response.

"He doesn't look so good," said O'Donnell.

"Lance? Nah. He the only one didn' get sick on the Vomit Comet," Freddy said. Nearly everybody had upchucked during the long series of parabolic maneuvers aboard the KC-135. The plane would dive and then nose up, giving the collection of fledgling space workers a few gut-wrenching moments of weightlessness before it dove again toward the lush green mat of central Florida.

Freddy craned his neck to take a look at Muncie. "Hey, man, you okay?"

"No. Terrible."

"Tha's crazy, man. You got the strongest stomach I know, except for my cousin Felix. And tha's because his wife can't cook."

"Maybe it's the excitement of being here for real," O'Donnell suggested.

Muncie started to shake his head. His face turned greenish.

"Tha's it," Freddy agreed cheerfully. "Okay, Lance, I leave you alone."

O'Donnell didn't feel so well himself. He attempted a few deep breaths, but found it impossible to fill his lungs. Loosening his harness did not help. He merely bobbed against the straps without any effect on his ability to breathe. Microgravity allowed his internal organs to shift upward, which seemed to restrict his lung capacity. He settled for concentrating on the clock, its LED digits moving in increasing speed from minutes to seconds to tenths of seconds to hundredths of seconds. In front of him, two Japanese technicians jabbered noisily. Behind him, an American technician and a Swedish scientist compared microgravity symptoms. The American complained of a severe headache and the Swede stated that she had trouble focusing on nearby objects.

Just after the forty-five-minute mark, the commander announced: "We are now about twelve miles in front and slightly above Trikon Station. You'll feel a few bumps and nudges as we use the RCS thrusters to kill off the drift rates and close in on the station. Then we'll make a low-z translation for berthing."

O'Donnell remembered that the RCS engines were the reaction control system jets that were used to make small maneuvering corrections. But what a low-z translation might be was a mystery to him.

The shuttle flew through night. The passengers ooohed and aaahed at the starlike patterns of city lights displayed on the portside monitor. Then came the real show—sunrise. It began with a faint rosy glow throwing the rim of the Earth into silhouette. Like a film run at fast speed, the glow boiled over the horizon, then separated into bands of brilliant colors —blues, reds, yellows, oranges. Finally came the golden bloom of the sun.

"Approaching Trikon Station," said Williams.

"There it is," said Freddy. "Looks like a giant silver diamond."

"Trikon Station," Williams called. "This is *Constellation*. Preparing for berthing."

"Roger, *Constellation*," spoke a voice from the station. "Damn happy to see you, too. That old bird never looked so beautiful."

The minutes inched by. The middeck passengers could hear Williams talking with the station, but it was all the clipped, incomprehensible jargon of professionals.

Finally Williams said, "Okay, folks. We are now station-keeping—hanging just outside Trikon's main docking port. They're cranking up their RMS to latch onto us and pull us up to the port. We'll be berthed in a couple of minutes."

O'Donnell pictured the spindly robot arm of the remote manipulator system reaching out to take the shuttle in its metal grip and slowly, gently bring it into contact with the airlock.

He felt a small thump.

"Bull's-eye," said the station voice.

Duncan, the second pilot of the shuttle, floated down from the flight deck and squeezed past the passengers to enter the airlock and complete the mating of the two ports.

Williams announced, "There will be a slight delay as we pressurize the connecting tunnel, check for leaks, and equalize pressure with Trikon. Might as well unstow your gear."

The passengers released themselves from their seat harnesses. In the cramped quarters of the middeck there was much bumping and banging, but eventually everyone managed to pull their flight bags out of the lockers. The shoulder straps were useless and wriggled like snakes until Freddy suggested wrapping them around the bag and holding the bag under the arm. The slight delay was much longer than Williams had predicted.

"Like deplaning at LAX," grumbled O'Donnell. He noticed that Muncie was still in his chair. Their eyes met momentarily. Muncie looked frightened, like a kid who had lost his mother in a crowded shopping mall. He closed his eyes tightly for a moment, as if trying to summon up whatever inner reserves of courage he had. Then Muncie unhooked his harness and eased himself afloat. He groped toward the lockers and did not seem to remember which one held his flight bag. When he finally located the locker, he fumbled with the latch until Freddy reached over to help.

"Was stuck, eh?" said Freddy.

"Yeah. Thanks." Muncie pulled out the flight bag and wrapped the strap as the others had done.

"Airlock is open," said Freddy. He placed his hands on Muncie's shoulders. "Man, you don't look so good."

"I still feel lousy."

"Happens to the best of us."

"But this is happening to me."

"You'll shake it."

O'Donnell followed as Freddy guided Muncie through the ribbed plastic tunnel connecting the shuttle's docking adapter to the station's airlock hatch. Floating awkwardly, bumping into one another, they entered the instrument-crammed command module, where a Trikon crewman hustled them through and out into the station's connecting passageway. O'Donnell felt the amused attitude of the Trikon technicians on duty in the command module, the typical knowing smirk of veterans eyeing newly arrived rookies.

The passageway was a confusion of greens, browns,

blues, and whites, bathed in intense light. O'Donnell
shaded his eyes. The blues gradually emerged from
the background as three figures dressed in flight suits.
The middle figure was a stocky man with a broken
nose and a red face. O'Donnell recognized him from
his pictures as Commander Dan Tighe. The other two
were a woman and a black man.

The last of the shuttle passengers floated into the
passageway. Then the twelve newcomers bunched up
around Tighe and the two others. O'Donnell noticed
that all three of them had their stockinged feet firmly
attached to loops set into the flooring.

"I want to welcome all of you aboard Trikon
Station," said Tighe. "I'm Dan Tighe, station commander. To my right is Dr. Lorraine Renoir. She's the
station medical officer, so I'm sure all of you will get to
know her."

Freddy nudged Lance in the shoulder. Lance
choked back a belch.

"To my left is Crewman William Jeffries. You
probably won't get to know him because, unfortunately, he is due to leave with the shuttle. Unless you want
to stay, Jeff."

Jeffries smiled benignly.

"You will all be assigned sleeping compartments in
Habitation Module Two. Hab Two is aft, behind me,
through hatch H-Two, second hatch on the port side.
That's your right side as you move aft, if your head is
toward the ceiling. If you get confused about orientation there are big arrows on the walls of the tunnels at
five-meter intervals. The red arrows point forward
and the blue arrows point to the ceiling. And they
glow in the dark."

Tighe hesitated a moment. When he saw that there
were no questions, he went on, "I want you to stow
your personal articles in the rumpus room until the
departing people finish packing. The rumpus room is

located at the far end of the connecting tunnel. You can secure your flight bags to the walls with clips or bungee cords. You may see some funny-looking plants floating around in there at the ends of tethers. They are bonsai plants. Anyone who touches them will be summarily executed."

Tighe smiled crookedly. A titter coursed through the new arrivals. Muncie did not laugh. Beads of sweat oozed across his brow. He struggled to loosen the collar of his flight suit.

"You all right?" whispered O'Donnell.

"I'm—" Lance Muncie's stomach contracted with the force of a small cannon. His mouth snapped open and, with a loud retch, out shot breakfast. It looked like a large, greenish yellow worm, expanding and contracting as it flew on a perfectly straight track toward Dr. Renoir. She spun out of the way. The vomit worm continued past, wriggling until it finally disappeared into the pastel recesses at the far end of the tunnel.

"Any other comments?" said Tighe.

The new arrivals laughed.

"I never get sick," Lance Muncie mumbled around the thermometer stuck in his mouth. Dr. Renoir's infirmary was cramped, but his addled senses welcomed the tighter perspective.

"Please don't speak, Mr. Muncie." Dr. Renoir pumped air into the collar of the blood-pressure gauge.

"What if I think I'm going to puke?"

Dr. Renoir closed his fingers around the plastic bag she had given him. One of the station's robots had vacuumed up the mess Muncie had spewed into the corridor and sprayed pungent disinfectant around the area. But the robot was too bulky to work effectively in this cubbyhole of an infirmary.

"Please be still and continue staring at that picture on the wall," she said. "Occupy your mind with pleasant thoughts."

There was kindness in her voice, thought Lance. An accent, too. German, maybe. No, French. Renoir was a French name. There was an artist named Renoir. He painted ballerinas. The picture on the wall was a small painting of a vase filled with flowers. Really pretty.

"Breathe deeply," she said.

The stethoscope was cold on his chest. He forced a breath and felt his stomach start to churn. Instinctively, his body tightened.

"Pleasant thoughts," trilled Dr. Renoir.

He tried, but his thoughts kept trailing back to his stomach. Thinking of the farm evoked the image of his father gunning his pickup toward a rise in the road to town. "Here we go, Lance, here we go. Your tummy. Wheeee!" Becky reminded him of a trip to Kansas City and the roller coaster that had delighted him and terrified her.

Dr. Renoir removed the thermometer. Lance gagged and hastily stuck his mouth in the plastic bag. Nothing came out, and after a moment he relaxed. Dr. Renoir instructed him to continue staring at the picture until the examination was complete.

"Haven't been sick in more than twenty years," he said.

"Is that so," said Dr. Renoir.

"I had a stomach virus when I was only a tyke. Couldn't keep anything down. I kept losing weight and losing weight. My ma and pa thought I was going to die. Then they heard about this faith healer that was going to be at a revival up near Alliance, Nebraska. Dr. J. Edward Moorhouse was his name. Pa drove all through the night to get there, with me tucked in the back seat and a throw-up pan on the floorboards."

Dr. Renoir turned to her desktop computer and pecked out a few numbers.

"I remember a huge tent way off in the middle of a prairie and people singing hymns as we drove up. My ma carried me down past all the people and up onto the stage. I was crying like crazy. And Dr. J. Edward Moorhouse wore this thin black skullcap with a point that came down the middle of his forehead. He had crooked teeth when he smiled. My stomach was rumbling and heaving, like there was a jackrabbit inside that wanted to get out. But Dr. J. Edward Moorhouse laid his hands on my stomach and I became as cool and as calm as I ever was. That was the last time I got sick before today."

"Sometimes we all need a little faith."

"You think so? I sure do."

"Psychosomatic healing," said Dr. Renoir. "The mind/body interface . . ."

"Those are all fancy words for faith, aren't they?" Muncie said.

"Perhaps."

"Well, I haven't been sick since then. I keep myself fit. I don't put anything in my body I think will cause me harm. Taking care of your body is doing God's work, isn't it?"

"I suppose so," Dr. Renoir replied gently.

Lance heard the ripping sound of Velcro parting. Then he felt something moist pressing against the ball of bone behind his right ear.

"What's that?" he said.

"Time-release motion-sickness medication."

"But Trikon doesn't want us using pads."

"You are under my care, not Trikon's. This pad is designed to release diminishing amounts of medication. By the time it is exhausted, you will be completely acclimated to space. And it won't harm your body." Dr. Renoir tore the blood-pressure collar from his arm. "You may stop staring at the wall now."

Lance turned his head and fixed his eyes on her. For the first time since reaching the station, his head did not continue spinning after his neck stopped.

A voice boomed over the loudspeaker:

"Attention. All new arrivals are to report to the connecting tunnel for sleep compartment assignments."

"You'd better go along now," said Dr. Renoir. "But don't rush. Take it easy for the time being."

Lance grinned at her. She's sure pretty, he thought. For a foreigner.

Habitation Modules 1 and 2 were located directly across the tunnels from The Bakery and Jasmine. Each habitation module housed twenty individual living compartments, four waste-management-system compartments (called Whits, after their inventor, Henry Whitmore), four full-body showers, and two enclosed hand basins. The compact living compartments were designed primarily for sleeping, but also were equipped for waking relaxation. Crammed into each one were storage cabinets, a toiletry kit, a foldaway desktop, reading lamp, and power outlets for portable computers, VCRs, and other small appliances. Screens set into the back walls served as "electronic windows" to minimize claustrophobia. Many employees brought tapes of scenery so they could look out at the cool green hills of Earth or a beautiful sunset over a tranquil sandy beach.

The "bed" was a mesh sleeping bag hung against one wall of the compartment. It could be zippered up, and there was a restraint band for the head. In microgravity the pressure of blood surging through the carotid arteries produced a gentle but persistent head nod when a person fell asleep. It awakened most people, nauseated some.

"Three and two-thirds cubic meters of living space," announced Jeffries as he peeled back the accordion door of an empty compartment. "That's one hundred twenty-eight cubic feet for the Americans in the group. Sounds like a lot, huh? The typical telephone booth is only a little over one cubic meter; forty cubic feet. Well, sometimes it feels like a lot and sometimes it feels smaller than a phone booth. Depends on your mood."

The newcomers hovered in the narrow aisle. Jeffries demonstrated the light switches, the power outlets, the sleep restraints, and how to prevent small objects from spewing out of the compartments when you opened the doors.

"Velcro, Velcro, Velcro," he said. "By the time you return to Earth, I guarantee you that you will never want to see another strip of Velcro again. And if you do happen to lose anything, check the nearest ventilator intake grid. They're located just above the floor along each wall. Everything ends up there sooner or later."

Jeffries then turned a dial on the back wall. The image on the screen changed from waves breaking at Waikiki to wheat fields waving in a summer breeze to an aerial view of snow-capped Mount Rainier.

"Any pictures of the Bronx?" asked Freddy.

"Not in this sequence. If you want it, we can arrange it," said Jeffries. "That ends the grand tour. I assume all of you learned how to operate the Whit and the showers back on Earth."

"I didn't," said O'Donnell.

"Well, my man," Jeffries grinned, "you are going to be in rough shape pretty fast without a lesson. Anybody else?"

The others answered that they were completely familiar with the personal hygiene facilities. Jeffries assigned each person a compartment, then led O'Donnell to the Whit.

"How does somebody come up here without learning this?" he said.

"I was a late addition," said O'Donnell.

"What the hell does that mean? Did you wander

onto the shuttle just before lift-off?"

"You might say that."

"Damn. Things sure have changed since I started to fly. Time was they wouldn't let anyone onto a shuttle without teaching you more things than you ever needed to know. Now they send people up who can't take a shit when they got to. Pull yourself in here." Jeffries opened the door of the Whit. The interior was a confusing array of tubes, levers, and siphons that looked like a piece of farm machinery designed at MIT. "We're going to start with number one. You remember number one from grammar school?"

O'Donnell entered the Whit and inserted his booted feet into the loops on the floor. Jeffries closed the door all but a crack.

"You're a Trikon scientist, right?"

"Right," said O'Donnell.

"Now unzip your flight suit. You know what happened a few days ago?"

"I heard."

"I thought with you being a late addition, maybe Trikon sent you up to keep an eye on these scientists."

"Not me."

"They can use a transfusion of common sense, the whole damn bunch of them." Jeffries saw that O'Donnell was out of his pants and closed the door completely.

"Okay," he called through the door. "You see that funnel right in front of you? Pull a urinal cover out of the dispenser on top of it and put it on the end of the funnel."

"Uh-huh," came O'Donnell's voice.

"Now turn that yellow switch on to start the fan and the centrifuge. Otherwise you'll end up with a pint-sized ball of piss on your crotch. Now stick your pecker into the funnel . . ."

"You sure this is safe?" O'Donnell asked over the whir of the fan.

"Are you Jewish?"

"No, and I don't want to be."

Jeffries laughed. "You'll be okay. We haven't lost anybody yet."

Feeling more than a little wary, O'Donnell did as Jeffries instructed. He relieved himself and felt the urine being whisked away by the airflow from the vacuum fan.

"Now I know how a cow feels in a milking barn," he said.

"Wait till we move on to number two," said Jeffries with a laugh that was nearly malicious. O'Donnell saw that there was a safety belt on the seat.

Dan Tighe watched the progress of the logistics-module transfer from the command center's view-ports. Standing beside him at the RMS console, a crewman operating the remotely controlled arm had already deftly detached the expended log module, stuck it on a temporary berthing mast, and was preparing to remove the replacement module from *Constellation*'s payload bay. Two other crewmen hovered outside in MMUs, manned maneuvering units, fondly nicknamed flying armchairs, ready to assist if the going got too tricky for the robot arm.

New food in, old garbage out, thought Tighe. Wryly he remembered some old soldier's maxim: The army is like the alimentary canal. No matter what goes in one end, nothing comes out the other end but crap.

Tighe had flown slot in the Thunderbirds, the Air Force's precision flying team. He had test-piloted jet fighters. He had commanded half a dozen shuttle missions for NASA. Now his flying days were over. Sure, he was still sailing clear around the world every ninety minutes. But as commander he didn't fly the station; nobody did. The station sailed around the world on its own, a diamond-shaped man-made moon. Tighe would never pilot a plane or a spacecraft again. He was fighting just to stay on as commander of this station.

This job was babysitting, not flying. There was a contingency plan for manually operating the complex system of translation and attitude thrusters in the event of a major gyroscope malfunction. He had trained for over a hundred hours with the hand controller that would override the automatic system in the event of such an emergency. But that had been on a simulator. Tighe doubted that the station could actually be "flown" the way its designers claimed.

What a laugh that would be, he thought bitterly. They won't let me fly because of my goddamned blood pressure, but maybe I could take control of this contraption and zoom her around for a while. Wouldn't that be sweet?

He pictured the look on Henderson's face and the frenzy at Mission Control if he suddenly started maneuvering the space station. It'd be like trying to fly a house. This station isn't going anywhere; just rolling around the Earth, time after time, day after day. Neither of us is going anywhere, are we?

His days were monotonous. He monitored the constant stream of data generated by the station's subsystems. He dispatched his crew to perform necessary tasks. He listened for alarms he prayed he never would hear. He refereed disputes between competing Trikon researchers. And all the while he struggled against being seduced by boredom. That was the greatest danger; not a meteoroid hit, not debris, not some weird chemical created in the labs. Simple boredom, a simple relaxation of vigilance.

Tighe frowned as he watched the two astronauts cavort in their MMUs. He missed the exhilaration of EVA. The media still called them space walks, and for once Tighe preferred the more romantic name. When he had first come to Trikon Station during the early shakeout phase, he would occasionally clamp himself into an MMU and jet outside the station. Strictly speaking he was not even supposed to do that much "flying," but if Dr. Renoir knew about it she at least chose not to make an issue of it.

One time he had parked himself beneath the station's nadir, where he could see nothing of the station, not the girders, not the modules, not even the shuttle that had transported him and his men to this outpost in the sky. He was completely alone and over Texas. Luminescent clouds scudded across the plains, tumbling before the wind, then curling into fishhooks where the Ozarks reared their craggy heads. He had a wife and a son down there, somewhere beneath those fishhooks. Three hundred miles away. Might as well be three hundred million.

He had made mistakes. Dammit, he had made mistakes. He thought he was being a good husband. When Cindy wanted to go back to school, after Bill was born, he made no objection. He was proud of her when she graduated, even if he was in the middle of a shuttle mission and couldn't attend the ceremonies. Sure, she was upset. She had a right to be. But when NASA grounded him over this stupid hypertension business Cindy had been tremendously supportive. He saw a whole new life starting for the two of them. Three of them; Bill was finishing high school, ready for college.

College costs money. The only firm that would consider a grounded astronaut had been Trikon International. It meant going back into space. Not as a pilot, but still Tighe accepted the offer without an instant's hesitation. When he phoned Cindy with the good news she went coldly silent. By the time he got back home she informed him that she had started procedures for a divorce. It hit him like a sniper's bullet.

But he was reasonable about it. He had to face the fact that he and Cindy had become a pair of virtual strangers. He had to struggle hard to salvage what was left of his career. Cindy wanted to move to Dallas, where she could start her new life and her own career. He was willing to let her sell their house, willing to pay all Bill's college expenses. There was no reason for them to fight, to snarl at each other, to drag themselves through an expensive and emotionally ruinous court battle. No reason at all. Except custody of their son.

"Commander Tighe?"

Dan's insides lurched with surprise. He snapped his attention to the here and now.

The two new crewmen hovered between the command center and the utilities section. Lance Muncie clenched a handhold with his massive fist and unconsciously bit his lower lip. His skin was several shades of green lighter than it had been when he blew breakfast down the length of the connecting tunnel. Tighe knew that Lorraine had fitted Muncie with a motion-sickness pad. This was in direct contravention of Trikon's policy that its people endure a few days of space sickness rather than become dependent on medication. But Trikon preferred a lot of things that just weren't practical in space, and Lorraine was judicious in her use of medication.

Freddy Aviles rocked gently from his center of gravity, which in his case was located near the solar plexus. His massive arm and chest muscles twitched as if only a supreme effort of self-denial prevented him from launching into a spin.

Tighe had selected them from a number of resumés Trikon had sent him. It was a damn fool way of manning a space station, but Trikon was the boss and constantly assured him that all candidates were top-notch space-worker material. Tighe doubted that anyone, especially Trikon's personnel department, could predict how a person would react in orbit, but he had to play the hand he was dealt. That same personnel section was on the verge of taking what was left of his career away from him.

His newest two recruits were very personal choices. Freddy Aviles had been born in the South Bronx and enlisted in the Navy after high school. As an electronics specialist he rose to the rank of petty officer, second class, on an Aegis destroyer before losing both legs when a missile broke loose from its mounting and crushed them while the ship rode out a typhoon. After discharge, he went to college for computer science and was working as a Pentagon analyst when he suddenly applied to Trikon for employment. Tighe had always believed that a legless person was well suited for life in micro-gee. The problem was that no space agency ever had recruited one. He was glad that Trikon had the vision, or the balls, to try.

There was nothing special to recommend Lance Muncie, other than that he was a fellow midwesterner. But one fact of personal importance had caught Tighe's eye: Muncie was a recent graduate of the University of Kansas.

Tighe acknowledged the two crewmen's salutes with a casual wave of his hand. He presented each of them with a set of thick laminated cards bound together by a plastic spiral.

"These outline your basic responsibilities. I'm sure you already know every word," he said. "Now for the unofficial stuff."

Lance Muncie's expression hardened into a frown. Freddy Aviles grinned as if expecting the punch line of an inside joke. His gold canine twinkled.

"There's been trouble among the scientists. I'm not going to bullshit you. It's getting worse. The official line is that they're working together on a project with environmental ramifications. The truth is that each one would slit the throats of the others in order to be the first to develop whatever it is they're trying to develop. I don't concern myself with the specifics, and neither should you. Our job is to see that the station remains in one piece and doesn't fall out of the sky.

"Now, some of these scientists may see you as possible allies in their games. Others may see you as enforcers. Others might not take any notice of you at all. You'll get a sense of it pretty damn fast. I want you to remember that you are not a policeman, a judge, or a jury. If you see anything that strikes you as odd, don't take any action. Report it to me."

"Odd like what, sir?" asked Lance Muncie.

"Odd like a Japanese scientist roaming through the American lab module late at night. Or vice versa. Or any permutation of scientists or their technicians in the wrong place at the wrong time."

"Oh."

"You'll get the idea pretty quickly, men. After a few days, you'll see who's staring daggers at who." Tighe paused long enough to look each crewman in the eye. "I'm sure you noticed that there are several women on board. Some are Trikon scientists or technicians, others are part of the Mars Project, and a few are members of the crew. There are no rules against fraternization, but I hope you'll use your common sense. This is a closed system. Emotions can run high even on the best of days, and there are damn few outlets for blowing off steam. I don't care how you conduct yourselves in your spare time. But if I see your performance suffering or the safety of this station compromised, remember one thing. I'm your commanding officer, not your father. I don't get paid for wisdom and understanding."

The two crewmen muttered in assent, although Muncie looked plainly disturbed.

"Aviles, I understand you are a computer whiz."

"I have a master's in computer science from *Columbia*. The Navy paid my way after the accident. Wanted me to be a useful citizen."

"The station has an emergency configuration for its computer system that makes sense only to people on the ground," said Tighe. "We can't shut off the mainframe without going to auxiliary power. If I get you the specs, can you reconfigure it?"

"I'm not on the ground, sir."

"Fine. Any questions?"

Muncie's brows knit slightly. "Sir—half the people up here are doctors, aren't they? Are we supposed to call them that? Or what?"

Smiling, Tighe answered, "It's all pretty informal. We call the medical officer 'Doctor.' Everybody else is 'mister' or 'ms.' Except the head of the Martians. He likes to be called *Professor* Jaeckle."

Muncie nodded, still frowning uncertainly.

"All right. That will be all," said Tighe.

Freddy flicked his wrists against the wall and bored like a torpedo toward the entrance to the connecting tunnel. Lance groped his way from handhold to handhold. The two new crewmen: a dour farm boy and a jive-ass Puerto Rican who had no ass.

"Muncie," called Tighe.

Muncie stopped himself and covered the pad behind his right ear with his hand.

"Sir, if it's about—"

"Forget it, son. I know about the pad and I know Trikon's policy. Dr. Renoir is a good doctor. You do what she says, okay?"

Lance dragged his lip beneath his teeth and nodded.

"You graduated from the University of Kansas, right? Ever run into someone named Bill Tighe?"

Lance knit his brow as if rummaging through his memory for a face to connect with the name.

"He would have been a freshman when you were a senior," prodded Tighe.

"No. Can't say I did. UK's a big place, sir."

"Yeah. I guess it is."

After mastering the use of the personal hygiene facilities, O'Donnell closed himself in his compartment and began to unpack. He was traveling light, even by space flight standards: socks, toothbrush, comb, and razor. No picture of a girl back home to attach to his compartment wall. No gold crucifix to drift out of his collar and dangle at the end of a thick chain. No blank minicassettes for video letters to home. Everything he needed was in his head—work, memories, dreams, and an invisible line he could not cross.

O'Donnell finished stowing his belongings and checked the time. It was early afternoon. His scientific gear was in the new logistics module and would not be accessible until the next day. He adjusted the sleep restraint, played with the reading lamp, and flipped through the selection of scenes on the viewscreen. He looked at his watch again. Four minutes had passed. The Cape began to look like paradise.

A knock on the doorframe relieved his boredom.

"Who is it?" O'Donnell pulled free of the sleep restraint and pushed toward the door, expecting either Freddy or Lance Muncie.

"Dr. Renoir."

He slid the door open.

"The medical officer," she added. She hung in the doorway, stockinged feet barely touching the floor, one hand on a grip set into the wall: good-looking, not quite beautiful, strong alert features, ample figure filling out her blue flight suit nicely.

"I remember," O'Donnell said, making himself smile at her. "From Commander Tighe's welcoming speech. You dodge projectile vomit very well."

"It comes with medical training," she said. She glanced down at the computer in her other hand. "You are required to report to me every day. Trikon's orders."

"I know. Does today count as a day?"

"It does."

He noticed her looking past him, taking in the entire compartment in one sweeping glance. He was accustomed to the probing eyes, the seemingly innocuous questions, the tricks. Was this visit a coincidence? Or had she come here as soon as Jeffries reported him safely in his compartment.

"We can talk here or you can come to the infirmary. It has slightly more room."

"I think I'll be seeing enough of this place."

"Fine. The infirmary is in the command module." She quickly turned and pushed through the hatch into the connecting tunnel.

Dr. Renoir's infirmary was larger than O'Donnell's compartment, but just barely. With the door closed, the only way for them to fit comfortably was for her to hover near the ceiling and for him to hook an arm through a foot loop on the floor. The positions were disorienting at first, but O'Donnell quickly adjusted his perceptions. Her legs, foreshortened from his angle, were tightly pressed together and crossed at the ankles. Excessively prim and proper. More like prudish, since she wore a trousered jumpsuit just like everybody else. He considered suggesting that she unwind, then thought better of it. There was a severity in her broad, blunt features. Her lips, pressed tightly together, seemed to be made of stone. Her brown eyes were narrowed in concentration and her dark eyebrows were shaped like the horns of a ram. She was too well scrubbed for O'Donnell's taste. In fact, her neatly wrapped French braid reminded him of a University of Oregon sorority sister he had tried unsuccessfully to bed. Then he laughed to himself. She'll look like Miss Universe in a couple of weeks, he predicted silently.

"Do you know why you are here?" she asked. Her voice was a rich mezzo, almost sultry despite the severity of her looks.

"On Trikon Station?"

"No."

"Seeing you? You want to make sure I won't get sick like Lance Muncie."

"Don't be flip, Mr. O'Donnell. You have already failed your first test by not admitting it." Dr. Renoir tapped on her hand computer. "July, 1995, you were arrested for possession of cocaine during a police sweep of a drug neighborhood in East L.A. Your car was confiscated but your case was dismissed on condition that you seek treatment for substance abuse. August, 1995, you checked into a private clinic in Encino, California. You were discharged in February of the following year and continued attending outpatient meetings for six months."

"That's when I started riding my motorcycle again."

Dr. Renoir furrowed her brows so that her ram's horns almost touched over the bridge of her nose.

"You and someone named Bob Rodriguez formed a chapter of a national motorcycle club for ex-addicts." Her tone was deprecating.

"You don't sound as though you approve."

"I don't think that a motorcycle club is the proper forum for treating drug abuse."

"It's worked for us, including the three physicians who begged to join."

Dr. Renoir ignored his comment. "You went to work for a Trikon subsidiary in August, 1996."

"I've been clean for three years."

She stared at him.

"I've been clean for three years. Does your report include that?"

Dr. Renoir stuck the hand computer behind a bungee cord. "Mr. O'Donnell."

"Hugh."

"Mr. O'Donnell," she repeated with emphasis. "I don't know why Trikon sent you here and I don't care to know. But I have my orders. You will report to me each day at oh-eight-thirty hours. If that time conflicts with your schedule for any reason, we will set a new time. You will be randomly tested for drugs once during each calendar month you are on the station. If any of the results are positive, I will immediately report you to your superiors on Earth. And if, despite negative results, I have reason to suspect that you might be using controlled substances, I will ask the commander to order a thorough search of your compartment and workstation. Do I make myself clear?"

17 AUGUST 1998
TRIKON STATION

TOP SECRET

To: The President and Staff
From: R. McQ. Welch, Executive Department, Drug
Task Force
Date: 11 January 1994
Subject: Eradicating cocaine

Ecgonine synthase *is the principal enzyme that ena-*
bles the coca plant to produce the chemical back-
bone of the alkaloid known as cocaine.

As experiments with tobacco plants have proven, it
is possible to create an RNA messenger molecule that
will instruct plant cells to stop manufacturing a
specific enzyme. The tobacco experiments, which
focused on the alkaloid nopaline, were highly suc-
cessful using this antisense RNA sequence treatment.
(The term "antisense" means that the RNA sequence
is instructing the cell to stop producing a certain
chemical, rather than start.) Nopaline production
was suppressed, and this trait was passed down to
the plants' offspring.

Our proposal is to develop and deliver an RNA
sequence that will turn off the gene responsible for
ecgonine synthase *production without affecting any*
other gene in the coca plant's cells. This genetic
agent will not kill the coca plants. In fact, its only
effect will be to suppress the production of the

enzyme, which will suppress the plant's production of cocaine and render the plants useless for cocaine processing.

We believe that this technique will be the safest, most successful, and most ecologically responsible method of eradicating cocaine from South American jungles.

Should such a research project be initiated, it must proceed under airtight security. To have the maximum impact on the cocaine cartel's raw materials, the coca crop must be treated in a single growing season. If the cartel learns of this plan they will disperse their growing fields and/or diversify into other drugs.

Security for the scientific personnel will also be important, both for their personal safety and to ensure the integrity of the program. Therefore the research should be conducted in a laboratory facility that is as secure and remote as possible.

THE STATION WARDROOM shared a module with the exercise and recreation area. The wardroom consisted of six galley stations and an equal number of chest-high tables. No chairs were necessary in microgravity. Instead, diners slipped their feet into the "stirrups" that were mounted on the table legs like the rungs of a ladder, so that anyone could find a height that was comfortable for his or her individual size and posture.

Each galley had three doors, two hinged to open sideways and one that swung down to provide a working surface. Behind the doors were a pantry, freezer, refrigerator, microwave oven, a supply of plastic trays with magnetized receptacles for utensils, and hot and cold water injectors. The predominant color of the fixtures was pastel yellow.

On the wall spaces between the galleys were larger versions of the video screens found in the living compartments. The screens almost always showed real-time views of the Earth taken by the station's TV cameras, accompanied by soft music.

The six tables poked up from the floor like truncated mushrooms. Above each table was an inverted bowl attached to the ceiling by thin pipes. Looking like Art Deco chandeliers, the bowls were actually vents that gently sucked crumbs and errant bits of food onto removable grids. Each table had four bins for holding the magnetized food trays. This limited the wardroom capacity to twenty-four; meals had to be staggered, since the station's normal population was more than double the wardroom's capacity. On rotation days it got even worse, with new personnel arriving before the old ones could depart.

Despite its high-tech ambience, the wardroom had the feel of a small-town general store. Except for a few days after a rotation, everybody knew everybody else. A nod or a glance often told as much as words; more, sometimes. Groups combined and recombined from meal to meal as alliances were forged and friendships made—or broken.

O'Donnell found the wardroom crowded when he pulled himself through the hatchway for his first meal. From the pantry he selected a tray of soup, smoked turkey, mixed vegetables, bread, strawberries, and apple juice. Just as he had been taught at his abbreviated preflight briefings, he attached his tray to the magnetic strips on the fold-down door of the galley, placed the turkey and mixed vegetables in the microwave oven, and rehydrated the soup by injecting it with a blast of hot water.

All of the tables were occupied, though none by four people. Three Japanese gathered around one table, their heads bobbing in unison as they efficiently moved precise cuts of food from tray to mouth with their chopsticks. A heavyset dark man with a billowing saffron shirt bellied up to another table, his spindly arms working his utensils like pistons. Lance

Muncie and Freddy Aviles were together near the doorway to the ex/rec room.

O'Donnell opted for a table occupied by a pudgy, bearded man wearing a Trikon USA T-shirt. He chose the table less for the man's nationality than for the amount of food remaining on his tray: He was almost finished with his dinner.

They introduced themselves. The bearded man was David Nutt. He explained that he was due to return to the States on *Constellation*.

"And not a day too soon, either. I'm not thrilled with the prospect of readjusting to gravity after six months, but this place is played out for me. You're a biochemist? Microbiologist? What?"

O'Donnell pushed a valved straw into his apple juice.

"That's the best policy. Don't answer any questions, not even those asked by compatriots." Nutt beckoned O'Donnell to lean closer and lowered his voice to a whisper. "Watch your ass and watch your data. See that Jap over there, the fat one with the crewcut? He's Hisashi Oyamo, head of the Japanese group. He'll kill you with politeness. All bowing and hissing. But one of those little pricks with him stole genetic data files from my computer."

"So I heard," said O'Donnell. "What happened?"

"Nothing," said Nutt bitterly. "Oyamo called Tighe's bluff and now the damned Jap's going back home with my data on a bugged disk. They'll figure out a way to get past the bug and then they'll have everything I've worked six months to accomplish. Fucking zipperheads."

"Racial epithets are not in the Trikon spirit," O'Donnell said, working to keep his face straight. "It says so in the orientation manual."

"Those fairy tales! And see that one over there with the yellow tent for a shirt? He's Dr. Chakra Ramsanjawi, the former pride of Oxford."

"He looks pretty dark for a Brit."

"He's the head of the European section."

"I thought the Brits weren't involved in Trikon," said O'Donnell.

"They aren't. Politics keeps them at arm's length from the rest of United Europe, so they decided to keep their scientists out of Trikon. Personally, I think they regret it."

"Then why is Ramsanjawi here?"

"He's had a hard-on for the Brits ever since he was dismissed as head of the biochem department at Oxford. Sex and drug scandal. You know, the type of story that keeps the tabloids in the black. He swears he's innocent of all charges. Trikon is his way of sticking it in the Brits' ear."

"Did he break into your computer files, too?"

"Not that I can prove." With some effort, Nutt forced himself lower and covered his mouth with his free hand. "When I came here six months ago the United Europe lab was a joke. They didn't know a microbe from a bathrobe. Then Ramsanjawi comes up here and bingo, they know everything we Americans and the Canadians took months to synthesize and more. You tell me they aren't stealing."

"I can't. But, Dave, how do you know what they know?" O'Donnell smiled impishly.

"Stick it, O'Donnell, willya?" Nutt yanked his food tray out of its bin and floated off.

Good thing he's leaving, O'Donnell thought. Guy's like a live bomb, ready to go off any minute.

O'Donnell ate slowly and carefully. Surface tension held the food in the containers and on his utensils, although the mixed vegetables escaped if he loaded too many onto his fork. Crumbs from his bread spiraled up into the vent like a lilliputian dust devil.

The music hid most of the dinnertime chatter. The only distinct voices he could hear belonged to Freddy Aviles and Lance Muncie.

"You din' finish, man."

"I've had enough."

"Thought you were feeling better."

"I am."

"So why don' you finish?"

"I know my digestive system better'n you do, okay, Freddy? I've had enough."

A wide-hipped man wearing a red flight suit emblazoned with the circle and arrow insignia of the Mars Project maneuvered through the tables. His eyelids blinked rapidly and his head bobbed like a chicken's. He looked at everyone in the wardroom, obviously considering and rejecting them as companions for his evening meal, then sank into footloops at O'Donnell's table. Despite his girth, his shoulders were narrow and his collarbones resembled a pair of twigs beneath the fabric of his flight suit. His brown hair was greased and plastered across his forehead for maximum coverage. Unbound by a hairnet, one strand had worked free and stood upright like an antenna. The name tag above the project insignia read: R. CRAMER.

"Howdy, pal," said O'Donnell. He extended his hand. Cramer did not look up from his tray, although O'Donnell detected a grunt that might have been a greeting. O'Donnell's hand dangled unshaken in the wash of the vent. He saved face by nipping at a bread crumb with his fingers.

Cramer went at his food like a man with palsy. No amount of surface tension could have bonded the food to his shaking fork. Crumbs and vegetables soon formed a cloud above his tray, drifting slowly upward. He tried batting an errant cube of brown mystery meat toward his mouth, and grew increasingly angry with each miss. Finally, he let it float up into the vent.

"Are these strawberries always this bad?" asked O'Donnell.

"You should have rehydrated them," said Cramer. He swiped at another cube of meat, but succeeded only in shooting it through the doorway to the exercise room. He slammed his fork against the table. "Damn!"

O'Donnell took his tray to the nearest galley and zapped his strawberries with a jet of cold water. He considered joining Freddy and Muncie. Even they would be better company than Cramer. But when he noticed Dr. Renoir hovering close to Cramer's ear, he glided back to his place and tried to look as if he weren't eavesdropping. Their topic of conversation seemed important, and they both kept their voices almost too low to hear.

"—supposed to meet at sixteen hundred hours," she was saying.

Cramer cast a wary glance at O'Donnell as he replied, "I was busy."

"Too busy to keep our meeting?"

He turned back to the doctor, whispering urgently, "I was at a very delicate point in an experiment. I couldn't just leave."

"You could have arranged another time."

"I can't foresee what I'll be doing every minute of the day. Jesus!"

Cramer unlooped himself and barreled toward the door, grazing the back of a Japanese tech with his foot. Startled, the Japanese flinched. Then he regained his self-control and discreetly did not react any further.

"Lover's quarrel or professional disagreement?" O'Donnell asked the doctor.

"Either way, it wouldn't be any of your business." A vein in her neck pulsed rapidly.

"Touché," said O'Donnell.

Dr. Lorraine Renoir considered her life to be a conflicting mix of opposing forces and conflicting situations. She had grown up in Quebec City, where French and English uneasily coexisted, where the ancient walled city towered over glitzy condominiums lining the St. Lawrence River, where the European elegance of the Château Frontenac competed with the New World efficiency of the Marriotts and Hiltons. The conflict followed her through McGill University, where she bucked the chauvinism of her male classmates and teachers to graduate summa cum laude in physics, tempered with a minor in French art. Later, in medical school, she was looked on as an oddity, a real scientist among all the younger pre-med graduates pursuing dreams of quick wealth. The clashing forces weaved through her own bilingualism and even showed themselves in her body: her thick legs and sunken cheeks on Earth, her shapely figure and full face in microgravity.

She had expected the post on Trikon Station would reconcile the opposing forces in her life. The station provided the perfect environment for a physician who had a keen interest in biophysics. This was not the mere practice of medicine. The effects of microgravity upon the human body permeated every aspect of a person's health from postnasal drip to heart arhythmia to calcium depletion.

Even her love of fine art found expression in the space station. The Earth, as seen from the observation blister, was the most splendid work of art she had ever seen. She thrilled at the thought of Monet or Cezanne trying to catch its ever-changing glory on canvas.

But what she had found was an even more complicated mix: a multinational population with different attitudes toward health and personal hygiene, ego clashes among the leaders of the various subgroups, and a rotation schedule that seemed to push people just slightly beyond their limits. Layered over these conflicts was a slowly disappearing region called medical ethics. On Earth she would never have dreamed of discussing a patient's problems with a third party without the patient's consent. But on Trikon Station, the doctor-patient privilege evaporated whenever she reasonably believed that withholding the information could jeopardize the safety of others.

Reasonable belief. She had no idea what the words actually meant. Did they mean the reasonable belief of a thirty-two-year-old female physician hurtling around the world in a closed system at more than twenty-eight thousand kilometers per hour at an altitude of almost five hundred kilometers? Or did they mean the cool judgment of an ethics committee meeting behind the closed doors of a Canadian Medical Association boardroom? Lorraine Renoir did not know.

And then there were the men aboard the station. Lorraine had been warned that Trikon, despite its technological sophistication, would be more like a frontier outpost than a modern research laboratory. That did not bother her; she almost enjoyed the attention she received, although it complicated her position of trust and authority even further.

Even the famous Kurt Jaeckle was beaming his photogenic smile at her. The one man who seemed to avoid her was the station commander. The only times they spoke more than a few words to one another were when she gave him his weekly cardiovascular exam. Even then he was guarded, almost hostile. Lorraine realized that Tighe saw her as an enemy, the woman who could have him fired from his post. In Dan Tighe, all Lorraine's contradictions and conflicts coalesced into a single whirlpool of turmoil.

It was evening according to the clock. The shuttle had returned to Earth, taking the departing rotation with it. The bulk of the station's population was in the wardroom or the ex/rec area. Hab 1 was quiet.

Lorraine knocked on the compartment doorjamb. There was a rumble, then the accordion door peeled back. Stereo headphones covered Kurt Jaeckle's ears and a pair of reading glasses bobbed on his nose.

"Lorraine, what a pleasant coincidence," he said, smiling. He pulled the headphones down around his neck and folded his glasses into a pocket. The strains of a Mozart piano concerto issued thinly from the headphones.

"I'm afraid I'm not here by coincidence or for pleasant conversation," said Lorraine. "I need to talk to you about Russell Cramer. He's been behaving strangely."

Jaeckle's smile vanished. "We had best talk in here," he said, sliding the door shut behind her. "We've all been out of sorts lately. That power outage two days ago on top of six months in space is not conducive to good humor."

"His behavior goes beyond just being out of sorts. Did you know that he consulted me about a problem?"

"I didn't," said Jaeckle. "When was that?"

"Four weeks ago. His complaint was that he couldn't sleep."

"Was our regimen the reason?"

"Actually, no. He said the trouble began with a dream of the station falling from the sky. He described the dream quite vividly. The dominant images were the modules glowing red from atmospheric friction and the screams of the people inside. He said he could identify each person from their cries."

"What action did you take?" Jaeckle asked.

"I'm hesitant to prescribe drugs unless absolutely necessary. So I suggested that he not exercise within three hours of his normal sleep time."

"I noticed that he altered his exercise schedule," said Jaeckle.

"It seemed to work until yesterday. He came to me with the same complaint. I'd never seen him so agitated, so I gave him a placebo and told him I wanted to see him at sixteen hundred hours today. But he never appeared. When I found him in the wardroom this evening, he said that he was unable to keep the appointment because he had been involved in an experiment."

"I can vouch for that," said Jaeckle. "When exactly did you say his trouble sleeping began?"

"Four weeks ago," said Lorraine.

Jaeckle removed a clipboard thick with papers from behind a bungee cord. He released one of the two clips attached to the board and the papers spread out like a fan.

"Cramer is our chief biochemist," he said. "He's been working with soil samples that one of the Martian landers brought back. Four weeks ago, he obtained a result in an experiment that he swears indicates the presence of microorganisms in the Martian soil. The evidence was fleeting at best, and had completely disappeared by the time I reached his workstation. He begged and pleaded with me to issue a media release, but I refused to do so unless he could duplicate the experiment. He's been trying ever since."

"Trying hard enough to be frustrated by failure?" asked Lorraine.

"Wouldn't surprise me. A day rarely goes by that he doesn't argue with me over releasing the original results. I would dearly love to issue that media release, but I simply can't until we are absolutely sure there is life in that soil. Cramer doesn't understand public relations."

"Whatever the reason, it seems to me that Mr. Cramer is showing the early signs of Orbital Dementia," Lorraine said. "He is agitated and cranky and his failure to keep his appointment with me is definite evidence of reclusiveness."

"Are you certain of your diagnosis?"

"One is never certain of Orbital Dementia," said Lorraine. "In its early stages the symptoms are far from clear."

"We wouldn't want to make a mistake," Jaeckle said. "I wouldn't want a run-of-the-mill bad mood to threaten a young man's career."

"No," said Lorraine. "But protocol requires me to report my concerns to the young man's immediate superior. If I'm not satisfied with the action taken by the superior, I am required to go to the commander."

"I appreciate that. The same protocol requires me to pass on my own report to the station commander. I will investigate Mr. Cramer's behavior at once. You may consider it done."

"Thank you." Lorraine turned toward the door.

"Lorraine," said Jaeckle. "I meant it that your visit here was a pleasant coincidence. I wanted to speak to you about something."

She slowly turned back and steadied herself by extending a hand to the wall.

"I need an assistant for my next several television shows. I would like her to be you."

Lorraine felt a mild shock of surprise. A pleasant shock. "But you already have an assistant."

"I know, but the producer wants a change. Something about it being necessary for ratings. It's all very esoteric."

"I'm not sure I have the time."

"I can promise you that it will not interfere with your duties. And if you would prefer, I can clear it with Dan."

"I can speak to him myself, thanks," said Lorraine. "Let me think about it."

She pushed herself out of the compartment, leaving a delicate spoor of perfume in her wake.

Jaeckle waited until Lorraine was gone, then made a beeline to his office in the Mars module. She's certainly good to look at, he thought. Nice throaty voice, too. Sexy. But how competent is she? Orbital Dementia is more of an accusation than a diagnosis. It could begin and end with Russ Cramer. Or it could infect the entire project like influenza. Or a witch hunt.

At his office, he quickly called up the project's computerized records and paged through Russell Cramer's personnel file. I've got to nip this problem quickly, Jaeckle told himself.

The Klaxons belonged to fire engines. Hugh O'Donnell lay in his bedroom with the windows open and the shades pulled back. Red emergency lights licked the ceiling as the engines passed.

He tried to push off the bed, but found himself restrained. The Klaxons whooped louder. He pushed harder. The restraints snapped. He sailed toward the open window, his fingers clawing for something to grab. He struck a solid wall. Still, the Klaxons whooped. He rubbed his forehead, stared at the unfastened straps of his sleep restraint.

"The first night," he groaned. "Shit."

Wearing nothing but his boxer shorts, he looped his glasses around his ears and dove out of his compartment. People swarmed in the aisle of Hab 2. Muncie. Freddy. Techs and scientists from the shuttle trip. Most of them in rumpled flight suits; a few in pajamas or skivvies. O'Donnell fell in behind them. Like a lemming, he thought, a goddamn lemming looking for a cliff.

They curved out of Hab 2 and flew down the connecting tunnel, arms pumping, feet kicking, everyone keeping pace. Chakra Ramsanjawi popped out of Hab 1 and joined the rush, his *kurta* flapping like a flag. The group bottlenecked at CERV Port 1. There were grunts, shouts, complaints, shoulders banged and knees skinned. Crewman Stanley, flattened against the tunnel wall and holding a stopwatch, yelled for everyone to hurry.

Eventually, they worked through the port and into the chamber beyond. O'Donnell found the last unoccupied harness and stretched the straps across his chest. Stanley strapped himself into the chair facing a tiny instrument panel.

"This is CERV One, officially known as crew emergency reentry vehicle one, affectionately known as a lifeboat," said Stanley, with just a trace of the outback in his voice. He had awkwardly turned himself around so that he could see the fifteen panting souls pressed shoulder to shoulder along the padded walls. One of the women was clutching a flimsy robe to her hunched-over body. A newcomer, O'Donnell recognized her from the flight up. This sure discourages you from sleeping in the nude, he told himself wistfully.

Stanley ignored the blonde's dishabille. "You'll notice that it is not very comfortable, not elaborately instrumented, and allows almost zero visibility. It isn't designed for sightseeing jaunts. It's designed to take sixteen people to Earth in case of an emergency.

"There are four CERVs docked at all times. Another one is across the tunnel, two more are at the far end of the tunnel. You are all designated for CERV One. In the event of an evacuation order, you come here from wherever you are. Understand?"

There were murmurs of assent. Ramsanjawi snorted. His hands worked at the harness, but the buckles kept bouncing away from each other.

"Problems, Dr. Ramsanjawi?" asked Stanley.

"This damnable buckle is defective."

"None of them ever seem to work for you," Stanley said.

O'Donnell, strapped into the harness next to Ramsanjawi, helped snap the buckle into place, his nostrils twitching at the cloying perfume that overlaid a more pungent body odor. Ramsanjawi scowled.

"This drill took forty seconds," said Stanley. "Excluding Dr. Ramsanjawi's continuing tribulations. Not bad, but there is room for improvement."

"When do we learn to fly it?" asked a tech.

"You don't. All you need to know is how to get into it, and fast. As for flying, each crewman is a certified CERV pilot. The training takes six months. All right —that's it until next time."

One by one, the people unharnessed themselves and filed out until only Ramsanjawi remained.

"May I have permission to linger and familiarize myself with these buckles?"

"Not a bad idea after tonight's performance," said Stanley.

Ramsanjawi fiddled with a harness until Stanley was gone. Then he settled into the pilot's seat. The controls were rudimentary—flat panel displays and two hand controllers, one a T-handle for maneuvering and the other a pistol grip for attitude control. Six months training in order to fly this contraption. Ridiculous! He could fly it right now, if the situation arose.

18 AUGUST 1998
LAUSANNE

Of all the problems facing space workers who spend months aboard a station such as Trikon, the worst is boredom. Although we designed Trikon Station with the help of a small army of ergonomists, environmental psychologists, and experienced astronauts, there was no way around the fact that a space station is a small, cramped, and terribly limited closed system.

The danger that this raised was, of course, that the space workers might resort to altering their internal environments in order to relieve the monotony. That is, they might turn to using drugs. Remember, we were dealing with very bright men and women, mostly young, mostly with personalities bordering on the aggressive side. In addition, most of them were biologists, chemists, and biochem technicians! They could invent new drugs easily; they had all the equipment and raw material that they needed.

I was very concerned about this possibility, so much so that I insisted that the medical officer of Trikon Station be equipped to test for narcotics of every type. I had Trikon's medical staff develop procedures for testing individuals suspected of drug abuse.

Some of the medical researchers wanted to go even further. They wanted to experiment with a controlled drug program for long-duration space flights, to develop specific recreational drugs that would have no dangerous aftereffects. I absolutely

*forbade it. I knew that such an experiment would be
both dangerous and foolish.*
>   —From the diary of Fabio Bianco,
>   CEO, Trikon International

FABIO BIANCO PEELED back the curtains on a bright
August afternoon. In the distance, a sliver of Lake
Geneva sparkled in the sunlight. The peaks of the Jura
Mountains fell away from Mont Tendre and formed a
scalloped horizon of white and gray against the bril-
liant blue sky.

Lausanne was so different from New York, Tokyo,
Berlin, Rome, or any of the other cities Bianco visited
in his capacity as CEO of Trikon International. The
Swiss city's cleanliness was seductive. Casting an eye
across that sweep of water, mountains, and sky,
feeling a snap in the midsummer air, one could almost
believe that the world was not collapsing into filth.

Bianco let the curtains fall together, and for a
moment the room went black. His tired old eyes
reacted slowly these days. The onset of cataracts? Why
not. He was afflicted by every other malady of old
age.

The room slowly brightened. As usual, he had taken
a suite: bedroom, bath, sitting room for solitary
meals, balcony, and an alcove with a desk, several
electrical outlets, and a telephone jack. On one side of
the desk was a laptop computer, its fuzzy white cursor
blinking slowly on the blue field of an otherwise
empty screen. On the other side was a portable laser
printer. A rivulet of accordion paper tumbled from
the printer to the thickly carpeted floor.

"You look tired, Uncle," said Ugo. He had dragged
an ottoman across from the deeply cushioned sofa
and leaned with his elbows on the desk.

"Mezzo-mezz'," said Bianco, fluttering a hand.

He was very thin, fragile, his wispy white hair
almost entirely gone. Once he had been able to glare

down anyone who dared stand against him, his face as haughty as any Caesar's with its proud Roman nose and penetrating brown eyes. Now, riddled with hypertension, ulcers, a weakening heart, he felt old and used up. But the will remained. The drive to master whoever or whatever stood in his way, even if it was his own slowly failing body.

He pulled open the mouth of a black satchel resting on the floor and plunged his hand into it. Made of the finest calfskin, the satchel was a gift from an old friend who was also Bianco's physician. It was stuffed with all manner of medical necessities: transdermal nitroglycerin pads, vitamins, anti-inflammatories, an extra pair of reading glasses, and pills to regulate blood pressure, heart rhythm, cholesterol, and water retention. He dug out his antacid and swigged it directly from the bottle. It tasted more like chalk than cherry.

"Your ulcer is bad today?"

"Always bad," said Bianco. "Meeting with the French makes it worse."

"I thought you were meeting with more than just the French."

"The French, the Germans, the Swiss, the Swedes, all of the member nations of the United Europe arm of Trikon will be present," said Bianco. "But it is from the French I expect the trouble. They have been miffed ever since the Board appointed Chakra Ramsanjawi over Jean-Pierre Delemonde as chief coordinating scientist of Trikon UE. I expect they will use the recent incident aboard Trikon Station as a pretext for pulling out."

"Let them," said Ugo. "If United Europe can survive without the British, Trikon UE could survive without the French."

Bianco looked at his nephew. The young man's shoulder muscles rippled defiantly beneath his open-necked shirt. His black hair fell like fine fur on his collar. His brown eyes gleamed in a sliver of sunlight poking through the curtains. The light projected a silhouette of Ugo's head on the alcove wall. His profile was strong, classical Roman. Family and friends often remarked that Ugo was the image of the young Fabio. Yes, I looked like that once, Bianco thought to himself. Long ago. Long ago.

With a sigh and a shrug of his frail shoulders he told his nephew, "We need everyone, Ugo, even the goddamned French."

"If it were up to me . . ." Ugo began.

The laptop suddenly beeped and its cursor began to run across the screen, leaving trails of characters in its wake.

"*Momento*. Rome is calling," said Bianco. He fumbled for his reading glasses.

The words scrolled up the screen in French, the language of Trikon UE: AN ADDRESS BY FABIO BIANCO, CEO, TRIKON INTERNATIONAL, TO THE BOARD OF DIRECTORS AND MEMBER CORPORATIONS OF TRIKON UNITED EUROPE. ANNUAL MEETING. 19 AUGUST 1998.

The printer started to hum. Rather than strain to read the letters on the laptop's screen, Bianco waited for the pages rolling out of the printer. The typescript was large enough so that he did not need his glasses. Bianco was not pleased with what he read. The French syntax was strained and the verbs were bland and weak. Worse, it attempted to avoid the truth. The sole allusion to the theft of the American computer files was a single sentence on page two: AN UNFORTUNATE MISAPPLICATION OF DATA.

As soon as the transmission ended, Bianco fired off a return message. I WILL NOT STAND BEFORE THE BOARD OF DIRECTORS AND DISPENSE OLIVE OIL. His forefingers hammered at the keys of the laptop. I WANT THE TRUTH, *LA VERITA. CAPISCE?*

The Rome office of Trikon UE acknowledged his ire. Bianco ripped the pages from the printer and tore the speech into confetti.

"Speech writers think they have words for all occasions. I expect enough displeasure without inviting the Board to brand me a weakling." He gripped his desk as pain ripped across his stomach like a bolt of forked lightning.

"Are you all right, Uncle?"

"Fine. Just some pain. I'll be—" With a trembling hand, he reached into his satchel. He gulped antacid ravenously.

"Do you want me to call the hotel doctor?"

Bianco waved away the suggestion. He placed the bottle uncapped on his desk and reclined his chair.

"You want to rest now? I can come back at dinnertime."

"No, Ugo. I am fine. I want you to stay. I want to ask you a question." Bianco closed his eyes. "Remember when we would sit in the garden of your mother's house and talk about the world in the year 2000?"

"I said there would be soccer games on the moon," said Ugo. "With a field six times as long and six times as wide and a dome pumped full of air. What a fool I was. Playing soccer on the moon! Now we can't even play in England."

"You were merely being a boy," said Bianco. "I was the fool, a grown man who foresaw an international consortium and a space station where the brightest minds from every nation could solve the problems created during centuries of ignorance."

"You have come closer with your prediction than I have with mine."

"But it is not good enough, Ugo. The space station is our perfect laboratory not because it is free of gravity but because it is free of borders and free of competition. It provides us with an endless view of the very world we are trying to save.

"But I learned too late that man is a stubborn creature. He will bring his politics and his competition with him. The people working on the project care only about dollars and lire and yen and who claims the glory."

"They are scientists, Uncle. They should know better."

"They know," said Bianco. "But they forget. I don't have the answer. Maybe I should return to research myself."

"You can't go to the space station with your condition."

"My doctor treats my condition with pills and warnings to avoid spicy foods. I do not obey because spicy foods are one of the few pleasures left me, other than watching beautiful women stroll the piazzas on a summer evening."

"There are no women strolling piazzas on Trikon Station," said Ugo.

"Nor are there spicy foods."

Bianco's voice trailed off. He breathed deeply and cleared his mind with a relaxation method suggested by an old friend of his from Bangkok. The reclining chair felt feather soft, almost like a cloud. He had an impression of Ugo rising from the ottoman and drawing the curtains tightly against the lowering sun. He heard, as if from a great distance, the door of the suite clicking shut. He pictured Ugo tiptoeing on the luxurious carpeting out in the corridor.

Bianco drifted off into a dream. He stood alone in the middle of a vast plain. Lightning flickered in the distance, backlighting gray clouds that boiled into thunderheads. He held a sledgehammer with one hand, a wooden stake with the other. A voice commanded him to drive the stake into the ground. But the soil turned to concrete wherever he placed its point.

He awoke to find Ugo reading a newspaper in the sitting room. His young nephew pulled open the curtains. The mountains stood purple against the faint orange of the sunset.

"What time is it?"

"Almost nine. You were tired, Uncle."

"Tired?" said Bianco. "Now I will be a cripple from this chair, eh?"

He shuffled into the bathroom to wash for dinner. The fluorescent bulbs raised a harsh image in the mirror. He almost laughed at himself. He certainly no longer resembled Ugo. His eyeballs were shattered with arteries, his strong nose had melted into a lumpy mass of flesh, his few remaining wisps of hair formed a tonsure on his freckled skull. Fabio Bianco, scientist-monk, Fra CEO.

They took a taxi to Ouchy and dined on a terrace overlooking Lake Geneva. The air was calm except for an occasional breeze that disturbed the reflections of shore lights on the glassy water. A jetliner's contrail, illuminated by the moon, passed through the bowl on the Big Dipper.

After they returned to the hotel Bianco lay on the bed long into the night with the lights out and the television playing without sound. He used the remote control to spin the dial. There were so many channels, so much information. Talk shows, game shows, police shows, music shows. When he was a boy, he would lie awake on a summer night with nothing but the music of his neighbor's mandolin floating through the open window. He would hear the mandolin telling him his future, the loves he would have, the great things he would accomplish, even the pain he would endure.

The local Swiss channel was showing a special report about the pollution that was strangling Venice. He watched mechanical harvesters scooping algae from the lagoon by the ton and still the water looked like a salad. He turned on the sound and heard that this summer was the worst ever. The smell was so terrible that the flow of tourists had dwindled to almost nothing. Swarms of flies thick as thunderclouds stopped trains when the wind shifted and blew them over Mestre. Their engineers could not see. Yet one of the harried scientists told the TV interviewer that Venice's lagoon was so polluted with chemicals that nothing should be alive in it.

With a pained sigh Bianco switched channels again.

An all-news station from Atlanta in the United States showed a man with gray curls and a rumpled tweed hat broadcasting from a rocky coastline. The sky was thick with rain clouds. *WHALE DEATHS* was superimposed on the screen. Bianco raised the volume.

"Aaron Weiss reporting. Behind me is the Bay of Fundy. Beyond that misty horizon, two Canadian trawlers are steaming home pulling a sad cargo behind them—four right whales found dead and floating fifty miles west of Sable Island. This brings to thirty-four the number of right whales that have died this summer on North American shores or in coastal waters."

The picture changed to show a blond woman wearing scuba gear and standing on the stern of a research vessel. Graphics identified her as Dr. Helga Knuttsen, marine biologist, Woods Hole, Massachusetts.

"The preliminary results of autopsies performed on two right whales found off Nauset Beach, Cape Cod, indicate that the cause of death was starvation. The ocean contains a wealth of food. Unfortunately, right whales can only eat a diet of plankton."

Weiss's voice-over returned to explain that not all marine biologists were convinced that starvation was the cause of death. The picture cut to a man with a white beard and a leathery face creased with deep wrinkles. He was Professor Theodore Adamski of Sea World, San Diego.

"The fact that these right whales may have died of starvation does not inexorably point to the conclusion that the main staple of their diet has disappeared. Each of these whales has been found a significant distance from summer feeding waters, which is equally consistent with a disease resulting in disorientation. Two or three dozen whale deaths sounds like a staggering number, and the general public as well as marine biologists are understandably concerned. However, the number is well within the normal range of attrition."

The picture returned to Aaron Weiss. His expression and voice turned somber.

"This reporter has dedicated the last ten days solely to investigating the story of the dying whales. It is too early to predict when these deaths will end and whether they have any hidden implications for the two-legged mammals that make their home on dry land. This is Aaron Weiss reporting from the Bay of Fundy, Nova Scotia, Canada."

Bianco clicked off the television and groped in the dark for his bathrobe draped over the foot of the bed. Knotting the robe around his waist, he shuffled out to the balcony. A couple crossed the street in front of the hotel, their arms around each other's shoulders. A taxi with a sputtering engine turned a corner, leaving Lausanne completely still. Bianco cupped his hands around his eyes in order to blot out the streetlights and gazed up at the sky. The moon was long gone, and thickening clouds scudded across the stars.

He waited, waited . . .

And there it was! A gleaming star, rising up beyond the mountains, brighter than all the others, moving steadily, purposefully, across the sky. Trikon Station.

Bianco fought down the urge to shout to the rooftops and wake up all of Lausanne so they could see and admire. He wanted to say to them all, Look! A man-made star is passing through our sky! Is it not beautiful?

Instead he watched in silence, a satisfied smile growing on his dry old lips, as the satellite sailed majestically, silently, across the night sky. He knew that tomorrow he would find the words to soothe the

French. That no longer worried him. Something else was gnawing at him.

The report from Venice and Aaron Weiss's story of the whale deaths. The two accounts twined together in his mind, not quite touching, but so close together. So close.

At last Fabio Bianco smiled to himself. He knew that once again he had heard the mandolin.

18 AUGUST 1998
TRIKON STATION

She packed my bags last night
Preflight
Zero hour, nine A.M.
And I'm gonna be high as a kite by then,
> —"Rocket Man"
> Elton John

Here am I sitting in a tin can
Far above the world
Planet Earth is blue
And there's nothing I can do.
> —"Space Oddity"
> David Bowie

Ashes to ashes
Funk to funky
We know Major Tom's a junkie
Strung out in Heaven's high,
Hitting an all-time low.
> —"Ashes to Ashes"
> David Bowie

HUGH O'DONNELL SEARCHED The Bakery, the wardroom, the exercise area, and the rumpus room without any luck. The tech who had been assigned the task of helping him unstow his scientific gear from the logistics module was nowhere to be found. O'Donnell parked himself at the end of the connecting tunnel and took a deep breath. The tunnel looked like a tropical aquarium at feeding time. Human fish dressed in iridescent reds and blues darted against the greenish backdrop. Some shoved bullet-shaped metal canisters while others shouted instructions.

A crewman hovered just outside the logistics entry hatch. As each canister was pushed out of the module, the crewman entered data into a hand-held computer. O'Donnell flattened himself against the wall as a procession of four Martians and two canisters surged past.

"I'm looking for Stu Roberts."

"The great songwriter?" The crewman laughed. "Check his compartment. Hab One."

O'Donnell navigated through the currents of moving bodies and pulled himself into the relative silence of Habitation Module 1. Moving slowly down the aisle, he read the names on the black-and-white plastic tags fixed to the bulkhead next to each compartment's door.

A sudden, ear-piercing screech sent a tingle up O'Donnell's spine. It settled into a throbbing whine that he followed to the last compartment. The passageway seemed to pulsate with rock music. The accordion door was vibrating from the sound volume.

O'Donnell braced himself against the opposite partition and pounded on Roberts's bulkhead. But knocking was no match for the noise inside. O'Donnell finally wrenched open the accordion door. Roberts was suspended in the center of his compartment, both feet kicked up behind his ass and his bandannaed head thrown back to expose a bony Adam's apple twitching beneath pale skin.

Roberts windmilled his right arm across the strings of an invisible guitar in rhythm with the pounding chords and wailed out the lyrics to "Acid Queen". On each revolution, his knuckles grazed silkscreen posters of ancient rock stars bellying from the compartment's wall.

"Excuse me, Mr. Townshend," shouted O'Donnell. "Can I interrupt your performance for about two hours?"

Roberts brought his arm down for a final, earsplitting chord. He writhed as if squeezing every decibel out of his imaginary guitar until the last note died away. Then he fell out of character.

"You knew who I was imitating," he said in awed disbelief. He turned off his portable CD player before the next song could begin.

"Sure. Peter Townshend. The Who. *Tommy* was a classic." O'Donnell mimed taking the guitar out of Roberts's hands and smashing it against the wall.

"Wow, they even trashed their instruments after every performance! Hey, who are you?"

O'Donnell introduced himself and offered his hand. He was not surprised when Roberts grasped it thumb to thumb in a handshake popular during the sixties.

"Hey, guess this one." Roberts untied his bandanna. His hair exploded into a wavy mass of red curls. He placed the invisible guitar on the back of his neck and started to twang a psychedelic rendition of "The Star-spangled Banner."

"Hendrix," said O'Donnell quickly, hoping that the correct answer would not encourage another round of Name That Rock Star.

"That's outtasight," said Roberts. "And you're a scientist working for Trikon? Where the hell they dig you up?"

"I've been around," said O'Donnell.

"Been around long enough to have gone to Woodstock?" There was awe in his voice.

"I was exactly five years old when the Woodstock Nation had its three days in the sun."

"Oh." Roberts's disappointment was palpable. "You look older." Then he brightened. "How come you know so much about old-time rock and roll? I thought I was the only one keeping the faith alive."

"I'm not keeping anything alive other than me."

"Dig that," said Roberts. "We have a real bunch of survivors up here. Anyway, it'll be more fun working with you than with Dave Nutt. What an uptight cat. Now *he* was old enough to have gone to Woodstock, and he didn't. Probably spent the weekend in the library, if I know him. Damn, I wish I could have gone. Joplin, Hendrix. All the great ones died before I was born."

"Time marches on," said O'Donnell, making a point of looking at his watch.

"Ain't that a bitch. I'm a composer, y'know. Been writing like mad. This job up here is just to put the bread on the table. Once I get back to the States I'll be the first rock composer to've been in orbit. I can't miss!"

"Good for you," said O'Donnell, without enthusiasm. Rather than prolong the discussion, he backed away from the compartment. To his amazement, Roberts took the hint.

"One thing you gotta remember about me," Roberts said as he tamed his wild mop with a hairnet. "I'm a real traditionalist when it comes to music."

The logistics module had been virtually picked clean of scientific-gear canisters by the time O'Donnell and Roberts entered the hatchway. O'Donnell found one canister with his name stenciled in black secured to the wall behind a waste drum. Roberts found another adjacent to the food supplies.

The canisters were made of medium-gauge aluminum. Each one was four feet long and three feet in diameter, the maximum size that could pass through

Trikon Station's interior hatchways. Inflatable bladders within the canisters cushioned the contents during lift-off. Depending upon the nature of the equipment, a fully loaded canister on Earth could weigh up to two hundred pounds. On Trikon Station, a person could easily lift the weightless canister with the touch of a finger. But maneuvering it was another matter. Regulations required that two people guide the bulky canisters from the logistics module to the labs, to avoid damaging equipment along the narrow aisles.

O'Donnell and Roberts guided the first canister through the connecting tunnel with little problem. The young tech chattered incessantly about rock music, and O'Donnell nodded at all the pauses. At The Bakery, Roberts directed O'Donnell past the people already at their workstations to a partitioned area located in the starboard forward corner of the module. The cubicle was almost the same size as Dr. Renoir's office, but it appeared much larger since it was totally empty.

"We called it our overflow storage room," explained Roberts after they jockeyed the canister through its narrow door. He switched on the drafting lamp bolted to a metal runner on the ceiling. "I wondered why they made us clean it out. It's gonna be your personal lab."

"Not very bright in here," said O'Donnell, seeing that the room was separated from the track of fluorescent lights running down the center of the module.

"I can rustle up a few more lamps for you."

"Do it. Full-spectrum bulbs," said O'Donnell.

"Don't worry, I'll get them." Roberts fingered a pair of clips attached to vertical runners on the walls. "You can attach equipment to these. I'd put all your bulky stuff here." He rapped his knuckles against the bulkhead of the module's exterior shell. "None of this shit weighs anything, but if you accidentally bump against something bulky you could dislodge the partition."

As they exited the compartment, O'Donnell realized that the other scientists and technicians were eyeing him from their workstations throughout The Bakery. Some were openly staring. He tried closing the door, but it did not latch properly.

"Is the canister safe in here?"

"No sweat," said Roberts.

They floated the second canister through the connecting tunnel and into The Bakery. Again, O'Donnell felt many pairs of eyes boring into his back as he and Roberts stood the canister on end and spun it into the storage room. His lab suddenly seemed quite congested.

"You must be O'Donnell," said a female voice, sharp as a whipcrack.

O'Donnell pushed aside the canisters and saw an unsmiling woman with a strong jawline, chiseled nose, and a salt-and-pepper crewcut.

"I'm Thora Skillen, coordinating scientist for this laboratory." She extended her hand through the open door. It was red and blistered, as if she washed with hydrochloric acid. Her lab smock was blotched with faint yellow stains like amoebae. "Trikon certainly threw us a curve adding you. This was the only space available."

"Tight, but I'll manage."

"Trikon informed me that you brought your own materials and supplies but will occasionally require use of our hardware." Skillen pressed her palms against each of the canisters as if to divine their contents. "Remember that my people have preference."

"You won't even know I'm here," said O'Donnell.

"I hope not," Skillen said. She seemed coiled with

an inner tension, almost vibrating with barely suppressed hostility. "I will cooperate with you as long as it doesn't interfere with my group's work. But I will not sacrifice my project for yours, whatever it is."

She jutted out her chin, nodded in a combination of warning and farewell, and sailed back into The Bakery.

"Charming, isn't she?" said Roberts.

"I've met worse," O'Donnell said, silently adding, But I'm not sure where.

"Thora baby is the hardest of the hard-asses. When I heard she wasn't going back Earthside this rotation, I almost decided to go back myself. Could have, too. I've been here six months."

"Why didn't you?"

"Not ready yet. Got to have a lot more songs down before I hit the studios. By the way, what are you working on that you rate your own lab?"

O'Donnell ignored the question as he studied the walls, figuring how he would arrange his equipment.

"Oh, shit!" Roberts blurted.

O'Donnell turned in time to see the lid of the first canister fly open. The effect was textbook jack-in-the-box. Books, diskettes, micro-gee vials, beakers, jars, bottles, test tubes spewed out and swarmed around the room.

O'Donnell lunged past Roberts and pulled the door shut before anything could escape into The Bakery.

"Sorry," Roberts said with a laugh. "You should see when that happens in the big lab. Sometimes we don't find things for weeks."

O'Donnell grunted, unamused.

"Don't sweat the details, man. If you ever can't find anything, check the ventilators. Everything ends up stuck to them eventually. Small stuff, anyway. You'll get used to it. Becomes second nature after you've been here awhile."

Roberts easily began picking objects out of the air. O'Donnell wasn't as dexterous and batted away as many things as he caught.

"Hey, what's this?" said Roberts. He waved a glassine bag containing powdery red soil.

"Dirt."

"I know it's dirt. Where's it from?"

O'Donnell squinted in thought. "Georgia."

"Georgia in the United States?"

"Yes, Georgia in the United States."

"You could have been talking about the Georgia in Russia." Roberts held the bag up to the light. "Never seen dirt like this before. This is redder than the soil from Mars. I know. One of my buddies has been analyzing the Mars soil. Says he found evidence of life in it, but nobody believes him. What're you doing with this?"

"Part of my experiment."

"Will you stop talking to me like I'm a kid," said Roberts. "I know this is soil and I know it's part of your experiment."

O'Donnell looked at the scarecrow face, the brick-red hair matted beneath its net, the bony elbows and knees. He had been with Roberts barely an hour and already he wished that the young tech had been scared Earthside by the personable Ms. Skillen.

"You people are working on phase one of a very complicated project," he said. "I'm working on phase two."

Roberts's face lit up with recognition.

"I get it. This soil contains toxic wastes already neutralized by microbes."

"Right," O'Donnell lied. "And I'm here to test whether it will be as useful as everyone expects."

They swept the rest of the flying objects into the opened canister and closed the lid. O'Donnell inspected the door that separated his lab from The Bakery. The latch was broken beyond repair, but the outside surface had a hasp and eyelet.

"Are there any padlocks lying around?" he said.

"Not lying. Floating around, maybe." Roberts's grin vanished when he saw that O'Donnell did not smile. "I'm pretty friendly with some of the crew. They might have one."

"See what you can do," said O'Donnell. "One with a combination rather than a key.

"Oh sure, I'll just trot down to the hardware store." O'Donnell frowned.

"I'm going, I'm going."

After Roberts sailed away, O'Donnell closed the door as best he could. He popped the lock of the second canister and opened the lid slowly. Simi Bioengineering, his immediate employer and a member corporation of the North American arm of Trikon International, had rushed it to Cape Canaveral after the incident that led to the station's power-down. It housed the most powerful and sophisticated laptop computer available. The station's mainframe and terminals were off limits to O'Donnell. No one would have an opportunity to steal his data files.

He deflated an air bladder. Behind it were several dozen plant sprigs tightly bound in glass jars. The roots were swaddled with moist cotton pads and the leaves were carefully positioned so they would not bend or break inside the jars.

He unbound one of the jars and spread it open. The leaves were oblong and shiny. Healthy. Lethal. A chill coursed through his body and he shuddered involuntarily.

He was damned glad Roberts hadn't seen these.

Thora Skillen's cubbyhole office was at the opposite end of The Bakery from O'Donnell's makeshift lab. She pushed herself past the open door and slid it shut.

Who is this O'Donnell and why is he here? she asked herself as she booted up her personal computer.

He isn't part of the ordinary Trikon staff. His work was to be kept separate from everyone else's, she had been told pointedly by the corporate brass in New York. Why? What will he be doing? Nobody back Earthside had been able to find out a thing about him, so far.

The only possible answer frightened her. He's been sent here to spy on me. They suspect me and they've sent a security agent to catch me up.

I'm all alone up here, Skillen realized. There's no one here to help me. It's all well and good for the sisters back Earthside to tell one another how much they hate the idea of bioengineering, how wrong and dangerous it is to tinker with genes, even the genes of microbes. They can sit back there and tell themselves how they'd blow up Trikon Station if they had the chance. But they're not here to help me. I'm alone. It's up to me.

Kurt Jaeckle forced his left hand down to the keyboard and saw a character appear on the screen of his word processor. *Z.* Goddammit, he had aimed for *A.* He found the backspace key, deleted the *Z*, and carefully moved his forefinger to *A.*

Typing had been tedious drudgery on Earth, but in micro-gee it was downright physically exhausting. He could not find a comfortable level for the machine and constantly fought the natural tendency of his hands to float above the keyboard. After a half hour of typing, he usually had a ribbon of sharp pain running from his shoulders to the tip of his forefingers.

Even on Earth, where gravity aided the fingers and secretaries were plentiful, Jaeckle insisted on typing his own scripts. He knew that words made dollars fall like manna and that dollars would shape the future of the Mars Project. He wanted no one fooling around with his words.

Strangely, he had found long ago that dictating into

a tape recorder never produced the results he wanted. His vocabulary was richer, his phrases stronger, when he wrote them out—even though the text was meant to be spoken aloud.

As usual, Jaeckle was three scripts ahead of schedule. This one, which was devoted to the practical problems of routine medical care in micro-gee, would be the first with Lorraine Renoir as his assistant. The transition was planned. He would broadcast his next show with Carla Sue, then inform her afterwards that the network no longer needed her services. She'd bitch, but he'd have prepared a host of reasonable excuses and arguments to blunt her rage. After all, this isn't Hollywood; it's a space station.

He would broadcast the second show by himself. That script was a beauty. Completely devoted to the practical benefits of a manned expedition to Mars, it advanced and then neatly punctured in classical Ciceronean fashion all of the arguments against such a trip. The medical show would be the perfect segue for Lorraine Renoir's debut. By then, Carla Sue's rage would have run its course. He hoped so, anyway.

Now all that remained was for Lorraine to agree to his proposal. He thought of the time he saw her pedaling the stationary cycle in the ex/rec room. She wore a tank top and flight pants. Her arm muscles strained and her stubby French braid bobbed against the nape of her neck. A thin saucer of sweat pooled in the depression between her shoulder blades and threatened to break free with each stroke of her legs. She stopped, dabbed herself with a towel, then unzipped the vents of her flight pants. When she resumed pumping, the vents spread like the petals of a flower to reveal round thighs and firm calves.

He imagined her speaking the words that slowly appeared on the screen. She had a breathy, throaty voice that rolled slightly over her *r*'s and *l*'s. It was much more pleasant than Carla Sue's twang, which lately sounded like an out-of-tune banjo.

A knock on the bulkhead interrupted his reverie. Without unlooping his feet, he pushed himself within reach of the door latch. From outside, fingers curled around the edge of the accordion door and swept it open.

Russell Cramer hovered in the doorway. The zipper of his nylon shirt was pulled down to the bulge of his stomach. Pencils bristled out of the pockets of his flight pants. His jowls glistened with sweat.

"I didn't see you in the wardroom this morning," said Jaeckle. "Nor did you help with the scientific resupply."

"I was in my compartment," said Cramer. "Everyone knew."

"Why didn't everyone tell me when I asked for you?"

"They knew," said Cramer. His upper lip quivered. "Did it arrive?"

"Did what arrive?"

"The new batch of Martian soil. It was supposed to be in our delivery."

"It was," said Jaeckle.

"Good." Cramer reached for a clip that usually held a gaggle of keys to various storage compartments in the Mars module. The clip was empty.

"The keys are in my pocket," said Jaeckle.

"I need them."

"You don't need them."

"How else am I going to get the new soil sample?"

"You aren't going to analyze that sample yet."

"But that soil is from the Martian south pole! If life exists there, it could be in that sample."

Jaeckle unlooped his feet. He was much smaller than Cramer and needed to bob up from the floor to face him eye to eye. "I don't want you testing that new soil sample for a few days."

"But, Professor, I was so close on the other sample!

This new one could yield the results we've been looking for!"

"Russell, I wish you would understand. This project still has eighteen months to run. You are the principal biochemist in our group. You are the top specialist for analyzing the Martian soil samples. No one else approaches your qualifications."

"I've tested the original sample every way I know how," Cramer wailed. "What else is there to do?"

"This isn't a race, Russell. The Mars Project is not designed to determine who will make the greatest scientific discovery. It is a test of endurance and mental toughness. Right now, you are failing."

The words seemed to sting Cramer physically. His head snapped back.

"You've been talking to Dr. Renoir," he said.

"She told me you consulted her about a problem," said Jaeckle.

"That bitch!"

"Russell—"

"She didn't tell me she was going to you. Goddamn her!"

"Now you wait one second, Mr. Cramer," boomed Jaeckle. "Dr. Renoir followed proper procedures in informing me about your medical complaint. And those same procedures require me to report to Commander Tighe *if* I feel your situation warrants it. So you had better remember who you are talking to. Okay?"

Cramer nodded meekly, but his mouth was still set in anger.

"Okay," said Jaeckle. "Let's start from the beginning. Dr. Renoir told me you are having trouble sleeping."

"Had trouble," said Cramer. "Not anymore. Hell, I slept all morning. That's why I was in my compartment."

"Glad to hear that," said Jaeckle. "But I've come

across something else. You haven't been taking the prescribed amount of time in the blister. Any reason for that?"

"I couldn't afford the time away from my work."

"I thought as much. Look, Russell, a good number of very intelligent people put a lot of thought into the Mars Project. Some of their ideas are damned good and some may be damned bad. But good or bad we're up here to test them so that when there is an actual manned flight to Mars—and I hope you and I are both on it—we know every inch of the psychological and physiological territory. Two hours per week in the observation blister may sound like an inefficient use of time, but it is very necessary. The records show that you haven't been in the blister in four weeks. I'm embarrassed that I didn't notice; that Dr. Renoir, an outsider, had to tell me there was something wrong with one of my people, my hand-picked people. I am ordering you to double up your sessions."

"Four hours a week! Professor Jaeckle!"

"The new soil sample will remain locked away until your blister time is brought current."

"That isn't fair," whined Cramer.

"It is completely fair. And it's damned preferable to you being sent Earthside on *Constellation* next time those Trikon clowns rotate." Jaeckle removed a folded sheet of paper from behind a bungee cord and handed it to Cramer. "That is your blister schedule. I want each session verified by a different member of the group."

21 AUGUST 1998
TRIKON STATION

In planning Trikon Station, much thought was devoted to whether the station should be constructed for a micro-gee environment or an artificial gravity environment. Artificial gravity could be induced by spinning the station around its center of mass. The resulting centrifugal force would create an artificial gravity gradient that would increase as one moved farther from the center.

Planners, however, opted for a micro-gee, or virtually weightless, environment in order to allow for the greatest adaptation for future use of the station's facilities. The term weightlessness is used to describe the orbital condition where all objects tend to float. Strictly speaking, there is only one point or line of reference in any sizable orbiting structure that allows true weightlessness. That point or line is along the structure's center of mass.

On Trikon Station, you will not be able to detect the subtle gradations within the micro-gee environment without highly sensitive accelerometers. However, for materials science and manufacturing, the minuscule differences can be crucial. Any experiment or process that requires very low gravity (on the order of one millionth of a g) can be ruined if the facility is displaced too far from the center of mass.

At the present time, Trikon Station is not devoted to crystal or pharmaceutical production or experimentation. Attempting such projects in the future will undoubtedly require a reconfiguring of the laboratory modules in order to obtain proper micro-gee management.

—from The Trikon Space Station Orientation Manual

DAN TIGHE LINGERED in the wardroom long after the end of the dinner hour. In his hand was a Mackintosh apple. Trikon dieticians routinely included seasonal fruits in the regular ninety-day food supplies. Fresh fruit was a luxury in orbit, and station personnel devoured it quickly. The Mackintosh was the first sign that summer was ending in North America.

The wardroom ceilings automatically dimmed with the pastoral sunset depicted on the viewscreens along the galley wall. Six identical sunsets, side by side. All six combined couldn't compare to being outdoors and watching the real thing, Dan thought.

He took a bite of the apple, slurping in the tart juices that oozed beneath the broken skin. Hisashi Oyamo and Chakra Ramsanjawi floated lazily through the wardroom on the way to their nightly chess match in the ex/rec area. Ramsanjawi threatened Oyamo with a new gambit he had devised on ELM's computer terminal. Oyamo laughed derisively. Neither paid Dan any attention.

Dan nibbled the apple down to the core with a minimum of juice and pulp escaping to the vents. Presently, the person he had been waiting for appeared. Lorraine Renoir mixed herself a squeeze bottle of coffee at the galley designated for after-hours snacks. She noticed Dan and floated in his direction.

"Eating all the fresh fruit, I see," she said.

"My procedure for preventing scurvy."

"Bad choice. Citrus fruits prevent scurvy."

"What do you expect from an old Air Force man?" he asked.

"Not much," said Lorraine, with a smile.

Her eyes searched him in a silence that lengthened past lighthearted banter. Dan drove his teeth into the apple's core, liberating a seed that bobbed against the roof of his mouth. Extricating the seed with his finger would be in poor taste, so he swallowed it.

"Tom Henderson tells me we have a health risk on board."

"Who might that be?" said Lorraine.

"New Trikon scientist named Hugh O'Donnell."

"What makes you think he's a health risk?"

Dan made a smile for her. "His standing orders to report to you every day."

Lorraine shot a quick burst of coffee into her mouth. She had sought out Dan to discuss Kurt Jaeckle's offer. But now she felt the same resentment that rose like bile in her throat whenever someone attempted to compromise her position as medical officer. The Russell Cramer issue was murky; the Hugh O'Donnell issue was clear. She might disapprove of his former drug use and dislike his irreverent attitude, but she had an ethical duty to keep his medical history in strictest confidence. No matter how much Dan smiled or crinkled the corners of his sky-blue eyes, O'Donnell's past was none of his business. At least not at this stage.

"You have standing orders to report to me every week," she said. "Does that make you a health risk?"

His smile vanished. "Only to myself," he muttered.

Without realizing it she leaned toward him, put her hand on his sleeve. "Oh Dan, your blood pressure's all right up here. Your hypertension is more an emotional problem than a physical one."

"Yeah, sure. And what happens if it goes up again?"

"It won't. Not in micro-gee."

"But if it does?"

She fixed him with her dark, serious brown eyes. "It won't. Trust me."

If I can't trust my own heart, Dan thought, how can I trust you? Or anybody else?

Lorraine seemed to realize she was clutching his arm. She released her hold and said, "At any rate, Hugh O'Donnell is not what you would consider a health risk."

Feeling glad that she had switched the subject back to its original theme, he replied, "Tom Henderson sent me O'Donnell's bio, and I was a little confused."

"What's confusing about his bio?"

"Nothing, so far as it goes," said Dan. "Except it doesn't go very far. He graduated from the University of Oregon in 1984, then he popped up working for Simi Bioengineering, a member of Trikon NA, in 1996. Nothing in between. Since he reports to you every day, it makes sense that you would know about his activities during those twelve years."

"I've seen him exactly five times, including the day he arrived. We haven't delved into his distant past."

"Will you tell me if you discover anything pertinent?"

"Pertinent to what?"

"The safety of this station."

"Do you see him as a safety risk?"

"I don't have overwhelming confidence in Trikon's selection of personnel."

Lorraine felt her brows knitting, felt the simmering anger that always came over her when someone tried to invade her professional territory. And she felt confusion, too. She did not want to be angry with Dan. Yet she was.

"Do you see him as a safety risk?" she repeated stiffly.

"Not yet."

"Neither do I," she said. "If and when I do, I will discuss the problem with his immediate supervisor and with you. But since I don't perceive him as a safety risk, I have an ethical obligation to honor his confidences."

"Thank you for your cooperation," Dan said icily. He pushed away from the table and sailed toward the wardroom hatch, pausing only to slam dunk the apple core into a waste receptacle.

Lorraine took another sip of coffee, but a constriction in her throat prevented her from swallowing. She forced down the coffee and realized that her hands were shaking.

"Dammit!" she whispered to herself.

She sailed to the hatch. He was at the far end of the connecting tunnel, swimming swiftly with an occasional stroke against one of the side walls.

"Dammit," she repeated.

Games came easily to Chakra Ramsanjawi. During his boyhood years in England, he had mastered physical games like squash, tennis, and cricket. He had even tried rugby, although his early years of malnutrition prevented him from developing the sheer body strength necessary to survive the violent scrums.

As he developed into manhood and the sedentary career that rusted his physical abilities, he turned his focus to mental games—especially those that required unorthodox modes of thought. Chess was his passion; he spent long hours huddled over a board in a dimly lit reading room of the London men's club he had joined along with Sir Derek.

On Trikon Station surprisingly few people played chess. Stu Roberts had challenged him to a game after boasting about having been dormitory champ in college. Ramsanjawi concluded that it must have been a dormitory full of cretins. Roberts's mind was too scattered, too full of frivolous songs to assemble the requisite concentration. He quickly knuckled under to Ramsanjawi's opening gambit, threw up his arms in mock despair, and never played again. Oyamo was the only worthy opponent on the station, and even the Japanese scientist was hardly fitting competition, Ramsanjawi thought.

As he floated through the wardroom, Ramsanjawi noticed Dan Tighe eating an apple by himself at one of the tables. It was not unlike the American station commander to eat in solitude, but Ramsanjawi sensed a special purpose in Tighe's presence. In the ex/rec room Ramsanjawi positioned himself so that he could watch the commander through the doorway.

Oyama settled opposite and began to set up the game. The magnetized figures had been designed with space-age motifs. The pawns wore EMU space suits. The knights were sleek aerospace planes. The rooks were fanciful third-generation space stations.

Ramsanjawi noticed Lorraine Renoir join Tighe at his table. He could not hear what they were saying, but it was obvious they were annoyed with each other.

Oyamo attacked with his knights and bishops. Ramsanjawi was so intent on the brewing argument that he failed to pay attention to the game. Oyamo's opening moves had him on the run.

A surge of adrenaline swept away Ramsanjawi's interest in the wardroom encounter. He moved swiftly to the attack, capturing one of Oyamo's bishops, both of his knights, and putting the space queen in jeopardy. Many an Englishman's competitive fire had been stoked on the playing fields of Eton. Ramsanjawi's had been fanned by the youthful Derek Brock-Smythe.

They had been an odd pair; Derek porcelain white and exquisitely tiny, Chakra dark and lithe despite a belly distended from years of poor diet. Derek's tongue was sharp and he was in constant nervous motion. Chakra was shy, his movements languorous, almost lazy. Derek resented the filthy interloper and only grudgingly obeyed his parents' commands to be civil to his Indian adopted brother. Cagily, he resorted to competition in order to make Chakra feel unwelcome. But Derek's problem was that he was not very good at sports. He challenged Chakra at tennis, squash, and croquet, and Chakra always won. He even challenged Chakra to a footrace, but his mincing gait was no match for Chakra's nimble strides.

As one unusually warm summer drew to a close, Derek challenged Chakra to golf, a game neither supposedly ever had played, at a course outside at Bath. During the round, it became apparent to Chakra that he had been duped. Derek had secretly played the game all summer and had received instruction from a battery of professionals.

Chakra did not know golf, but he knew physics. He hung in the match long enough for the increasingly nervous Derek to self-destruct, as he always did in their competitions. Chakra won the last hole, and with it the match. He could still see Derek, stomping furiously next to the flagstick in the orange light of dusk and shouting, "You may have beaten me. But you'll never be an aristocrat. You'll never be a true Englishman. Never! Never! Never!"

Ramsanjawi deftly removed Oyamo's space queen from the board and bore down on the king. The Japanese amused him, trying so hard to look inscrutable, impassive. Yet every time Ramsanjawi leaned forward across the board, Oyamo leaned back. As if an invisible force kept them apart by a rigid full meter. The Japanese are trained to remain that distance away, Ramsanjawi reflected. It is a cultural trait, quite unconscious. Like their fanatical insistence on cleanliness and bathing.

Oyamo allowed Ramsanjawi to pursue his king for eleven moves before finally placing himself in checkmate. It pleased this would-be Englishman to win at chess. It loosened his braggart's tongue.

As they set up for another game Oyamo deftly

moved the topic of their conversation to their work.
He knew that progress among the Europeans was
painfully slow, and for some reason Ramsanjawi did
not seem worried by it. The Americans would slow
down, too, now that Nutt had left the station. He had
been the only one among them with any flash of
inspiration, any drive at all.

Oyamo grunted and nodded and let Ramsanjawi
talk away in his strange mixture of Oxford and Delhi.
The bloated Indian thinks we are playing chess.
Oyamo knew better.

23 AUGUST 1998
TRIKON STATION

LAST TESTAMENT OF THORA SKILLEN

It seems strange to be writing to a dead person, Melissa, but you were always the only one I could confide in. Soon I will be joining you, but before I do I need to tell you how much I depended on you, how much I miss you, how much I love you.

You always thought I was the strong one, I know. But without you I would be nothing. I protected you against Father, true; that was easy to do. I hadn't the real strength I needed to protect myself.

When I watched you dying, week after week, month after month, I realized that my whole life had been a lie. At first I felt guilty that it was you who was dying, the good one, while I was being allowed to live. But less than two weeks after we buried you, they told me I had cystic fibrosis, too. A bad gene, they said. What irony! A molecular geneticist with a bad gene.

It was at that moment that I realized how much of a lie I had been living. My so-called brilliant career has been based on using their antidiscrimination rules against them. They couldn't refuse to hire me, they couldn't refuse to promote me. That would be discrimination against women, against lesbians, against the diseased. That's how I got here to Trikon Station over the heads of better scientists.

Of course, they saw a chance to use me as a guinea

pig in this weightless environment. They got something out of me, after all. So be it.

I belong to an organization of sisters now. Not sisters in the same sense we are, so close that not even death can entirely separate us. But my new sisters care for me, and I for them. They have helped me to advance through the labyrinth of male-dominated corporate organizations, helped me to get to Trikon Station.

The work here is the most advanced genetic engineering yet attempted. Not satisfied with having already ruined the Earth, they want to defile outer space and make more genetically altered microbes that will cause more problems for the world. My task is to keep that from happening, to make this research so painfully slow and expensive that they will eventually abandon it.

But another idea keeps running through my mind. How delicious it would be if everyone here died of some toxic microbe that they themselves have concocted! That will show the world how wrong it is to meddle with life. That will put an end to their constant interference with nature.

Do I have the skill to pull it off? I have the nerve—I think. When you know you're going to die anyway, what difference does it make?

Whatever happens, I will be with you soon. Our loneliness will end forever.

IN THE DARKNESS of his compartment, Dan Tighe unhitched himself from his sleep restraint, floating out like a dolphin leaving the womb. He flexed his shoulders and straightened his knees, savoring the welcome sensation of morning in his muscles and bones. Rather than switch on the light, he groped along the array of storage compartments for his toiletry kit and a fresh towel. Then he carefully pulled back the accordion door, still wearing the wrinkled, faded coveralls he had slept in.

Dan enjoyed early morning. Even though Trikon Station went through sixteen sunrises in every twenty-four-hour period, hardly anyone aboard the station saw the outside except through video screens. The planners had designed the interior system to cue normal circadian rhythms. The lights in the connecting tunnels and other common areas dimmed every evening and brightened every morning in an artificial approximation of dusk and dawn. The system effectively prevented the inhabitants from "going around the clock," the tendency to awaken and retire one hour later each day unless aroused by the morning sun.

At 0530 hours, the lights were still dim. Dan had the station to himself, a feeling of solitude that he cherished. The only sounds were the hum of the ventilation system and the occasional creaks of the module shells as they expanded or contracted in sunlight or darkness. They weren't cricket chirps or bird songs, but they were comforting just the same.

The personal hygiene facilities in Hab 2 were superior to those in Hab 1. The hot water was generally hotter and the pressure in one particular full-body shower was the most powerful on the station. Even the Whits were tolerable. The difference in quality and comfort certainly justified a swim from Hab 1 to Hab 2 first thing each morning.

Dan was surprised to discover that someone had beaten him to his favorite shower. He could hear the man singing tunelessly as the water removal vents sucked the millions of droplets out of the air inside. The singing broke into a torrent of curses, then subsided completely. Moments later, Hugh O'Donnell emerged from the shower. His neck and chin were mottled with splotches of blood.

"Up awful early," said Dan.

"Habit," O'Donnell replied.

"You also know which shower works best."

"I keep my ears open," said O'Donnell. He dabbed his chin; the towel came away dappled with blood. "Do you know any secrets to good shaving?"

"I nick myself every damn time. But I do find that long slow strokes draw less blood than short fast ones."

"I'll remember that tomorrow."

Dan closed himself into the shower and powered up the spray. The water drenched him from all directions, warm and fine, and for a moment he was a boy again, walking home through a sudden rainstorm on the last day of school. His bare feet squished in the mud of the dirt road that curved up to his house and a bead of water tickled his nose before dropping to earth.

He cut the shower and watched the vacuum vent suck away the water droplets hanging in the steamy air. The mist spiraled out, and with it the memory. He slapped shaving gel on his face, slipped his feet in the loops, and squinted one eye to focus himself in the aluminum mirror attached next to the shower head. The razor pulled slightly, and he concentrated on the long slow strokes he had suggested to Hugh O'Donnell.

Dan toweled himself dry and went to his compartment to change into his flight suit. He ate breakfast alone in the wardroom, then went to his office in the command module. He wasn't there long before crewman Stanley rapped on his bulkhead.

"Phone call, sir."

Dan looked at his watch. The station was set for central daylight time, which meant that it was 7:30 A.M. in Dallas, too.

"I think it's her," said Stanley.

* * *

Across the command module, Hugh O'Donnell floated patiently near the ceiling of Lorraine Renoir's tiny office.

"How do you find Trikon Station?" Lorraine asked. She slipped her feet into the restraining loops on the floor and opened a wall compartment.

"Not so bad," said O'Donnell. He had a perfect view of the razor-sharp line on the top of her head where her chestnut hair was separated and twisted into a neat French braid. "The scientists could be a little friendlier."

"I see," said Lorraine. An orange rubber tube slithered out of the compartment. She pinned it to her side with her elbow.

"Actually, I feel pretty damn good," said O'Donnell. "Haven't even seen the creepy-crawlies."

"What are they?"

"In my case, spiders." O'Donnell smiled at the worried look crossing Lorraine's face. "Not real ones. More like eye floaters. Saw them all the time in rehab. Now only on occasion, like if I'm knocked out of my routine. I thought I'd be bored here, but I feel just the opposite. I'm very focused."

"You've been here hardly a week," said Lorraine.

"Ah, but I can tell, Doc. This orbiting space lab was made for a workaholic like me."

"Is that what you are now? A workaholic?"

"Slip of the tongue, Doc. A mere slip of the tongue. What I meant to say is that there is nothing here to do except work. Consequently, I'm already a week ahead of schedule in my project. That is, how you say, *fantastique*?"

"Enough levity, Mr. O'Donnell. Push yourself down here and roll up your right sleeve."

"Already, huh?" said O'Donnell. He guided his stockinged feet to a second set of restraining loops and worked his sleeve toward his shoulder. His arm mus-

cles were wiry. The veins inside his elbow were
prominent.

Lorraine cinched the orange tube around his biceps
and rubbed an alcohol swab over a vein. O'Donnell
made a point of staring at the Monet print adorning
the wall.

"I didn't think you would be so squeamish," said
Lorraine.

"I've done my share of drugs," he said, "but nothing that required a needle."

Lorraine expertly drew a vial of blood and pressed a
bandage against O'Donnell's arm.

"What exactly are you testing for, Doc?"

"I use a screening panel for thirty different drugs.
Cocaine, amphetamines, MDMA, and a host of synthetics you probably never heard of."

"MDMA?" O'Donnell asked. "Ecstasy?"

"That's correct," said Lorraine as she tried to coax
the rubber tube into its compartment.

"Ecstasy on Trikon Station?"

"God forbid," Lorraine said.

Station personnel often joked that the sleep compartments were glorified telephone booths. The command
module, however, was equipped with two authentic
phone booths for the personal use of the crew, the
scientists, and the Martians. A call originating from
the station was transmitted by unsecured radio link to
any of several communications satellites in geosyn-
chronous orbits, then beamed down to receiving installations on Earth where conventional fiber-optic
lines carried the call to its destination. Calls from
Earth to the station went the same way, in reverse.
The system was fast but had two drawbacks. First, the
various links of the phone patch often distorted voices
beyond recognition. Second, although the phones had
voice encryption capabilities, Trikon regulations specifically prohibited scrambling except during opera-

tional emergencies. Any ham radio operator could eavesdrop on the calls by intercepting the radio signal.

Dan sealed himself into the booth. Conversations with Cindy were always tense. Knowing that strangers the world over could be listening made it worse. After one particularly violent argument over a child support payment, a female ham radio operator from the Shetland Islands had written to Trikon complaining about obscenities emanating from space.

Cindy cut him off one syllable into "Hello."

"I found something on Billy's dresser and I hope it's a joke." Her voice, even distorted, was coldly contemptuous. "A round-trip pass on a space plane."

"That is no joke," said Dan. His latest ploy in dealing with Cindy was to maintain a placid tone regardless of the topic of conversation. It did not always work, but it kept him from losing his temper. Sometimes.

"You can't take him away from me like that!"

"It's only a visit."

"I don't like the idea of him going up there. Riding a space plane. It's a glorified rocket."

"The aerospace plane is nothing of the sort. It has been tested and retested and shaken out in all kinds of conditions. Flying in it is safer than driving to the Seven Eleven."

"Maybe the way you drive it is."

Dan let the barb pinch him without answering. His driving record during their marriage had been checkered with speeding tickets.

"He's just a boy!" Cindy screamed into the silence.

"Bill is twenty years old. In most places and in most times, that qualifies him as a man."

"Not with me."

"When I was twenty I already had a thousand hours' solo flight time."

"You're always measuring him against your milestones. That isn't good for him."

"I'm no psychologist," Dan said evenly. "But is it bad for a young man to know what his father did with his life?"

Cindy grumbled. One of her subsequent gentleman companions had been a psychologist. "How did you get the passes to him?"

"Well, I knew I couldn't call him because you won't let him come to the phone. I knew I couldn't write because you intercept the letters. So I hired a process server to deliver them."

"He's not going!"

"You'll deny him an opportunity that every boy, as you like to call him, would love to have?"

"I'll call Ellis Berlow! I'll get a court order!"

"Without Bill knowing?"

Cindy mumbled incoherently, then the connection broke. Dan clicked the handset back into its receptacle. Not a bad performance. Reasonable, low-keyed, courteous. Still, he could not hear the name of Ellis Berlow without a raging sea of memories flooding back from his subconscious. He pulled himself out of the phone booth and headed for the rumpus room.

The rumpus room was another shuttle external tank, and its adaption to a pressurized, inhabitable volume had been a dry run for the later Mars module. The first station construction crew had burned the tank into orbit with *Constellation*. It had served as a "shanty" for the construction crews and later, as the station grew, was docked along with the other modules to provide additional space. When the Mars module was added to the station, the tank was moved to the leading end of the connecting tunnel to serve as a counterbalance.

The rumpus room had no "ceiling" or "floor," just a continuous dull silver wall that was particularly disorienting to people with sensitive middle ears. And it was *huge*. Even with the partition that separated it into two sections, even with the massive merry-go-round structure of the man-rated centrifuge and the other gym equipment, going from the station's lab and habitation modules to the rumpus room was like stepping from a crowded subway train to the great outdoors.

The variable-gravity human centrifuge had been installed for the Martians. Since opinion was divided over whether the eventual Mars spacecraft would provide artificial gravity or fly the entire mission in zero-gee, certain Martians were required to spin in the centrifuge each day while the rest were prohibited from using it at all. Mars Project medics on the ground closely monitored both groups to assess which might be better adapted for the nine-month trip to Mars.

Even with the centrifuge, there was still plenty of room for other activities. Kurt Jaeckle had transformed a section into the studio for his television show. A Swedish Trikon tech created a jogging track by attaching a ring of indoor-outdoor carpeting to the circular wall. And Dan Tighe used it to display his personal menagerie.

The rumpus room was empty except for the Swede, who ran the track in long, loping strides. Running laps in micro-gee required very little exertion, certainly not enough for a decent aerobic workout. But it was fun.

Three bonsai animals hovered on short leashes attached to the rear bulkhead: a turtle, a rabbit, and a squirrel. Dan examined each one, then dislodged a tiny pair of scissors from behind a bungee cord. As he snipped, he tried to imagine Cindy's next step. Would she try to dissuade Bill from the flight? Or would she actually hire Ellis Berlow to obtain a court order? Dan hated that fucker. He could still see him standing in the courtroom and arguing against his fitness as a father.

Rocket junkie, Berlow had called him, space vaga-

bond. This court must not be a party to this man
abandoning his child as he has his wife. After the
judge denied the petition for joint custody, Dan saw
Berlow in the courthouse men's room. The lawyer
would not acknowledge him. He simply stared into
the mirror and primped his smooth brown pelt of a
beard with a brush.

The scissors slipped and amputated a piece of the
squirrel's leg. Anger gurgled in Dan's chest. Memories
of his divorce evoked the worst kind of adrenaline.

"They're nicely done." Lorraine Renoir drifted
beside him, her voice a low purr.

"Sometimes they're too damn delicate." Tighe took
a deep breath to calm his rage at having ruined the
squirrel. He caught a whiff of Lorraine's perfume. It
smelled fresh, as if she had just come out of the
shower. He added: "Thanks. Glad you like them."

"Why animals?" She plucked one of the tethers.
The rabbit hopped in the air. "Why these animals?"

With a slow smile, Dan explained, "When I was a
boy I liked to pretend I saw creatures in cloud
formations. Most of them were silly, but one evening,
along about dusk after a full day of rain, the sun broke
through a patch of clear red sky just over the hills. The
clouds lit up and I saw a parade of perfectly shaped
animals: a bird, a rabbit, a squirrel, and a turtle."

Lorraine nuzzled each one, then set it slowly adrift.
She exuded a calm that seemed to affect everything
around her, even Dan, and he was glad of it.

"I'm sorry I snapped at you the other night," said
Lorraine. "You have to understand my position."

"That's all right," Dan said. "I was out of line."

"I have something to ask you, Dan." Lorraine
lowered her eyes as if marshaling the precise words,
then looked up. "Kurt Jaeckle asked me to assist him
in his TV broadcasts. I haven't given him an answer
yet. I wanted to talk to you."

Dan felt his guts wrench, but kept his face stony. "Are you asking me for my opinion or for my permission?"

"I'm not sure. Maybe both."

"Do you want to be on TV?"

"It isn't one of my great dreams, but I think it would be interesting."

"There's no regulation against it, if that's what you're asking."

"It isn't—" Lorraine turned slightly away from him.

"Well?"

"It's just that I know that you and Professor Jaeckle are not on the best of terms."

"That's irrelevant. The Mars Project is an integral part of this station. If you want to be Professor Jaeckle's TV assistant, there's nothing I can do about it as long as it doesn't interfere with your regular duties."

"It won't," said Lorraine. "So I guess you have no objection."

He did, but none that he could articulate. Lorraine looked at him as if she expected him to say something, but when he did not she pushed against the bulkhead and headed for the hatch.

Dan watched her sail away, pausing briefly to let the Swede pass on his endless run before slipping through the hatchway. Lorraine had a calming effect on him, all right. But why, after talking to her, did he always feel as though he had just fumbled the ball?

The last dinner shift was long over. The lights in the wardroom had dimmed to a glimmer. In the exercise area, Lance Muncie strained against a variable-resistance rowing machine. With every pull of his bulging arms, with every thrust of his sinewy legs, he grunted out the number of his repetitions. *Nine eighty-six, nine eighty-seven . . .*

Freddy Aviles pulled up to the doorway. He had a tool kit lashed to his chest and ten feet of fanfold paper snaking behind him. He gathered the paper into a manageable sheaf, then continued inside.

"Hey, Lance."

Nine ninety-one, nine ninety-two.

"Oh La-ance."

Nine ninety-seven, nine ninety-eight.

"Lance Muncie!"

Nine ninety-nine, one thousand.

Lance unhitched himself from the machine and drifted upward. His straw-colored hair was lined with dark streaks of sweat, his cheeks crimson from exertion. His teeth were set on edge, which made his chin protrude as if daring someone to take a poke at it. Freddy had seen this expression before; Lance was worried.

"You okay, man?"

Lance grunted in response. He removed his hairnet and toweled his hair.

"You not okay."

"I felt my calcium levels decreasing. I needed exercise."

"Oh, calcium. I see." Freddy nodded in exaggerated agreement. "You want to help me tonight?"

Lance patted his underarms with the towel, then braced his feet against the rowing machine while he slipped into his shirt.

"Sure, what else do I have to do?"

They drifted leisurely down the connecting tunnel and entered the Mars module. The computer circuits and multiplexers ran behind the ceiling panels in the module's internal tunnel. Freddy hooked his arm through a handhold and trained a penlight on the top page of his papers. The page was a spaghetti of colored lines and numbers. Freddy muttered thoughtfully as he traced his finger along one of the lines.

"I tried phoning Becky again tonight," said Lance. "She wasn't home."

Freddy directed the penlight at a tiny box set into a crease in the ceiling.

"That's three nights in a row," said Lance.

"Maybe she's away." Freddy tapped the box with his finger.

"Away where?"

"How would I know? People go places."

"I've never gone three days without talking to her. Never."

"You have an agreement with her?"

"What sort of agreement?"

"You know, an agreement. You up here for six months. She down there for six months. Six months a long time." Freddy opened the box with the blade of a screwdriver. "How long you been going out?"

"Two years," said Lance. "We met when we were seniors at Kansas. She was the prettiest girl I ever saw. Well, I showed you her picture."

Freddy hiked himself up until his eye was an inch from the inside of the box. Wires and circuits matched the diagram on the paper.

"You talk with her about you coming up here?" he asked.

"Of course we did. I told her that it was only six months, but that it would be very good for my long-range career plans. After that, we could talk about getting married."

"Hmmm. I see," said Freddy.

"What does that mean? Did I do something wrong?"

"No, I just found the relay I was lookin' for."

"Anyway," Lance continued, "now I'm not so sure about getting married."

"Because you can't get her on the phone?"

"Yeah. No. Well, yeah," said Lance. "That's never happened. It's like a sign."

"Sign of what?"

"That something is wrong. People don't always tell you. They give you signs."

"Maybe she just don' expect you to call."

"I always have before."

"You weren' in space before."

"But I always called."

"You know what you beginning to sound like, man? The catechism the nuns taught me in school. 'Who made me?' 'God made me.' 'Who God?' 'God the Supreme Being Who made all things.'"

"What's wrong with that?" said Lance.

Freddy shook his head. "Lemme see the next page."

They floated in silence, Freddy tracing computer circuits and Lance mulling over his crisis with Becky. The Swedish tech swam down the tunnel. He nodded to the two crewmen, then disappeared into the observation blister. As soon as the door closed, Freddy chuckled.

"What's so funny?" said Lance.

"Look at your watch and tell me when ten minutes is up."

Lance obeyed, assuming that the ten-minute period was related to Freddy's work. He signaled when the time had passed. Moments later, a female Martian appeared. She ignored the two crewmen and made straight for the observation blister. The door opened and she slipped inside.

Freddy laughed.

"Now what's so funny?" said Lance.

"I been in here the last two nights. Same thing. He goes into the blister and ten minutes later some chick shows up. Last night it was one of the Europeans. Wonder what'd happen if two showed up."

"There would be a fight."

"Or maybe our friend'd need some help." Freddy winked.

"Not from me," said Lance.

"Can you imagine? I had a waterbed once, till my cousin Felix used it one night and forgot to take his boots off. Thought I was floating then, but that'd be nothing compared to this. All kinds of tumbling, all kinds of angles. And with the Earth and stars right outside the window. Beats lookin' across an air shaft, eh?"

"I never have."

"Tha's right. No air shafts in Kansas."

There was a thud against the blister door.

"What's that?" Lance blurted.

"Newton's Law."

Freddy left Lance with instructions to keep a close eye on the circuitry, then headed for the command module to test the adjustments he had made to the relay. The project that Commander Tighe had assigned him was far less complicated than he had expected. If necessary, he could have reconfigured the entire computer system in two or three evenings. But Freddy was in no rush.

As he approached the command module, Freddy noticed two figures slipping out of The Bakery. Even at a distance of one hundred feet, he recognized the red mop of Stu Roberts and the ample ass of Russell Cramer. The two men entered Hab 1.

Freddy knifed past the command module. The test he was about to run could wait. As he passed the hatch to Hab 1, he could see Roberts and Cramer at the door to Roberts's compartment. Freddy cast his eyes up and down the tunnel. No one was in sight. He pulled himself into The Bakery. Like the Mars module, it was in nighttime illumination: pools of dim light and long stretches of shadow. Freddy nosed up to the tiny lab assigned to Hugh O'Donnell. The door was closed. The strip of cellophane tape O'Donnell stretched across the padlock each night to reveal signs of intrusion was undisturbed.

* * *

Dart throwing was easy in micro-gee, thought Hugh O'Donnell. Since the dart flew in a precisely straight line, rather than arc toward the floor in response to gravity, all you needed were an accurate aim and a correct release point in your throwing motion.

The darts were little more than plastic soda straws tipped with Velcro. O'Donnell threw three of them at the dart board, retrieved them, and returned to the foot loops at the far end of the ex/rec area. Over and over again. He never tired of throwing bull's-eyes.

Directly below the darts' flight path, Chakra Ramsanjawi and Hisashi Oyamo huddled over their chessboard. They played silently, although each one would chuckle when he removed one of the other's pieces from the board. Occasionally, Ramsanjawi cast a baleful glance in O'Donnell's direction, as if the incessant flight of the darts disturbed his concentration. O'Donnell ignored him.

"Care for a game?"

Dan Tighe hovered in the entryway.

"Why not?" said O'Donnell. He removed his three darts from the board while Dan rummaged through one of the recreation compartments for three more.

As they played, Dan scrutinized O'Donnell's every movement. The scientist threw darts as silently and as intensely as Ramsanjawi and Oyamo concentrated on their chess. He would close one eye, tense his body, and move his throwing hand back and forth repeatedly as if it were on an invisible track before he exhaled deeply and launched the dart on its dead-straight path. There was a rigidity about O'Donnell's movements that was completely at odds with his lanky, loose-jointed frame. Dan sensed an inability, or an unwillingness, to relax. He couldn't decide which.

"I see you're still shaving," Dan said between rounds. "I thought after a few days you'd grow a beard like everyone else."

"You haven't," said O'Donnell. He started to aim.

"I've mastered the long, slow strokes."

"Really?" said O'Donnell, taking his eye off the target. "I suppose your face is red from windburn."

"Yeah, well—I guess I really don't like beards."

O'Donnell said nothing. He fired one dart and settled into his aiming ritual with a second.

"I'm divorced," said Dan.

"And your ex-wife had a beard."

"Funny." Dan forced a laugh. "That isn't it. The lawyer who raked me over the coals had a beard. I can still see him running this tiny little comb through it like it was a mink stole. That was after my ex-wife won the custody battle for my kid. I wanted to talk to the guy, tell him what a lousy job he had done taking my son away from me. But he was too interested in preening his goddamned beard."

"I guess that would make me shave every day," said O'Donnell.

"You know, I hate those guys," Dan said with sudden intensity. His sky-blue eyes were focused on a point in his own past. "They come into your life, wreck it, and then go back to their offices to count their money. And what the hell are you left with? A mess. A big goddamn mess they made for you because they were charging by the hour."

"They don't always go back to their offices," said O'Donnell. "Sometimes they stay around and finish you off."

O'Donnell threw his last dart and slipped his feet from the loops. Dan took his place and fired three quick shots. None hit their marks.

"What the hell's that supposed to mean?"

O'Donnell floated slowly toward the board to retrieve his darts. He realized he shouldn't talk about his past, but sometimes he just couldn't keep it bottled up. Dr. Renoir was a woman. He could put his brain in neutral, disengage his mouth, and rap with her as he had rapped with chicks in bars. Dan Tighe was different. He might actually understand.

"My lawyer sold me out," said O'Donnell. "He charged me fifty grand for a settlement that I could have gotten myself when the case began. I had only twenty grand left, so he took my lady."

Dan grimaced.

"I guess she was worth thirty grand. I don't know anymore."

"Doesn't sound like the normal divorce case to me."

"It wasn't," said O'Donnell. A smile creased his face. Telling this story would be fun, as long as he avoided specifics. "You are looking at the first man to be completely and utterly rifkin-ized."

"Now what the hell is that supposed to mean?"

"It means that a bunch of know-nothings brought me and my company into court and obtained an injunction removing EPA approval of several genetically engineered microbes I designed for agricultural use. Of course, it happened just before my company was about to go public. The investors evaporated, the company tanked, and my lawyer waltzed off with my last dollar and my girlfriend."

"When was that?"

"A few years back. Lots of it is a blur, for one reason or another."

"How did you end up here?"

"I eventually went to work for a company large enough and established enough to have a high-powered set of lawyers of their own. The board voted to join Trikon NA. So here I am, property of Trikon."

They tossed several rounds of darts in silence. Ramsanjawi chattered happily as he chased Oyamo's king across the board and eventually proclaimed checkmate. Oyamo sulked and asked for another game.

Dan mulled over what O'Donnell had told him. The scientist seemed candid about career and women, the two most important aspects of a young man's life. But something was missing. Dan felt it in the vagueness of the dates and the blur O'Donnell said his life once had been.

"Tell me something," O'Donnell said.

"What?"

O'Donnell aimed and fired another bull's-eye. "The orientation manual says you grow taller in microgravity; your spine unbends when you're weightless."

"That's right," said Tighe. "That's why they make your flight suits extra long for your size."

"But I don't seem to be any taller, really."

Tighe chuckled. "If you had a full-length mirror you'd see why."

O'Donnell hiked his eyebrows questioningly.

"Well, look at me," Tighe said. Standing in the foot restraints, he knew he was bent over in the semi-question-mark posture known as the microgravity crouch.

"Am I doing that?" O'Donnell asked.

"Sure. Straighten yourself up. Go on, try it."

O'Donnell strained for a moment. His back straightened, his shoulders squared. But with a puff of held-back breath he quickly relaxed and went back to the more comfortable crouch.

"In micro-gee," Dan explained, "the spine does unbend. But the muscles tend to pull you into a sort of fetal crouch."

"O'Donnell the ape-man." Hugh grinned at himself and scratched under his armpit.

Tighe laughed. He was starting to like O'Donnell. Then he caught himself with the memory of who he was and what his responsibilities were.

"Play you for a drink," he said.

"There's liquor on board?" O'Donnell looked startled.

"No, but the loser can pay Earthside."

"Let's play for a soda," said O'Donnell.

Tighe nodded. Inwardly, he realized that he had expected just such a response from Hugh O'Donnell.

Freddy Aviles moved silently through Hab 1. Most of the sleep compartments were darkened. A few leaked pinpricks of light through the seals of their accordion doors. As Freddy drifted toward the rear of the module, he became aware of a dull, rhythmic vibration. The sound strengthened and finally resolved into music as Freddy steadied himself outside Stu Roberts's compartment. Freddy recognized the exquisitely clear electric guitar riffs that seemed to curl in arabesques against a heavy Latin backbeat. He had heard this music on boom boxes all over the South Bronx. Carlos Santana. Still a rock icon after thirty years.

Freddy slipped into the Whit, which abutted Roberts's compartment. He removed a tiny sound amplifier from a sleeve pouch and pressed its suction end against the wall. The music was so loud that Carlos Santana seemed to be picking guitar strings inside the convolutions of Freddy's brain. Freddy adjusted the amplifier to mute as much of the music as possible.

"This doesn't look like the same stuff."

"It is."

"But it looks jagged."

"The man downstairs didn't put any gelatin capsules in the last shipment. That's why it looks like a rock."

"It's yellower, too."

"Hey, take your business elsewhere if you don't like it."

"Sorry. It's all right. It's just that—"

"Goddammit, it's the same stuff. Take my word for it. Do you want the shit, or not?"

"Yeah, I want it."

Someone turned the music louder and drowned out the voices. Freddy coiled his amplifier into a tiny bundle and slipped out of Hab 1. Better run that relay test quickly, he thought. Otherwise, Lance might become suspicious.

27 AUGUST 1998
TRIKON STATION

Trikon Station has been equipped with state-of-the-art extravehicular mobility units (EMUs) designed through the combined efforts of NASA, ESA, and Trikon International's own aerospace division. These space suits are sleeker than the suits you may remember from photos of the Apollo lunar program or more recent American space shuttle flights.

The suit itself is constructed with layers of various insulation materials, a gas-tight bladder, a heat-resistant comfort layer, and protective outer layers of glass fibers and Teflon. The bubble helmet is made of a high-strength Lexan plastic.

The suit is ribbed at all joints and at the shoulders and waist to provide increased mobility. The self-contained life-support system will allow you to perform routine tasks safely and comfortably for up to six hours. There is an umbilical option if a longer duration is dictated. The suit also is equipped with multichannel communications units. During EVA, you may select one or more channels over which to conduct your communications. Special channels allow you to monitor the station's internal alarm system or voice traffic over the station's intercom.

The most innovative feature is the force-multiplier glove. Since all EMUs are internally pressurized, the limbs and appendages tend to become rigid in the vacuum of space. As a result, even the simple task of gripping a tool produces extreme fatigue since you must exert muscular energy just to keep the glove fingers grasping the tool. Force-multiplier gloves have solved this problem. Once you begin to move your fingers, the finger pressure is sensed inside the glove and the force multiplier's miniaturized servomotors will complete the movement and hold the position until a countermovement signals their release. In essence, the force-multiplier system is akin to the power steering system of an automobile.

One drawback of the EMUs you will be using is that they are pressurized to only six pounds per square inch. The atmosphere within Trikon Station, composed of 20% oxygen and 80% nitrogen, is pressurized to standard sea-level pressure of 14.7 psi. Since you will be going from a higher to a lower pressure when suited up for EVA, you must purge your bloodstream of dissolved nitrogen gas prior to depressurizing the airlock and being exposed to the vacuum of space. This is accomplished by prebreathing pure oxygen provided at the EMU servicing panel located in each airlock. Prebreathing oxygen will gradually remove the nitrogen from your bloodstream so there will be none left to bubble out of solution in the blood as the pressure drops during depressurization of the airlock.

A graph/chart is prominently displayed in each airlock showing the amount of prebreathe required if station pressure is less than normal. It is imperative that you follow these guidelines. Failure to do so may result in a potentially disabling gas embolism, such as the familiar "bends" experienced by deep-sea divers.

—from The Trikon Station Orientation Manual

HUGH O'DONNELL FELT intensely alive. He awoke each day without need of an alarm clock and performed his morning ablutions while the rest of the station slept. It occurred to him that he never explained to Dan Tighe exactly why he refused to grow a beard. Part of the reason was simple vanity: his beard contained far more gray than the hair on his head. But the main reason was the regimen stressed by the counselors at the substance abuse clinic: male patients were required to shave every day. The rationale was not predicated on some archaic notion equating facial hair with drug abuse. The idea was that each patient would forever be in danger of reverting to his habit if he allowed his life to wander from an established routine. For a male, a daily shave was the perfect object lesson.

It was the routine of life aboard Trikon Station that allowed O'Donnell to flourish. Each day, he accomplished three solid hours of work in his lab before reporting to Lorraine Renoir for his required session. Then it was a quick breakfast in the wardroom before returning to the lab for another three-hour stint. The lengths of his afternoons and evenings were dictated by the pace and progress of his work, but they rarely came to less than another eight hours.

After dinner each evening, he threw darts with Dan Tighe. He knew that the commander was pumping him for information about himself, and he deliberately refused to display any pique as he carefully sidestepped any questions relating to his former habit. He liked Tighe and sensed that Tighe liked him in the way veterans of the same war will appreciate each other. They played for sodas to be paid Earthside. The nature of O'Donnell's work never entered the conversation.

The fourteen-hour workdays began to show a cumulative effect. O'Donnell was confident that he would complete his project within the three-month period allotted him. After that, the world would never be the same. Or so he hoped.

O'Donnell cracked his lab door and peered into The Bakery. It was still early morning and the workstations were unoccupied. He slipped outside, one hand cupping a test tube filled with a solution approximately the color of seawater, and locked the door behind him. Even though he would be only a few feet away, he took no chances of unwanted eyes peeking into his lab while he was busy at the centrifuge. He anchored himself to the floor, slid open the clear plastic cover, and secured the micro-gee test tube to the centrifuge's arm. He adjusted the proper settings and pressed the button. Instantly, the centrifuge whirred to life. The arm and the test tube whizzed to a blur. After precisely one minute the motor cut off and the centrifuge wound down to a stop. The solution had migrated into three distinct bands: clear, green, and brown.

O'Donnell sighed with satisfaction. He brought the test tube back to his lab, where he placed it on a rack within a lightproof box, and removed another test tube from a different rack along the wall. The solution in this test tube was the color of beet juice.

Stu Roberts drifted into The Bakery while O'Donnell was watching the second test tube whirling in the centrifuge. Roberts's red hair was severely tangled beneath his hair net and his eyes squinted against the powerful fluorescents that illuminated the lab. Obviously, he had just tumbled out of his sleep restraint.

O'Donnell nodded to Roberts, then returned his attention to the centrifuge. The tech continued down the aisle, fussing with different workstations as he passed. He finally stopped at the sterilizer and began loading the previous day's dirty glassware.

As the sterilizer hissed and rumbled, Roberts watched O'Donnell bring test tube after test tube from his lab to the centrifuge. He spoke not a word to Roberts, and the technician remained silent also. The weirdo hasn't let me inside his lab since day one, Roberts grumbled to himself. Every time I offer to help him he brushes me off. He might know sixties music. He might be able to rap about The Who, the Stones, and Creedence Clearwater Revival. But he's just as much of an asshole as Dave Nutt, in his own way. Of course, there's always the chance . . .

"Need any help?" he called.

"No, thanks," said O'Donnell, his eyes fixed on the centrifuge.

"I mean, I could ferry that stuff back and forth for you."

"It's no trouble. Thanks."

Not this time, either, thought Roberts. He smiles, but he stays miles away. Damn!

Roberts clung to the door of the sterilizer and closed his eyes. I'm nothing but a glorified dishwasher to him, he told himself. The machine's constant vibration soothed the taut muscles of his back and neck. The serenity didn't last long. The shrill voice of Thora Skillen knifed through The Bakery.

"Dr. O'Donnell, what are you doing at that centrifuge?"

"Spinning test tubes," said O'Donnell.

"Did you obtain permission from me?"

"At seven A.M.? None of your people are ever here before eight."

"I don't care what time it is," said Skillen. She wore her usual stained smock. A vein stood out in the middle of her forehead, continuing the ridge formed by her chin and chiseled nose. "My people may require use of this lab's hardware at any time. That is why we have established procedures."

"I'm on my last tube."

"You're damned right you are. Next time you will be allowed a block of time no longer than fifteen minutes. Your tech is to arrange it for you."

Roberts floated toward the centrifuge.

"It's my fault," he said. "He told me that he wanted to use the 'fuge this morning. I was supposed to arrange it with you. I must've forgot."

Skillen's suspicious eyes darted from Roberts to O'Donnell and back again. The anger drained out of her face, as if berating a mere tech was less satisfying than a fellow scientist. O'Donnell maintained a poker face. He knew he hadn't told Roberts of his intention to use the centrifuge. He never told Roberts anything.

"Very well, Mr. Roberts," said Skillen. "See that it doesn't happen again."

She swept out of The Bakery. O'Donnell looked at Roberts. The tech smiled as if to say, You owe me one.

"Millions of you are sitting in kitchens across the United States, stirring no-cal sweetener into your instant coffee and listening to your soy sausages and cholesterol-free eggs sizzling in your microwave ovens. You watch me during breakfast as I babble incessantly about different aspects of our two-year Mars Project. You must wonder exactly how the manned exploration of such a distant world would affect you, if at all. Today, I plan to tell you."

"Cut!" shouted the meteorology payload specialist who doubled as camera and sound man for the weekly broadcasts to "Good Morning, World."

Kurt Jaeckle, suspended against a backdrop of full-color photographs of Mars taken from the Hubble Space Telescope, looked over the top of his reading glasses.

"The sound from the boom mike is weak," said the cameraman.

Jaeckle floated to the elbow of the aluminum boom, loosened a large wing nut, and tapped the arm with the heel of his hand.

"I don't want the mike in the picture," he said. "I want nothing distracting attention from me—and Mars."

"Don't worry," said the cameraman.

Jaeckle returned to his position and ran through the

opening lines of his script, this time from memory. The cameraman gave him a thumbs-up. Audio and video were perfect.

Jaeckle noticed a rustling in the black curtain that covered the rumpus room's entry hatch during broadcasts. A hand parted the curtain and Carla Sue Gamble sailed through, her blond hair floating freely like a globe of light. Jaeckle immediately resumed reciting his lines. He concentrated solely on the camera lens, but he could see Carla Sue in the background. With her slightly crouched micro-gee posture and skinny limbs wrapped in black exercise tights, she reminded him of a wingless four-legged mosquito flitting at the edge of his vision. Just as much a nuisance, too, he feared. He stopped his recitation and drew his finger across his neck.

"Take a break," he said. The cameraman shut off the equipment and knifed through the curtained hatch.

"You don't give me a script and now you're rehearsing by yourself." Carla Sue lurched forward, but stopped herself with a handhold before butting Jaeckle's chest with her head. "Am I supposed to draw my own conclusion?"

"Now, Carla." Jaeckle unhooked his reading glasses from behind his ears and slowly folded them into his pocket, all the while trying to remember exactly what he had told her. Two deep lines ran down the corners of her mouth, and for a moment he thought of her not as a mosquito but as a ventriloquist's dummy. "I meant to explain everything."

"What's there to explain? You're cutting me out. I understand. I just wish you had the balls to tell me."

"Carla, you misinterpret—"

"I haven't seen you in four days. Four nights, to be more precise. I'm no fool."

"The final decision wasn't made until last night," said Jaeckle. "Jared Lewis called me this morning to tell me. A marketing survey showed that ratings would improve if I went on alone."

"Alone?"

"Don't take it personally, Carla. Neither of us are media personalities, thank God. We don't need these cameras to put bread on our tables. We have Mars."

"Alone, you said."

"That's right," said Jaeckle. "I can't fathom how they arrive at these decisions."

Carla Sue's dummy jaw clamped shut. The two buttonholes that were her nostrils flared.

"If you don't need an assistant, why is Lorraine Renoir reading a script? Explain that unfathomable mystery to me, Professor Jaeckle. And don't give me any of your guff about it being a network idea to put Miss Florence Nightingale on television."

"She is a physician," said Jaeckle. "The next show is devoted to the problems of administering medical treatment in micro-gee. She is the only person on board qualified to discuss the subject."

"What else is she qualified for?"

"I resent your implication."

"You resent me hitting the nail square on the head," said Carla Sue. "But let me tell you something right now. I'm not one of your starry-eyed grad students who took a tumble with you for a grade. I never expected us to last. But I do expect to land on Mars someday. And if I don't, you can be damn sure that you won't either."

With that, Carla Sue spiraled away and punched through the curtain.

Thora Skillen reached her sleep cubicle and slid the door tightly shut. O'Donnell worried her. None of her contacts Earthside had been able to glean a shred of information about him. He was not a security agent, that much seemed sure. He certainly acted like a research scientist, and a damned reclusive one at that.

What is he doing here? The question pounded at her.

Her chest hurt. She knew it was psychosomatic, but the pain was real nonetheless. One of the things the Earthside medical people hoped to determine was how well she resisted infection. They had put her on antibiotics, of course. And then thrown her into this tightly confined space station where anyone with the slightest sniffle quickly spread it to one and all. It was like living through the first week of kindergarten every month; you could tell how long it had been since the shuttle's last docking by the coughs and sneezes echoing through the station.

She was providing them with the data they sought, Thora told herself grimly. They must be very happy with that. Their experimental animal is behaving well for them.

So far, she thought. So far so good. But time is running out.

She opened the compartment where she kept the antibiotic pills. The bottle was nearly empty, she saw. I'll have to get Lorraine to give me a refill. She'll probably want to change the prescription, too. Antibiotics lose their effectiveness over time; your body adapts to them.

Using a long-nosed tweezers, Thora extracted two of the pills from the bottle, then turned toward the door, intending to get a cup of water at the washroom. She stopped, turned back, and took two aspirin, as well. The pain might be psychosomatic, but it *hurt*.

Russell Cramer paused at the access door to the Mars module's internal tunnel. It was midafternoon and the module was abuzz with activity. Centrifuges whirred. Computer terminals chirped. The other Martians huddled in groups as they discussed findings about the meteorology and geology of the red planet. But his workstation was silent, and would remain so for another two weeks. They were all making progress but he was not.

Cramer opened the door and edged one foot outside as if testing the water of a swimming pool. He wanted someone, anyone, to see him heading for the blister, but no one paid him any mind. They were busy. They were working. He was about to spend two hours in solitary confinement.

Finally, one of the women noticed him.

"Have fun, Russell," she called.

Cramer hauled himself into the tunnel and slammed the door.

Cramer belonged to the group with Earth-viewing privileges. In the observation blister he pressed a button on the control panel and the lower portion of the clamshell peeled back. Trikon Station was flying over the eastern Atlantic. Cloud cover was sparse and the ocean was a brilliant, iridescent blue. The sun's reflection off the water traced a fuzzy round highlight eastward directly beneath the station. But Cramer was not interested in gazing at the spectacular scenery curving majestically beneath him. He was too angry at Kurt Jaeckle to enjoy anything.

Cramer didn't think he was sick. He didn't think he was crazy, Sure, he had some trouble sleeping, a few bad dreams. Nothing serious. Nothing that would have warranted discussion on Earth, let alone medical treatment. Everyone was too cautious up here.

But maybe caution hadn't been the reason for Jaeckle's order that he spend double time in the blister. People had warned him that Jaeckle's polished manners concealed a snake's cunning. Maybe he was less concerned with Cramer's health than with the newly arrived Martian soil sample. Maybe Jaeckle was using these two-hour time blocks to analyze the samples without him. He was screwing around with Carla Sue Gamble, the backup biochemist. Maybe he's giving the new soil sample to her!

Cramer dived out of the blister and back into the tunnel. He eased open the access door and peered into the laboratory section. His workstation was unoccupied. He closed the door and noted the time, deciding to check his workstation at fifteen-minute intervals. No one was going to discover life in that soil before him. Not Carla Sue. Not even Jaeckle himself.

The station crossed a thin band of green that was the coast of Morocco. Within minutes, the entire visible world dissolved into the burning browns and reds of the Sahara Desert. Sand dunes corrugated the surface in the long shadows of late afternoon. A dust storm formed a blurry corkscrew. Station personnel agreed that the Sahara, with its animated tableaux of shifting sands, was the most spectacular sight visible from the blister. The Martians had a special affinity for the desert because it resembled so much the spacecraft photos of Mars.

But Cramer was not interested. He felt antsy as hell. He shot himself from one end of the blister to the other in a micro-gee version of pacing the floor. Two hours in the blister. One and a third orbits of the earth. Thirty-five thousand miles. Some people didn't travel that far in their entire lives.

Cramer patted the breast pocket of his shirt. The tiny bottle felt hot to the touch, or was it his imagination? Three yellow rocks remained. One could make these two hours seem to pass in the blink of an eye. Thirty-five thousand miles in a second. Not quite the speed of light. But not bad, either.

He worked the bottle out of his pocket. It was less than an inch long and barely half that in diameter. Dark brown glass with a black plastic cap. He unscrewed the cap carefully. If the rocks jack-in-the-boxed out, they would be lost forever in the brightness of the blister.

Cramer had been stunned by Kurt Jaeckle's refusal to release the news of the discovery of life in the

Martian soil samples. He had spent a couple of days sulking in his sleep compartment and refusing to take exercise until he realized that he still held the key to his own success. He had found the microorganisms once; he could do it again.

He had thrown himself into the task, twelve, fourteen hours at a stretch at his workstation, wolfing down meals, skipping R and R in the blister. But he just could not repeat that one, slim result that had shown a trace of living cells in a sample of Martian soil. All the other soil samples were sterile, and the one glimmer of life he had found had been destroyed in the tests that showed it existed. All he had was a set of curves on a computer screen. Even that one soil sample refused to give any further positive results.

As his failures mounted he grew increasingly depressed. One night, while listening to music in Stu Roberts's sleep compartment, he confided his troubles.

"I know all about it," said Roberts.

"You do?"

"Sure. Everyone on the station knows you found living organisms in one of the soil samples. We're all waiting for you to duplicate the results."

"I can't," wailed Cramer. "I just can't."

"Sure you can."

"I can't, I tell you. I've done the experiment every way I know how. There's nothing in that soil anymore."

"You just need to think of things in a different way." Roberts fished a pencil and a sheet of paper out of a compartment. He pressed the paper against the wall and drew a figure. "What's that?"

"A hexagon," Cramer answered.

Roberts drew another figure and asked Cramer to identify it.

"A snake," said Cramer. "Eating its tail."

"Remember your freshman chemistry?" Roberts

asked. "The story about Kekulé being stumped by the molecular structure of benzene and then dreaming about a serpent eating its tail? Then he proved benzene's structure is hexagonal, right?"

"Yeah, but how does that relate to life on Mars?"

"You need to dream about a serpent eating its tail," said Roberts. "So to speak, that is."

"I don't dream of anything," Cramer said.

"That's where this comes in." Roberts wormed a small brown bottle out of his shirt pocket and let it hover in midair between them.

"What is it?"

"MDMA, better known as Ecstasy. It's a mild stimulant and hallucinogenic. Just the thing you need to get over your experimental hurdle. It heightens self-awareness, enhances sensory perceptions, generally helps you see things in a different way."

Cramer held the tiny bottle up to the light. Two capsules danced inside.

"Any side effects?"

"Not a one," said Roberts. "Hell, this stuff was legal until 1985."

"Where did you get it?"

"I use it when I'm stuck with my music. You know, I hit a block, can't get the notes down right. Just one swallow and the next thing I know I've got half a ton of paper covered with notes. Good stuff, too. Better'n I write cold."

Cramer licked his lips. "But it's illegal, isn't it? If anybody found out . . . "

"Hey, you don't want it, don't take it. I don't give a shit either way."

Cramer refused the capsules that first time. Roberts shrugged and changed the subject. But two sleepless nights later Cramer came back to the technician's quarters and asked if he could "just try out one capsule." Roberts gave him three.

With them he felt alert, brilliant, powerful. The

hallucinations were mild, just as Roberts had said. An inanimate object might wiggle in the corner of his eye. Flashing circles might appear, only to vanish when he blinked. An occasional bad dream might disturb his sleep. But these were mere trifles compared to the benefits of a keen mind.

Yet despite his enhanced perceptions, the Martian soil samples remained stubbornly, stupidly barren. He knew that Jaeckle and all the others were laughing at him behind his back. He knew that Mars was holding its secrets away from him deliberately.

Cramer stared at the reddening desert as he worked saliva into his mouth. The rocks were drier than the capsules Roberts usually gave him and needed lubrication going down. He popped one well back in his throat and swallowed.

The effect wasn't quite instantaneous. He had enough time for a second look at his workstation and Jaeckle's office. Both were as before.

He returned to the blister and steadied himself as best he could in its exact center. He closed his eyes, folded his arms, and crossed his legs at the ankles. Then he proceeded to drift, feeling great waves of energy course through his body as the drug entered his bloodstream. Time refused to speed up, but he didn't care. His senses grew, intertwined, then blossomed into pleasantly confounding combinations. He could hear the orange paint on the outer skin of the Mars module. He could smell the hum of the station ventilators. He could see the words of the other Martians oozing through the seam of the door like green gunk.

A flash of searing heat disrupted his fantasy. His eyes flashed wide. The Sahara was fiery red. Storms roiled, sending aloft great spirals of sand that buffeted the station like giant handfuls of gravel. A huge figure of a bearded man with long hair and a flowing robe loomed out of the clouds. He beckoned to Cramer with outstretched hands.

The heat was unbearable. Cramer tore at the collar of his shirt, ripped at the drawstring of his pants. His nightmare had come true. They were falling. The station was plummeting through the atmosphere. The entire sky glowed with the heat of their descent. The bearded man beckoned.

Cramer clamped his teeth over his wrist. He pushed his free hand against the dome. Molten plastic burned his fingers. The cries of his fellow Martians resounded through the station. The bearded man drew back his lips in a Satanic grin.

Cramer screamed.

Dan Tighe and Freddy Aviles were reviewing the progress of the computer reconfiguration project when a voice burst over the command module's loudspeaker.

"Emergency! Mars module! Emergency!"

Dan and Freddy locked eyes. A second later they were in the connecting tunnel, propelling themselves hand over hand toward a knot of people gathered at the Mars module's entry hatch. Shrieks echoed within.

Dan peeled bodies away and dove inside. At the far end of the internal tunnel, the door to the observation blister floated free of its broken hinges. Torn plastic seals bobbed in the doorway like the waving arms of an octopus.

"We're falling, we're falling!" someone was screaming.

Dan turned to the entry hatch and yelled at the circle of faces. "Find Dr. Renoir. Tell her to bring sedatives. Fast! Freddy, get something to restrain him."

Tighe dove headfirst through the nearest access

door and found himself beside Kurt Jaeckle. The
professor's normally olive skin was ghostly white, his
deep-set eyes wide in fear and confusion.

Near the aft end of the module, three Martians
cowered in cubbyholes formed by different workstations. A fourth drifted like a broken rag doll, his
face bloodied and his shirt tattered. Smashed lab
equipment and glassware hung in the air. In the
middle of it all Russell Cramer whirled like a dervish,
buck-naked.

"We're falling! The station is crashing! Don't you
feel it?" His voice was guttural as if coming from deep
within his chest. He grabbed the unconscious Martian
by the remains of his shirt and slapped his face.
"We're burning up! Do something!"

The Martian's head waggled. In disgust, Cramer
flung him toward the rear of the module.

"I don't know what happened," Jaeckle whispered,
his words coming in a rush. "He was in the blister for
about half an hour. He started screaming, broke down
the door, and attacked people."

Dan listened without taking his eyes off Cramer.
The Martian tumbled around the module, punching
equipment with fists that streamed ribbons of blood
and terrorizing his fellow Martians with threats of
death.

Freddy settled next to Dan. Draped between his
hands was a nylon net he had taken from a storage
compartment in the command module. Dan shot a
glance at the access door. Lorraine Renoir displayed a
syringe.

"Stay off my left flank," Dan told Freddy. "I'll try to
draw him in. When he goes for me, net him." He
turned to Lorraine. "Wait until we have him under
control."

Cramer acted as if blind to everything in the
module. He twisted his limbs and babbled a steady
stream of nonsense. Balls of white saliva spewed from

his mouth and gathered in tiny clouds around his head.

Dan and Freddy edged forward. Twenty feet, fifteen feet, twelve feet. At ten feet, they stopped. Cramer sensed they were close.

"Aye, Commander Tiger, come to see the fire, huh?" Cramer slowly turned his head toward them. His eyes rolled back in their sockets.

Dan tensed his grip on a handhold. He wanted to be able to fly backwards when Cramer lunged forward. But Cramer retreated toward the unconscious Martian, who bobbed against a workstation.

"Tiger sees the fire, the fire wants Tiger."

Cramer grabbed the unconscious man by the shirt and flung him like a missile toward Dan and Freddy. They tried to stop the Martian, but he barrelled through their arms. Jaeckle prevented him from crashing into the wall. Two other Martians pulled him into the tunnel.

"Tiger sees the fire, the fire wants Tiger."

Dan and Freddy resumed their careful approach. Cramer's eyes were unfocused, but he knew they were coming. His doggerel sounded more urgent with each repetition.

"Tiger sees the fire, the fire wants Tiger!"

Cramer suddenly gathered himself into a cannonball and shot forward. Dan pulled back and Freddy threw the net. It snared Cramer, but his fist shot free before Dan could react and caught him squarely in the jaw. Dan's vision blurred. When it cleared, Freddy's powerful arms had Cramer locked in a bear hug.

"Feet! Feet!" Freddy yelled.

Cramer kicked wildly, sending them into a tumble that smashed Freddy's back against a metal cabinet. Dan tackled Cramer and managed to pin both feet against his shoulder. He looped his other arm around a handhold to stop Cramer from moving. Lorraine Renoir swept overhead. Cramer yelped as she jammed the hypodermic into his buttock. A moment later, he went limp.

"Get some duct tape," Dan said to Freddy.

"Are you all right, Dan?" Lorraine asked, breathless, wide-eyed.

"I'm goddamn lucky it wasn't my nose," Dan said as he rubbed his bruised chin.

Dan summoned Muncie and Stanley to transfer the sedated Cramer into the rumpus room. Meanwhile, he ordered the Mars module cleared of all personnel to allow an inventory of the damage.

"I can't permit that," protested Jaeckle. "Six of my people aren't to interact with anyone. It would ruin the entire project."

Dan shook his head. Jaeckle hadn't been long in shedding his fear and resuming his contrary personality.

"Then lock them in their compartments," barked Dan. "*My* people have their own duties to perform."

Freddy volunteered to inspect the blister. The dome, normally so clear as to be invisible, was smeared with Cramer's handprints. A crimson shirt and flight pants wafted in currents of air. As Freddy gathered the clothes he felt something small and hard in the sleeve pocket of Cramer's shirt. He unzipped the pocket and scooped out the brown bottle. Two tiny rocks floated inside. Freddy stuffed the bottle into his own pocket and gathered the clothes into a bundle.

They were in the rumpus room. Cramer, still sedated, was bound hand and foot with duct tape and secured with bungee cords to the rear bulkhead not far from Dan's bonsai menagerie. A plastic helmet was tightly strapped under his chin to prevent him from injuring his head. Lorraine, Jaeckle, and Dan gathered in a circle near the centrifuge.

"You were treating him for what?" Dan asked.

Lorraine and Jaeckle looked at each other like game-show contestants deciding on the correct answer.

"Overwork," said Jaeckle.

"Sleep disorder," said Lorraine at the same time.

"Well, which is it?" Dan snapped.

Lorraine and Jaeckle each took a deep breath.

"He came to me several weeks ago complaining of bad dreams and an inability to sleep," said Lorraine. "I told him he should cease exercising at least three hours before sleep time. The complaints seemed to disappear. Two weeks ago, he returned and demanded that I prescribe sleeping pills. I gave him a placebo and ordered him to report to me on a daily basis. He never did. When I confronted him, his reaction was testy."

"Someone on the station was acting in this manner and you kept that information to yourself?"

"I didn't," said Lorraine. "I reported my observations to Professor Jaeckle as Cramer's immediate superior."

"That's right, Dan," said Jaeckle. "Dr. Renoir and I conferred at great length. I reviewed my records and discovered that Cramer had not been spending the required amount of R and R time in the observation blister. Instead, he had been working too hard on analyzing Martian soil samples. I relieved him of his research duties until he brought his blister time current. He was on his second two-hour stint in the blister when this happened."

"How did he behave during the first?" asked Dan.

Jaeckle looked at Lorraine and shrugged. "Fine."

Dan sensed something conspiratorial passing between Jaeckle and Lorraine.

"I don't like the way this was handled," he said.

"We complied with the regulations," said Jaeckle.

"Technically, but I expect more than a technical reading of the regs. From both of you." Dan looked at

Lorraine, but she refused to meet his eyes. "I want full written reports from each of you by oh-eight-hundred hours tomorrow."

"What do you intend to do with Cramer?" asked Jaeckle.

"A Trikon bigwig is coming up here by aerospace plane in a few days," said Dan. "Cramer will be on the return flight."

"You can't do that! He's vital to the project!"

"The hell I can't," said Dan. "Cramer trashed your module, trashed himself, and damn near killed one of your personnel. And all because he couldn't take a little R and R. Not on my station, Professor Jaeckle. Not on your life."

Stu Roberts peeled open the accordion door of Chakra Ramsanjawi's office in ELM and dove inside. He fought for breath with long rasping heaves as his trembling hands pawed at the retracted door.

Ramsanjawi was bellied up to his computer console. His *kurta* billowed out from his back and the ceiling lights glittered on the greasy sheen of his black hair.

"Close the door, please," he said without taking his eyes off the computer display.

Roberts, still panting, finally worked his fingers around the handle and slid the door shut.

"Cramer. Did you hear? Crazy. He—"

"Just one moment, please." Ramsanjawi's singsong voice matched the rhythm of his stubby fingers as they worked the computer keyboard. He typed unperturbed for several minutes, saved his work, then removed one foot from a loop so that he could turn his rotund body in Roberts's direction. Roberts was calmer now, but his eyes still had the terrified look of a hunted animal.

"As you were saying," said Ramsanjawi.

"Cramer went crazy in the observation blister,"

said Roberts. "He beat up a couple of Martians and had to be restrained by the crew. He's tied up in the rumpus room."

"I detected a disturbance in the tunnel," said Ramsanjawi. "That would explain it."

"He went crazy, man. He freaked out."

"That is truly unfortunate."

"You don't suppose—" Roberts's eyes locked as an idea slowly fit together in his head. "You don't suppose that the Ecstacy did it?"

Ramsanjawi said nothing. He smoothed the front of his *kurta* along the outline of his generous stomach. The loose garment was so much more comfortable than the ridiculous flight suit that had been issued to him.

"I mean, he didn't act like someone on Ecstasy," said Roberts, making a poor attempt at constricting his nasal passages as he spoke. "Did he?"

"I was not present to witness his behavior."

"He didn't," said Roberts, more to himself than to Ramsanjawi. "I mean, the stuff I gave him looked more rocky than Ecstasy because there weren't any gelatin capsules. But it was Ecstasy, wasn't it?"

Ramsanjawi shrugged.

"It was, wasn't it?"

"I'm afraid Mr. Cramer is a rather unbalanced personality," said Ramsanjawi. "I am mystified why NASA and ESA named him to the Mars Project."

"That's a lie! Russ Cramer is just as sane as anybody."

"I beg to differ, Mr. Roberts. Russell Cramer has a modicum of scientific intelligence that is hampered by a willingness to believe the unbelievable."

A Cheshire grin slowly spread across Ramsanjawi's dark face.

Roberts grasped its meaning. "You didn't? Did you? You planted the microorganisms in that soil sample? You couldn't have!"

"My actions with respect to that soil sample or to Russell Cramer are no concern of yours," said Ramsanjawi. "But what I choose to dispense to you is very much your concern."

"You wouldn't. You . . ." Roberts's voice trailed off and his eyes glazed over in fear as he remembered the time Ramsanjawi had given him a specially treated dosage of fentanyl that mimicked the symptoms of heroin withdrawal. For an entire night, Roberts writhed in his sleep compartment, his body racked by alternating currents of chills and sweats, cramps and nausea. And all because he had failed to deliver a sample from one of David Nutt's test tubes on time.

"Why wouldn't I?" Ramsanjawi's voice wove through the thick curtain of the memory. "You haven't held up your end of our latest bargain."

"I can't get close to him," said Roberts.

"That is absurd. You are his technician."

"But he works completely alone. He ignores Skillen's procedures and protocol. I haven't seen the inside of his lab since the day we moved in his equipment. Honest!"

"These are all routine hurdles," Ramsanjawi said. "My patience is wearing thin."

"A little more time," whined Roberts. "I promise. I'll get into his lab. I'll bring you samples of his work."

"Forget about his work. I have other plans for that when the time comes. Meanwhile, concentrate on his movements. I want a detailed log on everything he does, even something as innocuous as a sneeze."

"Okay. Yeah. I can do that. That'll be no sweat. No sweat."

"Enough simpering," said Ramsanjawi. With a flick of his hand, he sent a tiny brown bottle tumbling in Roberts's direction.

Roberts caught the bottle and fumbled with its cap.

"Don't take that here," Ramsanjawi said with disgust.

But Roberts did not listen. He pulled off the cap and hungrily devoured the white pill inside.

After Roberts left, Ramsanjawi reached for a bunch of grapes clipped to the wall. He pulled off a single grape and mashed it between his teeth, enjoying the sensation of the juice squirting inside his mouth. Most people are like grapes, he thought. They resist you at first, but once you break through their skin you find only the soft pulp of human weakness.

Ramsanjawi was skilled at identifying the weaknesses in people, and at conjuring ways of exploiting them. He knew that Roberts, with his absurd dreams of composing rock music, would see drugs as a necessary aid to the inspiration he so completely lacked; risky, perhaps, but controllable. A little knowledge is a dangerous thing, Ramsanjawi chuckled to himself. Roberts believed his pitiful understanding of chemistry could protect him against becoming addicted. Foolish boy.

Ramsanjawi knew that Cramer's obsession with finding life in the Martian soil made him receptive to the new avenues of thought drugs allegedly produced. Now, with the judicious use of synthetic drugs that he manufactured while his underlings slaved over genetically engineered microbes, he had reduced both men to his only true allies: fear and confusion. Roberts was too scared of withdrawal from his fentanyl dependency not to puncture Hugh O'Donnell's mysterious veneer; the rest of the station was confused about Cramer's sudden psychosis.

Ramsanjawi thrived on chaos. It reminded him of his birthplace—Jaipur in the northwest Indian state of Rajasthan. His father, a rug merchant, had been murdered in a dispute with a Pakistani trader. His mother, herself an orphan, was unable to arrange a new marriage that would have allowed her to support her five children. Chakra, the oldest, took to living in the streets of Jaipur. He was not alone. Depressed economic conditions, drought, and lack of arable land in Rajasthan drove people to Jaipur by the thousands. The broad avenues and colonnaded walkways, once the pride of northwestern India, disappeared beneath the huts of squatters and the ramshackle booths of sidewalk vendors. A bowl of rice or a piece of bread became luxuries.

But family ties are strong. Chakra's aunt worked as a cleaning woman for an agency that provided servants for tourists and business visitors. One English couple required a guide for their travels through the region. His aunt told his mother, and his mother bathed scrawny young Chakra and dressed him in the best western clothes she could borrow. He was presented to the English couple as their guide: old enough to know the area, young enough to be a tenth the price of a regular guide.

The man was Sir Walter Brock, the woman was Lady Elizabeth Smythe. They were quite wealthy and, Chakra could see, given to occasional bleedings of the heart. As they toured the countryside, he regaled them with the knowledge he had squirreled away during his last year of schooling—science, art, the history of this corner of the Commonwealth.

It was Lady Elizabeth who suggested that they bring this marvelous, forlorn boy back to England. Sir Walter wondered whether that was proper; they had their son Derek's feelings to consider. Nonsense, said Lady Elizabeth, Derek and Chakra would get along swimmingly.

Ramsanjawi pulled the empty sac of the grape skin from his mouth. How sweet, how naive Lady Elizabeth, his English mumsy, had been.

27 AUGUST 1998
NEW YORK

What attracted me was the ritual of the drug, not the drug itself. I'd buy half a gram, planning that it would last me the weekend doing a blow here and a blow there. On Friday night, after my shower, I would flip on the ballgame, take a picture frame off the wall, tap a small pile onto the glass, and chop it extra fine with a single-edge razor. I'd shape the lines, long thin ones that curved like the branches of willow trees. And each time a different batter stepped into the box, I'd trail my straw down another line.

By the time I left to pick up Stacey, the stuff would be gone. I'd be on the prowl again, not so much because I wanted to stay high, but because I craved the ritual. The tap tap tap of the bottle on the glass, the crunch of the fine grain beneath the edge of the blade, the pinch of the straw inside my nostril.

That's how I got fucked.

—Testimony of Jack O'Neill

FABIO BIANCO CONVENED a teleconference of the directorates of the three arms of Trikon International before leaving Lausanne. There was little resistance to his proposal to take personal charge of the research operation on Trikon Station. The vote was nearly unanimous.

Bianco thought wryly that they were probably hoping he would stay on the space station and out of their way.

He then leaned on the European Space Agency to use its good offices to obtain him a pass on one of the American aerospace planes. Although the space-plane fleet was slated to begin regular commercial flights to orbiting installations later in the year, passes were available to space agency employees, government officials, politicians seeking reelection, and well-connected members of the media.

Within twenty-four hours, every aspect of Bianco's trip to Trikon Station was arranged. His only problem was with his nephew Ugo, who told him upon boarding the Venice-bound train in Ouchy that flying into orbit with his ailments was suicidal.

"Nonsense," said Bianco, "Micro-gee will cure me."

He waved until the train went out of sight.

The aerospace plane was scheduled to depart from Edwards Space Center in California. Bianco decided to fly to New York, where he would receive final clearance for the flight and spend the intervening two days at Trikon International's offices near the United Nations.

He rose from the galley proofs spread across his desk and shuffled to the office window. Smoke from a New Jersey waterfront fire combined with a temperature inversion to paint the sky a flat gray. A tugboat chugged up the East River, its sluggish wake barely disturbing the purple oil slick that extended from shore to shore. Directly below, traffic on First Avenue was snarled by a bus-and-truck accident. Shirtless cabbies stood on the hoods of their taxis and yelled curses at the emergency workers trying to pry the vehicles apart.

The long, awkward galleys were for an article due to be published in an obscure Canadian scientific journal the following January. Bianco had heard rumors of the article while he was still in Lausanne, and upon his arrival in New York had ordered the Trikon staff to fetch him a copy. The article was as interesting as it was frightening. The media had been full of stories about a mysterious series of whale beachings a week or so ago. Now a research scientist had come up with a theory about the cause of the whale deaths. Bianco shuddered at the implications.

"Jonathan Eldredge is on the line," a female voice announced over the intercom.

Bianco turned away from the window just as Eldredge's image snapped onto the telephone monitor. Eldredge was a youthful-looking man with stylishly coiffed blond hair and an eternal tan. He was an expert in international finance rather than a scientist, and had been wooed away from the economics department of Stanford University shortly after Trikon International's founding to serve as president of Trikon's North American arm.

"I received a memo from Thora Skillen," said Bianco after the two men had exchanged pleasantries. "She complains about a man named Hugh O'Donnell. She says that he is uncooperative and disregards established laboratory procedures. She also says that her lab module is too small to accommodate two separate projects. Two separate projects? What does that mean? Someone is using Trikon facilities and is not contributing to our toxic-waste microbe project?"

Eldredge's normal smile faded from his tanned face. "Hugh O'Donnell is an independent scientist using the American/Canadian module by special arrangement with Trikon NA," he said. "The arrangement is similar to that of Trikon International with the Mars Project."

"It is not similar to the Mars Project if he is using Trikon facilities," said Bianco.

"It is part of the arrangement."

"Who is this arrangement with?"

"Fabio, it's a bona fide—"

"Who is it with?!"

Eldredge's beach-boy features darkened.

"If you want to know, I'll have to patch in someone else," he said. "Hold the line."

The screen went blank, although the subtle hum meant the connection still held. Goddamn these Americans, thought Bianco. How can they lease away precious lab space?

A split image formed on the monitor. Eldredge occupied one side; the other showed a man seated in a room with a blank white wall behind him. Eldredge introduced the man simply as Mr. Welch. The man nodded in acknowledgement. He had a bulldog's chin beneath a thin nose and narrowed eyes. His dark business suit was tight on his shoulders.

"You want to know about Hugh O'Donnell," said Welch. "He was specially selected by us to work on an extremely sensitive project. Trikon NA agreed to cooperate."

"Who are you?" said Bianco. "Besides being Mr. Welch."

"An employee of the United States government. That is all you need to know."

"Jonathan—"

"It doesn't matter who they are," said Eldredge. There was a strained tone in his voice that implied Trikon NA's cooperation was not completely voluntary.

"What is the nature of this project?" said Bianco.

"That is none of your concern," said Welch.

"It is my concern when my project suffers for his presence. And it is my concern when my space station is being misused."

Welch rolled his eyes as if mugging for a television camera.

"Another prima donna scientist who thinks he

owns Trikon Station," he said. He focused his attention squarely on Bianco. Even in the tiny telephone screen his eyes looked ruthless, dangerous. "I don't know where you come from, but we have a saying here that possession is nine-tenths of the law."

"What are you driving at?" said Bianco.

"I don't give a good goddamn who holds title to that aluminum shitcan. It's crewed by Americans. It's maintained by a support system based in the United States. And if any accidents happen up there, you can blame the Americans."

"Are you suggesting—"

"I'm suggesting you don't push me," said Welch.

Was this Welch really saying that the station would be destroyed if Trikon refused to cooperate? The thought raised a pinch of angina beneath Bianco's breastbone.

"Do either of you know about this?" demanded Bianco. He held up a handful of galley pages. "'A Chemical Assessment of Ocean Pollution and Its Long-Term Effects on Marine Flora.' Do you have any idea how serious this is? For everyone?"

Eldredge started to make placating sounds, but Welch cut him off.

"We know all about it," he said. "We are both doing important work, Professor. Unfortunately, there is only one station suited to both our tasks. You will have to work around O'Donnell. And don't try to interfere with him during your visit. He is being supervised."

The images disappeared.

Bianco stared at the suddenly blank screen. Mother of God, he thought, even Trikon Station is not beyond the grasp of an overreaching government. A stab of angina sent him crumpling into a chair. It was more necessary now than ever to journey to the station, for himself and for Trikon.

* * *

"Where the hell have you been?"

The connection was poor. Bob Rodriguez sounded as though he were speaking through a plastic bag.

"Working," said O'Donnell.

"You've been working ever since I've known you," said Rodriguez. "But you hardly ever missed a meeting, and when you did you called."

"Isn't that easy."

"Where the hell are you that you can't call? The clubhouse has a speakerphone. You installed it yourself."

"I know, I know," said O'Donnell. "Can you keep a secret?"

"That's all I fuckin' do," said Rodriguez.

"I'm on a space station," said O'Donnell. There was a long silence from the other end. "Bob?"

"Hugh, if you're having problems, the club can help. That's what it's for."

"This is no joke. I'm not in trouble. I'm on a fucking space station."

"Doing what?"

"Working."

"I didn't know you were an astronaut."

"Neither did I."

"So what's it like?"

"Weird," said O'Donnell. "Some people handle it. Some don't. A guy completely snapped today. He thought the station was burning up. He wrecked part of a module and beat up another guy."

"That just happened out of the blue?"

"Nothing just happens, Bob. The rumor is that he suffered from Orbital Dementia. That's a high-tech version of cabin fever."

"You don't like being shut in."

"You're right. But somehow I don't mind it here. I actually feel content. Maybe it's my work."

"Is there any sort of therapy for you there?"

"Yes, Mother Bob. I report to the medical officer

every morning. I talk. She threatens to draw my blood. It's very therapeutic."

"A she, huh? Nicer than looking at our mugs."

"She's a bitch. Cuts me no slack."

"Glad to hear it," said Rodriquez. "You had a strange visitor the other day. A woman named Stacey. She said you owed her money. Wanted to know if your bike was around. Said she had a court order said she could take it."

"Did you give it to her?"

"They need something stronger than a fuckin' court order for me to sell out a club member," Rodriguez snarled. "One funny thing, she called you by the name Jack O'Neill."

"She probably made a mistake. O'Neill, O'Donnell, all those names sound the same."

"Nope. Described you to a T."

"Did you tell her anything?"

"I was so confused—"

"Bob, did you tell her anything?"

"You know the rules. Nobody divulges anything about any club member."

"Damn right. Now if she comes back, you don't know me or this Jack O'Neill. Okay?"

"Okay," said Rodriquez. There was a long silence. "Why don't you call in during a meeting sometime? Sounds like you might need some support."

"Bob, I'm on a space station! You think there are extraterrestrial dope dealers hiding outside the airlocks looking to making a sale?"

"All right. Just don't kill yourself."

"Thanks for the advice, pal."

O'Donnell hung up the phone and made a beeline to the ex/rec area. Goddamn that Stacey! How the hell did she find him? Where did she get the balls to go nosing around the club? For the bike. The goddamn bike. Couldn't she just leave everything the hell alone?

He grunted a curt greeting to Dan Tighe and yanked

his set of darts from a compartment. He tossed his first round quickly, completely missing the board with two of his three shots.

"Something wrong?" asked Dan as he chased a tumbling dart through the exercise equipment.

"No. Does it look like something's wrong?" O'Donnell snapped. He shot himself toward the dart board, striking the far wall with a thump. Chakra Ramsanjawi raised his eyes from his eternal chess game.

"What the hell are you staring at?" snapped O'Donnell.

"Easy, Hugh," Dan said. "I already had to rope one psychotic today."

Dan's jaw was swollen from his struggle with Russell Cramer. His fists were knobbed with jagged knuckles that reminded O'Donnell of spikes on a medieval mace. They could do some damage.

"Sorry," said O'Donnell.

Ramsanjawi laughed and removed Oyamo's rook.

O'Donnell calmed as the dart game began in earnest. There was none of the usual banter, and Dan was content to let the silence linger. O'Donnell seemed intent on some inner struggle, going through the motions of the dart game mechanically while his mind fought its battle on its own interior landscape. Dan hoped that O'Donnell was gathering himself for a revelation. He didn't want to disturb the process.

O'Donnell knew that relating the conversation with Bob Rodriguez could open up a facet of his life he should keep buried at all costs. But sometimes you couldn't go it alone. Sometimes you just had to get things off your chest.

"Stacey," he finally said. "My old girlfriend. Every time I try to get past her, she stirs something up."

"You want to go back with her?" said Dan.

"Hell no! I want to fucking kill her!" O'Donnell said in an intense semiwhisper. "See, after my money problems began, but before Stacey went off with Pancho Weinstein, I wanted to buy a motorcycle. I couldn't put it in my name because I had lost my license and couldn't get insurance. So I put it in Stacey's name. I left it with a friend when I came up here. I just got off the phone with him. He said Stacey came looking for it the other day, saying I owed her money."

"Pancho Weinstein the lawyer?" asked Dan. Talking with O'Donnell was like piecing together a puzzle.

"You have a damn good memory," said O'Donnell. "Stacey doesn't want the money. What the hell could they get for my bike? Eight hundred? A grand? But Stacey knows that the bike is my salvation. That's why she wants it."

"How is a bike your salvation?"

O'Donnell looked at Dan as if he had lost his train of thought.

"You just said your bike is your salvation," said Dan.

"I did? Oh, well obviously you haven't ridden up the Pacific Coast Highway on a bike."

"Obviously not," said Dan.

"Riding it on a bike compares with driving it in a car or tour bus like being in this station compares with a space walk."

And that is your salvation, thought Dan as a few more pieces of the puzzle fell into place. Nice recovery, O'Donnell, but not good enough.

Kurt Jaeckle pressed a strip of rubber seal along the edge of the blister's door. The new hinges were so stiff he could set the door at any angle without it flapping like a wing. The Mars module was quiet except for tiny bits of debris occasionally pinging against the ventilator grids. He didn't notice Lorraine Renoir until she was at his shoulder.

"The chief scientist of the Mars Project is reduced

to menial repair work?" she said, with a slight smile.

Jaeckle let his eyes meander from her toes to her hair, taking every possible moment to think of a clever rejoinder. She was barefoot. Her flight pants had been altered into shorts that clung to her hips like a second skin. Her breasts rose beneath her blue Trikon T-shirt with each breath.

"This isn't repair work," he said. "I'm a parent healing my child."

"*Très* corny, Professor.

"I thought it was romantic," said Jaeckle, reaching for her.

Lorraine shrugged and slipped away from Jaeckle to peer into the open mouth of the blister. The clamshell was retracted and the blister was bright with Earthglow. She felt a sense of vertigo, as if she could dive through that doorway and not stop falling until she landed on the tiny cotton swabs three hundred miles below. She looked again at Jaeckle. His brown eyes were piercing, penetrating. Maybe it wasn't vertigo.

She always had been too analytical. She had never believed in Santa Claus. She never even believed in Bonhomme, which was astounding for a child growing up in Quebec City. During one Winter Carnival, she refused to join a group of classmates in front of the Ice Palace for a photograph with the seven-foot snowman who served as the carnival's traditional master of ceremonies. He's a figment of our imagination, she had said in English to her teacher.

Ever since Jaeckle had asked her to assist him on television, she had tried to look beyond the media personality that cloaked him like Bonhomme's costume. She knew of Jaeckle's reputation with women. She knew he wanted more from her than the TV show. Very deliberately, she decided to stop trying to analyze Jaeckle's motives. She was finished with analysis. It hadn't worked in her relationships on Earth, and it hadn't worked on the station with Dan. She was constantly waiting for moments when the music would rise, the lights would dim, and the unseen audience would hold its collective breath. Russell Cramer's episode and her accidental alliance with Jaeckle stripped away her complacency. This wasn't theater, this was life. Time to meet Kurt Jaeckle. Time to find out what he's really like—what I'm really like.

Lorraine flipped herself into the blister. Jaeckle followed, pulling the door closed behind him. The soft colors of twilight played through the dome.

"A parent healing your child," Lorraine murmured to him. "Perhaps that is romantic, after all."

"Am I a father figure to you?" he whispered back.

Before she could reply, his hands moved up her legs. His fingers were roughened from the repair work, and the scratchiness added to her excitement. He pulled her pants below her knees and kissed the insides of her thighs.

"Are you a naughty little girl?" Jaeckle crooned softly. "Do you want to be naughty for Daddy?"

Lorraine clutched at a handhold over her head and tried to move away from him, but Jaeckle held her legs firmly in the fading light as his tongue darted between her thighs.

The Rolls-Royce Corniche sped west from London on the M4. Early morning sunlight filtered weakly through clouds that bellied over the nearby hillocks. Rain hammered the pavement in a steady drone, punctuated by occasional cracks of thunder.

The Rolls was as large and sturdy as a fair-sized truck. Inside it, Harry Meade had no sense of the rainstorm lashing the south of England, hardly any sense of motion at all, the car rode so solidly on the smooth highway. The spacious rear compartment was completely soundproof and the windows were so darkly tinted that the streaking raindrops were invisible. He shifted his large frame within the cramped confines of the jumpseat. Sir Derek Brock-Smythe, dressed in a waistcoat, riding pants, and boots, reclined on a miniature leather chesterfield. A low mahogany table separated the two men.

Sir Derek traced esses in the air with a delicate finger as he speed-read several pages of typescript. On a shelf above the wet bar, brandy lapped gently in a Tyrone crystal decanter. Harry Meade licked his lips.

"Splendid," said Sir Derek. He removed a fountain pen from his jacket pocket and drew neat circles around certain words on the pages. "This touching conversation between Chakra and his wife contains the key to neutralizing two particularly dastardly toxic-waste molecules. Hisashi Oyamo has no inkling how intelligent and accommodating he can be."

Sir Derek hummed gaily as he continued extricating coded words from the transcript. Harry Meade pressed his face against the dark window glass. Within his pale reflection, there was only the barest hint of the Berkshire Downs. The island of hair left by his receding hairline looked scraggly. He wiped it with the palm of his hand.

Sir Derek's humming stopped like the disconnect tone of an old English phone box. Harry Meade had only a general knowledge of the complex code Chakra Ramsanjawi employed to smuggle biochemical information out of Trikon Station over unsecured phone lines. But he knew enough to have recognized that the latter portion of the conversation was devoted to Hugh O'Donnell. Sir Derek was reading that portion now; he did not appear happy.

Meade returned his attention to the window. But instead of searching for landmarks in the dim countryside or features on his lined face, he concentrated on the reflection of Sir Derek flipping through the transcript. After several minutes, Sir Derek cleared his throat.

"Ring up the lab and transmit these pages post-haste," he said as he tapped the first portion of the transcript into a uniform pile on the knee-high table.

Harry Meade scuttled off the jumpseat and took the pages in hand. Bending over double in a space tailored to Sir Derek's proportions, he opened the jumpseat adjacent to the limousine's communications center. The Lancashire lab's fax number was stored in the machine's memory. Harry secured a connection quickly. As he fed the pages into the machine, he cast an occasional glance at the window. Sir Derek was again busy circling words with his pen.

Sir Derek abruptly dropped the pages onto the table and got up from the leather couch. He was so tiny that he could almost stand erect inside the Corniche. Leaning forward over the mahogany table, he took the Tyrone decanter and a snifter from the shelf and poured a shot of brandy. Then he sat again facing Harry Meade, the snifter twinkling in his hands, the starched cuffs of his white shirt perfectly placed on his wrists, his booted heels pressed together on the exquisite Persian carpet, barely swaying as the Rolls negotiated a sweeping curve.

"What have you learned about Hugh O'Donnell?" he asked.

Meade heard the static that seemed to buzz between his ears whenever Sir Derek confronted him with the slightest bit of displeasure. What was the latest word on O'Donnell? He felt his fingers involuntarily gripping the lip of the jumpseat as he tried to gather his thoughts.

"We hacked into the computerized personnel files of Simi Bioengineering," said Meade. "It doesn't tell us anything we didn't already know. He graduated from the University of Oregon in 1984 and has been working for Simi since '96."

"No previous or intermediate employment listed?"

"None," said Harry Meade, suddenly uncertain of

the facts he knew to be accurate. "Just a date of birth."

Sir Derek daintily nipped at his drink. Harry Meade imagined the warmth of the brandy bathing his own tongue and throat.

"Chakra is very concerned about O'Donnell," said Sir Derek. "It seems that no one knows his purpose on the station. He has been given his own lab in the American module, which he keeps locked at all times. And he appears to be at odds with the American Trikon personnel. In fact, his only friend seems to be the station commander."

"Doesn't Roberts know anything?" Meade asked.

"Roberts?" said Sir Derek. "Oh yes, the gullible young man who has fallen into Chakra's clutches. Even he doesn't know anything, and he is supposedly O'Donnell's technician."

"Maybe O'Donnell isn't a spy," said Meade.

Sir Derek treated the comment as if it did not deserve acknowledgment. He finished his brandy and returned to the bar for a second tiny shot.

"How rude of me," he muttered. He placed a paper cup beside his snifter and poured in an equal amount.

"Chakra has a lead," said Sir Derek as he handed the paper cup to Harry. "Two to be exact. A Los Angeles lawyer with the inappropriate name of Pancho Weinstein and a woman named Stacey. She is O'Donnell's ex-girlfriend and is apparently in league with the lawyer against him."

The thick smell of brandy wafted past Harry Meade's nose. He knew it was impolite to drink before Sir Derek invited him.

"O'Donnell is aloof," said Sir Derek, leaning comfortably back in the couch. "Chakra needs to know something about him, preferably something personal. We all know how persuasive Chakra can be when he knows a person's secrets."

Meade shuddered; he knew only too well.

Sir Derek abruptly raised his crystal snifter.

"To Trikon," he said. "The finest multinational effort Great Britain never joined."

Meade muttered in assent and knocked back his tiny shot in one gulp. The matter was settled. It was his job to invade O'Donnell's personal life.

Sir Derek flicked the button of the intercom located in the armrest of his couch.

"Turn around. Heathrow."

The Corniche immediately decelerated, made a sweeping turn to the right, and resumed cruising speed.

"I hope you are not wearing long underwear," Sir Derek said to Meade. "You are leaving for Southern California."

In the dead middle of the sleep shift, Dan Tighe followed the dancing circle of a flashlight through the darkened rumpus room. Near the back wall, not far from the bonsai, Russell Cramer bobbed rhythmically in a sleep restraint. His wrists and ankles still were bound by duct tape and he had been drugged into bovine placidity by Lorraine Renoir.

Lorraine. Dan could not think of her without his stomach tightening. She was the exact opposite of his ex-wife: well groomed, subdued, coolly efficient in her approach to life's routines. He had been attracted to her from the moment they had met at the Cape. But he kept his feelings hidden, like the embers of a campfire at dawn. His bitter divorce and the aftermath of constant bickering had left him uncertain of his ability to understand the female psyche. He denied the signs of mutual attraction and retreated behind his mantle of authority whenever she threatened personal contact.

Now he was disturbed by the memory of Lorraine and Kurt Jaeckle casting sidelong glances at each other while he questioned them about Russell

Cramer. Obviously, they shared much more than knowledge of Cramer's gathering madness. Something passed between them right before his very eyes. Dan felt trapped in a funny little box of his own creation. How could he undo six months of rejecting her without looking like a petulant child?

Dan rolled up one of Cramer's sleeves and trained the flashlight on the inside of his elbow. Despite his wide hips, Cramer had thin arms with remarkably prominent veins. Dan pulled a syringe out of his pocket and, holding the flashlight with his mouth, attached a fresh needle from an antiseptic wrapper. He stuck a vein on his first try. Cramer moaned softly in his sleep. Dan drew out ten cc's of blood, then carefully removed the needle. A thread of blood spun in the beam of the flashlight. He blotted it with a piece of gauze and pressed an adhesive bandage to the hole in Cramer's vein before rolling down the sleeve.

Dan sailed toward the connecting tunnel, wondering whom the hell he could trust to analyze Cramer's blood.

28 AUGUST 1998
ATLANTA

The space probe Magellan, launched by NASA in May, 1989, was principally devoted to studying the surface geology of Venus. Its findings, however, suggested a dismal future for Planet Earth unless physical processes already set in motion can be reversed.

Although they are astronomical twins, Earth and Venus are environmental opposites. The atmosphere of Venus, composed of carbon dioxide (96%), nitrogen (3%), and trace amounts of other gases such as sulfur dioxide, is completely inhospitable to life. Earth's atmosphere, of course, is composed of nitrogen (79%), oxygen (20%), and less than 1% of carbon dioxide, water vapor, and other trace gases.

Most astronomers agree that the atmospheres of both planets were once composed of carbon dioxide, water vapor, and nitrogen. The condensation of Earth's water vapor dissolved the atmospheric carbon dioxide and trapped it in carbonate rocks. As a result, the proportion of oxygen increased to a level capable of sustaining life. Prior to the Magellan Project, the accepted view was that Venus's proximity to the sun prevented condensation of water vapor and the planet remained a "hothouse" of carbon dioxide and sulfur dioxide. Magellan has forced a reassessment of this view.

Geological data now suggests that significant amounts of water once existed on the surface of Venus. Therefore, Venus—with its surface tempera-

tures of nearly 1,000 degrees Fahrenheit, atmospher-
ic pressures 90 times that of Earth, and perpetual,
dense cloud cover—does not represent a divergent
development but a continuation of *processes already*
occurring on Earth.

The small decade-by-decade increases in the
amount of carbon dioxide and sulfuric acid (acid rain)
in Earth's atmosphere must be corrected. If not, there
is little doubt that Earth may one day become the
environmental twin of Venus.

> —Excerpt from the introduction to "A Chemical
> Assessment of Ocean Pollution and Its Long-
> Term Effects on Marine Flora"

"AARON, AARON." ED Yablon smacked his forehead
with the palm of his hand, sending a crack through the
cold dry air of his office. He swiveled his chair so that
he faced the window, turning his back to Aaron Weiss.
Twilight steamed over Atlanta. A thin band of dirty orange was all that remained of sunset. Ghostly hulks
of skyscrapers were dappled with yellow office lights.

Yablon could see the reflection of his own office in
the tinted glass of the window. His cigar stub glowed
weakly, like the sun through fog. Weiss paced on the
far side of Yablon's desk like a cat contemplating a
leap from a ledge. He twirled his Donegal walking hat
from hand to hand. Beyond Weiss, Zeke Tucker was
wedged into the only section of couch not littered with
papers and boxes. Yablon couldn't understand how
the equable cameraman had tolerated Weiss for seventeen years. He himself had been the reporter's bureau
chief for a mere three and he was certain the experience would launch him toward early retirement, if not
a coronary.

"You like the whale story," said Weiss. He sailed his
hat toward a coat rack where a faded cardigan sweater
dangled limply. The hat bounced between two hooks,

then landed on Tucker's lap. Tucker brushed it to the floor.

"I like the whale story," said Yablon. "I *love* the whale story. But I don't see the connection between dead whales and space stations."

Weiss's image disappeared behind the desk, then rose again into view, hat on head.

"Am I talking English, Zeke?" he asked the cameraman. "I mean, I thought I explained the connection."

Yablon slowly rotated his chair until he was facing Weiss. He leaned his elbows onto the desk and let his head hang between his hands.

"Tell me again." He spoke softly in an attempt to appear calm. Blue smoke curled toward the ceiling and bits of ash drifted down to his lap.

Weiss plopped into the creaking leather-covered chair in front of the desk. Leaning forward intently, he said, "Forty-six whales have died since the last week in July, and these are only the ones we know about." He swiveled the chair to glance at Tucker and then looked back at Yablon. When each nodded in mute agreement, he continued. "We also know that the diet of these whales consists of plankton." Another pause for more nods. "And we know that they died of starvation. Therefore, the level of plankton in the oceans has dropped."

"Wait a second," said Yablon. "There's no official word that those whales died of starvation."

"The people I talked to believe they did."

"Your people? English-lit students working at Sea World for the summer?"

"I had to start somewhere," said Weiss. "And you forgot Helga Knuttsen."

"Another fine example of the scientific mainstream," said Yablon. "What about Ted Adamski? Why didn't you start with him?"

"We aren't on speaking terms."

"He thinks the whales are suffering from an unidentified virus," said Yablon.

"Ted Adamski is a paid debunker of the truth," said Weiss.

Yablon smiled obscenely. There was no reason to mention the old court battle between Adamski and Weiss. The smile said it all.

"He's still a paid debunker of the truth," Weiss insisted.

"All right," said Yablon. "Let's suppose the whales did starve to death. What makes this any more than a typical August, slow news story?"

Weiss looked at Tucker and rolled his eyes as if asking heaven what he had done to be cursed with working for such an imbecile. Tucker shrugged.

"Right whales eat phytoplankton. Little plants," Weiss added sarcastically. "But those little plants contribute as much oxygen to the atmosphere as all the rain forests in Africa and South America. In other words, Ed: The story isn't one of no plankton, no right whales. The story is no plankton, no oxygen, and no oxygen, *no fucking human race!*"

Yablon let out a genuinely amused laugh. He leaned back in his chair and puffed smoke out of both sides of his mouth.

"Who told you that one?" he said.

"Peter Karlis. He's a professor at Colorado State University."

"That's great." Yablon's laugh grew heartier. "You want this network to broadcast a story that sounds damned alarming, if not outright apocalyptic, on the say-so of a whale expert located in the goddamn Rocky Mountains?"

"He isn't a whale expert," said Weiss. "He's a meteorologist who once worked for NASA. He's done lots of studies on the composition of the atmosphere fifty, a hundred, five hundred years in the future. He has computer models showing the depletion of the oxygen supply over different time frames. One of the factors involves a decrease in the total land covered by trees. The other is a decrease in the amount of phytoplankton. He tells me that the rate of plankton decrease already exceeds his worst-case scenario. The whale deaths are scaring the shit out of him."

Yablon turned back to the window. The orange light had completely left the sky. Atlanta glowed a sickly, muddy yellow in the humid air.

"If you think I will run a story based on Professor Karlis's doomsday predications, you are sadly mistaken," he said. "This is a responsible news bureau, not an electronic tabloid."

Zeke Tucker let out a long, plaintive sigh. He had warned Weiss that Yablon would be dead-set against running a story on Weiss's latest discovery. It looked as if he had been right.

But Weiss wasn't finished.

"Trikon International is working on a secret project with environmental ramifications," he said. "Maybe they have foreseen this problem. Maybe they caused it."

"Our average viewer doesn't give a good goddamn about Trikon," said Yablon.

"We know that."

"But the average viewer goddamn cares about the whales. We know that, too," said Weiss. "Look, I can't prove there is a connection between Trikon and the whale deaths. But I feel it. Trikon's CEO, Fabio Bianco, is going to Trikon Station on the aerospace plane. I don't think it's a coincidence. I want to be on that flight."

Yablon pulled the cigar out of his mouth and studied it closely. Suddenly, Zeke Tucker started to laugh.

"What the hell's so funny, Zeke?" Weiss snapped.

"You on the space plane?" Tucker struggled to form words around his laughter. "You don't even have a driver's license because you don't like cars."

"You're being a real pal, Zeke."

Yablon's chair squealed as he slowly rocked back and forth. Tucker's laughter died away into stifled snorts of amusement.

"Fabio Bianco's going up to Trikon Station?" Yablon muttered. "Are you sure?"

"I have it on the best authority. His personal secretary when he's in New York was once a big fan of mine. She told me about the arrangements."

"Did she say why he was going?"

"She couldn't be specific except to say that he was taking over control of a research project. Now the way I see it—"

"Shut up, Weiss." Yablon leaned back and stared at his cigar. "I wonder. Bianco needs a traveling drugstore with him wherever he goes. And now he's going into space. Hmmm."

"It can't be a coincidence. The whale deaths. Bianco taking charge. There must be a connection."

"I heard you the first time," said Yablon. He looked Weiss dead in the eyes for the first time. "Two seats on the space plane are out of the question. We don't have that kind of pull."

"Arrange with TBC for the use of their transmitter on Trikon Station. I can handle a Minicam myself," said Weiss.

"You're going by yourself?" Tucker wailed.

"Sorry, Zeke."

"You're going on the space plane and to Trikon Station without me?" Tucker seemed stunned.

"I don't like it any more than you do," said Weiss.

"Yeah, but you're doing it anyway."

"This is big, Zeke."

"So I've been hearing."

Russell Cramer was running out of time. Rather, Kurt Jaeckle's efforts at reversing Tighe's decision to send

Cramer Earthside were running out of time. Tighe refused to discuss the issue. Period. End of story. So Jaeckle turned his attention elsewhere. He spent an entire afternoon on his private comm unit lobbying everyone he could contact at NASA and ESA. Tighe was acting precipitously, he said. The project would be severely hampered without Cramer; he was the Mars Project's chief biochemist.

The effort was a failure. Everyone at both agencies deferred to the decision of Commander Tighe.

"For Chrissakes, Kurt," said one NASA bigwig who had been Jaeckle's staunchest supporter at the agency, "the guy went berserk! You can't expect to give him some aspirin and send him back to work."

Jaeckle was wounded by the rebuke. It made him feel like a little boy, and a boy he wasn't. He was a world-famous astronomer. He was a best-selling author. Millions of people recognized him by his face alone.

He needed to get his mind off Russell Cramer.

He decided to visit the observatory. The log showed that the Deep Space Study's instrument pod was due to be recalibrated. Normally, he dispatched the astronomy payload specialist to perform this menial task. But today he would go himself. And he would take Lorraine along with him. Otherwise, what was the point?

Lorraine accepted the offer. A little warily, Jaeckle thought, but at least she accepted. Somebody still likes me.

They met at the main airlock just after the dinner hour. The space suits were stored in lockers lining the connecting tunnel.

"I think a size Small will be best for you," said Jaeckle, floating along the row of lockers until he reached the end. Lorraine noticed that he picked out a Small for himself, too.

"Why do they have to call them EMUs?" she

complained, pointing to the letters stenciled on each locker door.

Taking her question literally, Jaeckle replied, "Government jargon," with a small sniff of distaste. "It sounds more official to say extravehicular mobility unit."

"I mean, why can't they just call them space suits, like everybody else?"

Pulling one of the empty suit torsos from its locker, Jaeckle repeated, "Government jargon," as if that explained everything.

The suits looked like haunted sets of armor, arms floating out slightly, as if occupied by a headless, handless ghost. The helmets bobbed loosely on short tethers attached to the shelf at the top of each locker. They towed the bulky gear to the airlock and sealed themselves inside.

Helping Lorraine to slip an oxygen mask over her chestnut hair, Jaeckle said, "We'll have to prebreathe pure oxygen for one hour."

Lorraine nodded. She said nothing, and Jaeckle did not see the look in her eyes that said, I know about the prebreathing requirements. I'm the station's medical officer, after all.

Neither of them was very adept at donning a space suit. Pulling on the legs was easy enough, although Lorraine had to wiggle her feet furiously to worm them into the attached boots. Then came the struggle of working her arms into the sleeves of the hard upper torso; it was like trying to pull on a sweatshirt made of armor plate. And it kept bobbing away from her. She finally had to ask Jaeckle to hold it still for her. When at last she popped her head through the neck ring Lorraine felt as if she had been underwater for half an hour. By the time they were safely buttoned in, with the life-support backpacks connected and all the seals and couplings checked out, the prebreathe was almost complete.

Jaeckle cycled the airlock. The pumps clattered for a few minutes, then Lorraine could no longer hear them. The hatch slid back to reveal utter darkness. Jaeckle stepped to the rim of the hatch, his suit looking gray and bulky in the dim lights of the airlock. He turned and extended a gloved hand to Lorraine. The glove was ridged with the metal "bones" of its force amplifier and knobbed with their tiny servomotors, like mechanical knuckles.

She took his hand and stepped out into black emptiness.

The station was on the night side of the Earth, but flying quickly toward another dawn. Lorraine had gone EVA only twice, and always on the day side. The scene—or lack of a scene—stretching below her was scary, chilling. She had gazed down upon the night side of the Earth from the observation blister. It was deep black with occasional flashes of lightning and the dim weblike patterns created by lights from larger cities. But viewing night from the protective bubble of the blister was nothing like experiencing it outside the station.

She was floating in emptiness, surrounded by the blackest black she ever had seen. Were it not for the sound of her own breathing within the bubble helmet, she would have been very close to total sensory deprivation.

"We'll wait until we're back in the light." Jaeckle's voice in her earphones startled her. "If we miss the observatory in the dark, the next stop is the moon." He chuckled at his little joke. Lorraine shivered.

Dawn was coming up quickly. Jaeckle and Lorraine backed themselves into manned maneuvering units mounted along the outer skin of the connecting tunnel. Lorraine felt the connector latches click into place on her space suit as she gripped the controls set into the MMU's armrests. Then, without needing instructions from Jaeckle, she pressed the control stud that unlocked the MMU from its mount. The astronauts called the MMUs "flying armchairs." But they were chairs with no seat and no legs.

The dawn broke swiftly, a breathtaking spectacle of colors rimming the Earth's curved horizon. Lorraine could not help but gasp with delighted awe as she watched the world below her come into the light, deep blue oceans and radiant swirls of white clouds, sparkling and fresh and gloriously beautiful.

With Jaeckle in the lead they jetted off, looping out a safe distance around the module raft and directing themselves toward the observatory at the zenith of the station's skeleton. Jaeckle chattered in her ear, using his lecturer's skill to highlight some of the more interesting stars and constellations.

Lorraine oohed and aahed, even though she could not see much of the stars through her tinted helmet visor. But flying an MMU was pure excitement. It was like a magic broomstick, a flying carpet from fabled Baghdad. The realization that she—Lorraine Renoir, the little girl from Quebec City who had dreamed of becoming an aerospace physician—was accompanying the great Kurt Jaeckle to the observatory only added to the thrill.

They parked the MMUs at the attachment points near the observatory's airlock and pulled themselves inside. As they waited for the airlock to repressurize, Jaeckle explained the scientific reason for the visit.

"The project administers an astronomical study of deep space. There's a pod of instruments here aimed directly at Polaris, the North Star. Due to effects such as thermal expansion, the pod occasionally becomes misaligned. So we inspect it periodically and, if necessary, realign it manually."

A green light on the control panel indicated that the air pressure in the airlock had reached a safe level. Jaeckle twisted his helmet off and took a deep breath

of air. Suddenly he started to shake, and for a horrify-
ing second Lorraine thought he had been stricken by a
seizure. Then she understood: he was trying to struggle out of his suit.

"Things are cramped inside," he said by way of
explanation. "You'd better take your suit off, too."

Lorraine soon saw that he was telling the truth.
Although the observatory itself was the approximate
size and shape of an old Apollo command module, it
was so crammed with instruments that the interior
was barely as large as a sleep compartment. It was
dimly lit, like a photographer's darkroom, with most
of the light coming from illuminated dials and
readouts. Lorraine drifted slowly along one wall, her
eyes drinking in the Christmas-tree colors of the
instruments.

"Where's the telescope?" she asked. Jaeckle did not
answer. When she turned she saw that he was staring
at her. He had shed his flight suit and wore nothing
but briefs.

"Here," he said, pointing at his crotch, where
something was telescoping indeed.

My God, Lorraine thought, he's like a twelve-year-
old. She was not quite surprised, but she felt somewhat cheated. Too bad you didn't stay in your space
suit, she berated herself. Too late.

Lance Muncie shot a jet of water to the back of his
throat, closed his mouth, and swallowed. The water
tasted like warm plastic from his having clutched the
thin polystyrene bottle in his hand for the entire shift.
He had tried letting the bottle float free in the cool air
as he watched Russell Cramer between pages of a
paperback thriller he had borrowed from a Trikon
scientist. But the bottle kept drifting into the dull
silver expanse of the rumpus room. Lance found this
tendency to be the most annoying aspect of micro-gee.

Objects did not remain where you put them, unless you bungeed them, or Velcroed them, or corralled them in a compartment.

Ten feet away, a sedated Russell Cramer hung silently in a sleep restraint that fit snugly over his pear-shaped body. His helmet was tethered to the wall to prevent his head from bobbing with the pulse of his carotid arteries. The zipper of the sleep restraint was locked.

Lance closed the book over a flattened straw he used as a mark and bound the covers with a rubber band. It was almost midnight, the time he would be relieved by Freddy Aviles. He pulled himself close to Cramer and stared intently at his face. Cramer's eyes were partially opened, the lids welded in place by dried white gunk. His jaw was slack. A strawberry-shaped bruise discolored one cheek.

"Hey, man."

Lance shot away from Cramer with a start. Freddy Aviles, trailing a flight bag from his shoulder, slowly spiraled through the rumpus room. He deftly arrested himself by hooking a handhold with a single finger.

"You get any closer to him, people goin' to talk."

Lance's face hardened. "That isn't funny, Freddy."

"Hey, man, don' look at me. I don' care. I'm very liberal, you know?"

"It's not funny."

Freddy unclipped the flight bag from his shoulder and attached it to the wall. He removed a banana and a squeeze bottle containing a bright red liquid.

"Hawaiian Punch," he said. "Wan' some?"

Lance waved away the offer. "Why did you say that?" he asked.

"Is a joke, okay?"

"You know I'm not like that."

"Forget it."

"I was looking at him because I'm interested in what happened."

"Lotsa people interested," said Freddy, "here and on the ground."

"What do you think happened?"

"Orbital Dementia. Tha's what the doctor's report said."

"What if that isn't the reason?" said Lance.

Freddy felt the hairs on the back of his neck bristle.

"Whatchyou mean?" he asked. "What else could it be?"

Lance shrugged.

"You made it sound like you knew something."

"Just a feeling," said Lance.

"Well, he had all the symptoms we learned in preflight. Cranky. Recluse."

"I know all that," said Lance. "But what if something else caused it?"

"Like what?"

"Something evil."

Freddy shook his head and took a bite of the banana.

"Something so evil and so clever that it makes itself look like Orbital Dementia."

"You reading too much of that shit." Freddy nodded toward the book tumbling slowly behind Lance's head. To accentuate the point, he fished around in his flight bag for a thin volume devoted to computer esoterica.

"I'm not talking about fiction," said Lance. "I'm talking about real evil. The devil, maybe."

"The devil is fiction, man."

"If the devil is fiction, why do you wear that crucifix?"

"Is a gift," said Freddy. He tugged at the chain until the crucifix popped out from under his shirt. "Besides, I can believe in Jesus Christ without believing in the devil. The devil is what we all can be if we don' got God."

"All right, suppose it isn't the devil. Suppose it is

Orbital Dementia. Maybe that's a sign we shouldn't be here."

"That sound awful strange from somebody who say he always wanted to be an astronaut." Freddy grinned as he stuffed the crucifix back inside his collar.

"I don't know," said Lance. "I was just thinking, that's all."

Freddy had relieved Lance at midnight three nights in a row. Each time, Lance had managed to linger well into the morning by starting some mildly philosophical conversation. Freddy knew that Lance had no intention of pursuing his half-baked theories on the cause of Russell Cramer's madness. Lance simply wanted to deflect attention from his loneliness.

"I talked to Becky tonight," said Lance.

"See? No problem, eh? Wha'd she say? She love you. She miss you. She can' wait to see you."

"She did, but—" Lance's features hardened.

"But what?"

"She laughs funny."

"Laugh funny? How you laugh funny?"

"It sounds different," said Lance. "Not like it did on Earth."

"Those phones are funny, not the laugh."

"I know that, Freddy. Believe me, this is different. It's like there's someone with her, someone she doesn't want me to know about."

"She lives with her parents, right? Who the hell with her there?"

Lance ignored the direction of Freddy's logic. "And she says stuff. Like about my birthday coming next month. She says she's attracted to older men."

"You getting older, no?"

"Freddy, I'm going to be twenty-four. She must be talking about someone else."

"Lance, I think this girl driving you cuckoo."

"You think so?"

"I know so," said Freddy. "Now my cousin Felix,

before he marry his wife she drive him crazy. She talk about this other guy, she stay out all night. But when he felt crazy, he din' sit around and think about she did this or she said that. He'd go out with another chick."

"You mean he would cheat on his girlfriend?"

"Not cheat," said Freddy. "He call it the fine art of getting perspective."

"I couldn't do that."

"Sure you could."

"Yeah, where? On Trikon Station?"

"Hey, man, there are chicks here. And you ain't exactly a bad-lookin' guy. Remind me of myself before my accident. I see these chicks checkin' you out in the wardroom."

"Like who?" Lance asked. A hint of a smile softened his features.

"All of them, man. Even the Swedes."

"Really?"

"Would I shit you?"

Lance's smile went into full bloom, creasing his face. Freddy plucked the paperback out of the air and pressed it into Lance's hands.

"Get some sleep, man. We talk more about perspective tomorrow."

"Yeah, Freddy," said Lance. "You really think these chicks like me?"

"Tomorrow, eh?"

Lance wedged the book and the bottle under one arm and used the other to propel himself across the rumpus room. He paused at the hatch to wave at Freddy before diving into the connecting tunnel.

Freddy washed down the dregs of the banana with a few squeezes of Hawaiian Punch. Lance wasn't a bad kid, he thought, just a little too hung up on his girlfriend. Maybe if he found some diversion up here he'd be a little less intense, and not so much of a leech.

Freddy removed a tiny aerosol can from an inner

pocket of his flight bag. The can contained a stimulant much more powerful than smelling salts. He took off the cap and inserted the can's thin rubber nipple into Russell Cramer's nose. Cramer snorted. Freddy pressed the nipple. Cramer's head shot back as if he had been punched in the jaw. His eyelids blinked and his lips trembled. Freddy shot more spray up the other nostril. Cramer groaned and shook his head. His eyelids separated. His eyes were bloodshot, but focused.

"Tha's good," said Freddy. He clamped one hand over Cramer's mouth, and slowly worked the tiny brown bottle out of his pocket with the other hand. He held the bottle before Cramer's face. The Martian's eyes bugged.

"Now we on the same wavelength, eh?" Freddy spoke into Cramer's ear. "You gonna talk?"

Cramer shook his head. Freddy held the bottle in his teeth while he shot more spray into Cramer's nostrils.

"Burn, eh?"

Cramer coughed and gagged against Freddy's hand. A giant tear loosened itself from his eye and floated away.

"Next one won' be so nice. Next one burn you right down to your lungs."

Cramer mumbled behind Freddy's hand. Freddy allowed him some space.

"Okay, okay," rasped Cramer.

"Good," said Freddy. He pressed the brown bottle between Cramer's eyes and held the aerosol's nipple up his nose.

"Who gave you this shit, eh?"

Sir Derek burst into the small room off the library that had been converted into the most sophisticated communications center in the whole shire of Avon. The operator on duty, a ruddy-faced man named Trane, snapped to attention.

"Any word yet from Ramsanjawi?" barked Sir Derek.

"Not a peep, sir," said Trane, removing his headset. "There's been a rather lengthy discussion progressing. A female and a private detective in the United States. All very hush-hush stuff."

"Goddamn him," muttered Sir Derek. Then he said to Trane, "I want the transcript of the conversation as soon as you get it."

"But, sir, I believe you have a houseguest on the way."

"I know I have a houseguest on the way! I want that transcript!"

Sir Derek stormed out to the closest of the many balconies that protruded from the limestone manor house like the parapets of a medieval castle. The sun was just down. The Mendip Hills humped toward a darkening horizon. Sir Derek took a deep breath of the evening air, then coughed it into his hand.

Objectively, the project was progressing far better than expected. Even the most pessimistic of the Lancashire lads agreed that the superbug was retaining its viability despite the enormous levels of genetic complexity engrafted by Ramsanjawi. Success hinged on Ramsanjawi, and Sir Derek was confident that his reading of Ramsanjawi's personality was accurate. The Indian's obsession with achieving a sense of belonging in English society far outweighed any of the personal enmity that had developed between the two men. Still, Sir Derek worried. There was always the slim chance that Chakra would do the unpredictable.

The trees beneath the balcony suddenly brightened. Gravel crunched loudly as an automobile ground to a halt. The Rolls-Royce Corniche, bearing Sir Derek's houseguest, had arrived.

Her named was Joanna Ames. She was a Latin instructor at Oxford, twelve years Sir Derek's junior, and the longest running of the several affairs he managed to conduct concurrently. She had green eyes, long sandy-colored hair, and a body that remained tautly slim from jogging thirty miles each week. She also had a flair for the dramatic and a high tolerance for pain.

Joanna had not always been so compliant. In the late seventies, during her first term at Oxford, she became enamored with the smoothly arrogant Chakra Ramsanjawi. At the time, Ramsanjawi was a faculty celebrity. He was on the fast track to the chairmanship of the world-renowned biology department and was treated as a guru by the more avant-garde elements of the university community. But in addition to dispensing wisdom, he dispensed drugs. They were mild synthetic hallucinogens he cooked up from common lab materials, and were supposedly harmless. He did not use them himself and he did not sell them. They were too new to be illegal. Ramsanjawi maintained until the end that he never accepted a penny for any of his wares, a claim no one could disprove. He would just bring them on the weekend party circuit and offer them to whoever expressed a desire to perceive an alternate reality.

Sir Derek, who was living not far from Oxford, attended several of these parties. The university scene was a refreshing change from his job as an under secretary in the foreign office. Relations with his would-be brother Chakra were cordial, almost friendly. That changed the moment his eyes found Joanna.

Thinking back, he was not sure whether he wanted Joanna for herself or because she was in love with Chakra. Perhaps the reasons were inextricably bound. She liked Sir Derek. He was, in her words, "comedically cute." But it soon became apparent to him that she never would take him seriously as long as Chakra was in the picture.

Sir Derek sent anonymous tips about an unnamed Oxford drug wizard to three Fleet Street tabloids. His avowed intent was to have Chakra plastered all over the gossip columns, thereby making him infinitely less desirable to the beautiful Ms. Ames. What actually happened was a full-blown sex-and-drugs inquiry that resulted in the expulsion of a score of students and the firing of a dozen faculty members, including Chakra.

Joanna was spared the sword even though she had indulged in more than one of Chakra's concoctions. The price was to agree to succumb to Sir Derek's unusual advances. By now, in the late 1990s, she had grown accustomed to his tastes. And his rewards.

Sir Derek leaned back against the pillows and admired the diamond choker Joanna wore around her neck. It sets off her other accoutrements quite nicely, he thought. She was naked except for the straps that bound her arms tightly behind her back.

"Will it be necessary to gag you?" he mused aloud.

"Please don't," said Joanna softly.

"I think I should."

"Won't you want to put something else in my mouth, instead?"

A fist thudded twice against the bedroom door. Joanna frowned and rolled onto her back. Sir Derek mouthed the words *important business*. He reached for a blanket and draped it over his bare legs and the hunched figure of Joanna huddled between them.

"Come in," he called after clearing his throat.

Trane entered with a look of pained embarrassment on his face and a neatly bound sheaf of papers in his hands. He crossed the room with his eyes fixed somewhere on the farthest wall, handed Sir Derek the papers, and left at double speed.

Joanna wriggled beneath the blanket. Sir Derek

pulled off the covers and gave her a sharp smack across her bare buttocks.

"You'll have to be still for a while," he said sternly. "Content yourself with thinking about what is to come."

She made herself look frightened and rested her head against his scrawny thigh.

Sir Derek quickly scanned the transcript. For the first time ever, there were no genetic data embedded in the code. Toward the end, he unearthed a message: The research pace had slowed to a crawl, especially in the American/Canadian lab module. Ramsanjawi suspected that this new American scientist O'Donnell was to blame. Perhaps he was protecting data under the guise of performing related experiments.

There were obstacles, thought Sir Derek, there always were obstacles. All the great ones had encountered them: Arthur, Alfred, Drake, Cromwell, Churchill. The true measure of a man was how he met those obstacles. He knew that he would do whatever was necessary; he always had. But he was earthbound, separated by an insuperable three hundred miles from the stage upon which this drama would be played. He wondered whether Chakra would have the nerve.

In his frustration and anger he threw the transcript to the floor and grabbed a handful of Joanna's dark hair.

"Now you'll pay," he whispered fiercely to her.

"Oh please," she whispered back, knowing they were Sir Derek's two favorite words.

29 AUGUST 1998
TRIKON STATION

MEMORANDUM

From: L. Renoir, M.D.
To: Cmdr. D. Tighe
Subject: Russell Cramer
Date: 28 August 1998

My conclusion is that the patient is suffering from an advanced case of Orbital Dementia. The patient's dedication to his work within the Mars Project induced him to conceal the early signs of personality breakdown.

The violent episode was most likely triggered by the scheduled arrival of the aerospace plane, which presented the patient with a means of returning to Earth outside the usual shuttle rotation. As demonstrated in studies of Antarctic "winterover" teams, the knowledge that escape from an isolated environment is possible forces the person to reexamine his reasons for being there. A conflict arises if the person cannot convince himself to remain.

In the case of this patient, his failure to duplicate certain experimental results may have hastened a complete personality breakdown.

DAN TIGHE WENT to The Bakery immediately after his morning shower. The main section of the module was empty. Lamps threw cones of light on the idle workstations. The padlock Hugh O'Donnell used to secure the door to his tiny lab was missing. O'Donnell was inside.

Dan knocked on the doorframe and heard a thud followed by a string of muffled words with the unmistakable cadence of obscenities. A moment later, O'Donnell poked his head out the door. His hair was still wet from his own shower and slicked back beneath his hairnet. His glasses magnified his eyes to the size of quarters. Oxidized quarters.

"Is this a business or social call, Dan?"

"Business," said Tighe.

O'Donnell opened the door enough to squeeze out. When he attempted to close it behind him, the runner stuck. The delay allowed Dan a snapshot view of the lab. One wall was covered with test tubes containing colored liquids labeled with polysyllabic names. Another wall was covered with plants bathed in strong white light from two lamps clipped to the ceiling. The thin green stems grew toward the lights, but the white roots looped aimlessly in specially designed beakers. The leaves were oblong, an inch to two inches in length. Some were healthy and green. Others were shriveled and brown.

O'Donnell gave the door a swift chop with the side of his hand and tugged it shut.

"Well, Commander, what can I do for you?"

"What is your specific scientific discipline?"

"Genetics," said O'Donnell. "And microbiology. I picked up some other areas of expertise along the way."

"Pick up any chemistry?"

"Some."

"Pick up any"—Dan paused—"medicine?"

"I wouldn't ask me for a diagnosis or treatment," said O'Donnell. "But I'd say I'm conversant."

"What's your opinion about what happened to Russell Cramer?"

"Is this a medical question?"

"If you want to treat it as such," Dan said. "I'll settle for a gut reaction."

"I honestly didn't give it much thought. Shit happens."

"Dr. Renoir thinks it's a case of Orbital Dementia. You know what that is, don't you? A mixture of boredom, confinement, and dislocation, layered over with the physical and mental stress from living in micro-gee. I understand he'd deluded himself into thinking he discovered evidence of life in a Martian soil sample. No one believed him."

"Sounds like a reasonable diagnosis," said O'Donnell. "I can't add anything."

"What if I told you I wasn't so sure it was correct?"

"I'd say that's very interesting, Commander, but I have a job to do. And standing here talking about Russell Cramer isn't helping me do it."

Dan pulled a vial from his pocket. The liquid within was deep crimson, slightly darker than the color of the Mars Project flight suits.

"Russell Cramer's blood," he said. "I need you to analyze it."

"Why don't you ask Dr. Renoir?"

"She's already rendered an official diagnosis. I need another opinion."

"Why me?"

"This station is riddled with professional politics, in case you haven't noticed," said Dan. "You're the only person I can trust."

"You've known me a matter of ten days or so. Why the hell do you trust me?"

"Because I know you better than you think." Dan paused. "There's something in your past. You talk about your ex-girl and your lawyer, but it isn't them you're running from. It's either drugs or booze. I can't make up my mind which, not that it matters."

O'Donnell almost smiled. "What makes you think that?" he asked.

"Things you say. Things you do. Like the way you throw darts. Shaving every day. The gap in your personnel file. Your orders to report to Dr. Renoir. Don't worry, she hasn't told me a thing. There's a lot she doesn't tell me, even things she should."

"Like what she feels about Jaeckle?" asked O'Donnell.

Dan's eyes snapped wide.

"You know something about me, I know something about you." O'Donnell's face broke into a dimpled grin. "It's obvious that you and Jaeckle are squaring off over the lovely doctor like a couple of bull moose."

"That has nothing to do with my request. And Jaeckle and I aren't squaring off. We both have our responsibilities. Sometimes they're at odds."

O'Donnell forced himself to stop grinning, but the two tarnished quarters behind his glasses still twinkled.

"Now that we've established how well we know each other, what am I looking for?"

"Anything out of the ordinary that can drive a man crazy."

"Blood analysis doesn't work that way. If you want me to test it, I need specific screening panels for specific substances."

"I can get the testing rig that Lor—that Dr. Renoir uses."

O'Donnell cocked an eyebrow. "Without her knowing about it?"

Dan nodded.

"But what am I supposed to be looking for?"

"Drugs," said Dan.

"Now you are talking about my field of expertise," said O'Donnell.

* * *

"You're in fine condition," said Lorraine Renoir, "considering . . ."

Thora Skillen smiled bleakly at the doctor. "Considering that I'm going to die in a year or two."

"That's not necessarily true," Lorraine replied, knowing that she was being evasive, at best.

Her slippered feet anchored in the floor loops, Skillen pulled the top of her sky-blue flight suit back over her shoulders and pressed its Velcro seam shut. For long moments the two women were silent, facing each other in the narrow confines of the station infirmary. Dr. Renoir floated near the display screen that showed an X-ray picture of Skillen's lungs.

"Cystic fibrosis isn't inevitably fatal," Lorraine said. "In your case the antibiotics seem to be working well. Your lungs are almost clear of infection."

"For how long?"

"If your immune system needs a booster shot . . ."

Skillen shook her head. "I watched my twin sister die of this. All that the doctors could do was prolong her suffering."

"I didn't realize you were twins."

"Yes. We were . . . very close. I wanted to die with her."

"But we're learning more all the time," Lorraine said, trying to make her voice brighter. "There's gene therapy now that looks very promising."

"There's always something in the lab that looks very promising," said Skillen, without rancor. "Has it ever occurred to you, Lorraine, that it's all these altered genes from all these labs that *causes* these diseases?"

Lorraine blinked with surprise. "Causes them? But cystic fibrosis has been with us since the beginnings of recorded medical history; long before anyone even started the earliest gene-splicing experiments."

"Do you believe that?"

"Yes. Of course."

Skillen looked almost amused. "You mustn't believe everything they tell you, Lorraine."

"They?"

"Men. Men write the history books, and they are not to be believed."

Lorraine smiled at her. "If I didn't know you better I'd wonder if you're starting to come down with Orbital Dementia."

"Cranky and suspicious?" Skillen smiled back, a rare expression for her. "There's nothing demented about being suspicious of men."

"I suppose not," Lorraine said, looking away from her. She edged away from the display screen.

"Are we finished?" Skillen asked. "I have to get back to The Bakery."

"Yes, we're done. Everything checks out well. The antibiotics are keeping you clear of infection."

Skillen nodded slightly, as though acknowledging a point she would rather resist. She turned and reached for the door.

"Thora?"

Skillen looked back at Lorraine.

Feeling torn, uncertain, Lorraine heard herself ask, "What would you do if—if you felt that someone was, well, using you?"

"A man?"

Lorraine nodded.

"Sexually?"

She nodded again.

Skillen's hard-bitten features relaxed into an almost tender aspect. "I'd stop seeing him," she said gently.

"But if you've agreed to work with him . . ."

"Work is one thing," Skillen said firmly. "Making love is something else. The two are completely separate. Or should be."

Lorraine nodded. "You're right. I know you're right."

"Keep your work on a professional level. Make it clear that your relationship will be strictly business and nothing else."

"I see," Lorraine said, uncertainly.

"If he insists on mixing sex with business . . ."

"Yes?"

"Kick him in the balls."

Flashing a wide grin, Skillen yanked the door open and sailed out of the infirmary.

Carla Sue Gamble simmered silently as she rubbed blush into her big cheeks. She felt her blood boiling. She was damned mad. She was goddamned livid. Nobody treated her so shabbily and got away with it.

She had always known where to find her men. As a University of Florida freshman, she had enrolled in an introductory "Rocks for Jocks" course because it was popular with the varsity football team. She snagged the starting quarterback by wearing pastel miniskirts that climbed the length of her tanned legs during lectures. The relationship barely lasted into basketball season, mainly because—much to her own surprise— she found chemistry much more interesting than the quarterback.

As a sophomore, she took as many science courses as she could. Her sorority sisters thought she had taken leave of her senses. Even the coolest science student was still a nerd compared to a varsity athlete. But Carla Sue found herself genuinely interested in biochemistry, of all things. And not all the guys in her science classes were nerds. They clustered around her like bees seeking a flower.

Kurt Jaeckle had been her biggest catch. The mission to Mars was destined to be her biggest prize, the coup that would set her up for life. The competition for the eventual mission was fierce; being a good scientist was nowhere near enough. You had to be the best, better than the best. Or you had to have strong connections to the men who made the decisions. Carla Sue made a strong connection with Kurt Jaeckle.

But now she was in danger of losing Jaeckle. And to whom? This mousy French Canadian, this glorified nurse, this twit with the phony accent. Well, she thought as she moistened her lips with her tongue, Carla Sue Gamble doesn't give up easily. And she still knows what makes men tick.

Carla Sue dragged herself into the wardroom. The hour was god-awful early, but she needed every minute. She selected a tray of dried peaches, sausage, scrambled eggs, corn flakes, and juice, then glided to a table that afforded her a view of the entire area. Dan Tighe was the only other person present. He nodded in solemn greeting, then returned his attention to his breakfast. His profile was attractively rugged and, at this distance, his eyes flashed like twin stars.

Carla Sue ticked through her mental file on Dan Tighe. Divorced. Embroiled in a constant battle with his ex-wife over their son. Not romantically involved with anyone on the station. More than six months away from Earth. By all outward signs he was ripe for an affair. And Kurt would go apeshit with jealousy.

But Carla Sue could not envision herself playing up to Dan Tighe; she could not imagine him snapping at her bait. Those eyes, at once so attractive and so remote, had the power to wither her with a glance.

Tighe left the wardroom. Carla Sue made herself a cup of coffee by injecting a blast of hot water into a squeeze bottle containing freeze-dried milk and coffee flakes. The wardroom filled up, then emptied as waves of people ate breakfast and moved on to their daily routines. Carla Sue, from her vantage point, assessed each of the males. She immediately discounted any of her fellow Martians. None would jeopardize his position within the Mars Project by crossing Kurt Jaeckle.

The Trikon group offered some interesting possibilities. Of all the people on board, Kurt considered only Chakra Ramsanjawi and Hisashi Oyamo as his intellectual equals. Carla Sue could twist a barb poisoned with professional jealousy by openly flirting with either of them. But with Oyamo's pimply obesity and Ramsanjawi's odorous presence, jealousy came at too high a price. The third chief scientist for this rotation, Thora Skillen, might be interested if the rumors about her were true. But Carla Sue wasn't prepared to go *that* far. Not even for Mars. Besides, that wouldn't make Jaeckle jealous; it would only drive him further away from her.

The new Trikon scientist, Hugh O'Donnell, had a lean and unpolished sexiness about him. But he also had the look of someone who had been around the block a few times. He would see right through her ruse. Besides, she sensed something inside him so tightly wound it was ready to snap. She did not want to be near him when the moment came.

That left the crew.

Carla Sue mixed herself another squeeze bottle of coffee as the wardroom crowd dwindled for the last time. Lance Muncie and Freddy Aviles prepared their breakfasts at different galley stations, then settled at the adjacent table. Forget Freddy, thought Carla Sue. He was a freak, a cripple. No telling how much his accident had taken away from him.

Lance Muncie. The name echoed slowly in Carla Sue's mind. She shaped it on her lips without making a sound. She had outgrown her taste for boys still wet behind the ears. But Lance seemed well suited for her plan. Physically, he was everything Kurt Jaeckle was not: young, tall, with the powerful body of a colt and the wheat-and-sunlight coloration of Middle America. He still wore the wide-eyed, slightly baffled expression of a kid seeing the world for the first time. Plus, the rumor mill said he had girlfriend trouble back home. Carla Sue patted her lips with a napkin. Lance Muncie was her man.

Carla Sue slipped her feet from the restraining loops and sailed over to the next table, her lips arranged in her Homecoming Queen's smile. Freddy greeted her and nudged Lance to do the same. Lance obliged, though not very warmly, then turned his attention to his rehydrated scrambled eggs.

"So what's your secret?" asked Carla Sue.

Lance was startled to realize Carla Sue was talking to him. He shot a nervous glance at Freddy, but saw only the gold canine catching a gleam from the overhead lights.

"Secret?" he asked. Halfway through a swallow, his voice was an octave higher than usual.

"For your muscle tone," said Carla Sue.

Lance had one arm crooked around his tray. The exertion of keeping his arm flat on the table exposed long cords of well-defined sinew. Carla Sue held her hand a half inch above that arm as if tempted but not daring to stroke it. Her fingers were long and elegant. The nails were short, shorter than Becky kept hers, but neatly manicured. Lance shot another glance at Freddy. This time Freddy winked.

"It must be the eggs," said Carla Sue.

"Eggs?" Lance guffawed. "It's not eggs ma'am. It's hard work."

"I work hard, too," said Carla Sue. She rolled up her sleeve and placed her bare arm alongside Lance's. Lance recoiled, but could move his arm only so far before it lodged against the side of the tray. Carla Sue persisted. She laid her arm right on top of his, wrist to wrist, elbow nestling into elbow. Lance felt the warmth of her skin. A chill rolled up his arm and coursed down his spine. He wanted to move, but his arm was wedged between hers and the tray. It would take effort to extricate himself; he did not want to appear impolite.

"But even allowing that you're a strong man and I'm just a weak little girl, I don't have your tone."

"Maybe you don' work right," said Freddy.

"Now that is a distinct possibility," said Carla Sue. She looked at Lance with her lips trembling between a pucker and a pout. "I follow the regimen, but the regimen just might not be right for me. I think I need a coach."

"Well—" Lance felt himself melting under the intensity of her blue eyes, the earnestness of her milky smile.

"Lance a good coach," said Freddy. "He know the body, the *human* body. He can coach you real good."

"Freddy—"

"Could you, Lance?" Carla Sue squeezed his hand. "I truly would appreciate it."

"Well, you see—"

"Sure he could," said Freddy. "You just name the time."

"I usually work out about nine," she said. "It leaves me plenty of time to cool down before bed."

"At nine I'm supposed to—"

"He'll be there," said Freddy.

"The exercise room at nine this evening. See you then." Carla Sue sailed out of the wardroom before Lance's stammering could resolve into a negative response.

"What did you do that for?" asked Lance.

"You need to get your mind off Becky."

"But I'm supposed to help you with your project. I do every night."

"I don' need your help tonight."

"I can't exercise with her. People will get the wrong idea."

"There's no idea to get."

"But she's Jaeckle's girlfriend. You remember what that guy said back at the Cape."

"Lance, my frien'," said Freddy. "That guy don' know shit. You work out with this lady at nine, eh?"

"This is how you do it," huffed Lance between pulls on the rowing machine. "Extend and pull, extend and pull. Full range of motion."

Carla Sue, wearing a white Danskin to set off the remains of her tan and hot-pink leg warmers to bulk up her nonexistent calves, floated beside his shoulder. She and Lance were the only people using the exercise equipment. In the farthest corner of the ex/rec room, Chakra Ramsanjawi and Hisashi Oyamo were at their nightly game of chess. Carla Sue could feel them staring in between moves.

"You try," said Lance. He released the belt and drifted off the rowing machine.

With her ankles and knees primly pressed together, Carla Sue positioned herself over the machine and pulled herself onto the seat. She cinched the belt at the last hole, but her waist was so thin that some play remained. On her first pull, she rose slightly off the seat.

"Extend," said Lance.

"I can't," Carla Sue said with a helpless trill. "I'm bobbing against this belt like a cork."

"Oh," said Lance. He brought one hand to his chin and inspected the situation. "Belt's as tight as it will go."

"I know that," said Carla Sue. "I'm too slim."

"Try again," said Lance. He spun so that he had a proper view of the seat and Carla Sue's butt. Carla Sue tugged at the oars.

"That's the problem," he said. "Belt's too loose."

"Does that mean I can't exercise?"

"No. It means we should fix the belt."

"Oh," said Carla Sue. She gathered her lips into a

classic pout."Fix the belt if you want, but a real gentleman would hold my shoulders down."

Reluctantly, Lance swung himself into position behind her. He hooked his feet to the bottom of the machine and placed his hands on her shoulders. He looked over at the chess game; Oyamo and Ramsanjawi stared at the board.

Carla Sue started to pull. Lance could feel the thin strands of muscle gathering and rolling beneath her skin with each repetition. He could hear the soft hum of her breath. He looked at the ceiling, at the other exercise machines, at the dart board, the chess game, anywhere but at the mane of blond hair and the thin thighs working below him. Chakra Ramsanjawi caught his eye and winked.

Lance felt something touch his hand. It was smooth and soft, with a hint of moist warmth. Carla Sue was nuzzling his hand with her cheek. He tried to move, but the pressure on his hand was too insistent.

At the urging of Freddy, Lance was wearing gym shorts and a tank top. He always hung loosely inside gym shorts and felt naked, as he often did in dreams. Now he was anything but hanging loose. He turned slightly so that Ramsanjawi could not see that he had an erection.

After the workout, Carla Sue suggested that they go to the observation blister.

"There is no better way to cool down," she said, "than to watch a few thousand miles of Earth turning below you."

Lance followed like a puppy dog.

They closeted themselves in the blister as Trikon Station passed over midday on the Indian subcontinent. Lance chattered about the jagged lines of rivers visible through large breaks in the cloud cover. Carla Sue dabbed a towel behind her ears. Whenever she moved too close to him, he seemed to drift away. But eventually, she maneuvered him to the edge of the bubble, against the bulkhead. Lance grew quiet, like a jackrabbit who senses a predator. Carla Sue hooked her ankle around his and, turning, wedged herself between him and the dome. He started chattering again, but she quieted him by pressing a toweled finger to his lips. She slowly withdrew her finger and replaced it with her mouth. He resisted with clenched teeth, but eventually he relaxed and accepted her tongue. She nudged her hand beneath the elastic band of his shorts. He tried to recoil, but there was nowhere to go.

"Feel good?" she said into his mouth.

"Uh-huh."

"Just wait until I wrap my lips around it."

"What?" A spasm coursed through Lance's body, dislodging Carla Sue from her position atop him and tumbling her across the blister.

"Lance!"

But he was hitting at the doorlatch with the heel of his hand, his gym shorts riding low enough to expose a block of firm flesh. He pushed open the door and flew up into the Mars module, his feet fluttering like a bullfrog's.

"Well, I'll be . . ." said Carla Sue. She felt like her grandmother.

Harry Meade poked his head out from the bristling shrub. The canyon wall was dark gray. Only a few bright stars and a smudge of moon were visible in a dirty sky turned orange by the distant lights of Los Angeles.

A breeze kicked up a dust devil near the footlights that fringed the driveway. Meade tucked his chin beneath the collar of his jacket, his two-day stubble grating like sandpaper on the leather. The days were hot, but the heat dissipated quickly in these canyons after dark. And everything was so dry. Even the plants seemed as dry and lifeless as theater props. They had spines and needles and branches that seemed to twist into barbs. One kept sticking him in the ass every time he moved.

The house resembled a Mexican hacienda, nestled between the loop of a circular driveway and the base of the canyon wall. A souped-up sport Jeep, its red finish reflecting the driveway's footlights, was parked at the front steps.

Meade checked his watch. It was nine-thirty P.M. local time, which meant that it was five-thirty A.M. in London. Sir Derek had ordered him to phone at eight o'clock sharp.

Meade nervously slapped a pair of black calfskin gloves in the palm of one hand. The front door opened and out walked a thin man with a mass of dark curly hair, wearing a dark leather jacket. The man threw a briefcase onto the passenger seat of the Jeep, then climbed behind the wheel. The engine ignited with an explosion that echoed off the canyon walls. As the Jeep sped down the driveway, Meade noticed its vanity license plate: PW ESQ.

Meade waited for the sweep of the headlights to disappear and for the roar of the engine to die away. He pulled on the gloves, working his fingers snugly into the soft leather.

The smooth rubber soles of his Clarks made no sound on the pavement. The front door was carved oak inlaid with brass. Meade removed a wire from a pouch that hung from his belt. He inserted it into the keyhole and twisted it around until the lock released.

The security system began to whine, warning Meade that he had sixty seconds to tap the proper four-digit code on the little keyboard mounted on the wall just inside the door. He swiftly pulled a tiny black box from his pocket and clamped it over the complaining keyboard. Four digits lit up in the box's tiny LED screen. Meade removed the box, tapped out the numbers. The whining stopped and the panel's blinking red light turned steady green. He let out a breath he had not realized he had been holding. Then he made a mental note to arm the security system again before he left.

The foyer of Pancho Weinstein's house was lit by brass lanterns hanging from exposed beams. The floor was terra-cotta tile. Meade crossed the foyer to a darkened room with an arched door. Shining a flashlight, he saw a glass-and-brass desk, oak file cabinets, and shelves stuffed with thick legal texts. Pancho Weinstein's office.

The cabinets were locked but opened with a twist of wire. The drawers rolled on silent bearings. Meade riffled through the files until he found one designated O'Donnell. It was empty except for a retainer agreement signed in a spidery hand by a Cornelius O'Donnell and several letters written by Weinstein in connection with a probate matter.

Meade squeezed the file back into the drawer. His breath was hot in his nostrils. Goddammit, he thought. He had to find out something about O'Donnell. Otherwise he would have to face an unhappy Sir Derek.

Meade searched through every drawer of every file cabinet. There was no other mention of any O'Donnell. He considered rushing into L.A. itself. Weinstein had another office downtown. Maybe the real O'Donnell files were stored there.

But there was scant possibility of making it in time to phone Sir Derek. He was about to fail, and Sir Derek's tolerance for failure had been rather low of late.

The voice of a woman singing drifted into the room, then faded. Meade held his breath. The voice rose again. It seemed to be coming from far away. Upstairs or outside, perhaps. Meade returned the flashlight to his pouch and drew his 9-mm Beretta from its shoulder holster. Carefully, quietly, he slid the action back to jack a round into the firing chamber. Then he walked out into the foyer, both hands on the gun, breathing checked, ears alert for sounds. The singing had stopped, but he could hear the faint lapping of water.

He stole up the stairs. Light was coming from the open door at the end of the upstairs hallway, slightly veiled by a billow of steam. Meade stepped into the bedroom, noiselessly. The air was filled with the dewy sweetness of a woman's bath oil.

The bathroom door was ajar. Meade edged along the wall until he could see inside. The floor was white marble, partially covered by an oval rug that looked like a black animal skin. In the center of the floor was a raised bathtub brimming with bubbles, and amid the bubbles was a woman. She had short blond hair, but after dipping her head back into the water it turned reddish brown. She lifted a leg and ran a razor along the back of her calf.

Meade leaned out of sight. The woman had to be Stacey, who Chakra Ramsanjawi discovered had once been O'Donnell's girlfriend but now lived with Weinstein. Maybe, he thought, he wouldn't need to read a file.

Meade pulled a nylon ski mask over his head. By the time he had all the holes lined up correctly, he could hear the slapping sounds of Stacey leaving her bath. He peeked around the door. She stood with her back to him, one foot on the floor and the other raised on the side of the tub as she toweled herself dry. She was small, almost boyish, with muscular legs and a lean bum.

His shoes made no sound on the marble floor. He grabbed her from behind, wedging her jaw in the crook of his arm and pressing the gun to the top of her head. Her scream died in her throat. She kicked back at him, but her heels bounced harmlessly off his shins.

He dragged her to the mirror. Condensation rolled

down the glass, but she could see well enough to make out the ski mask and the gun. Her body went rigid with fear.

"Now, little lady," whispered Meade. "All I want is to ask you a few questions about Hugh O'Donnell."

Stacey mumbled into his elbow.

"We're interested in the chap, you see. But we can't find out much about him."

Meade loosened his grip on her jaw so she could speak.

"Don't know him," her voice sputtered.

Meade raised her off the floor and leaned hard against her buttocks so that the sharp edge of the vanity's counter cut across her crotch.

"I don't have time for games, Stacey." He felt her body shudder at the sound of her name. "We know about O'Donnell's business, we know about the lawsuit, we know you threw him over for his lawyer."

"Don't know him," she gasped.

Meade slammed her against the vanity and traced the gun barrel along her quivering lips.

"Don't know him, eh? Well, he knows you. Talks about you all the time. He knows you went looking for him at the motorcycle club. Are we talking about the same person you don't know?"

With great effort she nodded, her delicate chin burrowing into the crook of his elbow.

"You talk and I leave. Understand?"

She nodded again; Meade relaxed his pressure a notch.

"His name isn't O'Donnell," she said with a trembling voice. "At least it wasn't when we were together. His name was Jack O'Neill. Owned his own biotech business. Had big ideas about turning it into a million-dollar company. Some environmental group took him to court and he hired Pancho to get him out of trouble. But they didn't get along. Pancho'd try to give him advice, but he'd never listen. Screwed the whole case up. He couldn't take things going bad. He used to dabble with drugs. Nothing much, maybe a gram of coke here and there. But that trial set him off. Did everything. Coke. Speed. Name it. Couldn't work. Borrowed money. Lost friends. Lost me. Disappeared."

"When?"

"Late ninety-five. Can't remember. Owed me a lot of money. Pancho too. For the case. I didn't care. Pancho did. Hired a detective. Found him at Simi Bioengineering. New name, but it was him.

"Pancho traced back. Jack was arrested on a drug charge under his old name, but the case was never prosecuted. Popped up at a rehab clinic in Encino as Hugh O'Donnell. Somebody was footing the bill. We never found out who. Then he landed the job at Simi. Started a motorcycle club for ex-addicts and ex-alcoholics. Yeah, I went looking for the motorcycle at the club. Title's in my name."

Meade noticed tears dripping down his elbow. Stacey was crying.

"That it?" he said.

"I don't know what else you want!"

Meade had ideas, but he didn't have time. He bent Stacey over with his elbow digging into her spine and her tiny breasts mashed against the countertop. His free hand groped through the equipment in his belt pouch until he found the syringe. It contained enough tranquilizer to knock out a hippopotamus.

Stacey saw the syringe in the mirror.

"What's that?" she cried.

"Just something to make you sleep."

"I don't want that! I don't know you! I didn't see you!"

She bucked against his elbow, wrapped her legs around his ankles, tried to kick his feet out from under him. He concentrated on her trembling buttocks. They were still reddened from the heat of the bath, so perfectly shaped, so firm, like two ripe apples. Her face was white with fear. Her hair swept back in reddish-brown swirls. A thin blue vein, just like Sir Derek's, beat beneath the china skin of her temples.

Meade jammed the needle into her ass.

Stacey yelped. Despite the pressure of the elbow on her spine, one hand shot up to her mouth. She bit her finger.

Meade stared at her face. It was so contorted in pain that it no longer looked feminine. He thought of Sir Derek with the same porcelain skin, the same reddish-brown hair, the same blue veins.

A hot rush of hatred surged through him. He tore open his pants and had it off with her. The syringe, still embedded in her right buttock, slapped at his waist as he pounded away at her slackening body.

29 AUGUST 1998
AEROSPACE PLANE *YEAGER*

"Cindy, Dan."

"I can't hear you."

"It's Dan!"

"You don't have to shout."

"Is Bill there?"

"No."

"This is very important, Cindy. I'm not calling to shoot the breeze."

"He's not home."

"Has he left for the space plane?"

"That'll be the day."

"Cindy, we have a slight problem up here. I don't think this is a very opportune time for Bill to visit the station. I've had his passes revoked."

"Trying to get back in my good graces, huh?"

"That isn't it at all. Is Bill there?"

"I told you he's not. What's your problem? Some young girl scientist think you're a big spaceman?"

"You wouldn't understand."

"I understand that as well as anyone."

"Tell him I'm sorry and that I'll make it up to him."

"Famous last words."

SHAPED VAGUELY LIKE a shark with wings instead of flippers, its eight hypersonic scramjet engines drinking up liquid hydrogen fuel, the aerospace plane *Yeager* accelerated past an altitude of 150,000 feet over the Great Plains. Nine minutes earlier it had taxied down the runway at Edwards Space Center in the high desert of California and vaulted into the crystalline blue of the early morning sky. Its itinerary: Trikon Station and Space Station Freedom.

Much to his relief, Aaron Weiss felt none of the crushing g-forces he had expected. The aerospace plane had taken off as smoothly as a commercial airliner. Which, in Weiss's catalogue of evils, was bad enough. No lover of high-speed travel, Weiss believed that roller coasters should be outlawed as dangerous instrumentalities. But he had traveled in bullet trains in both France and Japan, and was pleased to discover that the aerospace plane was no less comfortable. For a moment, he even forgot about the airsick bag dangling from his fist.

The seats were arranged four across, with an aisle in the middle. Weiss had demanded an aisle seat; he had no desire to see the world falling away from him. The window seat was empty. More than half the seats were empty. Nutty way to run an airline, Weiss thought, flying this expensive contraption without a full load of paying passengers.

Across the aisle sat Fabio Bianco. Weiss had heard that the elderly CEO of Trikon International looked like a monk; he saw that the description was not exaggerated. The frail old man seemed too small, almost childlike, nestled in his chair, his wispy tonsure splayed like a halo on the maroon velour of the headrest, his liquid brown eyes staring serenely forward, his lips quivering as if in silent prayer.

"Hell of a ride," said Weiss, realizing as he spoke that the cabin was much quieter than any plane he had ridden aboard.

Bianco smiled pleasantly and nodded.

"My first time on one of these babies." Weiss held aloft his airsick bag. "I thought it would be worse."

"The ride is very smooth," agreed Bianco, with just

a hint of Italian vowels at the end of his English words.

"Where are you headed?"

"Trikon Station."

"So am I. My name is Aaron Weiss." He stretched his hand across the aisle.

"I am Fabio Bianco."

"Bianco?" Weiss put on his most innocent expression. "Isn't the head of Trikon named Bianco?"

"That is correct. I am that person. It is a pleasure to make your acquaintance, Mr. Weiss of the whales."

"Recognized me, huh?" Weiss lifted a lock of gray hair from behind his ear. "Even without the hat?"

"I have been following your reports with great interest. I have been wondering how accurate they are."

"Accurate enough."

"Those deaths have brought me great sadness."

"Those deaths are pretty damned scary," said Weiss.

"What brings you to Trikon Station, Mr. Weiss? There are no whales on board, at least not to my knowledge."

"A hunch or two," Weiss said. "What about you? CEOs aren't noted for mingling with the peons."

"I have my reasons, Mr. Weiss. Now if you will excuse me, I need to rest. It has been an exhausting week for me. We can speak further on Trikon Station."

You bet we will, Fabio baby, Weiss muttered to himself.

Dan Tighe eyed Aaron Weiss suspiciously. The reporter wore white crew socks, baby chinos, and a denim workshirt with pearl buttons. His Donegal walking hat was attached to his head by a jerry-rigged system of rubber bands. A Minicam hovered at chest level, loosely tethered to Weiss's skinny neck by a loop of thinly braided cord. Dan didn't like the idea of a reporter nosing around the station. Especially the muckraking TV-tabloid kind. He didn't buy Weiss's protestations that he was now a legitimate reporter covering stories related to science and technology for CNN in Atlanta. To Dan, Aaron Weiss always was and always would be a parasite. But the parasite was on board with Trikon's permission, so Dan had to be cooperative, if not cordial.

Dan hovered in the doorway to his office. Dangling several inches above the deck of the command module just outside Tighe's office, Weiss gripped a handhold firmly, but didn't show any adverse effects of weightlessness. He had an airsick bag wedged under his belt. Kurt Jaeckle hovered next to Weiss. He had appeared the instant he learned that a reporter had arrived on the aerospace plane.

"The station comprises three distinct sets of personnel," Dan was explaining, his face taut with tension. "There is the station crew, the Martians, and the Trikon scientists. This last set is divided into three further subsets: the American/Canadian group, the United Europe group, and the Japanese group."

"I know all this," Weiss said.

"You are free to visit any of the lab modules," said Dan, putting more iron into his voice to discourage further interruptions. "But you cannot go beyond what the individual module's personnel will allow. In other words, you must honor their desires for security."

"You are welcome in the Mars module," piped Jaeckle.

"Furthermore," continued Dan, "certain modules will be strictly off limits to you unless you are accompanied by myself or a member of the crew. These include the command module and the logistics module."

Weiss nodded, although the expression on his

puffed-up face showed he was anything but happy
with Tighe's restrictions.

"Finally," Dan added, "Dr. Renoir is at your
disposal for any and all medical needs."

"She's already fitted me with a motion-sickness
pad," said Weiss.

"Fine," Dan snapped. He glanced at Jaeckle, then
returned his stern gaze to Weiss. "That's all I have to
say. I trust you will do your best not to interfere with
the smooth operation of the station."

Weiss mumbled something that did not sound like
wholehearted agreement, but Dan let it go.

"Do you want to start with the Mars module?"
asked Jaeckle, beaming the smile he reserved for
members of the media.

"Not really," said Weiss.

Hugh O'Donnell held the tiny strip of computer
printout to one of the lights in his lab. The blood
analysis unit Dan Tighe had pilfered from Dr.
Renoir's medical bay was programmed to screen
thirty distinct drugs, from common natural substances like marijuana to obscure synthetics like 3,4-
methylenedioxamphetamine. He had obtained one
positive result.

O'Donnell folded the printout into a pocket and
squeezed out the door. None of the lab workers
scattered throughout The Bakery paid him any mind
as he secured his padlock. Except for Stu Roberts. He
stared at O'Donnell with a cold, calculating eye as he
hovered at an oblique angle between the microwave
ovens fifteen meters away.

Dan Tighe was behind the closed door of his office.
O'Donnell could hear him talking to someone over
the radio. The topic of conversation was a TV news
reporter who had apparently arrived at Trikon Station
on the aerospace plane. Dan did not sound pleased
with his presence.

O'Donnell waited until there was a lull in the chatter before rapping on the partition. The door slid open half a foot to reveal Tighe, his broad face pinched by a set of headphones.

"Be right with you. Let me wind up this report."

The door closed and, after another minute of highly technical chatter, opened again. Dan no longer wore the headphones, although there was a white line where they had pressed against his roughened cheek.

"I have the blood work," said O'Donnell, keeping his voice low.

Dan released himself from the foot loops and drifted toward the rear of the office, giving O'Donnell enough room to squeeze inside the narrow compartment.

"Better close the door," he said.

O'Donnell obliged, then worked the printout from his pocket. Dan looked haggard. He had missed a spot shaving and his mouth was drawn down in an expression that in a lesser man would be worry, perhaps even fear.

"So what have we got?" he asked.

O'Donnell could tell from Tighe's tone that he was tightly wound.

"The panel allows tests for thirty different types of drugs, some common, some not so common."

"Get to the point," said Dan. "Was Cramer dirty?"

"His blood tested positive for PCP."

"I know that's bad," said Dan. "Now what the hell is it exactly?"

"Its chemical name is phencyclidine, but it's better known as Angel Dust. It's a hallucinogen that was developed in the fifties for use as an anesthetic. But it never was used because it caused bad dreams and aggressive behavior among the test subjects. It can turn a mouse into a maniac."

"How do you know so much?"

"I wasn't your normal doper," said O'Donnell. "I

would research a drug before I used it."

"Did you ever do this stuff?"

"Once. I didn't like it."

Dan took the slip of paper from O'Donnell's hand and peered at it like a suspicious man checking his supermarket bill. "Any chance of this being wrong?" he asked.

"There's roughly a ten-percent error factor. From the amount in the blood sample, I doubt it was a false positive."

Dan's eyes narrowed until they resembled two sabers glinting in sunlight.

"Could he have been using this over an extended period of time?"

"No way I can tell from the blood," said O'Donnell. "In low doses it could have a mild stimulant effect that might interfere with sleep. And the drug can build up in the fatty tissues of the brain and be released over time. But if you want to know the truth, one good dose can turn you into a psycho."

Dan stuffed the results into his pocket.

"Dr. Renoir hasn't missed her equipment yet. You'll get it back?"

"Soon as I can."

"Good."

"Can I ask you a question, Dan?"

"What?"

"Why didn't you have Dr. Renoir do this workup? After all, she's the station's medical officer."

For the flash of an instant Tighe looked angry, furious. But with an effort he controlled himself.

"I needed somebody with no political ties to anybody else on the station," he answered tightly. "Lorraine . . . Dr. Renoir . . . she'd been treating Cramer for sleep disorder without telling anybody but his supervisor."

"Without telling you?"

Tighe held himself to a single curt nod. "She was

following station regulations."

"Cramer's supervisor," O'Donnell mused. "That would be . . ."

"Kurt Jaeckle," Tighe snapped.

O'Donnell's lips formed a silent "Oh." He made a small shrug and turned toward the door.

"One more thing," said Dan, his voice still edgy. "There's a reporter on board. I don't want any of this getting out, understood?"

"Understood," said O'Donnell. "Who's the reporter?"

"Guy named Aaron Weiss from CNN. Looks like a pain in the ass. Trikon's given him limited access to the station. Damned if I know why."

"What's he reporting on?"

"Don't know for sure. Trikon, I guess. He surer than hell isn't interested in the Martians. He was pretty clear with Jaeckle about that."

"Am I required to talk to him?"

"Don't ask me. I'm not your superior. That's right. The grapevine says you have no boss up here."

"The grapevine says a lot," said O'Donnell. "I just won't talk to him."

"Suit yourself," said Dan. "Are you going to be all right?"

"What do you mean?"

"We just discovered that someone is cooking or smuggling drugs up here," said Dan. "I think the question is validly put to someone with your history."

"I'll be all right," said O'Donnell.

His hazel eyes, magnified by his glasses, stared into Tighe's intense sky-blue slits. Neither man wavered.

"That's good," said Dan.

O'Donnell opened the door and pulled himself into the comparatively cool air of the command module.

"And, Hugh," Dan called to him. "Thanks."

* * *

For all his work and dreams about Trikon Station, Fabio Bianco had never been to space before, never experienced microgravity.

As a scientist he understood the facts of near weightlessness. As a frail old man he hoped that he would adapt to microgravity quickly, without embarrassing himself by becoming obviously sick.

He never expected to enjoy the sensation.

Yet from the moment the aerospace plane coasted into orbit Bianco felt a strange exhilaration surging through his aged body. By the time the plane had docked with Trikon and he and his fellow passengers had disembarked into the station itself, Bianco was grinning broadly. For the first time in years, in decades, he felt truly alive. Strong, almost. Twenty years younger. Thirty, even.

The young men and women of the station's crew treated him with extreme deference. Bianco accepted their solicitude as his due as CEO of Trikon International, rather than because of his frail old age.

I'm not frail here, he marveled to himself as he floated effortlessly down the tunnel to Hab 1, following a ruddy-faced young crewman to the quarters he had been assigned. I'm strong again. Young again! I may never leave this place.

Within an hour of settling his meager luggage in his sleep compartment—and actually laughing when his clothes took on a weightless life of their own and floated almost out of his reach before he could corral them—Bianco used the intercom to call a meeting of all the Trikon personnel aboard the station.

The scientists and technicians gathered in the rumpus room at Bianco's command. He did not need to ask permission, nor did he need to ask where to hold the meeting. Bianco knew the station's layout in his heart, better perhaps than many of the scientists who had spent ninety days aboard. Bianco had spent years "seeing" Trikon Station in all its details.

Although the expended shuttle external tank that formed the rumpus room was the same size as the Mars module, its lack of scientific equipment made it the single most spacious area on the station, and the natural site for the meeting. Of course, there was no dais, and there were no chairs. Dan secured his three bonsai animals so they would not make a distracting backdrop for Bianco as he spoke. Lance Muncie and Freddy Aviles installed a portable floor grid on which the Trikon scientists and technicians could anchor their feet during the meeting.

Every member of the Trikon scientific community gathered in the rumpus room. Aaron Weiss joined the group, but rather than anchor himself to the floor grid he drifted above the assembly and slightly to one side so that he could see their faces without distracting them too much. His Minicam was loosely attached to his neck and he gripped a magnetized notepad in one hand.

Bianco looked small, almost shrunken in the light-blue Trikon flight suit he wore for the occasion. The open collar exposed the wrinkles and veins of his neck. The clinging pants revealed the sharp points of his knee and hip bones. Yet somehow he looked vital, eager. His eyes sparkled. He smiled gently at his employees.

"When I was a young man," he began, "I would sit in my family's garden at night and watch the stars track slowly across the sky. I dreamed of another star, not a glowing ball of hydrogen and helium hundreds of light years away, but a glittering diamond of aluminum and titanium that could circle our planet in a mere ninety minutes. And in that glittering diamond the finest minds from every nation would gather and direct their energies toward developing a second generation of science and technology that would solve

the problems created by our well-meaning but ignorant forebears."

Bianco hesitated a moment. The scientists and
technicians, anchored by their floor restraints, swayed
slightly like a field of brightly colored anemones
rocking back and forth in the tide.

"There are many in the world who blame all our ills
on science and technology. They say that we have too
much technology, that we must give up our sophisticated machines and return to a simpler way of life.
Otherwise the world will be polluted to death."

The light in Bianco's eyes changed. His voice became stronger, more urgent.

"But how can the human race go back to a simpler
life without allowing billions to die? Can we privi-
leged rich permit the world's poor to starve, to die of
disease? No. The answer, my friends, is not less
technology, but more. We need an entirely new type of
technology, second-generation technology, new and
clean and based on the scientific breakthroughs that
you are striving to create. Second-generation technology can feed the hungry without polluting the air and
the seas. Second-generation technology can give us all
the energy we need without destroying the global
environment."

Bianco studied their faces as he spoke. Only a few
seemed to be accepting his words. Most of them
looked impassive, indifferent.

"The most important task for our new scientific
capabilities is to learn how to clean up the filth that
the first-generation technologies have generated. That
is why we are here. That is our high purpose. To
cleanse the Earth of the toxic waste that is choking the
air and strangling the oceans of our planet. That is
why I created Trikon Station: to give you a place
where you can save the world.

"I am a lucky man. It is not everyone who can

board an aerospace plane and ascend to his dreams."

Eye pressed to his Minicam, Aaron Weiss scrutinized every face as Bianco spoke of his vision of Trikon. He saw blank-faced Japanese, dour Europeans, impassive Canadians, confident, almost arrogant Americans. He matched the faces with names he had memorized. The Japanese with the thick neck and rolls of fat visible up the back of his crew-cut head was Hisashi Oyamo. The Indian with the greasy hair and billowing yellow *kurta* was Chakra Ramsanjawi. The woman with the salt-and-pepper buzzcut and cast-iron features was Thora Skillen.

Most of the names meant nothing to Weiss. But he felt a vague tug in his memory when he thought of Ramsanjawi. There was something unseemly in the Indian's past, but Weiss wasn't exactly sure what it was.

"It is not my intention to sound a Biblical note," continued Bianco, "but there is a plague upon the land. We may not have as much time as we thought. Whales have been dying in the seas while we bicker among ourselves for the glory of ridding our world of toxic wastes. But this is not a problem that recognizes national borders. It does not even recognize different continents. It is truly a world problem."

Goddammit, I was right, thought Weiss. There *is* a connection with the whales. And that old bastard played it so cool on the space plane, asking me if the reports were accurate. He knew damn well they were accurate all along.

Weiss stifled his self-congratulation long enough to train his Minicam on each of the faces in the audience. Now they began to look troubled as Bianco elaborated on the whale deaths. There was a connection. Definitely. And Trikon had known about it for a long time. The level of toxic wastes in the oceans had become so high that it was killing the phytoplankton.

The whales were dying of starvation, just as Weiss had thought. Soon the atmosphere's supply of oxygen would start to dwindle.

"I must make it entirely clear to you," Bianco was saying, his voice now edged with sharp steel. "We are not talking in abstractions anymore. As the phytoplankton die, the human race will die. We are not talking about a problem that will manifest itself in a century or two. We have perhaps two decades, perhaps much less. We must find the way of destroying the toxic wastes in the oceans or they will destroy us. There is no third alternative."

They were all leaning toward Bianco now, their faces etched with worry, their heads nodding agreement and resolve. But as Weiss panned the crowd, he found two scientists who seemed totally unconcerned about the implications of the whale deaths, at least to judge by the expressions on their faces. One was Chakra Ramsanjawi. The other he did not know: Hugh O'Donnell.

Bianco continued, "The public perceives us as a gaggle of overgrown children joyriding across the sky in our expensive toy. Or worse, it sees us as fattened Neroes fiddling while Rome burns.

"I wish that our only problem was the public's perception. In that case, our public relations firms could help us. But, ladies and gentlemen, I need not remind you that our problem is not one of perception. Nature is not swayed by hidden persuaders. We are running out of time.

"For these reasons, and with the advice and consent of the Boards of Directors of each of Trikon's arms, I am assuming full authority to direct and coordinate our research efforts aboard Trikon Station. Each of the three coordinators will report directly to me from now on."

A murmur rose among the crowd. Weiss trained his

Minicam first on Chakra Ramsanjawi, then on Hugh O'Donnell. Neither reacted in any visible way to the surprise announcement.

Bianco adjourned the meeting. The audience drifted away, dispersing into knots of twos and threes, talking among themselves. Some seemed agitated, others almost stunned.

"Mr. Bianco, Mr. Bianco," called Weiss as he swam toward the end of the rumpus room. There were no other reporters for him to jockey with. Trikon Station was a reporter's heaven.

"I am consenting to speak to you on condition that my remarks are off the record," Bianco said to Weiss. It was evening and they were in the dimly lit wardroom. Through the portal of the ex/rec room came the jeers of two crewmen competing at darts.

"What's the point of talking if I can't use what you say?" said Weiss.

"Do you know the meaning of *lento*?" asked Bianco.

"It's a soup, right?"

Bianco slowly reared back his head and stared down the humped ridge of his Roman nose. Weiss felt the old man's brown eyes penetrate to the base of his brain. He wiped the grin from his face.

"It means to take things slowly," said Bianco. "In other words, I want you to have a comprehensive view of our work here before you file your report."

"Agreed," Weiss said easily. "Now how do these whale deaths connect with your work here?"

Bianco clasped his gnarled hands together and placed them on the table. Realizing that keeping them there required too much effort, he let them float before him like an inverted cradle.

"The main thrust of our project is to develop microbes genetically engineered to neutralize toxic wastes in our environment. The concept is called bioremediation."

"I've heard of that. Scientists have been doing that for more than ten years, haven't they?" Weiss asked.

"On a small scale, yes," said Bianco. "Bacteria have been used to devour chlorine compounds that were polluting aquifers. But in those efforts, the scientists used the bacteria that already existed in the ground."

"And Trikon's trying to develop new kinds of bugs through genetic engineering, right?"

Bianco nodded slowly. "Ten years ago, your American EPA published a study that identified one hundred twenty-eight different toxic chemicals and compounds that were present in dangerous levels in the world's oceans, lakes, and rivers. Ten years ago, Mr. Weiss. The situation has become much worse."

Weiss started to speak, but Bianco silenced him with a sharp glance.

"Now I know what you are thinking," said Bianco. "You are thinking that if there are one hundred twenty-eight chemicals, all we need do is pour the same number of microbes into the water and let them devour the chemicals to their hearts' content."

Weiss smiled wanly as if to say, Yes, that is exactly what I was thinking.

"The answer is not that simple," said Bianco. "These toxic chemicals are not floating around in the water in discrete little bundles. Some ride the surface, others are buried in sludge, others blend into insidious solutions."

"Are you getting to the whales?" said Weiss.

"Of course I am getting to the whales!" boomed Bianco.

Weiss flinched, completely surprised at the sudden power of Bianco's voice. Even the dart players peered silently out of the ex/rec room.

"We have been working to develop one or two,

maybe three, genetically engineered microbes with the capability of neutralizing all the major toxic wastes in the Earth's waters. To give you an idea of the enormous complexity of the task, the most complicated microbe we have been able to develop neutralizes only seven.

"We knew we were working against the clock, but until the whale deaths occurred and were investigated, we did not realize how little time actually remains."

"Do you really mean what you said at the meeting this afternoon?" Weiss asked. "We've only got ten years?"

"Perhaps less," said Bianco. "The level of toxins in the ocean waters is killing off the plankton on which these whales subsist."

"If that's the case," said Weiss, "why are so many marine biologists, big guns like Ted Adamski, saying that the cause of the whale deaths is a virus?"

"We have only recently satisfied ourselves that the deaths are from starvation and that the plankton supply has dipped below a level at which the normal whale population can sustain itself. We knew it would happen. But we did not anticipate it happening so quickly."

"But Adamski still says otherwise," said Weiss.

"Adamski privately believes the cause of death is starvation," said Bianco. "He is maintaining his original public stance at our request."

"Why?"

"To prevent wholesale panic," said Bianco.

"Professor Bianco, I love the whales. I donate to Greenpeace every chance I get. Why the hell would the death of a few whales cause a panic?"

"You talked to Professor Karlis," said Bianco.

"Karlis is a maverick," said Weiss, too disturbed by the drift of the conversation to appreciate the irony of turning against one of his sources.

"But in this regard, he is entirely correct."

Weiss tried to drum his fingers on the tabletop. They barely brushed the surface.

"Jesus H. Christ, you mean everything I've been saying is *true*?"

"Worse than that, Mr. Weiss. Phytoplankton not only manufacture oxygen. They also absorb carbon dioxide. For years, optimists in the great debate over global warming effects have looked to the plankton as our savior. The oceans might warm, yes, but then plankton would flourish and absorb more carbon dioxide, thereby preventing further warming. If the plankton die, the great leveling factor will be gone."

"What does this mean to the man on the street?" asked Weiss.

"To the man on the street, I would say that without plankton Planet Earth is well on its way to becoming another Planet Venus. The man on the street will choke to death. All the men, women, and children of Earth will die."

The Japanese tech watched impassively as Freddy Aviles traced a network of cables from Jasmine's main computer terminal to the relay box in the center of the module's ceiling. Freddy popped the cover with a screwdriver and inspected the innards of the box with a penlight.

"So then what happened?"

Lance Muncie, drifting beneath Freddy's abbreviated rump with a toolbox in one hand and pages of computer-generated diagrams springing out of the other, glanced back at the tech.

"Does he have to stare like that?" Lance whispered.

"Jus' doin' his job, man," said Freddy. "Like you an' me. Oyamo told Commander Tighe that we couldn't work in here alone."

"Nobody trusts anybody here."

"Nobody trusts anybody on Earth. Why should they be different here?" said Freddy. "So then what happened?"

Lance had hoped that the conversation would hop its tracks, but no such luck with Freddy. The man really *was* a computer whiz. He could talk, joke, sing, probably even dance if he had legs while working the reconfiguration project. He certainly didn't need any help other than someone to prevent the specs from snaking away. And he certainly would not forget the topic of this conversation.

"We went to the observation blister," said Lance. He waved away Freddy's long, suggestive whistle. "It wasn't what you think. We watched India pass beneath us and we talked about exercises and what the Mars Project was like."

"Yeah."

"We did, Freddy, and I told her about being part of the crew."

"You din' make a move on her?"

"Freddy."

"You were alone in the observation blister with Carla Sue Gamble, the way she was diggin' on you in the wardroom, and you din' make a move on her?"

"I'm not like that, Freddy. I'm saving—"

Freddy turned away from the relay box. Lance's cheeks were red; the muscles around his lips twitched. This time, Freddy's whistle did not drip with innuendo. It was full of sudden understanding.

"Oh my God," he said. "Oh my God, I shoulda figured it out long ago. You a virgin."

"Freddy, shh." Lance tilted his head toward the Japanese tech.

"He don' understand what we sayin', Lance. I can't believe this. I mean, I can believe it because I know you, but I can't believe it."

"Believe it."

"Well, well, well," said Freddy. "This puts a

differen' light on the subject."

"I wanted to, Freddy. I was really really tempted. She had her hands on me. She wanted to put her mouth on me."

"Not bad," Freddy said in a stage whisper. "Then what?"

"I left."

Freddy winced in embarrassment for his friend. "You get her pissed, no?"

"I guess so. I haven't had the courage to look for her."

"What you gonna do when you find her? Apologize?"

"Maybe," said Lance. "Maybe explain to her what I think about these things."

"And what do you think?"

Lance stuttered.

"You know, you full of shit, Lance. You talk about how you not like your folks. How you are space age and they are Stone Age. But here you are on a space station with a nice young lady hot for your bod, and you ain't taking advantage."

"Premarital sex is wrong no matter what the age," said Lance.

"Tha's a crock of shit," said Freddy, "You ever read Thomas More? He said people should see each other naked before they got married. An' he's a saint!"

"He was a Catholic, Freddy."

"Don' hold that against him."

"It's still no argument to say that everyone does it. I have myself to think about. Becky, too."

"Yeah," said Freddy. "And while you up here livin' like a monk, how do you know what she doin' down there?"

Lance's normally dark eyes flashed. His short hair bristled. His jaw clenched, making him resemble an avenging angel rather than a cute cherub.

"You take that back right now, Freddy!" Lance

released the toolbox and specs and pounded the fist of one hand into the palm of the other.

"Hello, gentlemen."

Aaron Weiss tumbled awkwardly through the entry hatch. The sound of his Minicam clanking against the floor echoed throughout the module. The Japanese tech hurried forward to intercept him. Weiss righted himself and inspected the camera for damage. The Japanese chattered shrilly and waved him away with the back of his hand.

"What? What?" said Weiss in response to the angry gestures. "I don't understand you."

"'Scuse me." Freddy left his screwdriver and penlight with Lance and dove toward the reporter and the tech. The tech was growling now, like a swordsman in a samurai movie, and obviously gesturing for Weiss to leave. The reporter, feigning ignorance, was explaining that he just wanted a few pictures of the equipment.

"Do you understand what this man wants?" Weiss asked Freddy. "He's not speaking English."

"He wants you gone, man. How's that for English?"

"Not very eloquent," Weiss said, noticing the thick muscles beneath Freddy's royal-blue flight suit. "But clear enough."

Freddy nodded to the tech as if to say everything was under control. Then he escorted Weiss to the entry hatch.

"Hey, I know you," said Weiss. "You're Freddy Aviles. I was supposed to cover your launch. But then a bunch of whales died."

"Out of here," said Freddy, slapping the rim of the hatch for emphasis. "Now."

With a sigh of resignation, Weiss eased himself through the hatch. Freddy watched him moving unsteadily down the connecting tunnel. Weiss stopped at The Bakery and looked at the hatch as if considering whether to enter.

"Not there either!" shouted Freddy.

"Sorry," said Weiss, a guilty grin on his face. "Thought it was my hab module. This is a very confusing place."

Freddy eyeballed Weiss until the reporter entered Hab 1. Then he returned to Lance and the relay box. Lance was still fuming.

"Sorry about what I said about Becky," said Freddy. "She prob'ly isn't doing anything like that."

"Definitely isn't," said Lance.

"But even so, you could still go back Earthside an' find her with another guy. Then what you gonna do, kick yourself in the ass for all the opportunities you let slide?"

Some of the hostility left Lance's face. He bit his lip as he considered Freddy's new tack. Stripped of the sexual issue, it made sense. Why did Becky sound so distant over the telephone? What type of person would he find when he returned?

"Take it from me, man. Don' let opportunities slide by. Look at me. I can' even kick myself in the ass anymore."

30 AUGUST 1998
TRIKON STATION

O'Donnell squirms inside his sleep restraint. The dream again. The same old dream. He is in his car. He is always in his car, and his name isn't O'Donnell yet. It is Jack O'Neill. The car is parked in the middle of a teeming barrio. Police and drug agents are swarming everywhere, riot guns in their hands, red and blue flashers strobe-lighting the decaying buildings and littered streets. People are running, shouting, scattering like roaches scuttling away from the light.

Two policemen, one black, the other Hispanic, both with mirrored sunglasses and thin mustaches like used-car salesmen, lean on opposite windows of his car.

"You can go," says the Hispanic, though his elbows and the elbows of his partner, each the size of a large ham hock, remain planted.

He needs two hands to turn the ignition key. As soon as the engine kicks over, the two policemen laugh.

"He isn't wearing his seat belt," says the Hispanic.

"He hasn't signaled to enter traffic," says the black.

The car disappears; the street fades, then re-forms as a police station. His chin clings to a desk while his feet float free. The desk sergeant's pen scratches, filling in answers to unasked questions. Two plastic bags swollen with white powder land beside his ears with a whump.

His chin slides off the desk. He spirals down in a long dizzying fall that ends in a chair. Across a table sits a man with a badge clipped to one lapel of his tight-fitting jacket and a name tag clipped to the other. The name tag says R. McQ. Welch. He has a pug nose and a bulldog's chin.

"When I was a kid," says Welch, "they had a saying, 'You fall in horseshit, you come up with a diamond.' I never believed it until just now."

No trace of a smile eases Welch's grim expression.

FOR THE FIRST time since he had arrived at Trikon Station, Hugh O'Donnell did not find The Bakery empty when he arrived shortly after artificial dawn had brightened the modules of the station. Microwave ovens buzzed, centrifuges whirled, techs floated from workstation to workstation like workers in a beehive. The entire American/Canadian contingent was present. Even Stu Roberts was awake, though he looked like he needed another couple hours of sleep.

O'Donnell grinned to himself as he floated past them all. Must be Bianco, he thought as he unfastened the padlock to his lab. From the first day of kindergarten through the last day before retirement, people constantly tried to fool the teacher, the boss, the authority figure. No one said a word to him, not even Roberts. It was if he did not exist, which suited him fine.

Once inside his own cubbyhole lab with the door pulled shut, O'Donnell pushed himself to the ceiling to inspect the dozen plants growing in the thin, saucer-shaped cases designed for micro-gee hydroponics.

"Goddammit." He sighed bitterly. As he had suspected when he closed up the lab the previous night, all of the plants showed definite signs of regeneration. He was back to square one.

O'Donnell booted up his computer and scrolled through the genetic structures of the microbes he had applied to each of the twelve plants. The three-dimensional diagrams on the screen were relatively simple, not at all as complicated as human genes, not even as complicated as the genes he had altered when designing microbes for AgriTech, Inc. But his previous work had been dedicated to promoting the growth of plants. This project was bent on rendering them impotent.

For well over an hour, O'Donnell stared zombielike at the screen as he used the cursor to rearrange molecules of RNA. There's got to be some sequence that will completely inhibit the chemical process, he thought as his fingers tapped the keyboard.

Aaron Weiss told himself that the real advantage to spending the morning with Fabio Bianco was that it kept Kurt Jaeckle off his neck. The leader of the Martians had cornered Weiss at breakfast in the wardroom and droned on about the importance of his team, his work, his dreams, his goals—himself—until Bianco had shown up and rescued the reporter.

But now Weiss was gasping as he struggled to keep pace with Fabio Bianco. The old scientist was supposed to be a walking catalogue of every geriatric malady known to Western man. Yet he seemed spry as a young chicken and agile as a cat as he led Weiss down the length of the connecting tunnel.

"Must be the weightlessness," Weiss muttered between gulps of air that never quite seemed to satisfy the aching in his lungs.

Bianco was in the middle of a lecture he had begun at breakfast.

"You ask why we need a space station for this research," he said as his spindly arms moved surely from handhold to handhold. "The truth is that ninety percent of the research conducted on this station for this particular project can be performed on Earth at far less expense."

"But not with as much fun," said Weiss.

Bianco brought himself to a sudden stop. Weiss crashed into him, then tumbled backwards. His Minicam tugged at the cord around his neck. He managed to snag a handhold.

"Fun? We are not here for fun, Mr. Weiss. What we do here is serious, perhaps the most serious work being done anywhere, by anyone. What we are doing up here is creating new life-forms that will be completely subservient to man. There are people on Earth who do not want this work to be done."

"Fundamentalists, creationists. I know the scene," Weiss said as he adjusted his hat.

"Those, of course. But also people with sophisticated academic backgrounds. They think we are creating monsters that will be set loose upon the land. They agree that our environment is in a sorry state, but they see science and technology as the culprits. To a certain extent they may be correct. However, they do not understand that the world has crossed the Rubicon. The die is cast. The answer to our problems is not to turn away from science. The answer lies in more science, but an intelligent, refined science."

Bianco gave himself a gentle shove in the direction of Jasmine. Weiss followed.

"Eventually, we will begin projects that will benefit from micro-gee," said Bianco. "But for now, the great advantage of this station is that it is not on Earth. No government controls us. We allay the fears of the ignorant by being in space, out of their sight. And it avoids their court battles."

The Japanese were very polite and not nearly as secretive as Weiss had expected from the previous night's abortive visit. Hisashi Oyamo forbade Weiss to film anything with his Minicam, but ordered a tech to take the reporter on a tour of the module. Weiss was free to ask any question that came to mind. His problem was that he didn't know enough about genetic engineering to formulate an intelligent question. The main activity seemed to be the spinning, shaking, cooking, and freezing of thousands of vials of colored liquids. In English that was clipped and formal, the tech explained that the liquids contained different types of genetically engineered microbes.

"Are they color-coded?" asked Weiss.

"Ah yes," said the tech with a toothy smile.

The second stop was ELM. Despite his space-sickness pad, Weiss felt a wave of nausea as soon as he passed through the hatchway. He first suspected the hideous color combination of pastel salmons and blah grays rather than the clean whites and yellows of Jasmine. Then he realized an additional reason for his disorientation: the equipment was placed higher on these walls to accommodate people of taller stature. The desktops of the workstations were higher, as well.

Weiss was not offered a tour of ELM. As Bianco and Chakra Ramsanjawi slowly drifted along the module's aisle, Weiss was confined to a corner under the humorless eye of a male tech. Weiss tried to cajole him into a conversation, but received only guttural German in response.

"Right. And you don't know English," said Weiss.

The tech bared his teeth.

This lack of hospitality was at odds with the demeanor of Ramsanjawi, who seemed to engage Bianco in warm conversation. Even the distance could not conceal the look of satisfaction on Bianco's face. He was obviously impressed by the work of the Europeans as he had not been with the Japanese. Maybe it was continental pride, thought Weiss.

The last stop was The Bakery. Weiss had managed only a quick glance into the dimly lit module the

previous night before being shooed away by Freddy
Aviles. Under the bright fluorescents, the interior was
a blend of pastel yellows and blues. The scheme was
far less disorienting than ELM's sickening decor, and
Weiss wondered whether Americans shared a genetic
predilection for these colors.

Thora Skillen rushed forward to meet them as soon
as they cleared the hatch. Her handshake reminded
Weiss of a slab of dead mackerel and her manner was
as sharply abrupt as her features. She informed Weiss
that he had the run of the module, but he could not
film or touch anything. Then she quickly ushered
Bianco toward her office, as if bursting to fill his ear
with news. Or gossip.

Weiss parked himself in the center of the module. A
centrifuge whirred to a stop, its arms slowly coming
into focus and folding down as if exhausted. A tangle
of multicolored tendrils appeared on a computer
monitor, the three-dimensional image rotating as a
woman worked the keys. Weiss decided that, except
for the color schemes and the heights of the workstations, seeing one orbital lab module was seeing
them all. Whatever Thora Skillen had been so anxious
to tell Bianco was probably far more interesting than
watching adults play with colored water.

Weiss moved slowly toward Skillen's office, which,
as with the other two lab modules, was located in an
aft corner. Pretending to be intensely interested in the
colored vials hanging from the inert centrifuge's spindly arms, Weiss strained his ears toward Skillen's
closed office. Through the accordion door he could
barely make out snatches of conversation. He edged
past the centrifuge and peered intently into a humming microwave oven.

"His presence is very disrupting," said Skillen. Her
voice sounded like fingernails on sandpaper.

"I do not like his presence any more than you do,"
Bianco replied.

Weiss felt a chill crawl up his spine. Were they talking about him?

"Can't you do anything about him?" Skillen asked.

"There is nothing I can do. It was all arranged without my knowledge."

"But you're the CEO."

"I am not omnipotent. The arrangement was made with Trikon NA. It is legitimate. We may not like it, but we must live with it."

"You read my memo."

"I did," said Bianco. "That is how O'Donnell came to my attention."

"Then you understand how disruptive he has been."

"Dr. Skillen," said Bianco, "I appreciate your ardent commitment to the project, but I do not appreciate your attempts to brand O'Donnell a scapegoat. The fact remains that you have fallen behind the research pace set by the other groups. O'Donnell cannot be the sole reason."

Weiss relaxed when he realized that Skillen wasn't bitching about his presence. As he listened to her defend the honor of The Bakery, he matched the faces he could see with the names he had memorized from the list of Trikon personnel. Only one was absent: Hugh O'Donnell.

A high-pitched whistle suddenly burst out of the microwave oven. Startled, Weiss kicked himself flat against the aft bulkhead. He was certain that the oven would blow, but no one paid any mind to the shrieking sound. Finally, a lanky young man glided over from a nearby workstation. He had a pale face and a mess of red hair tenuously held to his skull by a net.

"Shit," he said as he peered through the glass front of the oven. He opened the door and pulled out a miniature carousel, which he sent spinning in midair a scant three feet from Weiss's face.

"Keep your eye on that," he called over his shoulder

to Weiss. Then he looked back into the oven. "Shit."

Weiss could see that one of the vials had exploded. The young man used a hand-held vacuum cleaner to suck up globules of colored liquid and shards of tempered glass from the interior of the oven.

"How did that happen?" he asked.

"Bum vial. They get a hairline fracture, sometimes even a speck of dirt and they blow."

"You must be Stu Roberts."

"Crazy, man," said Roberts. He caught the spinning carousel and carefully slid it back into the oven. "How'd you know?"

"I do my homework," said Weiss. "Why didn't anyone react to that alarm?"

"Shit happens all the time."

"But what about those microbes? You just vacuumed them up."

"What'd you expect me to do? Leave that crap floating around the oven?"

"But isn't it important?"

"Mister, we have more of that stuff than anyone knows what to do with."

"Aaron Weiss is the name. Couldn't those microbes be dangerous?"

"They could, but they probably aren't. No one's died yet, anyway."

"Comforting thought," said Weiss. "Say, would you mind answering some questions?"

"You mean like an interview?" said Roberts. "Sure. I mean, no, I don't mind."

"Why is everyone so security conscious?" Weiss asked.

"Beats me. Seems pretty stupid to have everyone working up here if nobody trusts anybody else."

A woman scientist at the next workstation shot Roberts an angry look.

"That doesn't answer my question," said Weiss.

"People work hard," Roberts said, one eye on the eavesdropping scientist. He slammed the oven door. "I guess they don't want anyone taking advantage of their effort."

"But aren't you all working for the common good?"

"Hey, man, you don't need to convince me," said Roberts. "But I'm just a tech."

"You're right, Stu. Sorry. All this backbiting's thrown me. By the way, who is Hugh O'Donnell? Doesn't he work in here?"

"You won't catch him in the main part of The Bakery," said Roberts. "Not unless you get up real early in the morning. See that little room back by the rear hatch? That's his private lab."

"More security?"

"Nobody knows what the hell O'Donnell's doing. Not even me, and I'm supposed to be his tech."

And pissed about it, noted Weiss as Roberts propelled himself toward the front of The Bakery. Weiss allowed himself to follow. The reporter pretended to be casually studying the different workstations while keeping one eye on O'Donnell's lab. It wasn't very large, certainly not large enough for any of the equipment that dominated the main section of the module. Why was O'Donnell so unpopular? Why was his presence of such concern to Bianco and Skillen?

As if his thoughts had been translated into prayers and then immediately answered, Bianco and Skillen flew past him and stopped at the door to O'Donnell's lab. Skillen rapped sharply, visibly shaking the fiberglass partitions that formed the lab's walls. The door opened enough to allow Weiss to see O'Donnell eye his visitors from behind his wire-frame glasses. Weiss drifted closer.

Skillen introduced O'Donnell to Bianco. There was a smug tone in her voice, as if Bianco's presence fulfilled a threat she had long held over O'Donnell's head. O'Donnell squeezed out of his lab and pressed the door closed behind him. Weiss noticed that the door did not latch.

Skillen fired a salvo of complaints about O'Donnell's use of the module's hardware. This began a three-way argument, Skillen's shrill voice countered by O'Donnell's deeper growls, with Bianco's clear tenor in the middle. As the shouting intensified, the trio gradually drifted along the aisle. O'Donnell's lab door slowly opened, giving Weiss a partial view of the lab's interior.

With an exaggerated sigh of pained innocence, Weiss surreptitiously turned on the Minicam hanging on his chest and pointed his body at O'Donnell's lab. Vials of colored liquids lined one wall. A laptop computer displayed three-dimensional figures that Weiss now recognized as strands of genetic material. But the plants O'Donnell was growing under high-intensity lamps were like nothing he had seen anywhere on Trikon Station.

Nobody was paying any attention to him, so Weiss took the Minicam in his hands and zoomed in on the plants. But before his fingers could adjust the lens something hard crashed into the side of his face. The Minicam squirted out of his fingers. Another blow followed, this one to his midsection.

"No pictures, goddammit!" O'Donnell screamed. Weiss curled himself into a ball and tumbled beneath the onslaught of O'Donnell's punches. They caused more annoyance than pain; O'Donnell had not anchored his feet and his swings had no real power behind them. But Weiss sensed that O'Donnell had the strength and the inclination to kill him if his anger went unchecked.

Roberts and another tech pried them apart—after enjoying themselves watching for a while, Weiss thought. O'Donnell's glasses were skewed on his face. His hair poked through his hairnet like a forest of cowlicks. His shirt billowed about his chest, revealing a stomach that was lean and tautly muscled.

Weiss pulled his hat back onto the top of his head, adjusted the cord of linked rubber bands under his chin, and tucked the flaps of his denim shirt into his chinos. The Minicam was still tethered to his neck; it was not damaged.

"Give me the camera," said O'Donnell.

"The hell I will," Weiss said.

"You can see what I mean about Mr. O'Donnell," Skillen said to Bianco. "He's a troublemaker."

"Go squat on a fire hydrant," said O'Donnell. "I'm no trouble to you."

"*Basta!* Enough!" said Bianco.

The two techs released O'Donnell and Weiss. O'Donnell closed the door to his lab and held it shut.

"Mr. Weiss, did you take footage of Mr. O'Donnell's lab?" Bianco asked. Anger flared in his eyes. He was not a frail old wreck anymore, he was the man in charge.

"Sure I did."

"Hand me the camera."

"It's not your . . ."

Bianco's eyes were molten lava. "The camera, Mr. Weiss. Now."

Weiss felt a shudder go up his spine, as if he were facing an angry Mafia don. Reluctantly, he slipped the cord over his hat and handed the minicam to Bianco. Bianco passed it to O'Donnell.

"Since Dr. Skillen has not allowed Mr. Weiss to film her lab, I see no reason why he should be allowed to film yours," said Bianco. He responded to Skillen's grunt with an ironically friendly nod of his head. "Do you know how to operate this camera?"

O'Donnell spun the Minicam in his hands. It had two separate eyepieces, one for filming, the other for viewing what was on the tape. He told Bianco it seemed simple enough.

"Run the tape back until you reach the point where Mr. Weiss began shooting your lab," said Bianco. "Then erase whatever offends you."

O'Donnell ran the tape in reverse. Weiss had lingered on the plants while devoting comparatively little time to the vials and the computer. Was it coincidence? Dumb luck? Or did Weiss know exactly what he was doing? O'Donnell handed back the camera, thinking, I can't be too careful as long as Weiss stays on board.

News traveled quickly on Trikon Station; Dan learned about the scuffle in The Bakery within minutes after it happened. He was not surprised to hear the identities of the combatants. Aaron Weiss reminded him of a yelping poodle that deserved an occasional boot in the tail. O'Donnell was restrained enough to avoid a fight unless seriously provoked. Or unless . . .

Dan felt terrible thinking that O'Donnell's behavior might have been drug-induced. O'Donnell had been abused by a woman and screwed by a lawyer, just as he had. O'Donnell cared only about his work, just as he did. O'Donnell was the closest thing he had to a drinking buddy, and the irony was that they hadn't shared a drop of liquor.

But this was Trikon Station, and in light of the Russell Cramer incident Dan had no choice but to be suspicious, no matter how distasteful it felt.

Lorraine Renoir's office was empty, and Dan left his own door open so that he could see when she entered. Even though he was her commanding officer, he often wondered how Lorraine spent her days. There were reports to be filed and medicine to be dispensed. There were probably whole hosts of everyday complaints that he, in his intentional aloofness, failed to notice. But how else did she spend her time? What did she think about when her mind was not occupied with her work? He never knew. He always had given her a wide berth because he wanted to avoid any sort of entanglement. Now the answer to the question was easy: She was with Kurt Jaeckle. Word around the station was that they were a hot item. They spent long hours rehearsing Jaeckle's television scripts in the rumpus room. They reserved back-to-back sessions in the observation blister. They had even jetted to the observatory so that Jaeckle could show her spectacular views of the universe.

Dan was a master at suppression, sublimination, replacing people with animals shaped from bonsai trees. So he fought down the anger and bitterness that burned in his gut by concentrating on Carla Sue Gamble's reaction. She was one tough lady. She would not go quietly into the limbo of being an ex-lover. She was going to raise hell with Jaeckle, sooner or later. The thought almost put a smile on Tighe's face.

A blue flight suit flashed in the entry hatch. Lorraine flew into the command module in signature fashion—sideways in relation to local vertical. She reminded Dan of an Olympic diver the way she suddenly jackknifed and sliced through the doorway into her office. With a flick of his ankles, Dan propelled himself across the module toward her. He could see Lorraine groping with her stockinged feet for a pair of foot loops as she closed the door.

Dan knocked on the frame, his face hardened with the thought of his plan and the person he was asking to effect it. Lorraine actually smiled at the sight of him. But then, as if she had picked up on his demeanor, her smile vanished. Dan noticed that her normally neat French braid looked like a frayed rope. He didn't want to think why.

"I want to ask you something, Dr. Renoir." He hadn't called her *Doctor* in months and she seemed startled. The formality sounded strange to him, too. "I assume you will be seeing Hugh O'Donnell tomorrow."

"As I do every day."

"When was the last time you tested his blood?"

"What makes you think I test his blood at all?"

"I know about his past," said Dan. "I know the reason he sees you. He's told me. Now when was the last time you tested his blood?"

"Two weeks ago."

"I want you to test it again."

"Why is that, Commander?"

"I assume you heard of O'Donnell's altercation with Aaron Weiss."

A look of surprise crossed Lorraine's face. She hadn't heard. Dan coupled that with the disheveled braid and didn't like the connotation. *Everyone* should have heard about the fight by now.

"Weiss poked his video camera into O'Donnell's lab." Dan spoke quickly so that he would not lose his train of thought. Knowing Lorraine was screwing with Jaeckle was one thing; seeing the actual signs was something else. "O'Donnell attacked him and wrestled the camera away. I want to know whether O'Donnell's reaction was artificially induced."

"Maybe he just was angry," said Lorraine. "Everyone is so security conscious. It's sickening."

"I know. Maybe someone will develop a pill that will bring them all back to their senses. But until then, I have to deal with this situation the best way I know how."

"I haven't noticed any signs, either subjective or objective, that would lead me to believe that Hugh O'Donnell is using drugs," said Lorraine.

"Neither have I," Dan said. "But I have to be certain."

"Are you ordering me to test him?"

"I'm asking you to indulge me."

"I see," said Lorraine. "By the way, Commander—it's time for your blood pressure to be checked."

* * *

Hisashi Oyamo floated in the middle of his sleep compartment, legs tucked under him and hands resting on his knees in the classic meditative position. Actually his hands bobbed weightlessly several inches above his knees, but the calming effect on his mind was the same.

He had just returned from his evening chess game with Ramsanjawi. Once again he had swallowed his pride and allowed the bloated Hindu to best him. That did not bother him; even the greatest warrior retreats when it is to his ultimate advantage.

No, what bothered him was Bianco and his news about the whale deaths. The old man was convinced that the plankton in the seas were dying, killed by toxic wastes. Oyamo held no special fondness for whales. Not dolphins nor any other animals. His father had been a whaler, his livelihood destroyed by the smug Americans and Europeans who had forced an end to commercial whaling twenty years earlier.

But if the plankton die, the human race dies. Japan dies. My family dies.

Oyamo sighed deeply. Am I being realistic or have I merely fallen under Bianco's spell? The old man is a magician, surely. A great leader, even if he is not Japanese.

He sighed again. I will have to call Tokyo. I must inform them of this change in the situation. Perhaps Bianco has been right all along. Perhaps we should all be cooperating, without regard to nation or race. Perhaps the problem we face is so great that we must work together, fully and completely.

Tokyo, he knew, would not enjoy hearing that.

Long after disposing of Hisashi Oyamo in yet another chess game, Chakra Ramsanjawi stole into the dimly lit ELM. He unlocked a compartment in his office and dislodged the false wall that concealed a larger storage area behind. Attached to the sides by elastic loops were dozens of small brown bottles. Some contained fluids, others contained powders, still others tiny crystals. Ramsanjawi selected one labeled 3-methylfentanyl, another labeled lactose, and a third that was empty. Then he floated out toward the centrifuge.

In some respects, preparing a batch of designer drugs was more difficult in orbit than on Earth. In other respects, it was easier. He could not tap out a pile of powder onto a piece of glass and chop it into fine granules using a scalpel or a razor blade. That phase of preparation had to be done by the arduous use of a propeller-shaped blade rotating within a specially modified food processor. But once the drug was finely chopped, the lack of gravity assured a perfectly homogenous mix.

Ramsanjawi first spun the fentanyl to be certain that the grains had not clumped together since he had chopped them several days earlier. Then he added a precise amount of the drug to a precise amount of lactose and spun the mix in the third bottle for several minutes.

It was not possible, in microgravity, to simply pour the liquid out of the bottle. The bottle was designed with a piston inside it to force the weightless liquids into a microgravity vial of tempered glass. Otherwise Ramsanjawi would have had to use a syringe to suck its contents out.

Precise proportions were essential. Designer drugs were so much more potent than their naturally occurring analogs that the slightest mistake in synthesizing or the slightest error in cutting could result in a totally different drug capable of producing unintended, even deadly side effects. Ramsanjawi had seen this first-hand.

One night, just before Ramsanjawi was to depart for Trikon Station, Sir Derek called a meeting of the entire group he had recruited for his project. The

Lancashire lads, as Sir Derek called his Earthside lab workers, were present, as were the various messengers and henchmen Sir Derek thought were necessary. Early in the meeting, Sir Derek asked Ramsanjawi to create an opiate from a batch of chemicals present in the room. Ramsanjawi obliged. Toward the end of the meeting, a burly fellow named Meade dragged in the cringing and dirty figure of an emaciated young man. Sir Derek explained to the group that the man was a "volunteer" from one of the local flophouses "who would not be missed." He had consented to help demonstrate the power of one of Ramsanjawi's concoctions.

Sir Derek boiled the opiate over a burner while Meade stripped the man naked. The group muttered nervously among themselves, puzzled by what they were about to witness. Sir Derek filled a syringe with the liquefied drug. Not all of it, said Ramsanjawi, not all of it. But Sir Derek turned a deaf ear. He jammed the needle into the man's elbow vein and shot home the entire load.

Meade stepped back. The man stood completely still for a moment, as if listening for a faint sound. Then he began to shake. He fell to the floor, a fountain of urine arcing out of his penis, a flow of wet feces erupting from his anus. He thrashed in his own excrement, his eyes bulging, his tongue flapping, his face turning blue. Then he collapsed in upon himself and lay motionless.

"I trust all of you will honor our commitment," said Sir Derek. Then he ordered Meade to scrape up the body.

This time, the situation was far more delicate. O'Donnell or O'Neill or whoever he might be was not a starving derelict. He was a man of science, like himself. The method of delivering the drug would be tricky, but Ramsanjawi would find a way. O'Donnell was an ex-addict; he might even enjoy the ride. But

Ramsanjawi did not want to kill him. That would never do. O'Donnell might prove useful later.

The presence of Aaron Weiss was a propitious sign. For all his scientific pretension, the man still had the mentality of a tabloid reporter. He would bite at the worm of sensationalism.

Ramsanjawi shut down the centrifuge and returned with the bottle to his office. He chuckled at the thought of a neat little irony. Druggies and tabloid reporters had driven him from his rightful station in England. Now the chance encounter between an ex-druggie and an ex-tabloid reporter would lead him back.

30 AUGUST 1998
TRIKON STATION

BASILIO INVESTIGATIVE SERVICE
P.O. Box 127
Annapolis, Maryland 21401

MEMO TO FILE

CLIENT: C.S. Gamble
SUBJECT: Kurt Jaeckle

August 27, 1998, 11:15 A.M.—Spoke to a Mrs. LaVerne Nelson, who worked as housekeeper for subject and his first wife from 1986 through 1988. At first she was reluctant to talk to me, thinking that I was gathering information for a news article or book about the subject. When I explained the real reason for my inquiries, she became very talkative as if she was happy to find someone with a similar opinion on the subject.

Mrs. Nelson informed me of her belief that the real reason for the breakup of the subject's first marriage was not "irreconcilable differences." She claims the subject raped his eldest daughter, probably more than once, when she was twelve years old.

August 27, 1998, 2:30 P.M.—Went to the Anne Arundel Courthouse in order to review the court file on subject's divorce from his first wife. Was informed that these files were sealed by court order immediately upon the entry of the divorce judgment. At present, I am *unable to verify Mrs. Nelson's allegations and must regard them as hearsay.*

DINNER HAD BEEN unusually quiet for Aaron Weiss. The two Martians with whom he shared a table spoke to each other in hushed tones, ignoring him. It's like they're really Martians, Weiss grumbled to himself, and they don't want anything to do with an Earthling.

When they left, no one took their places. Weiss finished his meal alone and groped his way out of the wardroom, feeling distinctly like a leper.

His mood changed as soon as he reached his compartment. Wedged into the door was an envelope. There was something primitive about this method of communication in the midst of the station's high-tech ambience. But Weiss quickly forgot the irony when he read the note inside.

> I have reconsidered my refusal to consent to an interview. I will be at your disposal in the European Lab Module at 2200 hours. Feel free to bring your camera.
> Chakra Ramsanjawi

Weiss could hear the Indian's singsong manner of speech in the serpentine style of the handwriting. He was surprised by the invitation. During dinner, he had come to the conclusion that his fight with Hugh O'Donnell had resulted in the station's scientific community hardening against him. Now the one scientist he had considered least likely to talk was consenting to an interview. These bright boys sure are an unpredictable bunch, thought Weiss.

He swam into ELM at the appointed time, moving cautiously from handhold to handhold, his innards braced against the slight hint of nausea he had felt that morning. The threat of sickness bothered him more than the real thing; he almost wished his guts would get the damned job done, upchuck and have it over with. Almost.

Ramsanjawi was alone, floating at a workstation halfway down the length of the module. His billowing saffron *kurta* was a brilliant contrast to the salmon-and-gray color scheme. Weiss noticed a flash of the eyes in Ramsanjawi's dark face and thought he heard laughter echoing off the aluminum walls. He pulled himself closer. Ramsanjawi was staring at a centrifuge.

"Good evening, Mr. Weiss," Ramsanjawi said without turning around. "I am delighted you accepted my invitation."

Barely noticing the man's overly sweet, perfumed scent, Weiss said, "I was happy to receive it. Surprised, too."

"Why were you surprised?"

"You didn't exactly lay out the red carpet for me when I came in here with Bianco this morning," said Weiss, drifting farther away from the Indian. "And after my fight with Hugh O'Donnell, I assumed no one would talk to me. Least of all you."

Ramsanjawi nodded at each of Weiss's reasons, then dismissed them with a laugh that blended perfectly with the whir of the centrifuge.

"I will explain why I have once again decided to break ranks with my brethren," he said.

The centrifuge kicked off and Ramsanjawi reached inside to free a vial from the arm. The vial contained a liquid that shaded from aquamarine to deep blue in four distinct bands. Ramsanjawi motioned Weiss to the adjacent workstation, where a stoppered beaker was secured in a metal rack.

"Seawater from the North Atlantic," said Ramsanjawi, nodding toward the beaker. "The white filaments you see are particularly nasty polychlorinated biphenyl molecules, which you know as PCBs.

They are visually enhanced for what I am about to demonstrate."

He inserted the needle of a syringe through the top of the vial he was holding and pushed carefully until the tip of the needle entered the third of the four bands of blue. Then he drew a portion of the liquid into the barrel of the syringe.

"These are genetically altered *E. coli* bacteria," said Ramsanjawi, withdrawing the needle and holding the syringe so that Weiss had a clear view of the thin band of blue. "We use *E. coli* because they are easy to cultivate in large quantities. They are visually enhanced as well."

Ramsanjawi slowly pressed the needle through the stopper of the beaker. The needle appeared in the seawater, glinting among the filaments. Ramsanjawi pressed the plunger. The microbes dispersed throughout the water in thin blue whorls. The filaments seemed to dance as the microbes swirled around them. Slowly, the filaments broke apart, separating into a snowstorm of flakes. In a minute, the water was clear.

"Fantastic," said Weiss.

"A parlor trick," Ramsanjawi said.

"But the water is clear."

"Only of PCBs. There are dozens of other toxic substances I did not choose to visually enhance." Ramsanjawi sighed. "I am afraid this is a case of too little too late."

"Spoken like a true optimist," said Weiss.

"If I exude pessimism, it is only because I have been here too long."

Weiss studied the Indian's face for a moment. "Why don't the three arms of Trikon cooperate, Dr. Ramsanjawi?" he asked.

"Personality clashes, racial clashes, silly notions of national pride. There is a good deal of competition in science, Mr. Weiss. Ask anyone who has received a

Nobel Prize." He hesitated a beat, then, "But if you want my honest opinion, the root cause is money."

"No one's mentioned that before," Weiss said.

"Perhaps because it is not obvious. Or perhaps because it is so obvious that it requires no mention."

"Pretend I don't think it's so obvious," said Weiss. "How does money enter into it?"

"There are forces that want to prevent Trikon from developing these microbes," said Ramsanjawi. "It is not because these forces wish the Earth to be suffocated in toxic wastes. They simply prefer that *they* be the ones who own the means of cleaning it up."

"Forces? What forces? Who are you talking about?" Weiss demanded.

"I have no specific names to give you," said Ramsanjawi. "But you can guess where they reside. The United States of America."

"Dr. Ramsanjawi, that's absurd. American scientists have spearheaded the ecological advances of the last decade."

"I did not say American scientists. I meant American industry. Most of the pollutants in the oceans are by-products of American manufacturing processes developed in the middle part of the twentieth century. A patented microbe with the ability to neutralize these wastes would be worth millions of dollars to any scientist who can develop it. But it would be worth *trillions* to these industries because they would be able to continue using those old, cheap manufacturing processes, since they would have the means of cleaning up after them. They could even sell their manufacturing processes—and the cleanup systems—to the rest of the world."

Weiss thought a moment, then said, "Kind of like putting catalytic converters on automobiles instead of giving them nonpolluting motors."

"Exactly!" Ramsanjawi beamed at the reporter. "You grasp the situation very quickly."

Weiss thought the details were vague, but he liked the conspiratorial, antiestablishment flavor of Ramsanjawi's theory. It was like the stories he had unearthed for his old TV tabloid, but on a far more sweeping scale.

"How are these forces preventing you from doing your work?" he asked.

"They are not," said Ramsanjawi. "They are actually trying to promote our work so they can steal it and use it for their own purposes."

"How do they steal it?"

"We are not certain of their methods, but we are certain of the thefts."

"By who?" said Weiss.

"Different people." Ramsanjawi made a small wave of his hand. "They change from rotation to rotation, posing as scientists or technicians. We think they are close to fitting all the pieces of this microbial puzzle together."

"Is that so bad?"

"That depends on who you think should own the keys to toxic-waste cleanup—some giant corporation or a nonprofit consortium dedicated to the betterment of the world."

Weiss considered the alternatives and decided that he did have a strong preference. He flashed on the image of Ramsanjawi and Bianco speaking warmly that morning. Could it be that the Indian, of all the others, was Bianco's true soul mate, the genuine embodiment of what Bianco called the Trikon spirit?

"What makes you think these forces are close to developing the microbe?" he said.

"We think they have sent up a superspy," said Ramsanjawi. Lowering his voice, "Hugh O'Donnell."

"Why did I know you were going to say that?" Weiss asked, grinning.

"What impelled O'Donnell to attack you today?"

"I tried to film his lab. He got, as we say, pissed."

"When *we* say pissed, we mean drunk," said Ramsanjawi. He smiled as if the incident proved his premise that O'Donnell was a spy.

"Wait a second," said Weiss. "Everybody in the American lab hates O'Donnell."

"An elaborate act. He pretends to work on a separate project, they complain about lack of lab space. All the while, he is gleaning data from us and the Japanese and sending it back to the corporation he works for. His employer may not even be a member of Trikon."

Weiss remembered the conversation he overheard through Thora Skillen's door. The Americans had fallen behind in their research and Bianco was angry. Ramsanjawi might have a point, farfetched as it seemed.

"Is that the camera you used?" said Ramsanjawi. "May I?"

Weiss slipped the cord over his head and handed the Minicam to Ramsanjawi. The Indian aimed it around the lab like a tourist in midtown Manhattan.

"Extremely fine resolution," he said. "And good magnification."

"Only the best from CNN."

"What did you see as you filmed?"

"A computer, smaller than the ones in the main lab modules. It had some sort of genetic structure on the screen. Vials of colored liquids, which probably were microbe soups."

"You have learned much in your short time here," said Ramsanjawi. "Was there anything else? Any sophisticated communications equipment?"

"That's all I saw," said Weiss. Of course, there were the plants. But he wasn't about to mention them. He had a reporter's sense that Ramsanjawi was angling for something—information, a favor, maybe a deal. He wanted to keep one trump card up his sleeve. Besides, he had a damned good idea what those plants were. The sixty-four-billion-dollar question was what were they doing on Trikon Station.

"How would you like to film O'Donnell's lab?" Ramsanjawi asked.

"And get killed doing it? No thanks."

"What if I told you I could arrange it?"

"With O'Donnell? Fat chance."

"Ascend from the real world, Mr. Weiss, just for a moment. Theoretically, would you like to film O'Donnell's lab and have someone with scientific expertise interpret the images?"

"What I would like to do is ask O'Donnell a bunch of questions and have him answer them. But that isn't going to happen."

"Precisely. So answer my question."

"Do I look stupid?" said Weiss.

"What if I told you that I could guarantee you fifteen minutes without danger of being assaulted? Is that enough time?"

"How are you going to do that?"

"Is it enough time, Mr. Weiss?"

"I can manage with it."

"Would you be willing to cooperate, and bring the tape to me?"

"I might," said Weiss. "But why should I?"

"Because we both want the same information."

"How do you know I'm not a spy myself."

"I don't," said Ramsanjawi, handing the camera back to him. "But I can't be in two places at the same time, so I have asked you. I assume there are spies. If I discover you to be one, so be it."

Weiss took the Minicam from Ramsanjawi and slipped the cord back over his head. He wasn't sure about the offer. It was too easy, too coincidental with his fight that morning. But where would he be if he hadn't run down the other coincidences he had encountered in his life? Probably writing a police blotter column for a local rag and playing with himself. Fuck the whales. Big as they were, those plants in

O'Donnell's lab were the key to something bigger. He was going to have another look at them. Somehow. Some way.

"Why did you show me the parlor trick?" he asked.

"To establish credibility, Mr. Weiss," said Ramsanjawi. "Why else?"

The phone booths in the command module were open twenty-four hours a day. Crewman Stanley was on duty in the module when Weiss got there. He looked askance as the reporter swiftly explained that he had to contact his boss in Atlanta. The Aussie nodded okay, but the suspicious look stayed on his face.

Weiss closed himself in the booth farther from Stanley, then grumbled under his breath as his fingers refused to hit the right pads on the telephone keyboard. Damned micro-gee, he fumed. Nothing works right here, not even my hands.

Slowly, very deliberately, he pressed out the number of the network office in Atlanta. Zeke'll be there, he said to himself. He's got to be. Where else does he have to go to, without me?

Sure enough, Tucker was exactly where Weiss hoped: in the editing room helping a production assistant wade through miles of tape.

"How's outer space treating you?" Zeke's voice drawled in the phone.

"Never mind. Gotta make this fast, Zeke." Weiss kept his voice low, eyeing Stanley through the booth's clear plastic door, watching him from across the module. "I'm going to mention two names. I'm only going to say them once. After that, they are Number One and Number Two. I want you to dig out morgue files on both. I'm not looking for mainstream vanilla bullshit. I want the kind of dirt that used to pay our rent. Ready?"

"Yup."

"Number One is Chakra Ramsanjawi. I remember

something about a scandal in England several years ago, mid-eighties, maybe. Not sure of the particulars, but it was bad. The European Bureau should have it.

"Number Two is Kurt Jaeckle. I need something I can hit him with to get him off my back. Guy's a pain in the ass, begging to show off his Mars Project. Like I need Mars."

Tucker chuckled. "Only you would call a world-class scientist and media star a pain in the ass."

"I've seen the slimy undersides of too many world-class media stars in my day."

"Why, Aaron, you're a world-class media star yourself."

"Cut the crap, Zeke. This is important."

"Okay. Give me twenty-four hours. Hey, Yablon's pretty steamed he hasn't heard from you."

"Another pain in the ass," said Weiss. "I'll call when I'm damn good and ready."

"A real world-class attitude," Zeke Tucker said, laughing.

It's now or never, Thora Skillen said to herself as she slipped into the sleep restraint in her compartment.

Fabio Bianco himself is here. And a reporter from CNN. If I do it now it will get tremendous publicity all over the world. *Everybody* will see how wrong it is to conduct genetic research, even on a space station.

She could stop them, she knew. In the darkness of her compartment she squeezed her eyes shut and told herself that she would strike back at them for her sister's death.

But her dreams, when she finally fell asleep, were troubled. Her father stared down at her, cold and disapproving. "Melissa would never do that," her father said, in a tone that was more hurt than anger. "Why must you always be the bad one?"

Melissa told her, "It's all right, Thora. You don't have to do anything you don't want to do. I love you,

Thora dear. It's all right."

And she heard her own voice pleading, "I don't want to die. Oh God, please don't make me die."

"I reserved the observation blister," said Lance, "so we can cool down."

Carla Sue removed her hairnet and shook her head. Her hair instantly puffed out like a perfect sphere of yellow cotton candy. She patted the nape of her neck with a towel.

"Sure," she said. "Sounds fine."

Lance detected uncertainty in her voice, as if she were replaying their last visit to the blister. Be cool, be in command, Freddy had told him. You are the man.

He didn't give her a chance to reconsider. He led her to the Mars module, never once looking back lest she interpret the slightest glance as a lack of confidence. She stayed right behind him.

He opened the blister door with a flourish and invited her to enter before him. She smiled for him as if charmed by his gallantry.

They floated side by side. Three hundred miles below, a necklace of atolls gleamed in the brilliant blue waters of the Pacific. Lance felt a mad urge to apologize for his behavior their last time together. He wanted to tell her the truth, that he had been surprised and scared but that this time would be different. He checked himself. All the talk in the world don' mean *nada,* Freddy had told him. You deliver with action.

So they talked about their workout and the pleasant sensation of fatigue that followed exercise. Carla Sue wasn't as forward as the last time. In fact, as Freddy had predicted, she was downright prudish. Her knees were pressed together, her arms folded.

Thoughts of Becky tried to creep into Lance's mind. He suppressed them by talking faster and louder.

"Look how the water is a lighter blue around the islands," he said.

"Yes," said Carla Sue.

A lock of blond hair brushed against his cheek. He stole a glance at her and suddenly felt a giddy sense of ownership, as if all of this woman—the long legs, the blond hair, the lips shaped like Cupid's bow and red as a valentine—were his for the taking.

All the talk in the world don' mean *nada*, Freddy's voice said in his ear.

He pulled Carla Sue to his body, locked one leg behind her knees, and pressed his lips against hers.

Just get her started and don' worry.

31 AUGUST 1998
TRIKON STATION

I feel like Captain Kirk in the old "Star Trek" series I watched as a girl. "Captain's Log, Star Date August 1998." But the truth of the matter is that I am troubled, and when I am troubled I write down my thoughts in order to sort them out.

My relationship with Kurt Jaeckle is not going well. It's not just that he's so eternally self-absorbed, even when we make love. The trouble is, he's so childish! This world-known scientist and teacher turns into a high school boy when we make love. Even when we went to the observatory. I was so thrilled by the invitation, so interested in learning about the sky. But Kurt had other ideas. I feel used.

I am not a kid. I realize that love is not what is depicted in the movies. I have no illusions. I fully expect that one day he will regard me as a fling. The one on the space station. Doctor What's-Her-Name.

But at least the here and now, the lovemaking, should be better. Instead, I feel as though he would rather be playing with a teenager.

Would it have been this way with Dan?

—From the diary of Lorraine Renoir

O'DONNELL REALIZED THAT there was something wrong with Lorraine. Her hair was no longer twisted into a neat French braid. Instead, it was bound by a net that seemed poised to fly off her head with the force of her loosened chestnut tresses. Her lips, usually pressed together in an expression he called grim, were noticeably turned down into a frown. She refused to meet his eyes.

His daily meetings with Lorraine had diminished from a half hour to barely ten minutes. Their tenor had shaded from openly adversarial to politely civil, if not genuinely friendly. They would chat until Lorraine apparently satisfied herself that the whites of his eyes weren't bloodshot, his pupils weren't dilated, his speech wasn't slurred, and his limbs were not twitching uncontrollably. So he was surprised when she immediately ordered him to roll up his sleeve.

O'Donnell watched silently as Lorraine readied a syringe. Her breath sounded thick, as if she were congested. Still refusing to meet his eyes, she tied a rubber tube around his biceps and told him to pump his hand until his already prominent veins threatened to burst out of his skin. As with the last blood test, O'Donnell concentrated on the small Monet print fastened to the wall. He felt the coolness of the alcohol as she swabbed his inner elbow. He expected the thin prick of the needle. Instead, he felt as if his arm were being gouged by claws.

"Easy, Doc!"

Lorraine's hands trembled. The needle scraped across his skin, leaving a darkened line of blood behind. O'Donnell grabbed the syringe with his free hand and lifted the needle out of his arm. Lorraine wrenched the syringe away and, with the same motion, stuffed it into a waste receptacle.

"You okay, Doc?"

"Fine," she said. She didn't look at him and furiously prepared a second syringe.

O'Donnell thought he heard her sniffle. He pulled the tube from his right arm and tightened it around his left. This time he watched her. As she moved to stick him, he gently placed his hand on hers and guided the needle into his vein.

"Do you want to tell me what this is all about?" he said when she finished drawing his blood.

"It was time for a test."

"I'm talking about the butcher job on my right arm."

She was labeling the syringe. O'Donnell placed his hand on her chin and turned her head so that she faced him. Her brown eyes were wet.

"You want to talk to me for a change?" he said.

She hesitated, but only for a moment.

"Have you ever thought you loved someone and tried to make that person notice you?"

"All the time," said O'Donnell.

"Did they?"

"Sometimes, sometimes not. I never gave it much effort. I'm pretty lazy when it comes to that."

"Well, did it ever happen that after you gave up on the one person and started seeing someone else, you realized that the first person had noticed you all along. Only now, because you are with the second person, and because you may have done things that are not in the best interests of the first person, you realize that you can never go back."

O'Donnell knew the first person was Dan and the second person was Jaeckle, but he refrained from embarrassing her.

"I've been taught to think in absolutes," he said. "Black and white, yes and no. One drink or one snort and I'll be hell-bent for death and destruction. But when it comes to affairs of the heart, even I know that there are no absolutes. One day's great idea is another day's dumb mistake."

He grinned at her. "Some people say we react to the chemicals in our brains. Some believe in true love. Whatever, the situation can be as unpredictable as hell. You make decisions based on constantly changing conditions. It's worse than trying to predict the weather. But when you find yourself in a condition like the one you're in, there's only one reliable barometer." He patted her stomach. "How does this feel?"

"Like I have a fist in it," said Lorraine.

"You don't like the decision you made."

"I know that," said Lorraine. "What can I do about it?"

"Right now, nothing," he said. "You can't force these decisions. It's like trying to seed clouds. You can't seed them if they don't exist. You have to wait for the right time."

"When is that?"

"Hard to say," said O'Donnell. "But I do know one thing. The time always comes. They always come back."

Lance's innards trembled as he performed his daily inspection in the logistics module. The entire station seemed to be seething with a sexuality he had never noticed. The slender pipes looping across the ceiling were entwined arms and legs; their bright sheen was not from polished aluminum but from a fine glaze of sweat. The rounded bottoms of two oxygen cylinders lashed together were perfectly shaped breasts. Another pair were firm buttocks. The whole station was reeking with sex. It was everyplace, even in the very air. He tried to get his mind off last night with Carla Sue, tried to concentrate on his duties. But he could think of nothing else. His erection pressed against his flight pants.

A loud clanging interrupted his turmoil. Aaron Weiss hovered in the entry hatch, his ever-present hat and Minicam bound to him.

"May I come in?"

"I guess."

Weiss tumbled quickly into the module.

"Commander's orders," he said. "I need permission and the escort of a crew member to enter this module."

Lance shook his head as if perplexed by the rules.

"He must have a reason," said Weiss. "Nothing on this station exists without good reason."

"I suppose so," said Lance, warily.

"What the hell is a logistics module, anyway?" asked Weiss.

Patiently Lance explained about the materials stored in the module and described the computer-controlled system for utilizing them.

Weiss suddenly asked, "What is your opinion of the scientific research being conducted on this station?"

"Uh—It's important, I guess," said Lance.

"I get the feeling that the crew is not intimately involved with it."

Lance almost said that he personally was more intimately involved with the Mars Project. His thoughts surged between a giddy pride about last night and a gnawing fear that he had done something terribly wrong. But he couldn't tell Aaron Weiss about that. Weiss wouldn't understand.

"No, we're not," he replied. "Our main job is to keep the station flying. That's why we're here. That's what inspecting this here log mod every day is all about."

"Log . . .?" Weiss looked puzzled momentarily. "Oh, you mean logistics module."

Lance nodded. Moving around Weiss, he made a big show of testing the seals of a waste receptacle.

"It's an interesting project," said Weiss, adjusting himself so that he always faced the constantly moving crewman. "The creation of a superbug that will rid the world of toxic wastes."

"Sounds like a good idea," Lance said, though he didn't pay the idea much mind. He furtively passed a finger under his nose. Traces of Carla Sue's tangy smell were still there, even after he had scrubbed his hands several times. Could the reporter smell it?

"Looks to me," said Weiss, "that man for hundreds of years has played the devil in our Garden of Eden down below . . ."

"How's that?" A jolt of almost electrical intensity surged through Lance.

"We've screwed up the environment of Earth," Weiss explained, looking surprised at Lance's ferocious stare. "Now we have the chance to play God."

"Play God?" Something started churning inside Lance, an echo that reverberated with the guilty pleasures of the previous night.

"What these scientists are doing is altering the genes of common microbes so that they'll devour toxic wastes. They're creating new forms of life in the labs here instead of waiting for them to develop naturally. That's kind of like playing God, don't you think?"

"They're doing that here?" Lance looked surprised.

"What do you think all those tubes of colored liquids are? Oil paints?"

Lance swallowed bile. Trying to keep a calm appearance, he answered, "Well, like I said, all I'm concerned about is keeping the station flying. Anything else is none of my business."

"What about industrial espionage?" asked Weiss.

"I'm not sure what you mean."

"Spying," said Weiss. "This superbug is a very valuable little animal, you know. Or is it a vegetable? Anyway, someone might want to steal it for himself. What if you, as a crewman, witnessed a theft. What would you do?"

"I'm supposed to report it to Commander Tighe," said Lance, still shaking inside. "Those are the only orders we have."

"That's an awfully laid-back attitude, considering the nature of the project and its potential value."

"Commander Tighe says we're not policemen, or judges or juries, either."

"Is that why you were installing a security system the other night?"

Lance was confused. The other night was ages ago.

"In the Jap module. You and Freddy Aviles were there working on something when I wandered in."

"Oh, that night," said Lance. "That was no security system. See, Freddy's a computer whiz, so Commander Tighe is having him reconfigure the station's computer system. I don't know much about it myself. I just hold the tools and—"

"Lance!"

Freddy Aviles sailed through the entry hatch with his usual acrobatic flair.

"Hi, Freddy," said Lance.

Freddy ignored Lance and spoke directly to Weiss.

"You have a phone call in the command module."

"I do? Male or female?"

"A guy named Ed Yablon."

"Oh, him," said Weiss. "Tell him I'll be there in a minute."

"I ain't goin' there, and he don' sound like he got a minute."

"Bureau chiefs!" said Weiss with mock exasperation. "I'm going. Thanks for the tour, Lance."

Lance nodded silently. Freddy stared at Weiss until well after he had disappeared into the connecting tunnel.

"What was he doin' here?" Freddy asked.

"Nothing. He just wanted to see the logistics module."

"What was he askin' about me?"

"Nothing."

"I heard you mention my name."

"He thought we were installing a security system that night in Jasmine. I told him you were reconfiguring the station's computer system because you were a computer whiz."

Freddy stroked the thin strands of black hair that waved on his chin.

"That it?" he said.

"That's it," said Lance, confused by Freddy's reaction to such an innocent conversation. "He was here only about five minutes. He did most of the talking."

"Anything else he want to know?"

"About spies and the research project. I told him it was none of our business."

Freddy stared at the hatchway as if expecting Weiss to return.

"Freddy," Lance said. "Last night. I got to tell you what happened."

"Save it, Lance," said Freddy as he launched himself toward the connecting tunnel.

Lance hung in the middle of the logistics module, alone, surrounded by mute canisters and gleaming pipes, knowing that what he had done with Carla Sue was terribly wrong. Playing the devil in the Garden of Eden. That's what Weiss called it. And he was right. Lance knew he was right.

Lance knew one other fact. He wanted Carla Sue. Wrong or not, he wanted her with a desperate physical ache that hurt so much it was pleasure.

"What the hell are you doing up there?" screamed Ed Yablon. "I haven't heard a goddamn word from you."

"Easy, Ed," said Weiss into the phone. "It took me a while to feel my way around up here."

"Feel your way around? Where the hell are you? Goddamn New York City?"

"There's a very complicated social and professional structure on the station. I've had to weave my way through it to find the most reliable sources."

"Cut the crap, Aaron. When do I get the first report?"

"Not for a while."

"Aaron, if this is another of your goddamn schemes, I'll make sure you never come back." Yablon's voice was never sweet, even face-to-face. Over the phone connection it sounded sandpaper rough.

"Listen to me, Ed. I came up here looking for one thing and I think I found something else, something much bigger."

"Stop talking in generalities."

"I can't. These are unsecured phone channels. All I can say is I'm worming my way to the core."

"When the hell are you going to get there?"

"Soon."

"This better be worth the wait, Aaron."

"This is big, Ed."

Even the poor connection could not mask Ed Yablon's sigh of exasperation. "Everything is big with you. If you're not the death of me, I'm going to see that it's written on your grave."

"You're a bundle of laughs, Ed. Is Zeke there?"

"I'm in his office. He's the only one around here who goddamn knew how to reach you."

Zeke Tucker took the phone and stalled until Yablon left the office.

"What did you get?" Weiss asked impatiently.

"Number One," said Zeke. "The BBC sent us a taped report in 1985. Subject was implicated in an Oxford University drug scandal. Nothing ever was proven, but the university was *very* sensitive to its own reputation and dismissed him from the faculty."

"What types of drugs?"

"Designers," said Tucker. "Bunch of chemical names."

"Interesting," said Weiss. "What about Number Two?"

"Wait till you hear this one . . ."

Even Weiss, the old tabloid reporter, was shocked by the story.

"Who's your source?"

"A P.I. up in Maryland. Claims he was working for one of Number Two's recently jilted lovers. She stiffed him on his fee and he shopped it around the media to cut his losses. Nobody wants to use it, though, 'cause he can't provide anything more'n hearsay."

"That's a real humdinger."

"It's hearsay, Aaron," said Tucker.

"Yeah. A guy like that would probably go screaming to a lawyer."

"Sort of reminds you of the old days, don't it?"

Stu Roberts fingered the keypad of his hand-held computer. He had stored the data in a secured file and now was having difficulty gaining entry. Looming above Roberts, Chakra Ramsanjawi sighed impatiently. The Indian's sleep compartment felt small and fumingly hot.

"Be cool, man, I'll get it," said Roberts, perspiring.

Ramsanjawi smirked. He was growing tired of Roberts's jive talk. It made a bad combination with incompetence.

"Dig it," said Roberts as data played across the tiny screen. "Okay, O'Donnell works an average of three hours in his lab before breakfast. He eats at oh-eight-hundred hours, returns to Hab Two to brush his teeth, then reports to Dr. Renoir at 0830 hours. He does this every day. The amount of time with Dr. Renoir usually runs from five to ten minutes, but today it was close to a half hour. When he returns to his lab, he works an average of four hours before lunch. The actual time doesn't deviate by more than a minute or two. After lunch, he stops at his compartment, goes to the Whit, then returns to his lab by fourteen hundred hours. Not much deviation there, either."

"What does he do at the Whit?" asked Ramsanjawi.

"What do we all do at the Whit?" said Roberts. "Oh yeah, he brushes his teeth, too."

Ramsanjawi nodded.

"His afternoon time in the lab is more variable," said Roberts. "He never spends less than three hours, but there have been days he's spent four or five. You think he does timed experiments?"

Ramsanjawi, lost in thought, ignored the question.

"He always goes to the wardroom for dinner at nineteen hundred hours," said Roberts. "Always. If Commander Tighe is there, he'll eat with him. If not, he'll try to eat alone. If he can't, he'll sit with the Martians. Never with anyone from the American/Canadian group. I know. I tried to sit with him once. He left without finishing his food."

"Very discriminating," said Ramsanjawi.

Roberts grinned awkwardly, not sure whether Ramsanjawi's comment was an insult.

"After dinner he goes back to Hab Two, hits the head, I mean the Whit, and spends time in his compartment. Then usually, and I mean four out of every five nights, he meets Tighe in the ex/rec room for a game of darts. This is pretty boring stuff, huh?"

"Does he brush his teeth?" said Ramsanjawi.

"Before darts? Yeah, and after, too."

Roberts went on to explain how he had poked a pinhole in the accordion door of O'Donnell's compartment so he could time exactly how long O'Donnell kept his lights on before retiring. But Ramsanjawi wasn't listening. He had heard enough to realize that O'Donnell led a very rigid life within the patterned rhythm of the station. It would be frightfully easy to knock him out of sync.

"Can you bring me his toothpaste?" said Ramsanjawi, interrupting Roberts's discourse.

"Sure," said Roberts, fighting the impulse to ask the reason why. He did not want to know, he told himself.

2 SEPTEMBER 1998
TRIKON STATION

TINGO MARIA, Peru (AP)—A Peruvian Army helicopter crashed while spraying the herbicide Spike on cocaine fields in the upper Huallaga River Valley. The helicopter pilot, three Peruvian antinarcotics policemen, and an attaché from the United States Drug Enforcement Agency were killed.

An official at the American Embassy in Lima has confirmed that the helicopter crashed after being hit by a surface-to-air missile fired by Shining Path guerrillas. The Shining Path, a fanatical pro-Maoist guerrilla group, has protected coca growers from Peruvian and American military strikes in this coca-rich valley since the mid-1980s. It has been estimated that Peru contributes 75 percent of the world's coca leaf production and that 75 percent of Peru's overall production is grown in the upper Huallaga valley.

This helicopter was the third to be lost while attempting aerial application of Spike. The first crashed after being disabled by machine-gun fire in December, 1996. The second was destroyed by a SAM missile last March. DEA officials have conceded that the aerial herbicide program has been a failure.

In June, 1996, a combined force of coca growers, drug traffickers, and Shining Path guerrillas overran the highly fortified Santa Lucia base on the edge of the valley. This base, a combined effort of American and Peruvian antidrug forces, had been used as a

springboard for eradication efforts since 1989. Two
hundred people, including all 150 Peruvian and
American base personnel, were killed in that battle.
                                    —Newsday, 31 August 1998

IT WAS WORSE than Lance thought it ever could be.

It was like there were two people inside his head.
Just like the stories he used to see on video in Bible
school when he was a kid: a good angel and a bad devil
both talking to him, telling him what to do.

He knew that Carla Sue was bad, a temptress, evil.
He knew he should have nothing to do with her. But
he could not stay away. It was as if there was some
power in his body that moved him no matter what his
good angel told him.

Maybe I'm bewitched, Lance thought. Like Samson.

Talking with Freddy had been no help at all. Freddy
just laughed at his fears and told him, "Forget about
all that Sunday School crap, man! Nail her while she's
hot for you."

Each time he saw Carla Sue he meant to tell her that
he was finished with her; he wasn't going to touch her
or even talk to her again. Each time his resolve
disappeared in an explosion of animal lust.

Becky will never want me now. She'll know. She'll
sense it as soon as she sees me.

Still, he headed for Hab 1 the instant his shift was
finished, looking for Carla Sue. He knew that her shift
should be over, too. This time he would really tell her.
Definitely. As soon as he saw her he would end this
agony once and for all.

Kurt Jaeckle was in the corridor. Lance hung back,
watching. Jaeckle floated right to Carla Sue's door and
tapped gently on it. No response. He slid the door
open a crack. Lance started down the corridor toward
him, fuming to himself. He's not going to bother Carla

Sue again. Not ever. Jaeckle looked over his shoulder and saw Lance approaching.

Both men felt flustered. Lance stopped himself a few feet before Jaeckle, his face set in a hard frown.

The scientist backed away from her door a bit. "Um, do you know where Carla Sue might be?" he asked.

"No," said Lance.

"I received a message that she wanted to see me," Jaeckle said.

Lance did not reply. If Carla Sue wanted to see him she would do it in the Mars module, he thought.

"Well. Um, if you see her, would you tell her that I got her message and I'll be in my office in the Mars module. Please."

Lance nodded. Jaeckle pushed off the wall with one hand and headed down the corridor. Lance watched his small, red-suited form disappear through the far hatch.

Then he started after Jaeckle. Sure enough, the scientist headed down the central tunnel and into the Mars module. Lance followed behind him, then hesitated in the open hatchway.

Jaeckle must have sensed him. He turned, looking curious, concerned.

"Do you have official business in this module, crewman?" Jaeckle asked.

"No, sir," said Muncie. "I'm off duty now."

"Then I'm afraid I'll have to ask you to stay out of this module. Unless you have time reserved in the observation blister, of course."

"No, sir. Not at this hour."

"Then . . ." Jaeckle made a small shooing motion with both hands. The exertion moved him backwards, away from Lance.

"Yes, sir," said Lance. He turned and started back up the tunnel. But after only a few meters, Lance

grabbed a handhold and turned back again toward the
hatch.

Along the length of the Mars module's central
tunnel he could see Jaeckle swim past the door that
led to his office and head straight to the hatch of the
observation blister. He knocked sharply against the
metal hatch once and it was opened from inside. By a
woman. At this distance Lance could not be sure who
it was, but he was certain there was a woman in there
waiting for Jaeckle. Carla Sue.

There wasn't any message and he didn't go to his
office. He's in the blister with Carla Sue, Lance
realized, his insides flaming. She was *waiting* for him.

It unsettled Jaeckle to have the burly, sulky crewman
hanging around the hatch to the Mars module. I'll
have to speak to Tighe about this, he thought. We have
protocols. His people are not supposed to be in my
module.

He thought for a moment that he should have asked
the crewman why he was there. But Lorraine was
waiting for him in the observation blister and Muncie
looked too glowering, too bellicose, to speak to without an argument erupting. Tighe's probably sent him
in here on some pretext or other. I'll speak to the
commander about it. Later.

He rapped on the hatch and Lorraine swiftly
opened it for him. Putting on his highest-wattage
smile, Jaeckle entered the observation blister.

Lorraine was not smiling. She backed away from his
reaching arms.

"There's no easy way to say this, Kurt." Her voice
was tense, her hands knotted into tight little fists.

"To say what?" he asked, gliding toward her.

"We're finished," Lorraine blurted. "It's over."

Jaeckle felt his breath catch in his throat. Finished?
She's telling *me* it's over?

* * *

As she finally pushed herself away from the biochemistry bench, Carla Sue realized she was playing a losing game. Wearily she nodded farewell to the other late workers and headed back to her compartment in Hab 1. Even though she had spent two extra hours on the soil samples she could still find nothing to confirm Russ Cramer's supposed discovery.

Worse than that, she was no closer to her goal of penetrating the arrogant, self-absorbed psyche that encased Kurt Jaeckle like a suit of armor than she had been when she first tried to seduce Lance Muncie. Her failure was not for lack of effort. She had spent every possible minute of the last three days in Lance's dubious company. They ate meals together, exercised in tandem, and spent a well-advertised double session in the observation blister.

The rumor mill, which Carla Sue knew to be more efficient than the station's computer system, seized on this morsel of gossip with its usual speed. Her fellow Martians whistled when she floated to the biochemistry workstation in the Mars module. Trikon techs smirked when they passed her in the connecting tunnel. Freddy Aviles peered out of the labyrinth of cylinders in the logistics module and flashed a smile dripping with forbidden knowledge.

Everyone on the station noticed—except Kurt Jaeckle.

Carla Sue's resolve was beginning to ebb. Her choice of Lance seemed more blunder than brilliance. There was something weird about Lance Muncie. It was as if there were actually two of him: he was awkward, reticent, almost afraid to be alone with her—until she touched his body. Anywhere. Then he exploded in a passion of animal fury that left her gasping and a little frightened. Lance was a big guy; when he threw away his self-control he could hurt you.

Other than those wild bursts of ardor he was as dull as a wheat field. No, not dull, exactly. No matter how boring his conversation, or lack of it, there was always something lurking just beneath the surface—something scary.

I've created a Frankenstein, Carla Sue said to herself, trying to make light of her predicament. But then she thought of how Kurt must be laughing at her behind her back. *That* she could not tolerate.

Carla Sue finally reached her compartment. She slipped inside, but kept the door open a crack to peer down toward the aft end of Hab 1. Kurt Jaeckle would be coming down this way, heading for his own compartment. Carla Sue hoped he had nothing important planned for the rest of the day. She didn't expect he would be able to concentrate once she finished with him.

Within minutes Jaeckle floated into view. Carla Sue pulled back her door. "Oh, there you are, Kurt."

"Hello, Carla Sue," he replied. He trailed his fingertips along the opposite door as if wondering whether he should stop. "I understand you want to see me."

"I certainly do."

"Well, I'm on my way back to the module," he said.

"This'll only take a minute."

Jaeckle eyed her up and down, then looked past her as if suspicious of her intentions, wondering if she had already found out that his affair with Lorraine was finished. She was fully clothed and her compartment appeared to be in order. Satisfied that she was not bent on seduction, he decided to grant her a minute, no more. He turned his body to face her wide-open door, and pushed himself inside.

Carla Sue closed the door behind him. She switched on the viewscreen and turned up the stereo. Snow swirled on a New England countryside to the strains of Leroy Anderson's "Sleighride."

Jaeckle frowned with sudden suspicion. "Why do we need music?" he asked.

"You'll understand the reason," said Carla Sue. "I wanted to talk to you about LaVerne Nelson."

"Who the hell's that?"

"LaVerne Nelson was your housekeeper during your first marriage," said Carla Sue. "I've been in contact with her. Not directly, through a private investigator. I know all about her role in your divorce proceedings."

Jaeckle blinked several times, rapidly. Then he reached over and turned up the volume of the stereo.

"LaVerne Nelson is a pathological liar," he said, leaning closer to Carla Sue to be heard over the cheerful music. "I fired her for stealing."

"I don't doubt that's true, Kurt. But there is the small matter of the deposition she gave before you and your first wife decided to settle your differences out of court."

"A deposition by a liar and a thief is not the most believable document in the world," said Jaeckle. His lower lip quivered slightly. "Besides, that deposition is sealed by court order. I insisted on it."

"Well, my investigator tells me that LaVerne's memory is still very fresh. And she's still in need of a few dollars."

"Carla Sue, this is a poor way of getting attention."

"I don't want your attention, Kurt. I decided that long ago. I just don't want you to forget me."

"Forget you?" he said, summoning a smarmy smile onto his face. "How can I forget the times we had? The Cape. Do you think I could forget the time we—"

"You fool!" Carla Sue snapped. "I don't give a damn about that sentimental guff. I want you to remember me when it comes to Mars."

Carla Sue knew that Jaeckle regarded himself as the sole deed holder to Mars. Everyone else, even his colleagues in the Mars project, were squatters. Her statement had the desired effect: Jaeckle's phony warmth was transmuted to a more authentic iciness.

"What do you mean?" he asked, like a professor quizzing a student.

"I want to take over Russ Cramer's position, now that he's gone. And when it comes time to pick the team for the first mission to Mars, I want to be the chief biochemist."

Jaeckle had been unconsciously backing away from her. He thumped against the closed door; he could retreat no further.

"The standards for the real Mars crew will be very high," he said, trying to regain his dignity.

"No they won't, and you damn well know it," said Carla Sue. "They'll be just as cockamamy as they were for this project. Carla Sue Gamble in space? You thought that was funny at first, didn't you? But I'm here. And now that I've come this far I'm going all the way."

"Your work will have to . . ."

"Never mind my work! It's good enough, we both know that. I want to be on the first team and you're going to make damned certain that I am."

"Carla, I won't have the power to select the actual Mars team."

"You know, you're probably right," said Carla Sue. "You won't have any power at all once people start seeing your face plastered over every supermarket checkout in the country. I don't think anyone would want a man who raped his own daughter to plant the flag on Mars."

Even though she was in her own compartment, Carla Sue realized she had just uttered the perfect exit line. Exaggerating a smile, she opened the door a tad and slipped out.

Jaeckle was too dumbfounded to follow. He stared blankly at the video screen and replayed the conversation over and over again in his mind, oblivious to the music and the images of evergreens laden with snow.

The stereo was playing "Rudolph the Red-Nosed Reindeer."

He unfurled a handkerchief from a shoulder pocket of his flight suit and mopped at the film of sweat oozing across his brow. A minute later, his brow still wet, he realized that he had twisted the handkerchief into a knotty coil.

Hovering in the shadows by the hatch to Hab 1, Lance felt his skin crawling with hatred. He had been right. For two hours he had waited here watching Carla Sue's compartment. Ever since he had seen Jaeckle go into the observation blister.

I was right, he kept repeating to himself. First they spend two hours in the blister and then they come straight back here to her compartment. They think they're pretty smart, coming back separately. But they're not smart enough to fool me.

Lance edged closer to Carla Sue's compartment, his insides blazing. He saw that the accordion door was tightly sealed. Music played inside. Christmas music!

Something—someone—thumped against the door. Lance remembered Freddy's comment the first time they had seen the observation blister: Newton's Law.

Lance felt a surge of nausea as he hung in the aisle. A chill spread out from his spine. His mouth filled with bile. He thought first of the Hab 1 Whits; they were only a few feet away. But he wanted to be out of this module, as far away as possible from Kurt Jaeckle and Carla Sue Gamble and whatever was going on behind that door. So he bolted and threw up his guts in the Whit of Hab 2.

Dan Tighe ate alone at a table in the rear of the wardroom. As was his custom, he divided his attention equally between the food tenuously adhering to his tray and the people occupying the other tables. He was particularly interested in Aaron Weiss. The reporter had not developed into the pain in the ass Dan had expected. Except for the incident with Hugh O'Donnell, the only complaint had been from Jaeckle, who was insulted by Weiss's lack of interest in the Mars Project.

Weiss was sharing a table with Stu Roberts on the far side of the wardroom. Roberts's bony Adam's apple was in constant motion, either from slurping his food or from whining about long-forgotten rock stars. Weiss looked as bored as a gelding at a stud farm, thought Dan with an amusement he barely could contain. If Weiss spends much more time with Roberts, he'll beg to return Earthside. Not a bad idea. Maybe I should assign Roberts to escort him wherever he goes.

Jaeckle, Ramsanjawi, Oyamo, and Bianco ringed another table. A formidable quartet. Jaeckle orated, Ramsanjawi snickered, Oyamo listened politely, and Bianco drank it all in with a twinkle in his dark eyes. Good thing we're in micro-gee, thought Dan. Otherwise the table might collapse from the combined weight of their egos.

Funny the way Bianco's adapted to microgravity, Dan thought. Trikon's Earth-bound medics had sent a long worried report about the old man's ailments and medication needs. Yet since the moment he had come aboard the station Bianco had seemed strong, alert, healthier than some of the scientists half his age. Maybe it's poetic justice, Dan said to himself. Bianco created this station; it's treating him kindly. It's as if he was always meant to be here.

Freddy Aviles was alone at an adjacent table. There was no sign of Lance Muncie or Carla Sue Gamble. More precisely, Lance Muncie *and* Carla Sue Gamble. Word was that the two towheads had fallen for each other.

O'Donnell sailed into the wardroom. He hastily

prepared a tray at one of the galleys and joined Dan at his table. Dan had read Lorraine Renoir's report on O'Donnell's latest blood test. Negative. Dan felt relieved. Still, he found himself scrutinizing every movement of O'Donnell's hands and analyzing every word of small talk.

"No darts tonight," said O'Donnell.

"Work?"

"Yeah. I need to log more lab time."

"Problems?"

"A few unexpected snags."

"Sometimes it's a good idea to step back when you've run into a wall," said Dan. "Makes it easier to find your way round it."

"I'm sure you're right," O'Donnell said. "Sometimes."

There was a general shift in the wardroom crowd. Stu Roberts finished eating, to Aaron Weiss's obvious relief. Oyamo rose from his foot loops, executed his patented micro-gee bow to each of his three dinner companions, then propelled himself toward the hatchway. Freddy Aviles checked his watch as if waiting for a train that was long overdue. After another minute, he departed as well. Three Japanese techs settled at a table adjacent to Weiss. They grinned at the reporter and he grinned back. Ramsanjawi and Bianco fell into a deep conversation that excluded Jaeckle and attracted the attention of Weiss from the far side of the room. The reporter stared at the scientists as if hoping to provoke an invitation to join them. Instead, Jaeckle moved across to Weiss's table and started talking to him earnestly, urgently. Weiss stood it for a few minutes, then abruptly pushed himself away from the table and left the wardroom. Jaeckle glared after him.

In the midst of all the movement of bodies and clanging of trays, Lance entered the wardroom. His flight suit was askew and his hair was mussed as if he had just got out of bed. His skin was as pale as it had been his first day on board. But Dan paid less attention to these details than to the simple fact that Lance was alone. He looked at O'Donnell and mouthed the name Carla Sue. O'Donnell shrugged as if to say, Search me.

Lance hung in front of a galley for a full minute before attempting to remove a tray from the magnetized stack in the cabinet. He seemed to grab blindly at the first packets of food that his hands could reach, then stuffed them into the nearest microwave unit. He fumbled with the hot water jet, then missed his cup entirely and sent bubbles of scalding water spraying everywhere. All the while he kept glancing nervously in the direction of the entry hatch.

The bubbles of water floated up toward the overhead ventilator grill. The microwave pinged. Lance attached the meal to his tray and pushed himself away from the galley, still looking over his shoulder toward the hatch. There was one empty table and two others occupied by single people. But Lance chose the last available spot at the table with the three Japanese.

"You see what I see?" muttered Dan.

"Carla Sue's dumped him?" said O'Donnell.

"I'd bet on it."

"Do you think he realized she's a shark?"

"That doesn't take a hell of a lot of insight," Dan said.

"It might for someone like Lance," said O'Donnell.

Lance ate quickly and not very cleanly. The Japanese scrupulously ignored the fine spray of crumbs and gravy spiraling from Lance's tray to the table vent. Lance suddenly grabbed the edge of the table. His stomach heaved and his cheeks puffed out like the throat of a bullfrog. He shot upwards, banged his head on the ceiling, then dove out the hatch.

"Young love gone bad." Hugh shook his head sadly.

"What the hell," said Dan. "Saves me from giving him some fatherly advice."

Lance managed to keep his stomach under control long enough to reach the Whit in Hab 2, where he heaved a yellow-brown ball of gravy, bread, and bile into an airsick bag. This was his third attack since seeing Carla Sue and Jaeckle together. He wiped his face with a moist towelette and stared into a mirror. His normally cream-smooth skin was splotched and seamed like the surface of the moon.

When Lance exited the Whit, he found Lorraine Renoir waiting for him. He felt an immediate flash of anger.

"Commander Tighe sent you, right?"

"Actually not, Lance. I saw you rush in here. Are you okay?"

"No I'm not okay. I just puked like crazy."

Lorraine reached out her hand to touch his shoulder, but he spun away. His arm slammed against the door of the Whit. The bang echoed throughout the module.

"Perhaps I should examine you," she said.

Oddly, the impact calmed Lance. He was still angry at Dr. Renoir for meddling with his pain, but he found that stifling his anger was easier than swallowing back his dinner.

Lorraine brought him to her infirmary and told him to remove his shirt. His stomach, chest, and arms seemed terribly lean, as if he hadn't eaten for a week instead of merely a day. Lorraine listened to his heart and took his blood pressure and stuck the end of a digitalized thermometer into his mouth.

"I believe you have a virus," she announced.

Lance wanted to scream. He wanted to shout that he didn't have a virus at all, that if anything he was heartsick at the thought of that bitch-woman Carla Sue lying to him, using him, and then betraying him.

He was sick at the thought that right now she was with
Jaeckle in her compartment, doing all the things she
had done with him, that she had promised she would
do with nobody else but him. What right did she have
to draw him in, to use her body, to say the things she
said? Didn't words mean anything? Didn't lovemaking mean anything?

But Lance kept quiet, partly because he didn't want
to call attention to his shame, mostly because he
remembered Russell Cramer bellowing in the Mars
module. He knew that if he said one word about Carla
Sue, he would not be able to stop. He accepted a
package of breath mints from Lorraine and nodded
meekly at her admonition to stay in his compartment
and drink plenty of liquids.

Lance slowly made his way back to Hab 2. Airsick
bags billowed from his belt like animal pelts. People in
the connecting tunnel stared at him with faces that
looked like images in carnival mirrors. Lance felt
another surge of anger, this time at the thought that
everyone knew the real reason for his sickness. He
crossed one arm over his stomach, tucked his chin
against his chest, and pulled himself toward home
with one hand.

Once inside his compartment, something stronger
and more bilious than undigested food rose from his
stomach to his throat. He punched his head into the
sleep restraint.

"Bitch! You goddamned lying bitch!" he muttered
into his dark cocoon.

He called her every filthy word he knew; every
damning curse he had ever heard he spoke in the
darkness, his voice murderously low, intoning anathe-
ma on Carla Sue like an ancient priest casting out a
traitress, a villainess, a carrier of loathsome disease.
He kept up his deadly chant until, exhausted, he fell
asleep.

* * *

O'Donnell took Dan's dinnertime suggestion to heart. But rather than return to the ex/rec area for a game of darts, he wandered into the Mars module. The observation blister was empty.

He had spent little time in the blister. The long hours he logged in his lab were more than enough solitude. On the few occasions he had signed up for R and R, he found the view to be overwhelming. He had heard about "second sight," the unexplained ability of astronauts to discern increasingly minute surface features with the unaided eye, but he had not detected any improvement in his visual acuity. In fact, he rarely knew what the hell was down below. The real world did not display political boundaries and neatly lettered names trailing away from perfectly circular cities. But on this evening he knew exactly where he was: three hundred miles above the Andes, whose spiny backs looked razor sharp beneath the broken cloud cover.

One of those valleys corkscrewing through the green was the Huallaga, the coca-producing capital of the world. He remembered the short days and endless nights of his own addiction. He would read of the DEA or the border patrol seizing tons upon tons of cocaine discovered in safe houses or barns. The law of supply and demand should have pushed the street price upward after such massive seizures. But the price never rose; sometimes it even declined. Were the drug kingpins dumb? Did they fail to notice that oil companies routinely used the news of even a minor spill as a pretext for jacking up prices? No, O'Donnell finally had realized. There was so much shit around that a twenty-ton seizure was as annoying as a fly alighting on the back of a bull.

The Andes slipped below the edge of the wide window, their spines deepening in the dying sunlight. O'Donnell activated the control that closed the clamshell. The session in the blister had not lit a path around the wall that suddenly had sprung up in front of him. But he felt strong enough to resume bashing his head.

O'Donnell headed toward the lab by way of Hab 2. The turkey he had eaten for dinner had been tough and stringy. He could feel the strands between his teeth.

He anchored himself in front of a hand basin and worked his toothbrush over his teeth and gums. The toothpaste had a slightly milky taste and seemed grittier than usual, but he didn't mind. The grittier the paste, the cleaner his teeth. He rinsed his mouth with a jet of water that he spit into the vacuum vent of the basin. He was ready to attack his lab.

A strange sensation coursed through his body. The air around him suddenly thickened to the consistency of gelatin. His legs went numb. His arms filled with sawdust. The aisle tilted upward.

By the time he reached his compartment, he felt as if a helmet had closed over his head. His vision diminished to a pair of blurry pinholes swimming in a sea of purple. He groped for the door latch and tumbled inside, crashing into the far wall with enough force to cause pain. But the impact of the metal on the base of his neck felt like a punch through a pillow. The toothpaste and brush bounced out of his numb hand, whirling in the suddenly dazzling light from the passageway outside his compartment. The light was so bright that it hurt his eyes. He pawed at the door until it somehow closed.

In a detached way he knew what had happened. Someone had slipped him some shit. Powerful shit, and a lot of it. He tensed his muscles, gulped air into his lungs, tried to keep those two blurry pinholes from dissolving into the purple.

But it felt so good. So damned good. Why fight it? Fuck the lab, he thought. So what if I lose a day. So what if I miss the deadline. I've worked hard. So very very hard. I need to rest.

The words seeped slowly through his brain, like heavy oil through a ton of cat litter. They stretched like long, never-ending strands of taffy. All he wanted was to drift . . . and drift . . . and . . . drift . . .

The sound of laughter awoke Lance. He could not tell if it had been in a dream or real. His eyes snapped wide open in the darkness. His compartment felt like the inside of a coffin, too confined, too close to the other people who shared Hab 2. He heard conversations, laughter, music. He knew that if he could find a quiet place away from everyone else, he would feel much better.

He eased himself into the aisle, still in his sleep-rumpled coveralls. At the aft end of the module, two Japanese techs spoke quietly as they waited to use the Whits. He did not return their waves.

The connecting tunnel was in its nighttime lighting mode. Circles of light played out from the hab and command modules. Lockers and compartments cast jagged shadows. Lance wanted to find the most secluded area of the station. He glanced at his wristwatch: 2107 hours. The ex/rec area usually was occupied well past midnight. The rumpus room was usually lit regardless of the hour. And the Mars module definitely was out of the question.

His eye caught a flash of movement. A lanky figure topped by a head of blond hair knifed through the alternating bands of light and shadow from the vicinity of the Mars module. Lance shuddered. She was coming. Carla Sue was coming. A thousand thoughts raced through his head, everything from tearful forgiveness to unbridled rage.

But Carla Sue proved to be a trick of the eye and the heart. As the figure moved closer, it resolved into one of the European techs. He waved cheerfully at Lance before turning into Hab 1.

Lance shoved off toward the labs. Jasmine was lit and occupied as usual, but both ELM and The Bakery were dark and empty. He decided on ELM for a start. He groped his way down the aisle and tucked himself into a cubbyhole beneath a workstation. He kept his eyes trained on the hatch. Occasionally someone flitted past, but no one entered. ELM was far more quiet than Hab 2, and for the first time since that afternoon he felt relaxed.

But he could not keep Carla Sue out of his mind. Eventually they would meet; the station was just too small. Scenarios played before his eyes like waking dreams. In each, he was a gallant warrior and she was a weak woman begging for forgiveness. His hair streamed in the wind and his narrowed eyes were fixed on a distant horizon while she clung to him from behind, weeping and bussing his shoulders with kisses.

2 SEPTEMBER 1998
TRIKON STATION

CYSTIC FIBROSIS CORRECTED IN LAB

Two teams of investigators have used gene transfer to correct the cystic fibrosis defect in cells in culture, opening the door, at least a crack, for gene therapy.

"We are talking about years, not decades any longer," said a clearly elated Robert Bealle, vice president and medical director of the Cystic Fibrosis Foundation. "We hope this will move CF up the list of diseases that are candidates for gene therapy." Cystic fibrosis is the most common fatal genetic disease in North America.

—Science, 28 September 1990

WHEN AARON WEISS returned to his compartment after dinner, he found an envelope containing a note and a small power-driven screwdriver. The note instructed him to remain in his compartment until 2345 hours. If he had not received any further instructions in the meantime, he could proceed with the plan. O'Donnell's absence was guaranteed; but if anyone else wandered into the vicinity, he must refrain from entering the lab. The screwdriver was needed to remove the door hinges; it would be cleaner than fooling with the padlock. He also was to destroy the note.

As Weiss waited for the further instructions that

never came, he entered every fact he could muster into his laptop computer. Then he ran a program popular among investigative reporters. The computer played out a series of hypotheses in flowchart fashion. But each hypothesis found a dead end. Question marks filled the screen. The cursor blinked maddeningly as if unsure where to go.

He didn't need the goddamn program to tell him there was an unknown, an x factor, something other than Fabio Bianco's superbug waiting to be uncovered on this station. The plants in O'Donnell's lab were the first sign; Chakra Ramsanjawi's checkered past the second. The connection between these two men will be very interesting, Weiss thought as he closed the laptop. Very interesting indeed.

At 2340 hours, someone rapped on the compartment bulkhead. Despite himself, Weiss jerked with surprise and a little fear. Something's gone wrong, he thought. His first instinct was to hide the screwdriver. Looking rapidly around the narrow compartment, he shoved it into the belt of his jeans. Then he slid the door open.

Kurt Jaeckle floated obliquely in the aisle. Weiss felt a rush of relief, then hostility. Before Jaeckle could say a word, Weiss snapped: "Look, I told you in the wardroom, I'm not interested in Mars."

"But I have a story that will make you famous," Jaeckle said.

"Stories don't make me famous."

"This one will." Jaeckle shouldered his way into the compartment. "Some weeks ago one of my scientists discovered signs of life in a Martian soil sample."

"How interesting," said Weiss. He checked his watch. Four minutes.

"Didn't you hear me? Life! On Mars!"

"I heard you."

"The story is yours, exclusively, if you'll feature the Mars Project."

"I don't have time," said Weiss.

"Look, I'll be candid with you." Jaeckle anchored himself in the doorway. "My man's finding was very tenuous—too tenuous to report through the usual scientific channels. But you could report it! You'll be the first man to break the story of life on Mars!"

Weiss could have barreled through Jaeckle's feeble blockade, but the scientist would have yapped at his heels all the way to The Bakery. It was time to play the trump card Zeke had dealt him. He opened the compartment's desktop and unfastened a tape recorder from its Velcro stay.

"All right," he said, starting the tape. "I'm here on Trikon Station speaking to the man many believe will lead the first human expedition to Mars."

Jaeckle arranged himself as if posing for a camera.

"Dr. Jaeckle," continued Weiss, "what benefits would an expedition to Mars offer the man in the street?"

Jaeckle blinked once, as if he had not expected exactly that question, but he immediately launched into his reply, "Economic reasons leap to mind first." His voice resonated in the tiny compartment. "The project itself will employ hundreds of thousands of people. There are also scientific reasons. We can learn much about our own planet by studying the geological and meteorological history of Mars. Then there are the intangibles, the idea that mankind has spread its seed to another planet. And—"

"Interesting image," said Weiss, cutting Jaeckle off before the scientist became too wound up in his own oratory. "What about the idea that Mars may be a penal colony, like Australia was centuries ago."

Jaeckle was not flustered. "Well, of course, there are societal aspects—"

"I'm talking specifically about a penal colony for perverts and sociopaths. For men accused of having incestuous relations with their daughters?"

Jaeckle's sunny smile turned to a trembling, white-faced mask of hatred.

"So she got to you, huh? The bitch already got to you."

He pulled himself into the aisle and sailed away.

"Au revoir, Kurt Jaeckle," muttered Weiss. He still had two minutes to spare.

At precisely 2345 hours, Weiss left his compartment. Hab 2 was silent except for the hiss of a full-body shower. The screwdriver was still tucked into the belt of his jeans, and he held the Minicam with one hand to prevent it from banging against the lip of the entry hatch.

Shadows ribbed the pastel-green walls of the connecting tunnel. Weiss shot himself to the hatch of The Bakery. No one was in sight. The only sounds were the whoosh of the ventilator and the occasional groan of the module's skin stretching in the sunlit void of space.

Weiss pulled himself through the hatch. His heart thumped at the base of his throat and he steadied himself in the corner opposite O'Donnell's lab until his anxiety passed. The hinges were each held to the door frame by two screws. Their rounded edges reflected tiny beams of light filtering in from the tunnel.

Enough time had passed for anyone who might have seen him enter The Bakery to follow him inside. Weiss opened a button and wedged the Minicam beneath his shirt. Then he worked the screwdriver out of his belt. Cupping it to his chest, he gave the tool a burst of power. The blade spun slowly and silently.

And Weiss spun in the opposite direction, just as slowly and silently, until he whacked the ceiling with his hip. He stifled a string of curses as he realized that, in micro-gee, he who is not firmly anchored by foot loops will be spun by a power screwdriver while the screw remains stubbornly unmoved.

Grumbling under his teeth, Weiss straightened himself out and started to slide his feet into the nearest floor loops. Then the module groaned, and once again his heart rushed to a gallop. He pushed himself into the corner formed by the lab and the forward bulkhead, his eyes fixed intently on the entry hatch. He remained frozen until he was certain no one was coming. Listening carefully to the groans and whooshes, he familiarized himself with the harmless sounds and hoped he would hear nothing else. Slowly, he rotated himself into position at the lower hinge. He wormed his stockinged feet firmly into the nearest loops. He had to lean forward and sideways quite a bit to fit the screwdriver's blade into the notch of a screw. He applied power. The screwdriver's blade danced across the door with a series of agonizingly loud scratches.

Weiss gathered himself into the corner again. He had performed several routine micro-gee tasks since boarding the station, but had not imagined loosening four screws could be a major project. The problem suddenly seemed obvious: the screwdriver imparted its torque to the object providing the least resistance.

Weiss cast a quick glance out the hatch before resuming. The connecting tunnel was still empty. He returned to the hinge, anchored himself in the loops, and this time braced himself with his back against the forward bulkhead. He applied a shot of power; the screw turned slightly. Aha! He adjusted himself for leverage and shot again. The screw rose out of its hole. Worried that it would fly free, he performed the last few turns with his thumb and forefinger, then discovered that the screw was tethered to the hinge by a fine plastic wire that revealed itself only on the very last turn. These astronauts thought of everything.

The second screw came out quickly. He pulled the hinge away from the frame, leaving its other half still attached to the accordion door itself.

The loose hinge allowed some play in the door. Weiss pulled it back enough to see inside. The leaves of the plants floated in the strong beams of the lamps. Some of the leaves were shiny, almost waxy; others were curled, drooping, their edges brown.

He went to work on the top hinge. As he removed the first screw, he thought he heard a sound in the back of the module. Dismissing it as the groaning of The Bakery's walls, he turned his attention to the last screw. The blade of his screwdriver never reached the slot.

The blow to his neck hurt for only an instant. In the split second before darkness fell, the chemicals of his brain formed an illogical memory. He was a boy, climbing a tree toward a nest that held three blue robin's eggs. As he reached out his hand, the branch beneath him snapped.

3 SEPTEMBER 1998
TRIKON STATION

WASHINGTON, D.C. (UPI)—Democrats in Congress garnered enough votes last night to override a Presidential veto of the controversial foreign aid bill. The bill, as originally submitted to the President, indefinitely suspended all foreign aid to Bolivia, based on its failure to eradicate 100 million acres of coca-producing fields in 1997.

Aid to Bolivia reached a high point of $200 million in 1993. Virtually half of the aid went to equipment and training for security forces and cash subsidies for farmers. Farmers received onetime payments of $2,000 for every 2.47 acres on which coca plants had been eliminated. Continuation of the aid in subsequent years was conditioned upon the Bolivian government certifying that acreage quotas had been met.

Earlier this year, the DEA reported widespread fraud in the subsidy program. Farmers reportedly pocketed the subsidies, then returned their acreage to coca production with the complicity of local officials.

In 1995, Bolivia ranked second to Peru in world coca production. It has been estimated that production in 1995 yielded $2 billion, one-quarter of which circulated the country in the form of hard currency. National foreign-exchange earnings for the same year totalled $500 million.

In vetoing the foreign aid bill, the President urged

*that suspending aid to Bolivia would be tantamount
to creating an official safe haven for international
drug traffickers. In pleading for the override, both the
Senate Majority Leader and the Speaker of the House
stated that the American public could no longer
afford to pay for another nation's corruption.*
          —*The Washington Post*, 2 September 1998

SLEEP CAME IN fits for Lance. Each time he awoke he
felt the pattering of his heart and sensed with animal
certainty that something evil was pursuing him. He
tacked about from module to module like an animated chess piece. His thoughts, even when he was
certain he was awake, were as disjointed as dreams.
He saw himself as a child, his head hanging in the
chipped enamel bedpan his mother kept under his
bed. He saw the toothy face of Dr. J. Edward
Moorhouse perched atop a pair of tiny shoulders,
his long arms sweeping down beneath the folds
of his purple robe, his scaly hands cold on Lance's
stomach.

"There is evil in this place," intoned Moorhouse.

He saw Becky on the moonlit porch on her farm-
house, her eyes closed, her lips slightly parted as her
face curved up toward his. Before their lips could
meet, a hand wrenched him away and cast him down
into a large enamel tub of putrid-smelling vomit. He
tried to pull himself out, but a horde of gnomes with
blistered skin fought him back with pitchforks.

"Man has tried to be God," gibbered Moorhouse
from afar. "But he has created devils."

Lance sloshed to the other side of the tub, his mouth
choking with the stink. The gnomes rushed to head
him off, stabbing at him with their pitchforks. Lance
grabbed one of the gnomes by the neck and squeezed
until he felt the tiny bones crumble between his hands.
He flung the limp body at the others and they retreated. Using every remaining ounce of his strength,

Lance vaulted over the side. He plummeted through a cold dark void. Above him, a tiny Trikon Station spun like a wobbly top between the huge eyes of Dr. J. Edward Moorhouse.

"The woman is weak, Lance. But you are strong. You are strong."

Lance awoke with a start. Gradually, he realized that he was in the logistics module, safely nested among empty science-supply canisters and secured by a sleep restraint jerry-rigged out of his belt and shirt. He fumbled for a breath mint. As it melted on his tongue, he released himself from the restraint and peered over the top of his nest. It was morning; the connecting tunnel was brightly lit through the entry hatch. He hastily donned his shirt and hitched his belt around his waist. Speed was all-important. He wanted to be well into the day's routine before anyone tried to talk to him. Freddy. Carla Sue. Commander Tighe. Anyone.

Lance started to disassemble his protective nest. As he pushed the canisters aside, one of the lids popped open. For a moment, the face that floated out seemed perfectly normal. The eyes were open and the lips were drawn back in a smile. It was only when he saw the purplish indentation on the side of Aaron Weiss's neck that reality set in.

Lance tilted his head back to scream. All that came out was a torrent of bile.

Freddy Aviles guarded the entry hatch. The Aussie crewman Stanley carefully, almost gently, pulled the contorted body of Aaron Weiss from the aluminum canister into which it had been crammed. Lorraine Renoir hovered close by, dictating medical observations into a minicassette recorder.

"Let's have that again," Dan said to Lance. His face looked as grim as death itself.

"I was doing a routine inspection of the supply

cylinders," said Lance. "I had to move some canisters around. I accidentally bumped the latch and it opened."

"You were working at this hour?"

"I know, sir, it's early. I skipped breakfast. I haven't been very hungry lately."

"I see." Dan assumed that Carla Sue Gamble was the reason for Lance's loss of appetite. He made no comment. The affairs of his crewmen's hearts paled in comparison to the discovery of Weiss's body.

"All right, get this mess cleaned up."

Lance used a vacuum cleaner to suck up globules of bile that drifted around the module like tarnished Christmas ornaments. Meanwhile, Dan instructed Stanley to hold Weiss steady. As Lorraine continued her dictation, Dan eyeballed every inch of the body. Weiss was frozen in fetal position. One arm seemed to clutch the backs of his raised thighs, the other was drawn across the front of his shoulders like a movie Dracula tossing his cape. His neck was loose and his head bobbed with each inadvertent movement made by Stanley. The tweed hat remained attached to Weiss's ear by a single rubber band. The Minicam floated on its tether, still looped around the reporter's broken neck. Weiss had been wearing his denim shirt with the pearl buttons. There was a small tear in the chest, and near the tear a button was missing. A few threads were still in place. Lorraine concluded her monologue.

"Broken neck," she said in answer to Dan's unspoken request to translate her medical jargon. She shoved the recorder into her pocket.

"When did it happen?" said Dan.

"Very hard to tell. Blood doesn't pool in micro-gee, so I have to base an estimate on the rigidity of the body. I'd say no less than eight hours ago, but that's a gross estimate."

They both stared at the body. Dan thought of the

fight between O'Donnell and Weiss. He remembered O'Donnell's anxiety over his work the previous night. O'Donnell had skipped darts to spend time in his lab. Weiss was given to roaming the station at all hours. Dan tried to crowd the implications out of his mind.

"What now, Dan?" asked Lorraine. For the first time in what seemed to be several weeks she spoke to him without a trace of sarcasm in her voice.

"You and Lance get him into a body bag and stow it in the auxiliary airlock. Stanley, you take over for Freddy at the hatch. No one enters, no one asks questions, you don't know anything."

Dan exited the logistics module and signaled for Freddy to follow. As he flew toward the command module, he wondered if his orders had sounded as uncertain as he felt.

Once in his office, Dan inserted an encryption chip designated for operational emergencies into his comm console and called ground control in Houston. The accordion door to Dan's office was closed. Freddy Aviles hovered against it, his normally jolly face somber, his eyes flicking back and forth between his commander and the image of Tom Henderson on the monitor.

"We have a real problem up here, Tom," said Dan. "A fatality."

Henderson smiled crookedly, as if hoping Dan suddenly had developed a warped sense of humor and would follow up with a punch line.

"Aaron Weiss, the CNN reporter," continued Dan. "Looks like a broken neck."

"Jesus Christ," said Henderson. "How did it happen?"

"It wasn't any damned accident. One of my men found him stuffed in an empty canister in the logistics module. Been dead about eight hours."

Henderson let out a long whistle. "What are you going to do? The shuttle—"

"I don't know what the hell I'm going to do! We don't have a goddamn protocol for murder on an orbiting facility!"

"Easy, Dan," said Henderson. "Let me get some people over here."

Henderson disappeared from his console. Dan took a deep breath and looked at Freddy.

"They on the ground, man," said Freddy. "They don' know nothing."

Dan nodded in agreement. That was the problem. People on the ground thought like people on the ground. No matter how much they claimed to understand, they didn't realize that simply being in orbit— confined, weightless, entirely dependent upon a fragile web of technology to keep you alive—automatically transformed every facet of existence into an abnormal environment. Now the station was faced with the worst possible scenario: an abnormal situation in an abnormal environment.

Tom Henderson returned to his console. Several other people stood behind him, some in shirtsleeves, others in suits. All wore headsets with tiny microphones in front of their mouths.

"I have some people here," began Henderson.

"Listen, Tom," said Dan. "I know you can't get a shuttle here anytime soon."

"Or an aerospace plane, either," said Henderson. "They—"

"Doesn't matter. But you still can help me. I'm going to cut off all comm links between us and the ground." Dan shot a glance at Freddy as if to say that he was the person who would actually effect the blackout. "Make up some bullshit as a cover. Tell 'em we've had another goddamn power-down. That'll give you time to contrive some sort of story about Weiss's death. Don't say it was a murder. Not yet, anyway."

"What are you going to do?" asked Henderson, running a nervous hand over his bald pate.

"Try to find out who did it."

Henderson's response was interrupted by one of the men standing behind him. He spoke with the man briefly, then returned his attention to Dan.

"What have you done with the body?" he asked.

"It's in a body bag," said Dan. "I'm going to stick it in the auxiliary airlock."

The man behind Henderson leaned down into the screen. He looked like a lawyer-type in a baggy gray suit.

"I don't think that is a proper method of preservation," said the man as he adjusted his horn-rimmed glasses. "The authorities will want to inspect all evidence, including the body."

"Quigley is right, Dan," said Henderson. "You should try to preserve the body somehow. Maybe refrigerate it."

"Tom, you know how we're equipped up here. Do you think we have a walk-in freezer?"

Freddy chuckled.

"You could put the body in an EMU," said Henderson. "The air conditioner will help it keep better."

"I don't believe this," muttered Dan. Then he said to Henderson: "I may need all my suits."

"Are you expecting trouble?" said Henderson.

"I have a murderer on board! Does that sound like trouble to you?"

Quigley started to protest, but Henderson pushed him out of the screen.

"Okay, Dan, it's your ball game," said Henderson.

"The auxiliary airlock's in shadow almost all the time," Dan said. "We can keep the outer hatch open, so it stays in vacuum. That ought to be as good as a refrigerator. Maybe better."

Quigley looked skeptical. Henderson said, "I hope you know what you're doing, Dan."

"I'm the only one who can do anything, Tom. We're going to blackout in five minutes. I'll talk to you as soon as I know something. Out."

Dan broke the link before Henderson could acknowledge.

"That was helpful," he said to himself, then turned to Freddy. "Five minutes enough time?"

"You got it, boss," said Freddy.

After Freddy reported that all the comm links between the station and Earth were shut down, Dan announced over the loudspeaker that an extremely dire emergency had arisen. All personnel, regardless of their current activities, were to assemble in the rumpus room immediately. He expected that everyone would comply; the heavy tone of his voice was obvious.

Five minutes later, Dan pulled himself into a rumpus room that seemed to have shrunk around the press of floating bodies. The Japanese contingent was neatly dressed and wide awake, hovering by the big centrifuge in order of their rank. The Americans, Canadians, and Europeans seemed to have been taken by surprise. Some obviously had been rousted out of their sleep. Bianco hovered up at the front in a pair of handsome red-and-gold silk pajamas.

Kurt Jaeckle and Thora Skillen accosted Dan and demanded to be told the nature of the emergency. Dan was preoccupied with taking a head count and suggested absently that they wait along with everyone else. When the two scientists pressed him, he nodded toward Freddy. The crewman sliced between Jaeckle and Skillen and placed his powerful hands on their shoulders.

"You listen to the man, eh?" he said.

Jaeckle and Skillen backed away, then sought out Bianco. The Italian listened to them and nodded, but made no move toward Dan. Yet their insistence had affected Dan. Most of the people on the station had been through the emergency power-down. Some had grumbled and some had complained, but most simply rode out the three hours of semidarkness. Today he had called them without explanation into the rumpus room. This mysterious emergency was not a power-down that would disappear after tinkering with the mainframe computer. He could not bring Aaron Weiss back to life.

Dan stopped counting heads. The people who were here deserved an immediate explanation. Then he would seek out any absentees.

"We have had a very serious and tragic incident," he said. "Aaron Weiss, the CNN reporter who has been visiting the station, is dead."

A current of shock coursed through the ranks. Dan could read it on their faces; stunned surprise that made eyes go wide and cheeks pale. He could hear it in the collective gasp of indrawn breath followed by the eerie silence that fell over the rumpus room. The silence deepened for a long moment. Everyone was shaken. Then a murmur rose as people whispered among themselves.

"The crew and I will be conducting an investigation until the authorities arrive," Dan said, silencing the whispers. "We intend to keep our interference with your science projects to a minimum, but we expect your full cooperation if and when it is requested."

Stanley, Muncie, and Lorraine entered the rumpus room. Lorraine's nod indicated that the body had been stowed in the auxiliary airlock.

Bianco drew himself to his full height and said in a voice powerful enough for everyone to hear, "I assure you, *Commandante,* that the entire Trikon scientific staff will cooperate with you in every way."

Dan nodded at the old man. "Thank you, sir." Then he stared pointedly at Jaeckle. The chief of the Martians made no such guarantee on behalf of his people. He seemed pale, shaken.

"All right, then," Dan said. "I am asking all of you

to remain here for a few minutes longer while I report to ground control." Dan ignored the rumble of protest, ordered Stanley and Muncie to prevent anyone from leaving the rumpus room, and waved for Freddy to follow him. He had completed his mental head count during his announcement. Seven people were missing. Six were the segregated Martians no one ever saw. The seventh was Hugh O'Donnell.

Freddy knew exactly whom they were looking for. "We split up. Compartment and lab. Is faster, eh?"

Dan agreed. Freddy volunteered for the compartment while Dan went for the lab. Dan hoped that O'Donnell was so engrossed in his work that he hadn't heard the announcement.

The Bakery was still in its nighttime lighting mode. A few lamps cast weak cones of light in the shadowy recesses of the module. Dan listened carefully for any sound in the darkness. None came. He pulled himself through the hatch and pressed the manual switch that operated the main column of overhead lights. The module was completely empty; the door to O'Donnell's lab was padlocked. Dan's stomach felt hollow with apprehension. Still, he let himself drift halfway down the aisle, then reversed direction. Before leaving for Hab 2, he took a close look at the lab door. There were two long scratch marks in the fiberglass surface adjacent to the lower hinge. The screws for that hinge seemed slightly raised as if they recently had been unseated. The screws for the upper hinge were flush.

Dan heard a metallic ping from somewhere near the floor. Instinctively, he focused on a ventilator intake and saw a shiny object adhered to the grid. Forcing himself down like a swimmer going for the bottom of the pool, he picked it off with his thumb and forefinger: a pearl button.

Dan's apprehension swelled. He tucked the button into a pocket and shot himself through the hatch. He

found Freddy in O'Donnell's compartment.
O'Donnell was in his sleep restraint. His eyes were
closed and Freddy was trying to awaken him.

"What's the problem?"

"Don' know. He won' wake up."

O'Donnell moaned softly. His eyelids fluttered. His
teeth were clenched down on his tongue, exposing a
portion that resembled dry leather.

"Get Lorraine on the double," said Dan. "Then
head over to the rumpus room. Those scientists will
be ready to riot before long."

As Freddy flew off, Dan hurried to the personal
hygiene facility and returned with a handful of
towelettes. He pressed O'Donnell's tongue back into
his mouth. O'Donnell gagged and sucked air. Dan
slapped his cheeks with the towelettes. O'Donnell
groaned.

"C'mon, buddy, wake up," said Dan. Then he
muttered to himself, "What the hell is going on?"

O'Donnell was still only semiconscious when Lorraine arrived. To facilitate the examination they removed him from the sleep restraint and splayed his
ankles and wrists to the walls with Velcro bracelets.

"Well?" said Dan, hovering just outside the door.

Lorraine turned off the penlight she had used to
examine O'Donnell's eyes.

"Mr. O'Donnell is suffering from intoxication,
most likely due to a narcotic drug." Her voice was flat,
professional. Yet Dan thought he detected a note of
disappointment, almost anger.

Dan's breath had been threatening to leave his body
ever since he first realized that O'Donnell had not
reported to the rumpus room. Now it escaped in a
rush.

"Are you sure?"

"Look, Dan, I know O'Donnell is your friend. I've
actually grown quite fond of him myself recently. But
by all outward signs, the causative factor is a drug. His

breathing and heart rates are low. His reactions are dulled. His speech, when he does speak, is slurred. There are no visible wounds on his body. And we're both aware of his history. The fact that he was found in his sleep restraint means that he probably ingested the drug just prior to retiring."

"Any idea when that may have been?"

Lorraine shook her head.

"But if it is a narcotic," said Dan, "wouldn't there be some sign?"

"Like needle tracks?" said Lorraine. "They aren't that obvious. Besides, there are other ways to ingest drugs."

She attached a needle to a syringe.

"What are you going to do?" said Dan.

"Give you the benefit of a doubt. I'll test his blood."

"How long will it take?"

"I'll have the results before he's fully awake."

Lorraine was better than her word. Within fifteen minutes she sailed through the hatch with tightened lips. Dan did not have to ask; he knew the results were positive.

"Three-methyl-fentanyl," she said.

"What the hell is that?"

"An analog of fentanyl, which is synthetic heroin. Far more potent and much longer lasting than the real stuff."

Dan gripped a handhold, as if he could draw strength from the frame of the station. The evidence that was quickly mounting against O'Donnell seemed overwhelming: the previous fight with Weiss, absence from the nightly game of darts, the missing button stuck to the ventilator grid outside the lab, O'Donnell's drugged condition. A logical conclusion was that O'Donnell had encountered Weiss at his lab—perhaps in the act of trying to gain entry— killed him during a struggle, hid the body, then concocted an alibi by filling himself with this 3-methyl-fentanyl crap. Or maybe he was already on the stuff when he ran into Weiss at his lab.

What did he really know about O'Donnell? Who knew what he was doing in his lab? He could have cooked up the drugs himself. Maybe he was some sort of special agent sent to test the effects of illicit drugs in space. After all, hadn't Russell Cramer's problems mushroomed once O'Donnell arrived?

Dan felt ensnarled in a web of uncertainties. Police detectives used this line of thinking. So did prosecutors, judges, and juries. Suddenly, he was all of them rolled up in one. And he hated it.

"Orders are he is to be sent Earthside," said Lorraine. "Even for a minor slip."

"I know, I know," snapped Dan. The problem was what to do in the meantime. "Get Freddy in here. And have him bring duct tape."

O'Donnell mumbled and moaned but did not break through into consciousness as Dan and Freddy bound his wrists and ankles with the duct tape. When they finished, Lorraine carefully fit a padded helmet onto O'Donnell's head. Dan and Freddy then maneuvered O'Donnell into the command module and tethered him to a handgrip outside Dan's office door. Lorraine closed herself into the infirmary to prepare a report.

"I need my comm link back," Dan said to Freddy. "Then stretch duct tape across Weiss's compartment, O'Donnell's compartment, and his lab. I don't want anyone tampering with anything inside."

It took Freddy less than two minutes inside the utilities section to reestablish a link with ground control. Then he flew off to follow the rest of Dan's instructions. Meanwhile, Dan called Tom Henderson.

"I didn't expect to hear from you so soon," said Henderson.

"Maybe I'm just damn lucky," Dan said sarcastically. He recognized Quigley and the other consultants milling behind Henderson. "I have a question for you, Tom. It isn't necessarily related to the murder. Okay? What's Hugh O'Donnell's business up here?"

"He's a Trikon scientist."

"Trikon may have sent him, but Trikon business isn't what he seems to be about," said Dan. "Unless Trikon's working with drugs."

"I wouldn't know."

"What about them?" said Dan, indicating the group behind Henderson.

"They don't know, either," said Henderson. "What the hell, you got a Trikon honcho on board. Ask him."

"I will," said Dan. "I have someone in custody who I believe may be Aaron Weiss's murderer."

"O'Donnell?"

"I said the question about O'Donnell wasn't related."

"Who is it?" said Henderson.

"I'm not going to tell you."

"What?!" Quigley's face appeared beside Henderson's. "You're not going to tell us? With all due respect, Commander Tighe, a murder in an orbiting facility is a complicated matter."

"Damned right it is."

"There are all types of considerations: political, international, diplomatic, not to mention legal and ethical."

"I know all that, goddammit! That's exactly why I'm not telling you."

"But the implications—"

"Look, Bigley or Quigley or whatever the hell your name is. The victim is an American, the suspect is an American, the death occurred in the American lab module, and the body was hidden in an American scientific-supply canister. It's an American problem, okay?"

Quigley's jaw hung slack.

"I want to talk to Tom," said Dan.

The lawyer's face slid from the screen.

"I hope you know what you're doing, Dan," said Henderson.

"I wish you'd stop saying that to me. I don't know what I'm doing, but I'm doing what I think is best for this station." Dan hoped no one overheard him. Admitting that he was treed could be a station commander's fatal mistake. "And that includes safeguarding all personnel, allowing them to continue with their work, and preserving evidence for the proper authorities. In that order. Now when can you get someone up here?"

"Days," said Henderson. "One aerospace plane is in for overhaul. The others are committed to a series of suborbital flights. That leaves *Constellation*."

"What about Trikon's retainer contract with NASA?"

"That only covers resupply emergencies. I could ask ESA about *Hermes*, but they've only had one orbital flight with the little bugger so far. I don't think we ought to risk a rendezvous with the station, even if the French would okay the mission. Besides, it would take weeks for them to make up their minds." Henderson spread his hands in a helpless gesture.

"Okay. Then here's what I'm going to do. I'm going to tell everyone on board that the investigation is over. They can go back to work. Did you announce Weiss's death yet?"

"Not yet. We haven't had time."

"Good. Don't mention it was murder. We'll let the investigators handle that whenever they get here. Meanwhile, I'm going to continue the blackout of all comm channels. You'll probably get complaints about that."

"We'll handle them," said Henderson. "What about your suspect?"

"I'll keep him segregated until your boys get here."

* * *

Freddy Aviles could hear angry voices erupting from the rumpus room as he flew down the connecting tunnel. He didn't know how long Tighe would talk to ground control and it was obvious that the scientists were on the verge of mutiny, despite Bianco's assurances. He had to work quickly.

His first stop was O'Donnell's compartment. Before entering, he snapped on a pair of latex gloves. He had searched the compartment on a few occasions and knew exactly how O'Donnell arranged his meager belongings. His movements were swift and sure. The search uncovered nothing that could even be adapted into drug paraphernalia. He latched the accordion door and stretched two strands of duct tape in a giant X across the frame.

Weiss's compartment, located a few doors down, took slightly longer to search. Time prevented Freddy from rifling all the storage compartments, so he concentrated on the laptop computer attached to the foldaway desk. He copied the entire contents of the hard disk onto a floppy. He would sort through the files later.

Freddy zoomed into The Bakery. He knew the exact nature of the work O'Donnell had been conducting in the tiny lab, and until this morning he had no reason to inspect the project for himself. It was now essential that he get inside. Bracing himself with one arm, he pressed his ear against the padlock and turned the four number circles. One by one, he heard the tumblers click into place. The lock sprang open.

Under perfect circumstances, Freddy would have taken samples from each of the vials that lined one wall. He would have taken clippings from each of the plants. Conditions were far less than perfect. He booted up O'Donnell's laptop and frantically scrolled through the directory. O'Donnell had created many files on the hard disk. Since few ran more than one or two kilobytes in length, Freddy assumed that each contained the structure of a different genetically engineered microbe.

Freddy inserted a floppy into the disk drive and copied all of O'Donnell's data. Then he crashed the system. No one else would ever see what O'Donnell had been doing.

3 SEPTEMBER 1998
TRIKON STATION

NEW DRUG APPEARS IN EUROPE
BUT NO ONE REMEMBERS USING IT

LONDON (Reuters)—Health officials and clinics in several large European cities have reported that a powerful new hallucinogen is gaining popularity among the avant-garde elements of the European drug culture. The new drug is called Lethe, after the mythological river whose waters induced amnesia. Not surprisingly, one of the side effects of the drug is loss of memory.

Little is known about the drug because few people seeking treatment have any recollection of ingesting it. Blood analyses of people exhibiting the symptoms of giddiness, depressed inhibitions, and memory loss suggest that it may have a methamphetamine base.

In the early 1980s, another drug with a methamphetamine base, Ecstasy, enjoyed widespread popularity in both the United States and Western Europe. Technically legal, it became the drug of choice in discos and nightclubs, where it was purchased and used openly. The drug's mild stimulant and hallucinogenic effects supposedly allowed users to function rationally while under its influence. In 1985, the United States classified Ecstasy as an illegal narcotic.

A similar fate may befall Lethe—if investigators can determine its chemical composition. Much of what is *currently known about the drug is anecdotal. Accounts of its use first appeared in an anonymous pamphlet in Basel, Switzerland, in the mid-1990s. Shortly thereafter, it was rumored to have surfaced in Amsterdam, Rotterdam, Paris, London, and Berlin.*

An Interpol source recently stated that Lethe definitely was a synthetic or "designer" drug and that it was being manufactured in a single laboratory. The source, however, declined further comment.

Meanwhile, the mythology of Lethe grows daily. A fortunate postscript to the story is that the drug's effects, though strange, are not particularly lethal.
—The Philadelphia Inquirer, 8 November 1997

DAN TIGHE ANNOUNCED over the intercom that all Trikon personnel and Martians were free to leave the rumpus room. Everyone quickly obliged. Most of them were still in the connecting tunnel when Dan and Freddy guided a groggy Hugh O'Donnell out of the command module.

Everyone stopped and flattened against the tunnel walls, staring. No one asked a question; no one spoke. Everyone was too unnerved by the sight of O'Donnell, trussed and helmeted, with his eyes rolled back in his head and his mouth trailing tendrils of drool.

"Aft bulkhead," said Dan as they squeezed through the entry hatch of the rumpus room. Lorraine Renoir and Lance Muncie, who had joined the procession along the way, followed them inside.

Dan secured his bonsai animals while Freddy hooked a strong arm around O'Donnell's waist. O'Donnell grimaced and groaned but did not break through into full consciousness until after he was tethered to the bulkhead.

". . . the hell . . ." he muttered. His gummy eyelids opened. "Dan . . . Doc . . . what the hell?"

"That's what we want to know," said Dan.

"Feel like shit." O'Donnell shook his head as if testing the limits of a headache. Then he realized that he was bound. "Why am I tied?"

"Aaron Weiss is dead," said Dan.

"Huh?"

"Murdered. A broken neck."

"What?"

"Outside your lab. Sometime around midnight."

"So what . . ." Realization flickered in O'Donnell's eyes. "Dan, you don't think—"

"Doesn't matter what I think. *Constellation* will be here in a few days with a team of investigators. They'll do the thinking."

"My job . . ."

"You're finished with it."

"But—"

"You did it too well, if you ask me."

"There is another factor," said Lorraine. "The fentanyl you ingested."

"Fentanyl? What?"

"No sense lying about it," said Dan. "We tested your blood. You had enough in you to send half the station into never-never land."

"But I didn't—"

"Save your breath," said Dan. "I've already made my decision. You're staying right here until *Constellation* arrives. Then the investigators will take over."

He spun away and motioned for Freddy and Lance to join him at the far end of the rumpus room. O'Donnell looked at Lorraine. Without his glasses, his eyes seemed small, watery, pleading for help. Lorraine bit her lip.

"You knew the rules," she said.

"Someone must have slipped it to me."

"You can't charm your way out of this one," she said. "Sorry, Hugh."

* * *

Like all the others, Fabio Bianco had been stunned by the announcement of Weiss's death. But when he saw the station commander towing Hugh O'Donnell, bound and unconscious, down the tunnel toward the rumpus room, Bianco immediately leaped to a conclusion: Weiss had been murdered and O'Donnell was suspected of being the killer.

Making his way slowly back to his own cubicle, Bianco played the evidence of his eyes over and over again in his mind. Weiss was too young and healthy to just suddenly die of natural causes. The reporter was not in the best of physical condition, true, but the flinty look on Commander Tighe's face clearly said that Weiss had been murdered. And O'Donnell was bound hand and foot, like Samson taken by the Philistines.

Murder. Aboard Trikon Station. Murder in this haven of peace and scientific research. I created an Eden for them and they have fouled it with the most heinous crime imaginable. Murder. Here. On *my* station.

By the time Bianco reached his compartment he could hardly see for the tears that filled his eyes.

Chakra Ramsanjawi gazed down the length of ELM through the open door of his office. There was little activity in the module. Scientists and technicians occupied the various workstations, but no one was doing anything constructive. Some stared at blank computer monitors or at racks of colored vials. Others whispered to each other. Death is like that, thought Ramsanjawi. It sobers people quickly.

The death had sobered Ramsanjawi himself, though not in so philosophical a manner. He was scheduled to report to Sir Derek, and for the second consecutive time he had no data to send. The pace of research had not merely been choked off to a trickle; it had screeched to a halt. He had hoped Aaron Weiss would discover something significant, perhaps a cache of data that O'Donnell had been hiding. Now he had nothing, not even Weiss. And every possible avenue of espionage had been sealed by Tighe.

Ramsanjawi removed a tiny booklet from its hiding place at the rear of a storage compartment. The booklet contained the code Sir Derek had devised. He placed it under his *kurta*, then looped a leather belt around his waist. Ramsanjawi swam through ELM without acknowledging any of his underlings. The two public telephones in the command module were unoccupied. Ramsanjawi sealed himself into one of the booths and unhooked the sleek handset from the wall. It was dead. He tried the handset in the other booth. That one was dead as well. He poked his head out the door. The only person in sight was the doctor, Lorraine Renoir, who was just exiting her office.

"These telephones are not operating," he said.

"All the comm links are blacked out until further notice," said Lorraine.

"Is that wise?"

"It's Dan's order," she said.

She dove out the hatch before Ramsanjawi could say another word. He ignored her rudeness. Engaging the female doctor in an intelligent conversation about station procedures would have been a futile activity. He sank back into the booth and contemplated the pitfalls that had suddenly opened in his path. The pace of research had fallen off; O'Donnell, undoubtedly the culprit, had been "arrested" and his lab sealed; Aaron Weiss, the contact he had cultivated, was dead; and now the phones were shut down.

He remembered a boyhood Christmas, soon after his arrival in England. Sir Walter had ordered motorized bicycles for both Derek and Chakra, but the merchant had cocked up the order and delivered only one. Sir Walter was properly angry at the merchant and properly embarrassed in front of the two boys. He suggested that they take turns at riding the bike on the path that wound through the gardens behind the manor house. Derek rode first and relinquished the bike after one tour through the garden. However, his subsequent turns lengthened until he completely disobeyed his father's admonition to share the toy. Chakra turned to Lady Elizabeth. She placed her arm around his shoulder and smiled down at him.

"Derek is silly," she said. "Be patient. Good things happen to those who wait."

Those words had followed him into his manhood. Her assessment of Derek was correct, but the rest seemed to be pure rubbish. His experience had not borne out the idea that good things happened to those who waited. He had waited and he had been royally screwed up the arse, swearing fealty to the adopted brother he despised in order to return to his rightful place. His last chance might now be slipping away. He already was too old to wait.

Dan found Fabio Bianco waiting for him in the command module. The old scientist looked as shriveled as a dried pepper as he hung in a micro-gee crouch outside the door to Dan's office. He smoothed his hairnet over his wispy tonsure.

"May I have a word with you, Commander?"

"I was hoping for the same with you."

"I suppose we have an even exchange," said Bianco.

Dan anchored himself in front of the communications console, realizing even as his feet slipped into the loops that the desire to attach himself to something solid was becoming a habit. He wondered what the psych–types on the ground would think.

"Okay, Professor, who should begin?" he said.

"I defer to you," said Bianco. "In this realm, you outrank me."

Dan grunted in cautious agreement. "You probably

gathered that I am holding Hugh O'Donnell under suspicion of murdering Aaron Weiss."

"I had assumed as much."

"I also suspect that O'Donnell's work was the reason. That is, Weiss wanted to investigate it and O'Donnell wouldn't let him." Dan paused to gauge Bianco's reaction to his words. He saw nothing. The old man was as blank-faced as a Mafia don in front of a Senate investigating committee.

Tighe continued, "No one seems to know exactly what he's doing here: not me, not Dr. Renoir, not the American scientists, not the ground. Do you know?"

"I regret that I do not."

"You're the Trikon CEO and you don't know what O'Donnell's doing here?"

"I am CEO, not *Il Duce*," said Bianco. "There are things that pass under even this nose."

"I suspect he is working on an experiment to test how people in orbit react to certain drugs."

"Trikon is conducting no such work," said Bianco. "*That* I can say with confidence."

"I didn't say Trikon, Professor."

Bianco shrugged. "I am very saddened about Mr. Weiss. He was a good man. Had you ever seen him on television?"

"A long time ago," said Dan, sensing that Bianco had dug in his heels.

"He struck me as someone who could be very diligent in his pursuit of the truth, though not always well advised in his actions. He was learning something up here. I could see it in his eyes when we spoke. They started out as laughing eyes, as if nothing we did here could impress him. But he was impressed, Commander. He was in awe of our work."

Dan mumbled noncommittally.

"You do not seem overly concerned with our work here, Commander Tighe."

"I didn't sign on to conduct experiments, Professor."

"What did you sign on for?"

"Uh-uh, Professor. You're not going to get me to say that this is the last frontier. The last perfect environment where man still can dream and all that crap."

"Isn't it?"

"It is and it isn't."

"I agree with you, Commander. Our work is what it is and Aaron Weiss's untimely end is what it isn't." Bianco smiled. "I did not come here to trade philosophies with you. There is concern among our coordinating scientists. I told them I would request a meeting with you."

"Is that why you wanted to see me?"

Bianco nodded.

"No need to be so formal, Professor. I'm at your disposal."

The meeting took place in the area outside Dan's office and included the three coordinating scientists, Bianco, and Kurt Jaeckle. There was some discussion among the scientists about whether Jaeckle should be allowed to participate since he technically was not a Trikon employee. Bianco pointed out that Jaeckle's presence could be helpful because he had been on the station longer than any of the other scientists. So Jaeckle remained.

As the meeting was about to begin, Freddy Aviles poked out of the utilities section. Dan motioned for him to stick around. Thora Skillen was the first to speak.

"We have requests and recommendations regarding this newest development." She had been the most strident in her dislike of O'Donnell, and she fairly quivered as she fought to contain her I-told-you-so grin. "We had to rearrange The Bakery to accommodate O'Donnell's lab. And as you know, space is at a premium."

"His lab is not to be disturbed in any way until the investigators arrive on *Constellation*." Dan nodded toward Freddy. "My crew will enforce that order. Anyone violating it will be sent down on *Constellation*. I don't care who it is."

Dan looked to Bianco for support. Bianco picked up on the cue and nodded.

"And after that, I assume O'Donnell's lab may be dismantled," said Skillen.

"Lab space is an issue for Trikon, not me," Dan replied.

Hisashi Oyamo raised his hand. "What about O'Donnell's data?"

"The data would be ours," said Skillen.

"With all due respect, I disagree," said Oyamo. "First, O'Donnell has been treated as an outcast the entire time he has been on Trikon Station. Second, this project is a cooperative effort, which indicates that whatever data he has obtained should be shared."

Everyone's eyes instinctively turned toward Bianco.

"I am not sure who would be entitled to O'Donnell's files," said the old scientist. "It should be subject to prior review."

"Do we hear you correctly?" asked Oyamo, plainly astonished. "Fabio Bianco, the champion of international cooperation, siding with the Americans?"

"I have not sided with anyone," Bianco said. "I simply expressed doubts pending a further determination."

Oyamo turned toward Chakra Ramsanjawi. The Indian had been completely silent since the meeting began. His *kurta* was belted and his clasped hands rose and fell with each breath that passed through his nostrils.

"What do you think?" asked Oyamo.

Ramsanjawi looked for a long moment at each of his Trikon colleagues. He deliberately ignored Jaeckle, Dan, and Freddy.

"I defer to the wisdom of Professor Bianco," he finally said.

Skillen and Oyamo started to protest, but Dan cut them off.

"Is there anything else that concerns me or the crew?" he said.

"There is," said Jaeckle. "What precautions have you taken to protect us from O'Donnell?"

"He is bound and tethered to the aft bulkhead of the rumpus room. That's where he'll stay. He also has a full-time guard."

"You had Russell Cramer bound and tethered and guarded," said Jaeckle. "And you saw fit to have him drugged, too. And he hadn't even killed anyone."

"Different situations," said Dan. "At the time, we thought Cramer was suffering from Orbital Dementia, and the medical officer sedated him to prevent any injury to himself and others. O'Donnell ingested a huge amount of fentanyl. Lorraine believes sedation at this point could be harmful."

"What do you mean that you thought at the time Russell Cramer was suffering from Orbital Dementia? Was there another cause for his behavior?"

"I meant exactly what I said."

"You mean you don't think so now?" Jaeckle pressed.

"What I think and why I think it is no concern of yours."

"Russell Cramer is one of my people."

"Russell Cramer is no longer aboard this station, which makes him completely irrelevant to this discussion," said Dan. He pulled loose from his foot restraints and glided toward the open doorway of his office. "Any other requests or suggestions?"

No one said a word. The only sound was Jaeckle snorting angrily at having been rebuffed.

"Good. I have work to do." Dan pulled himself through the doorway and slid the door shut. He was pissed off himself. A few moments later, as the voices of the scientists receded toward the tunnel, he thought about his reference to Lorraine. In connection with Russell Cramer, she was "the medical officer"; now she was just Lorraine. He wondered what the psychtypes on Earth would think about *that*.

Activities in the Mars module had returned almost to normal. Cautious, fearful talk about the murder of Aaron Weiss soon enough gave way to more animated discussions of Mars-related experiments. Kurt Jaeckle, however, felt anything but normal as his mind circled endlessly within the narrow confines of his office. Unlike his colleagues, neither Mars nor Aaron Weiss was uppermost in his mind. His main concern was Carla Sue Gamble.

Throughout his entire life, Jaeckle always had been careful in his dealings with women. His watchword was *power*. Never allow a woman to have power over you. Be charming and gallant, witty and intelligent. But never reveal the part of yourself that is most important to you. Knowledge is power, and what every woman wants is power over men.

Now Carla Sue had the power. She had disguised her all-consuming jealousy as a desire to travel to Mars, but the fact remained that no one wanted—no one deserved—to stand on the surface of the red planet as much as he. And now, in this empire that bore the imprint of his hand, in this first way station on his lifetime journey to Mars, he was being victimized by the most primal of human instincts.

The communications blackout might actually be beneficial, he thought as he cracked his accordion door for a peek at the module. He had time to reason with Carla Sue before she could set any foolish plan in motion.

Jaeckle closed the door and booted up his computer. Carla Sue had been working on a long-term project of trying to cultivate terrestrial bacteria in samples of Martian soil returned by the unmanned space probes. The purpose was to determine if earthly life-forms could survive under the subzero temperatures and desert-dry conditions on Mars. If they could, it would be important evidence that native life might exist in those frozen red sands. It would also be a warning that astronauts from Earth could contaminate the planet's soil with their own microbes.

Her progress seemed to vary in direct proportion to his interest in her. It had lagged seriously during his ill-fated affair with Lorraine Renoir.

Jaeckle summoned Carla Sue's project files to his computer screen and hastily reviewed her work. A thrill coursed through his body. The microbe-growing project was completely stalled. He quickly tapped out a message for Carla Sue to report to his office immediately. She did not acknowledge, but two minutes later there was a sharp rap on the doorjamb.

Carla Sue had her hair pulled back and knotted, which made her face resemble a beachball with a face painted on it. It was not a happy face as she eyed Jaeckle with her arms folded in front of the hint of breasts that puffed out her uniform shirt.

"I think we have a problem," said Jaeckle. "I've been reviewing your microbe contamination project. Your work has been inadequate."

"In what way?" said Carla Sue. "I surely haven't conclusively proved that bacteria can grow under Martian conditions. But I didn't expect to at this point. *You* didn't expect it, either."

Jaeckle fought the impulse to wince as Carla Sue

spat an almost exact quote back in his face. He immediately reversed field.

"That isn't the point," he said. "You haven't logged any tangible results in the past several days."

"The hell I haven't, *Professor* Jaeckle."

"The computer doesn't lie," said Jaeckle, directing her attention to the screen with an arrogant wave of his hand.

Carla Sue squinted at the data display. "That's all wrong."

Jaeckle laughed. Without asking permission, Carla Sue brushed past him and quickly typed in a set of commands. The screen changed several times, showing page after page of fresh data.

"You obviously didn't look at my work very closely, did you, Kurt?" she said. "I guess even my scientific work is yesterday's news in your book."

Jaeckle's embarrassment blossomed into raw anger. He envisioned his face on supermarket tabloids, the brutality and depravity of his private life at once trumpeted and trivialized along with stories of UFOs, alien kidnappings, and Bigfoot. He grabbed her by the shirt just above the bump of her breasts.

"Listen to me, goddammit!" he hissed.

Carla Sue, six inches taller, managed to slip a foot into an anchoring loop. She brought her hands up between Jaeckle's arms and, with a snap of her wrists, broke his grip. He sailed backward into the rear partition of the office.

They stared at each other—Jaeckle with the horror of realizing he had just lost his composure, Carla Sue with a measure of sad understanding, even pity. She opened the door and slipped out of the office.

Jaeckle did not pursue her. There was no sense in losing his dignity in front of the rest of the Martians. He waited until he knew she would be at her workstation, then keyed an urgent, heartfelt apology into his computer. The stress of the mission was beginning to take its toll, he stated. He was only human.

The more he typed the better he felt. Grabbing Carla Sue was not the end of his world. It was a minor faux pas, something he certainly could repair with politeness, a few well-chosen words, an exaggerated respect for her scientific abilities.

He almost convinced himself.

Fifteen meters away, Carla Sue saw the apology gushing across her screen. She had realized when she embarked on her gambit that her position among the Martians would be changed forever. But she was surprised that Jaeckle had overreacted so quickly.

She wiped Jaeckle's words from the monitor and stared at her keyboard, wondering whether she should respond.

You've already rolled the dice, Carla Sue, she said to herself. You're in this for the duration.

Her fingers moved across the keys: YOU HAVE JUST PROVEN LAVERNE NELSON'S ALLEGATIONS.

Satisfied, she transmitted the words to Jaeckle.

Now I need to get me some protection, she thought.

O'Donnell did not even attempt to speak during the first few hours of captivity in the rumpus room. His body seemed to be processing the last remnants of the fentanyl in spasms. At different intervals his limbs went numb, his vision blurred, and his whole body shuddered.

In between these episodes, he tried to piece together what had happened. The last thing he remembered was brushing his teeth. The toothpaste had tasted funny, and as an ex-coke addict he knew that the gums were efficient at absorbing drugs into the bloodstream. But the method was less important than the motive. Who would want him drugged? Did that same person want Aaron Weiss dead? And why?

By the time O'Donnell felt well enough to speak,

Lance Muncie was on guard duty. Lance did not come very close, preferring to hover near the variable-gravity centrifuge. Although nothing seemed to occupy him other than his thoughts, he pointedly refused to meet O'Donnell's eyes. Still, O'Donnell decided to venture a question. "What happened, Lance?"

"I'm not supposed to talk to you."

"Who told you?"

"Commander Tighe. It's his orders." Lance pulled himself to the other side of the centrifuge.

"You mean you people are going to keep me tied up here and no one's going to tell me what's going on?"

"You already know."

"The hell I do."

"I can't talk to you."

"Then listen to me. Dan thinks I killed Weiss. Now why would I do a thing like that?"

Lance did not answer. He positioned himself on the carpeted surface of the jogging track and began to run. He moved slowly at first with bent legs and a stooped torso.

"You know me, Lance," continued O'Donnell. "We did the Cape together. We bounced around in the Vomit Comet together. We flew up here together. Do I look like a person who'd kill someone?"

Lance's strides grew longer and more fluid. His posture straightened as he gained speed.

"Just shake your head, Lance. If you can't say I didn't do it, at least let me know you hear me."

But Lance ran on. His thundering feet created such a racket that O'Donnell gave up trying to prod him into conversation. Lance eventually slackened his pace. He hunched forward and bumped the heels of his hands against the running surface to dampen his momentum. As Lance drifted in a long lazy circle around the inside of the track, O'Donnell noticed Carla Sue hovering in the tunnel. Lance saw her at the same time.

"This module is off limits," he snapped.

But Carla Sue squirmed her sleek body through the hatch.

"Lance, I just need to see you for a minute."

"It's off limits," he said. "No exceptions."

"Well, you'll just have to make an exception for me." Carla Sue pulled up in front of him and arranged her lips in a pucker. Lance dodged her kiss.

"My, my, we're all business, aren't we?" she teased.

"What do you want, Carla Sue?"

"I was scared, what with all this talk about murder and such."

"There's nothing to be scared of." Lance nodded in O'Donnell's direction as if to say the situation was under control.

"Well, I was worried about you."

"Worried about me?" Lance blurted.

"Why, yes," she said, rubbing both hands along his biceps. "I know you're a big strong man, but I worry just the same."

"You can't stay here," Lance said. He was virtually pleading.

"I've booked an hour in the observation blister," she whispered, patting his chest. He grabbed her wrist, then quickly released it.

"Okay, Lance," she said. "I won't trouble you none. But when you're off duty, come to the blister. I'll be waiting."

She gave him a quick peck on the cheek and flew out of the room. O'Donnell could see that Carla Sue's visit had shaken Lance. His face was flushed as if he had just been sitting in front of a raging fire.

"What's she into you for?" called O'Donnell.

"I don't know what you mean."

"You remember the bartender at the Cape," said O'Donnell. "He said Carla Sue belonged to Jaeckle."

"She does not."

"Well, I wouldn't know about that," said O'Donnell. "But he made sense when he said to keep away from Carla Sue."

"She's okay," Lance said.

"If she's so okay, why did you chase her out of here?"

"Orders."

"Orders my ass. If I had someone like her puckering those lips at me, I'd forget orders pretty damn quick," said O'Donnell. He paused to let the words sink in. "Unless of course I thought she was using me too."

"She's not using me," said Lance.

"I guess you'd know," O'Donnell said with a smile.

Lance suddenly flew at him. He crashed into O'Donnell's chest with his shoulder, then grabbed two wads of O'Donnell's shirt.

"You think it's funny, huh?" he yelled. "You think it's funny she used me!"

Lance braced himself on the floor and punched O'Donnell squarely in the stomach. O'Donnell's head snapped forward. A gasp of saliva shot out of his mouth and the top of the helmet banged against Lance's cheek and jaw, opening a large red gash.

"Son of a bitch!" screamed Lance.

O'Donnell felt Lance's knee explode into his groin. Stars obliterated his vision, and he sagged away from the bulkhead as far as the tethers would allow. A hand grabbed his chin as if lining up his head for a haymaker.

"Lance!"

Through his blurry vision, O'Donnell saw Dan and Freddy hurtling toward them. They pulled Lance away.

"What the hell is going on here, Muncie?" Dan barked.

Lance sniffed back a wad of snot and tamped his sleeve against the gash on his face.

"He suckered me, sir. Said he couldn't breathe and wanted me to loosen the tape a little. When I tried to, he butted me with his head."

O'Donnell was gasping desperately, eyes rolling with pain. Could he be that crazy? Dan asked himself. Start a fight with his hands tied? Can drugs scramble your brain that badly?

"You damn fool," Dan said to Muncie. "Go get cleaned up."

By midafternoon, the people on Trikon Station had returned to a semblance of their normal daily routines. Stanley relieved Freddy, who had relieved Lance, and accomplished the tricky maneuver of feeding O'Donnell from a collection of squeeze bottles. O'Donnell, still smarting from Lance's attack, meekly cooperated.

At 1500 hours, Dan called Lance and Freddy to his office. He had attended several meetings, both in person and over his comm link Earthside, since the discovery of Weiss's body early that morning. He hoped that this one would be the last.

"Keeping O'Donnell in the rumpus room is causing logistical problems," he said. "And some of the scientists are concerned for their own safety."

"Like who?" Freddy asked.

"Jaeckle, for one."

"Wimp," said Freddy. He looked at Lance and nodded.

"Maybe he has a valid point for a change," said Dan. "Anyway, I've decided it's best to move O'Donnell."

"Where to?" said Freddy.

"The observatory."

"Ain't that going a little too far?"

"Not after this latest incident," Dan said. "Putting him in the observatory poses the fewest logistical problems and requires the least manpower."

"Hokay," said Freddy. It was obvious he disagreed with the decision, but it was just as obvious that Dan would not be swayed. "Who gonna move him?"

"I don't want to leave the station and Stanley's had some EVA problems lately. That leaves you two." Dan leveled his steel-eyed gaze at Lance. "There will be no repeat performance, right?"

Lance stared at the floor.

"There will be no repeat performance even if O'Donnell provokes you. Correct, Mr. Muncie?"

"Correct, Commander," said Lance without raising his eyes.

"Get going," said Dan.

Freddy dispatched Lance to the wardroom to assemble a four-day supply of food and water. Meanwhile, he toted an EMU into the rumpus room and started to prepare O'Donnell for transfer.

"I gonna release you," said Freddy as he snipped the duct tape with a pocket scissors. "You fuck aroun' and what Lance did to you feel like a massage. Right?"

"Sure, Freddy, no fucking around," said O'Donnell. He watched the suit tumbling slowly in the air behind Freddy, like the victim of an ax murderer: disembodied head, legless torso, disconnected legs. "Where are we going?"

Freddy pulled a pair of eyeglasses from his shirt pocket and handed them to O'Donnell. "To look at the stars."

They initiated the transfer procedure as the station passed out of the Earth's shadow, to take full advantage of the light. Freddy was the first to exit the airlock. O'Donnell, with tethers attached to his suit, was second. Freddy gripped the tethers while Lance backed in to one of the six MMUs docked to ports along the outer skin of the tunnel. Then Freddy backed into one of the flying armchairs and felt its latches click into place against his suit. O'Donnell was not to be given his own MMU. Freddy and Lance pulled him along between them.

Jesus Christ don't let go of me, O'Donnell begged

them silently. He gaped at the emptiness that stretched out forever, the gleaming Earth so far below, the black infinity of space swallowing his tiny frail being. His breath caught in his throat. He could hear his pulse thundering in his ears. He saw himself spinning into the dark yawning void endlessly, spiraling out into nothingness, cast away until the end of time. For the first time he could remember since childhood, Hugh O'Donnell found himself praying.

But Freddy and Lance held him firmly for the several minutes it took to cover the two hundred meters between the raft of modules and the observatory. As they slowed to a stop outside the airlock, Freddy radioed Lance to remain in his MMU while he took O'Donnell inside. Lance acknowledged with a thumbs-up.

Freddy and O'Donnell sealed themselves in the airlock, waited for the pressure to equalize, then opened the inner hatch to enter the observatory itself. Freddy was more familiar with space suits than O'Donnell and removed his helmet quickly. O'Donnell tried to detach his own and spun into a tumble. Freddy eventually pried it off, dislodging O'Donnell's glasses in the process.

"So this is exile," said O'Donnell, reattaching his glasses and looking around the cramped quarters. He shuddered slightly, remembering his terror outside. "It's cold in here."

"I gonna level with you, man," said Freddy. "I know you didn' kill Weiss."

"Thanks for your confidence, Freddy. Why the hell am I here, then?"

"Commander don' wan' you hurtin' anyone."

"Like Lance? He attacked me, pal. That kid is nuts."

"Well, he ain't gonna attack you no more," said Freddy. "You an' me got a big problem, man."

"You're half right, anyway."

"I'm *all* right. I'm with Welch."

"You're what!?"

"With Welch, man. I'm supposed to watch you. Make sure you do your work. Make sure no one fuck around with you. And we both fucked up, man. You because you had that shit stuffed down your throat, me because I didn' stop it."

"This is a helluva time to tell me!"

"Orders, man," said Freddy, unhappily. "They don' want you to know you got a security man with you. They figure you give us both away if you knew."

"Shit," O'Donnell muttered.

"In spades."

"What exactly happened?"

"Don' know exactly. I found Weiss outside your lab aroun' 0115 hours. He already dead and somebody, maybe him, tried to get in your lab by removin' the hinges. I fix the door and hide Weiss in a canister in the logistics module until I figure out what's goin' on. Then I look for you. You trashed in your compartment. I din' know why, so I fix you in your restraint and hope you wake up. Lance found the body and Tighe called everybody into the rumpus room. When you don' show, we go look. I found you where I left you, but you still trashed."

"So why does Dan think I killed Weiss?"

"You the best bet, far as he can see. He knows your lab tampered with and found a button ripped off Weiss's shirt outside it."

"That won't hold up as evidence."

"We ain't in court, man."

"So who do you think did it?"

"Don' know. Same guy gave stuff to Russell Cramer, prob'ly."

"How did you know that Cramer had drugs in him?"

Freddy tapped his temple with a finger. "I had a talk with Cramer before they sent him down. He wasn' much help. I think he got it directly from Roberts. But I don' know where Roberts got it from."

"Roberts? That twit?" O'Donnell said. Then he took a breath. "I guess there aren't too many possibilities."

"There's enough. We don' have much time."

"Say that again. So someone tried to fuck me up because they know what I'm working on."

"Maybe. Anything possible with these lulus."

"Weiss?"

"Nah. Too stupid. An' we ran a check on him. Somebody use him, if you ask me."

"What about my lab?"

"Sealed it myself. Copied all your computer files, then crashed the system." Freddy patted his chest to indicate the disk. "Rest of the stuff a problem. Skillen wants the space. Oyamo wants the data. They all think you working on the toxic-waste superbug. But no one doin' anything till the shuttle get here."

"Then what?"

"Don' know. I gotta have a little talk with Bianco, case things get outta hand later. Meanwhile, I gotta report to Welch. Make sure he can get some friendlies on the shuttle." Freddy thumbed an encryption chip from his flight suit pocket and pressed it into a slot on the comm console. "This's the only link I left open, besides Tighe's down in the command module. You wanna talk to Welch?"

"Nah," said O'Donnell. "I never liked the bastard."

While Freddy reported the situation to Welch, Lance remained parked outside the airlock. He was suspended between the dazzling beauty of the Earth and the cold, star-specked darkness of the firmament, but he paid little attention to either view. Freddy seemed to be taking an awfully long time in the observatory. Maybe O'Donnell had tried to overpower him and right now they were banging around inside.

Lance felt a tingle as he remembered his own battle with O'Donnell. The sensation was not unlike what he had felt with Carla Sue, before she proved to be a dishonest, lying, cheating slut. He had not merely punched O'Donnell. He had smote him as if his own hand were the hammer of God.

Lance decided to swing around to one of the observatory windows. His right forefinger accidently touched the MMU's pitch control, and a jet of cold nitrogen gas sent him into a tumble. Blue-white Earth and deep black space flashed past him like a giant stroboscope, bright-dark, bright-dark, until he nudged a series of opposite thrusts to arrest himself.

Wow, he thought, that was fun. He jetted away from the observatory and tried it again. And again. And again.

3 SEPTEMBER 1998
TRIKON STATION

The bar was empty at that time of the morning except for the two men sitting side by side at the far end, away from the windows. They were a strange pair: a short, round, heavyset bald man who exuded nervous energy and a long, lean, lanky, lantern-jawed guy with his elbows on the bar and his head drooping between his hands.

"I still can't believe it," said Ed Yablon. "I mean, I know it's true—but in my gut I expect to see him come waltzing through that door and pull up a stool beside us."

"Yeah," muttered Zeke Tucker.

Yablon picked up his beer and drained it. Smacking the empty glass on the bar's gleaming surface, he motioned for the bartender to fill it up again.

"I ought to be glad, in a way," Yablon said. "The sonofabitch was nothing but trouble."

"Yeah."

"The biggest pain in the ass I ever had to work with."

"Yeah."

"You remember the time he snuck into the Kennedy compound in Hyannisport and . . . well, hell, Zeke—you were there with him, weren't you?"

Tucker did not answer. Yablon saw that the photographer was softly, quietly sobbing as if his own father had just died.

AFTER REMOVING HIS space suit Freddy went directly to the command module to report on the transfer of O'Donnell to the observatory.

"How would you describe his behavior?" asked Dan.

"Din' give me no trouble."

"Lance?"

"Not so good with the flying armchair. I found him spinning aroun' when I left the observatory."

"Lance's EVA skills are the least of our worries," Dan said. "Better get some rest."

Freddy shoved off, but not for the relative comfort of his sleep compartment. The commander's suggestion did not countermand the direct order he had received from Welch. Safeguarding O'Donnell's work was of paramount importance. O'Donnell himself could be replaced, or even neutralized, if the situation dictated. But if his work fell into the wrong hands, the result could be disastrous. According to Welch, Fabio Bianco had a general awareness of O'Donnell's purpose on the station. His authority could be useful in preventing the other scientists from scavenging O'Donnell's lab. Freddy had permission to use all available avenues to ensure Bianco's cooperation.

Freddy found Bianco in ELM. Bianco floated with his arms folded and his eyes narrowed in concentration while a fellow Italian chattered about data displayed on a computer monitor. Freddy wanted to avoid entering ELM itself. Chakra Ramsanjawi had a history of complaining to Tighe about intruding crewmen, and Freddy could see the Indian lurking in his office at the far end of the module. Fortunately, Bianco's attention wandered toward the hatch.

At first, Bianco ignored Freddy's hand signals. When Freddy became more insistent, he broke away from the conversation. Freddy could read the reluctance in the old scientist's eyes. Nothing a crewman said could possibly be of any interest to Bianco.

Freddy decided on a direct approach.

"Mr. Welch says hello," he whispered when Bianco was within hearing range.

"Who?"

"Mr. Welch. Hugh O'Donnell's friend. You spoke to him before comin' up here." Freddy paused until recognition sharpened Bianco's features. "We gotta talk."

"Yes, we must. Excuse me." Bianco sailed back to the Italian and spoke with emphatic hand gestures that obviously were instructions. Then he joined Bianco in the connecting tunnel. "Where shall we talk?"

"My compartment," said Freddy.

Freddy's compartment was completely bare of decoration except for a crucifix that floated at the end of a heavy gold chain clipped to the wall over his sleep restraint. Freddy motioned for Bianco to be silent, then turned up the volume of the stereo. The music had a Latin beat. Bianco winced.

"Mr. Welch very interested in O'Donnell's lab," said Freddy. He spoke directly into Bianco's ear and carefully kept his voice below the music.

"I imagine he would be," said Bianco.

"I was at your meetin' this morning. You didn' sound like you knew what to do with the lab."

"That is correct. I still do not."

"Is no one's business what's in there."

"Perhaps not," Bianco said. "It is difficult to tell without knowing exactly what it is."

"Can' say. Is very important. Sensitive," said Freddy, placing equal stress on each syllable.

"Sensitive enough to commit murder over it?" Bianco's eyes bored into Freddy.

Surprised at the meaning of the old man's words, Freddy answered, "Hey, I din' do it! I wanna find out who did."

"Yes," said Bianco. "Of course."

The man was angry, Freddy saw. As if the murder had taken one of his own family.

Bianco said, "Mr. Welch told me he had a watchdog up here with O'Donnell. Are you the only one?"

Freddy nodded with a slight tilt of his head as if to say, At your service.

Bianco eyed him carefully—the stump, the well-muscled torso, the gold canine embedded in a grin that was tired, almost bored. Freddy certainly was capable of strong-arming him, but he had not made any threatening moves. He was polite, even deferential. It was obvious he sought cooperation rather than confrontation. And why not? With O'Donnell exiled to the station's astronomical observatory, Freddy was alone in his mission.

"The toxic-waste project that my people are working on is very important," said Bianco. "It does not qualify as a state secret; in fact, much of the world does not seem to care. In my official capacity, I can prevent the American team, or anyone else, from taking over that lab. But it would be at the expense of my project. I would like to know exactly why I am being so compliant with your Mr. Welch."

Freddy considered the offer for a long moment.

"Hokay, Señor Bianco," he finally said. "I tell you. You familiar with the work of a Professor Rothstein on tobacco plants?"

Bianco furrowed his brow as if sifting through his memory.

"About ten years ago," prodded Freddy.

"Was that the antisense RNA treatment to prevent the production of nicotine in tobacco leaves?"

"You say that good," said Freddy. "What O'Donnell doing is jus' like that, only different."

Kurt Jaeckle remained in his office for a long time after reading Carla Sue's reply to his apology. He slipped out of the Mars module and peered into the wardroom. Only a few stragglers remained from lunch, but it was still too crowded for his present state of mind. Deciding to kill some time in his compartment, he made his way down the connecting tunnel.

As he passed the logistics module, he heard a hissing sound from within. Thinking it might be a gas leak, Jaeckle decided to investigate. It took a moment of peering down aisles formed by canisters and cylinders to find the source of the noise. It was not a gas leak. Lance Muncie floated in the fetal position, his hands cradling something that resembled a bouquet of yellow paper flowers. All around him, smaller bits of yellow tatters danced in eddies of air.

"She loves me, she loves me not. She loves me, she loves me not." Lance was whispering harshly, a sibilant, strangling murmur hissing from between his teeth.

Jaeckle edged backwards. The sight of Muncie was terrifying. The man was totally insane. He wanted to get away as quickly and as quietly as possible.

Lance suddenly paused in his counting.

"I'm okay, I'm okay, I'm okay," he whispered to himself. Then he attacked another paper flower. "He lives, he dies. He lives, he dies. He lives, he dies."

Jaeckle's knee banged against an empty cylinder; the clang echoed like a church bell. Muncie jerked upright. His eyes lit on Jaeckle and his face broke out in a maniacal grin.

"Speak of the devil," he said.

The words turned Jaeckle's bones to ice. His heart froze in his chest. Jaeckle spun and dove into the tunnel. He reached his compartment before he realized that his heart was thumping so hard he feared it would burst his rib cage.

Even with things falling apart around him, Dan Tighe stubbornly refused to abandon established station procedure. After learning from Freddy that O'Donnell had been installed in the observatory, he ensconced himself in the command and control center and in his patient, painstaking manner, checked and rechecked every system within the station's operation—life support, station attitude, orbital configuration, fuel supply, and waste management. The atmospheric replenishment system would be low on oxygen in a few hours. Dan left a message for Freddy to replace the expended tank. As he completed his recheck, he sensed a presence. Lorraine Renoir hovered a few feet from him, holding two squeeze bottles of coffee.

He started to reach for one of them. "Thanks, Lorraine."

She pulled back slightly. "I hate to do it, Dan, but I've got to get a blood pressure reading on you."

Tighe felt his shoulders sag. "Now?"

"Sooner or later."

"Okay," he said. "Let's get it over with."

She still withheld the coffee. "Afterward. Caffeine raises the pressure."

"What the hell doesn't?" Dan grumbled. He kicked free of the anchoring loops and followed her the length of the command module to her infirmary.

Lorraine quickly and efficiently wrapped the cuff around his left arm and took a reading. She glanced up into his eyes.

"Let's try the other arm."

"That bad, huh?" Somehow Dan didn't care. Almost. As the doctor inflated the cuff again he told himself, Let them take the station away from me; it'll be a relief. But he knew he did not truly believe that.

Lorraine smiled at him. "I don't understand it."

"What?"

Her smile widened. "Your pressure is down into the normal range."

"You're sure?" Dan blurted.

"High normal, but normal."

"I'll be damned."

"Let me try another reading."

She puffed up the cuff once again and stared at the numbers. "I think you thrive on trouble, Dan." She seemed delighted. "Or perhaps responsibility."

"It's really down?"

"Really."

He grinned back at her. "Can I have my coffee now?"

They sipped and talked, and even though the conversation eventually turned to O'Donnell, Dan felt a quiet ease settling gently over them. My pressure's down! He marveled at the news. Lorraine wouldn't fake the readings, he knew. But she sure seemed happy about it.

For more than an hour they traded information they had gleaned from their independent conversations with O'Donnell. The twelve-year gap in his biography slowly shrank. But when it reached the three years starting in 1995 it would close no more.

"Maybe Weiss knew something about O'Donnell that O'Donnell didn't want anyone else to know," said Lorraine.

Dan's eyes focused on infinity for a long moment. "Maybe."

"You looked troubled, Dan. Is it because he's your friend?"

"Friend, buddy, whatever. You spend time with a guy, you kid around with him. You want to think that he's leveling with you and that you can read him. When you find out you've been wrong, well, maybe he's been bullshitting you or maybe you just can't read people. Either way, that can be a dangerous proposition up here."

"Don't feel bad about having misread him," said Lorraine. "I did, too. Addicts are con artists. It's part of their survival instinct. Even if they clean up, those other habits die hard."

"I know something about addicts," said Dan, forcing himself to brighten the somber mood. "My ex-wife was addicted to her career."

Lorraine laughed. "And you weren't?"

Dan grinned back at her, ruefully.

"You know," she said, more seriously, "that's the first time you've mentioned your ex-wife to me."

"Someday I'll tell you the rest of the story."

"I'd like that."

Before Dan could say anything more Kurt Jaeckle appeared in the infirmary doorway. Jaeckle looked more than grim; he looked scared.

"Has either of you seen Lance Muncie?" he asked.

Dan and Lorraine looked at each other.

Dan said, "He just completed transferring O'Donnell to the observatory along with Freddy Aviles."

"I think he's suffering from Orbital Dementia," said Jaeckle. He described his encounter with Lance in the logistics module. The account was disturbing enough in itself, but Jaeckle's narrative skills made it sound chilling. Throughout, Lorraine hovered close to Dan. At the mention of the tattered flowers, she nudged softly against his shoulder. Jaeckle concluded: "I'm certain he was referring to me."

Dan scrutinized Jaeckle suspiciously. He knew that Jaeckle often blabbed to the other scientists that the station commander "had it in for" the Mars Project and had sent Russell Cramer Earthside as part of some convoluted personal vendetta. He also knew that Jaeckle and Lance were inextricably linked by Carla Sue Gamble. Lance had fought with O'Donnell. But he said he had been provoked and O'Donnell hadn't contradicted him. Was this a poor attempt at payback by Jaeckle? Or was it a legitimate report?

"Lorraine?" he asked.

"No harm in examining him," she replied.

Dan nodded abruptly, then looked at his wrist-watch. "We all have jobs to do," he said.

"Yes," said Lorraine. "I've got to log in the results of the latest test I performed."

Dan wanted to kiss her, right there in front of Jaeckle. Instead he settled for a grin. My pressure's down, he said to himself again as he sailed toward his own office. And Lorraine's just as happy about it as I am.

Lance responded without any hesitation to Lorraine's suggestion that he come to the infirmary. That was a positive sign, she thought. Russell Cramer had routinely avoided her.

She studied Lance's appearance between glances at his personnel file. The gash on his cheek and jaw was starting to scab. His blond hair was neatly tucked beneath a hairnet. His uniform was in good shape. He seemed slightly edgy, occasionally biting his lower lip or running his tongue along the outside of his front teeth. But everyone was a little edgy. Lance had better reasons than most.

"Have your stomach problems persisted?"

"Nope. Eating fine now," said Lance. "Are you seeing me because you think something else is wrong?"

"I believe it's a good idea to talk to everyone on the station," said Lorraine. "I wanted to start with you because you've been at the center of these events."

Lance rubbed his jaw with his knuckles. "I'll say."

"Do you feel troubled at all?"

"I'm troubled that a man got killed," said Lance. "But you don't mean that."

"That's right, Lance. I mean that you more than anyone are carrying images of what happened. You discovered the body and you were the victim of an attack. Will those images interfere with your work?"

"Nope," said Lance.

"Would you want to return to Earth?"

"I have more'n two more months to go up here."

"I realize that," said Lorraine. "But this is very important now, Lance. Does the fact that *Constellation* will be here shortly put the idea in your head that you might want to return now?"

Lance emphatically shook his head.

"Thanks for stopping by, Lance. You'll contact me if you want to talk?"

Lance nodded and left the office. Lorraine noted in his chart: *Somewhat agitated, but not beyond the normal range indicated by recent events. Diagnosis— no signs of O.D. observed.*

Lance hurried to Hab 2 and sealed himself in his compartment. His stomach and chest felt like an overloaded steam pipe. He buried his head in his sleep restraint. Once again, his angry words spewed forth in a hissing hot torrent.

Chakra Ramsanjawi's plan was simple. Fabio Bianco believed in open cooperation and free exchange of data among the three arms of Trikon. It was a naive belief, but one that Bianco had espoused consistently since the creation of the consortium. Yet Bianco definitely had balked at Oyamo's suggestion that O'Donnell's data be shared by everyone. Ergo, Bianco was privy to the data. All Ramsanjawi needed to do was ask.

Of course, executing the plan was not so simple. Despite the great mutual respect that existed between the two men, Bianco was unlikely to answer Ramsanjawi's questions willingly. Which was why Ramsanjawi had two syringes hidden beneath his *kurta* when he closed his office door. Drugging Bianco was a huge risk; the old man might collapse and die on him. Or worse yet, he might remember being interrogated. Ramsanjawi shrugged massively inside his *kurta*. Perhaps the old man will indeed die—after he has answered my questions. After all, he is already a physical wreck. Who would suspect anything more than the stresses he has encountered here in his very own haven of scientific research?

As Ramsanjawi pulled himself through ELM's hatch, he noticed a disturbance in the shadows of the connecting tunnel. Stu Roberts was being shoved into the logistics module. His attacker was Freddy Aviles.

Ramsanjawi quickly scuttled along the floor. The interior of the logistics module was dimly lit, but he could see Roberts and Aviles silhouetted against a pair of area lights.

"You gave shit to Cramer, no? An' you gave it to O'Donnell, no?"

"I didn't," blubbered Roberts.

"Don' you fuckin' lie to me, man."

"I'm not lying!"

Ramsanjawi's eyes slowly adjusted to the dimness. Freddy's back was to the hatch. One hand grasped the handle of a receptacle while the other clenched a wad of Roberts's shirt. Roberts faced Ramsanjawi, but his terror-stricken eyes were fastened on Aviles.

"Why you fuck up O'Donnell? Huh? You interested in what he doin'? Huh?"

Roberts tried to answer but his voice was cracked by Freddy's fist pounding his chest.

Ramsanjawi decided that Bianco could wait; Aviles was the more pressing problem. Squirting a few drops from a syringe onto the material of his *kurta,* Ramsanjawi then clamped the syringe in his teeth and used both hands to sling himself through the hatch.

Roberts had no time to react; Freddy had no time to move. In one motion, Ramsanjawi pulled the syringe from his teeth and jammed the needle into Freddy's rump. Freddy managed one solid punch to Ramsanjawi's midsection. Ramsanjawi drew himself into a ball, bracing himself for another blow. But it never came. When he lifted his head, he saw Freddy tumbling slowly near the ceiling.

Roberts cautiously peeked out from behind a wall of canisters.

"What was that all about?" asked Ramsanjawi.

"I don't know! He jumped me as I came out of the Whit."

"Did you tell him anything?"

"No! Nothing! You got here just in time."

"Then we are both fortunate," said Ramsanjawi.

"What are you going to do with him?" Roberts asked. He touched Freddy's neck as if testing for signs of life.

"That is my affair," said Ramsanjawi. "Return to your compartment."

Roberts moved slowly to the hatch, took a final look at Ramsanjawi and Freddy, then shot into the tunnel.

Ramsanjawi grabbed Freddy by the shirt and held his serene face to the light.

"Well, my abbreviated friend, we have much to discuss."

Ramsanjawi used an empty canister to transport Freddy from the logistics module to ELM. It was near midnight, and he encountered no one during the short journey. He brought the canister into his office, sealed the accordion door, and popped the lid.

Freddy groaned as he spilled out, his arms unfolding like the wings of an injured bird. After a few minutes, his groans sharpened and his movements strengthened. Ramsanjawi readied the second syringe. This one did not contain a tranquilizer. It contained sodium pentothal—truth serum.

Ramsanjawi rolled up Freddy's sleeve and injected the serum into his arm. Freddy faded for a moment, then regained consciousness. His eyes were glazed and his speech was slurred and halting, but he accurately answered Ramsanjawi's preliminary questions. Then Ramsanjawi turned to more important matters.

"What do you know about Cramer?"

"He din't have Orbital Dementia . . . Drugs made him crazy."

"And O'Donnell?"

"Drugs make him crazy, too. Differen' drugs."

"And you think that Roberts gave them the drugs."

"Roberts friend of Cramer. Make sense."

"But who gave the drugs to Roberts?"

"Don' know."

"Why are you interested in Roberts's interest in O'Donnell?"

"My job. . . . Protect O'Donnell. Protect his work."

"So you killed Aaron Weiss."

"No."

"Who did?"

"Don' know."

"What is O'Donnell working on?"

"Impor'ant stuff."

"Not part of Trikon's work?"

"More impor'ant."

"What?"

"Can' say."

"But you can tell me."

Freddy paused. His features twisted as his better judgment struggled unsuccessfully against the sodium pentothal.

"Bug . . . to use against . . . cocaine."

"The product or the plants themselves?"

"Plants."

"Bah. That has been tried. It was unsuccessful."

"Not this one."

"And I suppose *you* know how it works."

"Not me. O'Donnell."

"O'Donnell is not here, Aviles."

Freddy hovered weightlessly, silent, slack-jawed, while Ramsanjawi thought furiously.

At last he said, "O'Donnell has his own computer, does he not?"

"Yeah."

"And all his data is stored in it?"

"It was."

"Was? What do you mean?"

"Crashed his files."

"You *what?*"

"So nobody could copy," Freddy muttered.

Ramsanjawi wanted to slap him. Then he realized, "*You* made a copy, didn't you?"

"Sure."

"Where is it?"

Freddy's hand flopped against his chest. "Here."

Ramsanjawi removed a diskette from an inside pocket of Freddy's shirt and loaded it into his computer. There had been several attempts to destroy cocaine production at its source—chemicals, herbicides, even insects specifically crossbred to feed only on coca leaves. None of these plans had worked, and to Ramsanjawi's knowledge the United States government had ceased trying.

O'Donnell's attempt proved to be different.

Ramsanjawi perused the computer files and immediately grasped the thrust of the project: the development of a genetic sequence that would block the production of a specific enzyme necessary for cells of the coca leaf to manufacture cocaine. O'Donnell had not quite perfected the sequence. But he was close. Very close.

Ramsanjawi stored the data in his computer and returned the diskette to the pocket in Freddy's shirt. He prepared another dose of tranquilizer to keep Freddy asleep through the rest of the night. Freddy might remember this encounter; he might not. It mattered little to Ramsanjawi. The plan that was coming together in his head would be executed quickly.

Ramsanjawi placed Freddy in his sleep compartment and returned to his office. In less than an hour of reviewing the data, he knew exactly how to apply

O'Donnell's groundwork. With just a few basic alterations to the genetic sequence and to the RNA messenger molecule O'Donnell had developed, he would possess a unique commodity. Sir Derek was welcome to the toxic-waste superbug. The ability to destroy the world's coca supply would be far more valuable.

Then a new insight flashed into his mind. How much would the drug cartel pay for this information? And the techniques for guarding against it? Ramsanjawi felt himself glowing like the sun. Or better yet, I could use this technique to alter ordinary plants and make them produce cocaine! How much would the cartel pay for the ability to insert the coca-producing enzyme into ordinary plants? Chakra laughed aloud. Cocaine-yielding potatoes! Spinach! Watermelons!

He pictured himself living like a maharajah in a splendid villa on the Riviera. Who needs Oxford, and its airs of shabby gentility? With this kind of money I can buy all the respect I want.

Chuckling happily, Ramsanjawi shut down his computer and prepared himself for a long night of designing. Perhaps Lady Elizabeth had been correct after all. Good things happened to those who waited. And his long wait was finally over.

3 SEPTEMBER 1998
TRIKON STATION

TOPANGA DEATH BAFFLES POLICE

Police in the Los Angeles suburb of Topanga are investigating the mysterious death of a 32-year-old woman. The nude body of Stacey Hollis was discovered last Saturday night in the Topanga Canyon home of her fiancé, attorney Phillip "Pancho" Weinstein, shortly before midnight. The death has been termed suspicious, but no charges have yet been filed.

Weinstein told police that he left his home at about 9:30 Saturday night to pick up some files at his Los Angeles law office. When he returned, he found Ms. Hollis on the bathroom floor. There were no signs of a struggle and no evidence of a forced entry.

The Medical Examiner's report is expected to be released tomorrow.

—Los Angeles Times, 3 September 1998

LANCE SLIPPED INTO the Mars module at 2330 hours. From previous reconnaissance, he knew that Carla Sue had reserved a two-hour block in the blister commencing at 2300 hours. No one else had reserved a slot until morning. He would have plenty of time.

He knocked on the door. His heart quickened when he heard no immediate reply. Maybe Carla Sue wasn't inside; maybe Jaeckle was with her. He knocked again.

"Who's there?" Her voice was muffled only slightly by the flimsy door.

"Lance."

The door slid open. She was not wearing her usual Danskin, just a white cotton T-shirt and blue nylon shorts. Her hair was unbound and swayed like yellow grass in a river. The lights were low, but the massive cloud-decked curve of Earth glowed brilliantly through the observation windows.

"Oh, Lance, I'm glad you could come."

Her smile looked genuine enough. Ignoring it, he pushed past her into the blister. She floated demurely at arm's length from him. "I've missed you," she said softly.

Lance's chest constricted into a steel cage that squeezed the breath out of him. He could not speak. His stomach began to knot. He nodded wordlessly at Carla Sue.

"You poor dear. Here I am thinking only of myself when you've been through so much."

"I'm fine," he managed to gasp out, rubbing his lips and the scab of his gash with the same hand.

"After all that's happened—"

"Nothing happened to me," Lance said. "God, why does everyone treat me like a child?"

"Why, Lance, you're not a child to me."

"I'm not, huh? What were you doing with Kurt Jaeckle yesterday?"

"Yesterday?" Carla Sue cocked her head as if searching the distant cloud cover for the answer.

"In your compartment, dammit!" said Lance. Forgetting himself, he pounded the bulkhead for emphasis. He went into a spin, but quickly stopped himself.

"Right, right, yesterday," said Carla Sue. "You see, Lance, I didn't want to tell you, but a long, long time ago, before the Mars Project even began, Kurt asked me to marry him."

Lance opened his mouth as if to speak. In his mind,

she had just proven his point. He had been less than a child; he had been a toy.

"I didn't say yes," Carla Sue added quickly. "I was a little leery, what with him being married twice and me never even being engaged. So I told him we should put off making plans until after the Mars Project. Meantime, I hired a private detective."

"Why'd you do that?" Lance asked, unsure that he was hearing the truth.

"Suspicion, caution. I've known my share of sweet talkers, but none as smooth as Kurt Jaeckle. It turned out to be a good idea because the detective discovered things about Kurt that weren't quite right."

"Like what?"

"Unsavory things. Exactly what they were don't matter. The point is I found out in time."

"Is that why you got interested in me?"

"Why, Lance, I would have been interested in a big hunk like you anyway. Learning about Kurt just cleared the field."

"So what did you want with him the other day?"

"I wanted nothing with him. He keeps trying to explain himself to me, hoping I'll reconsider. But I won't. He's gone, good-bye, for me." Carla Sue smiled sweetly. "Is that why you've been avoiding me?"

Lance stared at the long legs, the nipples suddenly upright beneath the T-shirt, the glistening lips. Base desire and righteous anger battled within him as he weighed her explanation. She was talking sweet to him, saying what she thought he wanted to hear. There was no private detective. There were no unsavory things in Jaeckle's past. They were face to face in the very room where they had made love, and she still couldn't tell him the truth.

He forced a smile as sweet as hers.

"Yes," he said, opening his arms.

She flew to him. They kissed long and deep. He locked his ankles behind her knees. She worked the

Velcro of his shirt. He pressed his cock against her pelvis. She moaned. He caressed her neck as her tongue probed his ear. Her breath was hot.

He jammed his thumbs into her throat, choking off her scream.

They tumbled around the blister, their backs scraping the door, their elbows butting the dome. She kicked her feet and pounded his sides with her fists. But his thumbs dug into the ribbing of her trachea and his mouth sucked out her last puff of breath.

He slammed her head against the bulkhead for good measure. "Lying bitch!"

Carla Sue's eyes were wide open. Her perfect lips formed a perfect, soundless O. Two splotches of angry red gathered where his thumbs had closed off her windpipe.

Lance looped one of her arms through a handhold so she would not float around the blister. He peeked out the door. No one was in the tunnel. He slipped out and cracked the access door. The Mars module was empty. A supply canister protruded from a cubbyhole beneath a nearby workstation. It was empty except for the inflatable bladders used to cushion its contents during lift-off. He deflated the bladders and guided the canister into the blister.

Carla Sue's T-shirt had floated up to her shoulders. Lance folded her legs, pressed her thighs against her breasts, then pulled the T-shirt over her knees to lock her in fetal position. As he stuffed her into the canister, her neck bent at an impossible angle. He was overwhelmed by a momentary sense of déjà vu, then he shook his head and closed the latch.

He never had murdered anyone before. At least, he didn't think he had.

At 0800 hours the next morning, Dan was in his office talking to Tom Henderson over a secured comm link.

"As normal as can be expected," he said in answer

to Henderson's opening and most obvious question. "How about with you?"

"Been fielding a slew of phone calls from CNN," said Henderson. "In particular from a guy named Ed Yablon. He's Weiss's bureau chief."

"I'm sure you can handle it," said Dan. "How's *Constellation* coming?"

"On the pad at Kennedy. Still will take two, maybe three days before she's cleared for launch. One good break, the weather looks like it will cooperate."

Thank heaven for small favors, thought Dan.

"All the personal communications for the Trikon people are piling up here," Henderson said. "My people think you ought to let the incoming messages through."

Dan shook his head. "If I do then they'll start pressuring to send down their replies. No deal."

"Some stuff for your crew members, too. Including the medical officer."

Hesitating a moment, Dan grudgingly answered, "Okay, I guess you can send that through. Nothing else, though."

"Okay."

Before either Dan or Henderson could say another word, an alarm buzzer sounded in the command module.

"—the hell is that?" said Henderson.

Dan did not answer. He flew into the command and control center. A warning light on the life-support instrument panel flashed yellow, indicating that the oxygen supply in the atmospheric mix was nearing a dangerously low level. Dan tapped the blinking button and the angry buzz of the alarm switched off. But the yellow light still flashed balefully.

"Freddy!" he shouted.

No one answered.

Dan launched himself to the infirmary and banged on Lorraine's door. She had a European tech inside with her; they both looked more curious than apprehensive.

"Was that an alarm we heard?" she asked, with a slightly puzzled smile.

"You seen Freddy anywhere?"

Lorraine's smile evaporated. "No. Why?"

"What about Lance or Stanley?"

"Haven't seen them either."

"Thanks. No big deal. Sorry."

Dan sailed back to his office, where Henderson's image waited on the screen.

"Minor problem, Tom. A crewman forgot to replace an oxygen cylinder. I'll do it myself. You have anything else?"

"Not now. If I do, I'll holler."

"Rog," said Dan as he cut the comm link.

He went directly to the logistics module without searching for any of his crewman. It was unlike Freddy to ignore an order, especially one so vital to the station's life support. But then again, the conditions on the station had been abnormal. Anything could get lost in the shuffle. I've got to get this tin can running efficiently again, Dan growled to himself.

He located the nearly depleted oxygen cylinder and quickly replaced it with a fresh one. As he was about to exit the module, he noticed a science-supply canister attached to a bulkhead in a position reserved for waste receptacles. Stencil markings on the canister identified it as belonging to the Mars Project.

"Goddamn Martians act like they own the place," muttered Dan. He detached the canister and shoved it gently in the direction of its proper storage area. The canister wobbled slightly and struck a dry-goods cylinder with a loud thud. Dan instantly realized the canister held something far more massive than usual.

He opened the lid. Carla Sue Gamble stared back at him.

"Jesus Christ," he muttered. "Jesus H. Christ and a half."

They were in the deepest recess of the logistics module, well hidden from anyone who happened to float past the hatch. Dan had waited until after Lorraine completed her therapy session with the European tech before asking her to accompany him. He did not want to arouse suspicion.

"Asphyxiation. Eight, maybe ten hours ago," said Lorraine, her voice dropping in response to Dan's urgent gestures. "I'll get another body bag."

"Not yet," whispered Dan. "We're going to leave her right here."

Lorraine held her hands palm up as if asking why.

"I know I didn't kill her and I'm pretty sure you didn't either. After that, I'm not certain about anyone. Every innocent person on this station thinks we have a killer locked away at the observatory. If they learn otherwise, we'll have a real panic on our hands. And the shuttle is still at least two days away."

"But someone will notice she's missing."

"We'll deal with that problem when it comes up. Help me with this."

They closed Carla Sue in the canister.

"Lorraine, can you take over for me for a couple of hours?"

"Me?"

Nodding, "Stanley's on watch at the command module. If you have any problems, he can help. I don't know where the hell Freddy Aviles or Lance Muncie have gotten to."

She saw the anxiety on his face, heard it in his voice. "Sure, Dan. But where will you be?"

"I want to visit O'Donnell. Maybe I was wrong about him."

* * *

In the main airlock, Dan sucked oxygen from a mask as he worked himself into an EMU. Prebreathe was a pain in the ass. The pure oxygen was so dry it felt like sandpaper rasping his sinuses. And it was boring. He usually fumed about NASA, ESA, and Trikon's joint inability to fashion a space suit pressurized to one atmosphere, but this time he actually welcomed the forced inactivity. At least he wouldn't discover any more dead bodies.

His thoughts turned to O'Donnell. What did he expect to accomplish by traveling to the observatory? Would O'Donnell have any answers, any clues about what the hell was happening on Trikon Station? Did he expect to return O'Donnell to the station? And if so, as what? An advisor? An ally? An instant source of panic?

Dan snapped his helmet into place and called Lorraine over channel D, the secured comm link he had designated for their chatter.

"I'm all gassed up and ready for egress," he said. "Any of my crew show themselves?"

"Just Stanley," said Lorraine, her usually husky voice sounding thin over the tiny speaker. "I haven't seen Lance or Freddy."

"Any other problems?"

"Not a one. No one's asked about Carla Sue yet."

"I won't be gone long. Out."

"Take care," she replied before he cut the link.

Outside the airlock, Dan backed himself into an MMU and ran a quick check of its propulsion and guidance systems. Finding everything in proper order, he undocked and jetted off on a path that looped around the raft of modules at a safe distance. The brilliant wash of sunlight and earthglow exhilarated him, and he found himself thinking not of Weiss or O'Donnell or Carla Sue but of Lorraine. For reasons he could not fully understand, he sensed that their relationship was about to change. Everything that had happened before—the early days of their stint on the station, the blood-pressure testing, her fling with Kurt Jaeckle—slowly diminished into irrelevance. He did not know exactly what lay ahead for them, but he felt certain that a new relationship between them was beginning. It almost made him smile.

The sight of the observatory growing smoothly beyond his visor returned Dan to the problems at hand. He nudged the translation control, brought the MMU to a stop less than a meter from the airlock, and docked to a fitting next to the airlock entry hatch. After some trouble disengaging himself, he tethered the MMU to the docking port and entered the observatory. As the airlock slowly repressurized, Dan stared down through the mesh-covered porthole. The raft of modules—so massive and labyrinthine when viewed up close—seemed like insignificant Tinkertoys against the luminescent Earth.

After the pressure equalized, Dan removed his helmet and pulled himself through the hatch into the observatory. O'Donnell floated near the apex of the conical interior. He obviously realized he had a visitor, but he kept his eye nestled against the lens of an optical telescope. His hair, which normally gave a slicked-back appearance when restrained by a net, floated out in a nest of spikes. His free hand twirled his glasses by the eyepiece.

"You ever see any of this stuff?" he said without taking his eye off the telescope. "Makes you appreciate how much our atmosphere distorts light rays."

"Carla Sue Gamble has been murdered," said Dan.

O'Donnell turned slowly, deliberately, toward him. "That's funny, I don't remember killing her."

"You didn't."

"Whew, what a relief." O'Donnell fixed his eye back on the telescope. "You have any idea where

Neptune is? Been looking for that bastard for hours."

Dan braced himself, then wrenched O'Donnell away from the telescope.

"Look, Hugh, I didn't come here to bullshit about the sky. I want some answers. Now what in the good Christ is happening on my space station?"

"I fucked up," O'Donnell said with sadness. "No, to be more precise, someone fucked me up."

"That's what you were trying to tell me back in the rumpus room?"

"I did a lot of drugs in my day, but I never fooled around with fentanyl. Too strong. No margin for error. People die doing that shit," said O'Donnell. "It was in my toothpaste. Somehow. I remember it tasted funny. You can check it. There's a trace left."

"I will," said Dan, knowing that the investigators would test it Earthside. "But who? Why?"

"Who could be anyone. Anybody on the station is capable of synthesizing fentanyl, except maybe you and your crew. And why? Well, there's a damn good reason."

"Such as?"

O'Donnell swam for the telescope, but Dan grabbed his shoulder. O'Donnell stared at him for a full minute. Then he told him.

He started with the legal assassination of his company, Agritech, Inc. His name was Jack O'Neill then, and he had already long been using drugs—principally cocaine and amphetamines—as a way of coping with his myriad personal and legal problems. But the injunction that the Foundation for Assessing Technology had won against his company accelerated his downward spiral into a plummeting nosedive. One night, after eluding a repo man who had come to claim his BMW, he tooled the barrios of East L.A. looking for a bag of blow. He scored five minutes before being arrested in a police sweep.

He spent a night and a day in an open-air holding

pen in the Los Angeles Coliseum. His polo shirt and penny loafers marked him as an outsider, maybe a police informer, and gangs of suspicious, angry detainees beat the shit out of him repeatedly. As dusk reddened the sky, two officers dragged him to a makeshift courtroom for arraignment. He was battered, bloody, and mumbling incoherently. A man in a blue suit, whom he took to be his court-appointed lawyer, spoke to the judge. The next thing he knew, he was seated with the man in the back of a gray car that hurtled away from the Coliseum.

The man identified himself only as Welch and stated he had posted bond for him. If O'Neill played ball, his arrest would be expunged and he would be given a new life and a new identity. If he didn't play ball, he could spend the next ten years as a homicidal weight lifter's jailhouse wife.

So he became Hugh O'Donnell. Welch supervised his therapy in a thousand-dollar-a-day substance abuse clinic and monitored his aftercare. One year later he was clean, and Welch installed him in a lab in the Tehachapi Mountains. The lab was supposedly owned by a company named Simi Bioengineering, but O'Donnell was convinced it was a government installation. He worked on several projects, each involving the removal of enzymes from various plants by genetic means. He suspected that these projects were mere dry runs for something much more important.

He stayed at the lab for two years, leaving only for meetings of a motorcycle club for recovered addicts he had cofounded. At the beginning of July he was informed by Welch that he had been selected to conduct research on a top-secret project so potentially dangerous that it could only be performed on Trikon Station.

"You know the rest," O'Donnell concluded.

Dan was reluctant to agree. The story may have jibed with information he and Lorraine had pieced together. But he still heard her cautionary words: Addicts are con artists. Even if they clean up, those other habits die hard. Dan wanted to question him, but before he had a chance a call came over the observatory intercom.

"Hi, Dan. Oh, I can't believe I'm saying this." The voice belonged to Lorraine. She sounded giddy, like a giggling little girl. "I want you to know that I really do care about you. Maybe it's because—"

"Lorraine!" shouted Dan.

"—it's because I can't see you right now. Sometimes it's easier—"

He flew to the comm console. "Lorraine, this is Dan. Acknowledge."

"—to say things over a gadget rather than in person." Her voice faded.

"What the hell was that all about?" said O'Donnell.

"Lorraine, acknowledge," Dan repeated. But all he raised was silence. "Damned if I know."

Dan pulled himself to the airlock and peered through the portholes.

"Crazy broad must have O.D. too," he said, hoping that explained the message. He moved his head around the porthole, focusing on the silhouette of each of the modules one at a time. Everything appeared normal.

"Aw hell, Dan. There you go selling yourself short. A woman doesn't need Orbital Dementia to be interested in you. She needs to be totally insane."

Dan answered him with a grunt as his eyes scanned from The Bakery to Jasmine to ELM.

"Anyway," said O'Donnell, trying to win back his audience, "I think whoever slipped me the mickied toothpaste knows what he's doing."

Dan nodded absently. The Mars module, which jutted out beyond the trailing edge of the diamond as a continuation of the connecting tunnel, seemed to be askew. Dan blinked. The module still seemed bent.

Thinking it was an anomalous reflection on the glass, he moved his head. The module was not merely out of line. It was completely broken from its mooring.

"Holy shit!" he said. "The goddamn Mars module just separated from the station."

"What?" said O'Donnell.

"You heard me. Get your ass suited up. We've got to get back there."

As O'Donnell struggled into the EMU, Dan tried to raise Lorraine on the comm unit. Channel D was silent. He opened all the channels. A synthesized ringing made his flesh crawl: a life-support alarm.

"You and I will talk over channel C," he said to O'Donnell as he put on his helmet.

O'Donnell grunted. Dan helped him struggle into his suit, the need to hurry fighting against the need to make certain the suit was safely sealed and working properly. There was no need to prebreathe. The pure oxygen of the observatory was the same pressure as the EMUs. And entering the higher pressure of the station itself would pose no danger of embolism.

Dan led the way out the hatch and fit himself into the MMU. "Sit on my lap," he instructed O'Donnell.

"What lap?" But the space-suited figure backed against Dan, who wrapped his legs around O'Donnell's waist.

"Lock your arms around my knees," Dan said.

"Just like biking," O'Donnell said. "Almost." His voice in Dan's earphones sounded full of doubt, if not outright fear.

The station shuddered. Like a giant sail suddenly caught in a crosswind. Like a man startled by danger.

"Did you see that?" Dan heard a voice yell, high-pitched with fear. His own.

"Looked like the whole damned station . . . shook," O'Donnell said, hollow-voiced.

Dan fought back murderous fury and the terrible fear that clawed at his chest as he watched the space station begin to wobble and sway. Through the heavily tinted visor of his helmet he saw the bulbous, burnt-orange structure of the detached Mars module begin to drift away, like a rudderless ship caught by an evil tide. The broad wings of the solar panels were swaying, undulating visibly. Dan knew they would break up within minutes.

We're all going to die, said a voice inside his head. We're going to die and it's my fault. All my own goddamned stupid fault.

The Mars module was about five meters starboard of the station's leading edge and drifting slowly. Dan flew the MMU into that gap. Both hatches appeared to be properly sealed. Dan jetted around to the aft end of the module. The only way to see inside was through the observation blister—if the lid of the clamshell was retracted.

It was.

Inside the blister, a male and a female Martian clutched each other while their crimson flight suits, turned inside out but still attached to their wrists and ankles, billowed around them.

"What the hell!" Dan yelled into his helmet microphone.

"Don't know," said O'Donnell. "Look there."

Beyond the Martians coupling and through the open door of the blister, Kurt Jaeckle bounced between the floor and ceiling of the module, cushioning each landing with his hands and feet. There was an unmistakable expression of glee on his face, the kind Dan expected Jaeckle would wear if he ever landed on Mars.

"This module isn't going anywhere," said Dan as he tapped out a tiny blast from the retrothrusters. "We'd better get inside."

"But it's drifting away!" O'Donnell's voice in his earphones sounded demanding, urgent, but not panicked. That's something, at least, Dan said to himself.

Aloud, he answered, "It's sealed tight. It's got no propulsion. It'll drift, but we'll be able to get it and reattach after we get the station straightened away."

O'Donnell did not answer. Dan hoped his tone of command instilled more confidence than he actually felt. Maybe they could get the Martians back before the damned ET drifted too far. Maybe. It depended on what the hell was going on in the station itself.

Dan looked carefully at each of the other modules as he and O'Donnell looped toward the main airlock. Nothing else was obviously amiss. There was no voice traffic over any of the comm channels and the single life-support alarm still blared.

It seemed to take hours to get to the airlock, detach the MMU, open the hatch, and go inside. Dan looked through the tiny portholes of the airlock's inner hatch as he started the repressurization pumps. Halfway down the connecting tunnel, Stu Roberts jerked about as if holding the end of a live wire.

"What the hell's he doing?" Dan muttered over the clattering of the pumps.

O'Donnell nudged Dan away.

"Giving a rock concert," he said matter-of-factly. "Does that every day."

O'Donnell's interpretation lent a crude logic to Roberts's movements. The young tech windmilled his arm across the strings of an air guitar, pounded invisible drums, and ran his fingers along the keys of an imaginary piano. Two pairs of European couples, their lab uniforms disheveled and torn, popped out of ELM. They whirled and tumbled, their faces contorted in silent laughter. Hisashi Oyamo followed, bare to the waist. He pounded his beach-ball gut with his fists as he drifted near Roberts.

Dan tried calling Lorraine. Static crackled on Channel D. O'Donnell cut in on Channel C. "Green light, Dan." The airlock pressure had equalized.

"Don't open your helmet!" Dan snapped. "We're

keeping the suits on. I show one life-support alarm sounding. Everybody's acting so weird, maybe there's something in the air."

"Like what?"

"Who the hell knows? But the suits stay on."

Suddenly, Dan's comm unit exploded into a synthesized cacophony of Klaxons, horns, buzzers, and bells. The airlock seemed to slide sideways and both men tumbled toward its outer hatch.

"What—?" O'Donnell gasped.

Outside the hatch's porthole, the stars seemed to slant dizzyingly across the black sky. But Dan didn't need a visual to know what was happening.

"The station!" he yelled. "It's gone into a tumble!"

4 SEPTEMBER 1998
TRIKON STATION

SOMETIME EARLIER, WHILE Dan was prebreathing pure oxygen in preparation for visiting the observatory, Chakra Ramsanjawi had sailed forth from his compartment in Hab 1 wearing an emergency breathing mask and a tank strapped to his back that held a three-hour air supply. The time was 0945 hours, and no one was in the connecting tunnel to notice him. The Martians and Trikon scientists were at workstations in their respective science modules. Freddy Aviles was still sleeping off the side effects of the previous night's interrogation. Stanley was on duty in the command module in Tighe's usual place.

Ramsanjawi slipped into the logistics module. From beneath his *kurta,* he removed a small cylinder made of rubber and plastic. With a flick of his hands, he broke the impermeable inner partition that separated the two highly reactive gases he had toiled through the night to create. The cylinder seemed to come alive in his fingers as the two gases combined with a hiss.

He spent a minute analyzing the spaghetti of wires, hoses, and ducts that comprised the veins and arteries of the life-support system. Then, using the same type of screwdriver he had provided Aaron Weiss, he quickly removed a protective collar and sliced open a duct. An alarm would sound in the command module, but that was no matter. The surprise he had dreamed up for the people of Trikon Station was so fast-acting that he doubted anyone would have time to respond.

He pushed the cylinder into the air duct, punctured its rubber seal with the blade of the screwdriver, then quickly replaced the collar over the slit.

The hatch darkened; someone had reacted quickly to the alarm. Ramsanjawi hid himself behind a wall of cylinders and watched crewman Stanley trace along the duct system in search of the problem. Within minutes the sandy-haired Aussie found the collar and inspected it carefully, rubbing his jaw and comparing the actual duct work with a binder of specs tethered to his belt. He was about to detach the collar when he suddenly began to whistle. He flung his screwdriver away. It clattered among the supply cylinders, bouncing so close to Ramsanjawi's head that the Indian flinched.

Stanley's whistling quickened into a snappy polka. He locked his hands at the base of his spine and moved his legs like a figure skater.

Ramsanjawi stole out of hiding. He edged past Stanley, carefully avoiding the strong, fluid movements of the crewman's feet. Stanley did not miss a note. His eyes fell directly on Ramsanjawi without acknowledging his presence, preferring, Ramsanjawi knew, the pageant playing within his mind.

Ramsanjawi waited at the hatch, smiling behind his oxygen mask. Another minute or two and everyone would be occupied with their own personal dreams. The treasures in O'Donnell's lab would belong to him.

Kurt Jaeckle had taken the scent wafting through his office to be lilacs. His nose trembled as if he were about to sneeze, but he pinched his nostrils and the urge passed. The scent seemed stronger, and for a moment he thought he saw a thin purple plume curling out of the air vent. He waved his hand and the plume—if it ever existed—dissipated. He drew two long draughts of air deep into his lungs. The air was sweet, so sweet.

Suddenly, Jaeckle had an idea. It was such a great idea, such a fantastic notion, that he wondered why it had not occurred to him long before. He opened the accordion door and twirled out his office.

The Martians were at their workstations, but no one seemed interested in work. They moved their hands toward their gaping mouths as if the air were made of custard.

"Friends, Romans, fellow Martians," Jaeckle called in his most stentorian voice. "This is the day we have hoped and prayed and worked for over so many long, hard years. We are about to set out for the red planet Mars, at last. This is history! All in favor, say aye!"

The response shook the entire module.

"All opposed, say no."

The Martians fell silent, except for a couple of giggles.

"Fantastic!" Jaeckle clapped his hands. "Let's take this sucker to Mars."

As the Martians applauded, Jaeckle pressed the two closest males into securing the twin hatches at the junction between the module and the connecting tunnel.

"Where's Carla Sue?" one asked with a laugh.

"Yeah, I haven't seen her," giggled the other.

"She didn't want to come," said Jaeckle. "Imagine that. She said she didn't want to come to Mars."

"Well, fuck her, then."

"I did," Jaeckle said, grinning. "Early and often."

He felt he would burst with laughter.

Fabio Bianco had been arguing with Thora Skillen in The Bakery when the scent of flowers tickled his nose. The topic of the argument was O'Donnell's lab. Skillen still insisted that the American/Canadian contingent was the rightful custodian of O'Donnell's data and threatened to present the issue to Jonathan Eldredge as soon as communications with the ground were restored. Bianco remained adamantly opposed and privately thought it quite amusing that Skillen would invoke the very person who had arranged for O'Donnell's presence on the station.

The scent immediately reminded Bianco of the perfume worn by a waitress who worked in a Venetian café he had frequented as a young man. Imagine that, a part of his mind marveled. I have not even thought about her in fifty years, yet she returns to me. No matter how hot and crowded the café may have been, she always seemed as clean and as fresh as dew on a morning flower. Young Fabio would drink espresso until his nerve endings sizzled just for the pleasure of gazing at her.

Bianco breathed deeply, reveling in the memory from his youth. The edges of his vision purpled, then cleared. Thora Skillen's marble-white skin had deepened to the color of mocha. Her sharp, angular features had softened into graceful curves. Her salt-and-pepper buzz cut had sprouted into long auburn tresses sparkling with a hint of Mediterranean sunlight.

"Bella," he said, brushing her cheeks with his knuckles. *"Molta bella."*

In Skillen's eyes, Fabio Bianco was her father, the father she feared and hated, the father she loved beyond all others. Just as she had always longed for him to do, her father embraced her lovingly. Skillen took her father's trembling hand and worked it beneath her lab smock.

Lance Muncie had taken almost half an hour to don his EMU. He wasn't about to let the rock music that suddenly boomed outside his compartment destroy his concentration. With great care, he took the helmet in both his hands, gazing upon it for a solemn moment as he imagined a Crusader knight would have gazed on his armored headpiece.

A flowery smell filled the compartment. Lance coughed so hard the helmet popped out of his hands. He hated flowery perfumes, and this one made him feel light-headed. But he passed it off as excitement. This was the greatest day of his life, the day he would leave his mark. Carla Sue had been punished. And now the rest of these godless scientists would meet their deserved end.

He secured the helmet and activated the suit's air supply. The rock music faded to a muffled drumbeat. After a few breaths, his light-headedness disappeared. He felt strong as a bull, keen as a knife.

He swept aside the accordion door of his compartment.

He felt worthy.

Chakra Ramsanjawi had waited inside the logistics module until he was certain that everyone on board was under the influence of the Lethe. He heard the distant echo of the Mars module erupting into a series of cheers led by Kurt Jaeckle and saw the two male Martians closing their hatch. Guessing what Jaeckle intended, he made certain that the connecting tunnel was properly sealed from his side before he moved on. There was no sense stealing the anticoca gene if he did not survive to profit by it.

As he swam down the connecting tunnel, he heard the blare of music from Stu Roberts's portable CD player. Roberts himself twitched like a one-man band, and a pair of Japanese techs cavorted in something that resembled a piscine mating dance. Even Oyamo, so stoic and staid during their chess matches, cut loose. He accompanied Roberts's performance by pounding his bare belly with his fists.

Ramsanjawi stopped in ELM to grab a small satchel from his office. The scene inside the module was as raucous as in the connecting tunnel. Finally, he pulled himself into The Bakery. The module was decorated with multicolored clouds as the techs and scientists, laughing uproariously, tossed broken vials between workstations. In the center of the aisle, Fabio Bianco and Thora Skillen had found each other.

Ramsanjawi hastily removed the hinges from the lab door. He had not been able to synthesize a great quantity of Lethe from available materials. The drug's effects would begin to wear off soon after the ventilation system purged itself and everyone breathed clean air again.

He first concentrated on the coca plants. He noted those that flourished and those that ailed and the covered culture dishes of microbe colonies that O'Donnell had employed to deliver the genetic mechanism. The ailing plants were O'Donnell's failures; the healthy ones were possible successes. He snipped a leaf and a portion of root from each healthy plant. He labelled the samples, bound them in plastic, and placed them in his satchel. Then he turned to the flat round culture dishes. From his review of O'Donnell's computer data, he knew that only a dozen or so of the glass dishes contained promising genetic material. Using tiny pneumatic test tubes, he began taking samples of each. Since liquids did not pour in microgee, the task was far more tedious than simply lopping off a leaf or snipping a section of root.

He was nearly finished collecting his samples when a Canadian scientist banged into the lab.

"We're havin' a party, eh?" said the scientist. His lab smock was so splashed with colored liquids it looked like a tie-dyed shirt.

Ramsanjawi waved him away. The scientist stared at him oddly, as if confused by Ramsanjawi's breathing apparatus.

"Some mask you have there, eh?"

Instinctively, Ramsanjawi moved to protect the

flexible plastic tube that looped over his shoulder and connected with the air tank on his back. He picked a greenish vial from the wall rack and ceremoniously smashed it against the Canadian's shoulder. Most of the liquid sailed in a flurry of tiny green balls, but some was absorbed into the cotton of the smock.

"Hey, that's cool," said the Canadian, gaping at his newest splash of color. He snatched a yellow vial from the wall. "This one is pretty."

It also was one of the solutions Ramsanjawi wanted to steal. The Canadian held it up to the light with one eye closed like a stupid drunk. Ramsanjawi carefully extricated the vial from the Canadian's fingers. The Canadian did not protest. He simply started to look for another pretty color.

Ramsanjawi had a brainstorm. Rather than close up the lab and feign ignorance about its missing contents, he would induce The Bakery's revelers to destroy it. He scooped a handful of vials from the wall and tossed them out of the lab. The Canadian, laughing, sailed after them. Ramsanjawi heaved another batch. Then he returned to the task of collecting the last of the samples.

Lorraine had been talking with Stanley when the alarm sounded, indicating a problem with the life-support system. Stanley explained that the problem was undoubtedly minor—the computers were so sensitive they sounded alarms for virtually any reason—but he sailed off to investigate. It was then, as Lorraine watched the yellow light flashing within the computer-generated diagram of the logistics module, that the aroma of flowers enveloped her like a shower of rose petals.

Suddenly, Lorraine had the maddest, most uncontrollable urge to be with Dan. Her heart swelled in her chest. Soft laughter bubbled in her throat. This was utter nonsense. She was a doctor, a medical officer on a space station. She wasn't a schoolgirl.

Nonsense aside, she sailed to Dan's office door. Biting her lip to keep her laughter at bay, she peeled off her hairnet and opened the collar of her shirt enough to reveal a hint of cleavage. Steady now, she told herself, no time to be immature.

Poised to dive into his arms, she gracefully swept open the door. The office was empty except for the bonsai bird fluttering in the sudden breeze. Of course, she remembered, he had gone to the observatory for some silly reason. But she could reach him on Channel D. D for Dan. She unclipped the headset from the comm console and called to him over the radio.

"Hi, Dan. Oh, I can't believe I'm saying this. I want you to know that I really do care about you. Maybe it's because I can't see you right now. Sometimes it's easier to say things over a gadget rather than in person."

"Lorraine," he said.

His voice sounded so sweet, so kind. She wanted to caress him, nuzzle him, press her lips over every inch of that beloved face. Instead, she hugged the headset against her breasts. She closed her eyes and rocked her arms as his words poured directly into her heart. He was shy, he told her, and unsure of himself after his divorce. For months he had watched her from afar, wanting her but uncertain how to approach her. So he clothed his words in jargon and buried his feelings in a professional relationship. But all that had changed— he had changed. He had developed a new appreciation for her. Oh hell, he might as well say it. . . . He loved her.

"I love you too," she whispered as she cuddled the headset. "I love you too."

She had no idea how many times she repeated her words. A hundred times, maybe a thousand. She felt her body swaying back and forth, as if she were in her grandfather's wonderful old rocking chair. She opened her eyes and saw him at the command and control center, still dressed in his space suit, like a knight in pure white armor.

She flung herself out of the office, and suddenly the module tilted drunkenly. Lorraine put out her hands to cushion her fall to the floor. Dan's feet were anchored beneath the computer console, his gloved fingers flicking across the keyboard like a grand maestro, but he too swayed and had to grab at the edge of the console to steady himself.

"Dan," she said. "Oh, Dan, you've come back!"

He paused, the gold visor of his helmet regarding her like the eye of a strange god. The reflection of her own distorted face smiled stupidly in the heavily tinted glass. Then he turned back to the keyboard.

She could not believe her eyes. He was ignoring her, rejecting her, mere minutes after professing his love for her. He couldn't be Dan. He couldn't be the man she loved.

She dove at him, pressed her eyes against the helmet. The face that loomed out of the shadows was hard, cruel, set in anger.

Lance ripped her from his shoulders and sent her spinning. She leaped back toward him, but he swatted her backhand across the mouth. Her eyes seemed to pop out of their sockets, and then they slowly closed.

Lance shoved her down the aisle. Then he went back to the command console and continued pecking out a new program for the translation thrusters.

4 SEPTEMBER 1998
TRIKON STATION

SUSPECT KILLED IN ESCAPE ATTEMPT

COALINGO, CA—A murder suspect being transported from San Francisco to Los Angeles by sheriff's deputies was killed early this morning while trying to escape on a lonely stretch of Interstate 5 in Fresno County.

Deputy Luther Green and Deputy Hector Andujar were returning the suspect to Los Angeles to face charges in connection with the murder of a Topanga woman.

The suspect, Harold Meade, reportedly worked free of his handcuffs. He slugged Deputy Andujar, and in the ensuing struggle with Deputy Green the car overturned in a roadside gully.

Police said Meade disarmed Green and was preparing to kill him when Andujar shot him through the neck with his service revolver. The deputies sustained only minor injuries in the struggle.

Meade was arrested in San Francisco yesterday in connection with the sexual assault and murder of Stacey Hollis, a 32-year-old Topanga woman who died from a massive injection of an animal tranquilizer. Meade, a British national, was apprehended at San Francisco International Airport while attempting to board a flight to Melbourne, Australia. In a routine inspection of luggage, airport security officials found

a supply of the same type of animal tranquilizer used in the Topanga murder.
                              —*Fresno Bee,* 4 September 1998

DAN AND HUGH O'Donnell felt as if they were in a runaway elevator. The airlock surged with sudden weight again and they tumbled against its outer hatch in a flurry of flailing arms and legs and curses.

Dan cut his EMU comm link with the station's alarm system. He didn't need those damn bells and Klaxons to remind him that all hell had broken loose. The other channels were silent except for an occasional crackle of static.

"What's that noise?" O'Donnell's voice muttered in Dan's helmet earphones.

Dan heard it. A low-frequency hum, like a giant bronze statue of Buddha intoning its mantra. The feeling of weight shifted again and they both slid to what had once been the airlock's overhead.

"What is it?" O'Donnell repeated.

"The whole damned station is vibrating," Dan replied grimly. "Like a big tuning fork."

"Jesus! Will it break up?"

"If we let it." Dan climbed to his booted feet. "Come on."

He guesstimated the station's sudden gravity to be around one-sixth g, like that of the moon. It didn't sound like a tremendous change—theoretically, he was capable of jumping six times farther or lifting objects six times heavier than on Earth. But after nine months of micro-gee, he felt like the circus fat man.

"We've got to get through the hatch," Dan said. "Give me a lift."

Grunting, O'Donnell boosted him within reach of the inner hatch. Dan reached for the small wheel that controlled the locking mechanism. The airlock lurched again and his gloved fingers slipped from the wheel. He came banging down hard, O'Donnell sprawling painfully beside him.

The suits aren't built for punishment, Dan knew. But they sure hand it out when you thump around inside them.

"Laurel and Hardy open a hatch," O'Donnell muttered. Dan did not need to tell him to get up and start again.

It took two more tries, but finally the wheel turned, the lock released, and the hatch popped open. O'Donnell pushed Dan through. Then Dan reached down and hauled O'Donnell into the connecting tunnel. They were both drenched with sweat.

"Command module," Dan said.

"I'm going to The Bakery," responded O'Donnell. "My lab."

In microgravity the tunnel had been a long corridor that they could swim through. Now it was a long slanting tube that they had to climb up. Laboriously, on their hands and knees, they started up opposite sides of the tunnel. The space suits felt as if they weighed tons.

"Like climbing Mt. Everest," Dan grunted.

O'Donnell's panting voice answered, "Look out for the Abominable Snowman, pal."

For Chakra Ramsanjawi, the first indication that something was amiss occurred when an orange-colored liquid spilled out of a vial. Rather than separate and disperse into a thousand orange beads, the liquid held together like a tongue-shaped river and streamed toward the bulkhead. It formed a puddle into which Ramsanjawi, suddenly drifting himself, splashed belly first. The lab door, still held by its padlocked hasp, slammed shut against its disconnected hinges.

Alarms clanged over the intercom system. A synthesized female voice calmly intoned: "Emergency.

Emergency. Major malfunction. All personnel to CERV stations. All personnel to CERV stations. Prepare to abandon the station."

"What the bloody hell is this?" Ramsanjawi grumbled to himself. He tucked the satchel under his arm and scrambled upright. He found himself standing on the bulkhead nearly perpendicular to the module's usual vertical. Several vials cascaded slowly out of the compartments that once corralled them. They tinkled around his feet.

He felt heavy. Ramsanjawi tried pushing the door with one hand. He had not bothered with Trikon's suggested exercise regimen, and he was unpleasantly surprised to learn how much his muscles had atrophied. He placed the satchel in a nearby compartment and used both hands along with a slight bend in his knees to throw open the door. Grabbing the satchel, he climbed out.

The Bakery looked even more a mess than before. Every loose object had slid to one side of the module. No one seemed concerned; gravity only added to the fun of Lethe. Scientists and technicians tumbled and frolicked in the multihued mayhem.

Ramsanjawi hoisted himself through the hatch. Something was very wrong. He could not imagine the exact cause of the problem, but he knew one thing very clearly: he was getting the hell out of The Bakery.

Lance stared through the command module's viewport. The Earth had slipped completely out of view and now the stars slid across his field of vision.

He had done it—seized control of the command module, blasted the station into a cartwheel that would tear it asunder. But there was one minor problem, one detail he hadn't foreseen: no one seemed to care. Where were the Trikon scientists, the Martians, his fellow crewmen? Why weren't they jamming the command module, whimpering, pleading, begging for their lives?

He stole a glance at Lorraine, hovering in the area between the command center and the utilities section. Her face was pretty in repose. And she had been so kind when he was sick and when he was troubled. Damnation, why did he always go for the bad ones, the Beckys, the Carla Sues, the ones who looked so fine and talked so fine and stabbed you in the back. Maybe he should save her. There would be more than enough room in the lifeboat.

Suddenly he realized why everyone was avoiding him. They were using psychology. That was it. They were ignoring him. Ignore him and he'll go away. Ignore him and he'll stop fussing. Ignore him and he'll go to sleep. His parents had used that psychology whenever his stomach hurt him. He would hear them from his bed, carefully raising their voices so he would hear. Ignore him and he'll go to sleep.

He fired off more commands to the translation thrusters. Let them ignore this one!

Ramsanjawi staggered out of The Bakery's hatch directly in front of O'Donnell. Or maybe it was above him. Goddamn, thought O'Donnell, this place is more confusing with gravity than without it.

Ramsanjawi's eyes, above the breathing mask, popped wide as he recognized O'Donnell through the tinted visor of his helmet. He scuttled along the wall, one hand clutching a black satchel, the other groping for handholds. O'Donnell tried to tackle him, but the Indian slipped free.

Fuck him, thought O'Donnell as he bent himself through the hatch. The Bakery looked like the aftermath of a fingerpaint fight. In any other context, the sight of grown adults gamboling among the drifting and sloshing wads of color would have been hilarious. But O'Donnell felt cold terror clutching at him. Then he caught sight of his lab and his heart stopped.

The vials, the culture dishes, the test tubes—all of them—broken, smashed. Their contents oozed along the bulkhead in a purplish-gray mass. And someone had tampered with the plants. Each was missing exactly one leaf.

O'Donnell tried to jump out of the lab, but a sudden surge of gravity sent him crashing against the bulkhead. He tried again, and this time managed to claw his way first through the lab door and then out the hatch and into the connecting tunnel.

Across the tunnel, a space-suited figure dangled from the open door of a locker.

"Dan, is that you?" O'Donnell called.

In his helmet earphones he heard, "Yeah." Dan was breathing hard, trying to climb up the tunnel wall toward the command module.

"You okay?" O'Donnell asked.

Dan grunted. "Yeah." And kept struggling up the tunnel wall.

Ramsanjawi, meanwhile, was nothing but a saffron dot diminishing toward the other end of the tunnel.

"Bastard stole my work," huffed O'Donnell as he lurched after him.

Dan had been climbing laboriously. With each upward lunge, he ticked off a possible reason for the station's predicament. Thruster misfire. Gyroscope damage. CERV engine ignition. Collision with the errant Mars module. But there was another possibility, and given the weird behavior already evident it was also the most likely: someone was trying to destroy the station.

Then came the surge.

It blasted him off the wall and sent him tumbling ass over teakettle down the tunnel until he managed to catch hold of a swinging locker door. Even through his helmet he could hear the station's metal frame groaning. Roberts, Oyamo, and the four Japanese techs somersaulted past, screaming like a sextet of banshees until they landed in a series of thuds against the bulkhead at the end of the tunnel.

O'Donnell emerged from The Bakery. "Dan, is that you?" he called.

"Yeah." Dan acknowledged, starting up the tunnel wall again toward the command module.

"You okay?" O'Donnell asked.

"Yeah."

"Bastard stole my work," O'Donnell growled. He disappeared down the tunnel.

Alone again, Dan scrambled around until he was belly on the wall, heading for the command module once more. Climbing was tougher, which meant the station was spinning faster. More g-forces, more weight. He heard something go *ping!* like a taut steel cable snapping. Dan moved a foot, then a hand. Then the other foot and the other hand. Like the old comic-book hero Spiderman scaling the face of a skyscraper. He paused to catch his breath. The force was weakening. A little. He was almost at the command module.

Ramsanjawi felt a sudden giddiness as he scurried past the command module's hatch. He knew that he was weightless again. But then, just as suddenly, his guts surged and he was bumping headlong toward the far end of the tunnel as if sucked into the maw of a giant vacuum cleaner. Petrified, he clawed at the storage compartments winging past him. Scrambling, fingernails screeching along metal, he banged and thumped against walls and doors until he finally managed to stop himself, bruised, battered, bleeding. But the satchel bounced crazily down, down, down.

"No matter," he breathed as a bead of sweat rolled down between his eyes and paused itchily at the rim of his oxygen mask. There were lifeboats in that direction as well.

O'Donnell glided through the micro-gee zone where the command module joined the connecting tunnel and felt the artificial gravity grab him from the other side. He could see Ramsanjawi's *kurta* bobbing in the distance. No time to rappel down the face of the tunnel, he decided. He tucked himself into a ball and let himself fall like a bomb.

Dan gripped both of his gloved hands securely on the lip of the command module's hatch. He swung his feet out toward the far end of the tunnel, the momentum ripping one hand from the hatch. Clinging desperately with the remaining hand, he painfully mustered the strength to pull himself inside.

The module was spinning like a fun-house barrel. Lorraine floated limply in the narrow aisle alongside the utilities section. Her eyes were closed and a thread of blood curled away from the corner of her lips. But she was breathing and a pulse was visible in her neck.

A flash of motion reflected in Dan's helmet visor. Someone clad in an EMU was banging at the keyboard of the main computer. The sonofabitch is deliberately wrecking the station. My station! Deliberately! I'll kill him!

Dan barreled down the aisle like a heat-seeking missile and struck the EMU solidly in the shoulder, tearing it out of the anchoring loops and sending it crashing against the viewport. Quickly bracing himself with his hands against the console behind him as the space-suited figure righted itself, Dan jackknifed and, with all the fury burning within him, kicked both legs into the soft area of the suit's midsection. He could feel muscles and ribs giving way beneath the impact of his kick.

I'll kill you, you sonofabitch, Dan snarled inwardly.

But the figure folded into a fetal position and went limp, drifting slowly upward above the instrument panel.

His hands shaking with barely controlled rage, Dan unfastened its helmet and yanked it off the EMU. Lance Muncie's head lolled around in the collar of the suit, his youthful face almost cherubic in unconsciousness.

"Oh, for God's sake," Dan said out loud. The anger drained out of him. Muncie. He must have gone berserk.

Dan shoved Lance out of the command center and anchored himself at the control panel. The instrument panel was ablaze with warning lights. Even with the alarm channel shut off, the whooping and ringing seeped into his helmet. His fingers tapped out a set of commands. The data readout showed that the tumble had begun with a short burst from the port zenith translation thruster at 1015 hours. The control moment gyroscopes had automatically tried to contain the torque generated by the burst, but they were quickly saturated and shut off automatically. A second firing command was issued seven minutes later. That's what caused the surge that knocked me back through the tunnel, Dan realized. The computer indicated that the thruster was still firing. The station wasn't only spinning. It was twisting and twanging like a paper kite caught in a high wind.

Can't abandon the station, he realized. The whole damned crew is too high to even hear the warning signals.

Muncie hadn't done that, he knew. One of the wiseass scientists had put something in the station's air. That was the only explanation.

"You're going to have to bring her back under control, mister," he muttered to himself. "You used to be a flier. Let's see if you still have the good stuff."

Strangely, he felt no fear. No more anger. He was as

calm inside as he had ever been in the cockpit of an airplane or spacecraft. There was no room for emotions when he had his hands on the controls of a dangerously careening craft. There was hardly any room for Dan Tighe to think about himself. He was one with the vehicle he was trying to control; he and this beautiful piece of machinery beneath his hands merged into a single being, nerves melding with electrical circuits, mind and machine, flesh and metal becoming one living entity.

Dan looked out the viewport and located the nadir trailing edge of the diamond against the dizzying sky. The solar panel and radiator were flapping like slow-motion bird's wings. The blue-and-white curve of the Earth slid past, then disappeared from his view. He could see a few stars in the darkness out there, whipping by so fast it almost made him dizzy.

Got to work fast. The solar panels were useless without proper orientation. Once the station lost power there would be no hope of regaining control. The station would spin and spin until it tore itself apart.

Something flashed in the corner of his vision. Leaning forward to get a better look out the window through his helmet visor, Dan saw the RMS arm weaving back and forth against the black background of space like the long, thin, bony arm of a gigantic Halloween skeleton. It's pulled loose of its restraint, he realized. Soon it would wrench free altogether and start bashing the station like a battering ram.

The Earth spun into view again. Dan keyed in a command for a display of attitude rates calculated by the inertial measurement unit. If the spin rates haven't already exceeded the ACS's limits, Dan told himself, maybe we can bring this Tinkertoy to heel. If not . . .

For a brief moment, the spin rates flashed—one revolution per minute, one point two—then the numbers exploded into garbage characters. The ACS's limit had been exceeded; the primary system was out of commission. The station was in a three-axis tumble.

Dan disengaged from his foot restraints and frantically rummaged through a nearby tool compartment. The cabin lights winked out. The command module darkened as the viewport spun away from the glow of the Earth. Dan whirled to the computer. A warning flashed: "Solar panel drive failure." Then the screen died.

Ramsanjawi lay flat on the bulkhead next to the rumpus-room hatch. With his lungs heaving and his legs as shaky as rubber, he struggled upright. His hands just reached the hatch of the CERV port.

The hatch seemed as heavy as a bank vault's. His first pull yielded nothing. The second opened the hatch briefly before it slammed shut again, nearly taking his fingers. He took a deep breath and steeled himself for one monumental pull. Slowly, the hatch peeled back. One inch, two inches, six inches. Then gravity was on his side, and the hatch snapped open.

Ramsanjawi crawled through the port and into the lifeboat. Six months' training, he thought; what a laugh. With a mere few hours of observation during and after those mindless evacuation drills, he had deduced the method of piloting the lifeboat to Earth. And even if he drifted in orbit, there was little to fear. NASA certainly would not forsake the sole survivor of Trikon Station.

Above the constant din of the alarms came a loud crash. The entire lifeboat shuddered.

The force of the landing stunned O'Donnell. When he saw the open CERV port, his senses cleared. He bounced up, hooked the port's rim with his gloves, and jerked himself through. His helmet smashed against the CERV hatch as it swung shut. O'Donnell used all his strength to prevent the hatch from locking. Wedging himself in the connecting station hatchway that Ramsanjawi had struggled to open a few moments earlier, O'Donnell pushed and pushed against the CERV hatch, feeling a slight give. Suddenly, the hatch released and he flew into the lifeboat. He landed against the far bulkhead and became entangled in the loose harnesses. Ramsanjawi gathered his satchel and fled the CERV, billowing into the connecting tunnel. O'Donnell freed himself and bounded after him.

Ramsanjawi had no time to open the other lifeboat port; O'Donnell was right on his heels. He clawed his way up the wall of the connecting tunnel and dropped into the wardroom. O'Donnell followed.

The centrifugal force had turned the module's wall into its floor, and both men clambered like harbor seals over the newly horizontal galleys. Ramsanjawi opened a galley door and began winging trays. They flew like lethal frisbees, crisply slicing through the air as O'Donnell instinctively ducked away from them. One hit the shoulder of his suit and bounced off, wobbling through the air.

Then the wardroom was plunged into darkness.

"Oh, shit," O'Donnell snapped. A tray clattered against the galley behind him. A single emergency light, glowing weakly from what had been the ceiling, cast thick slabs of shadow. O'Donnell carefully raised his helmeted head. No other trays came whizzing at him.

Ramsanjawi was nowhere in sight. O'Donnell climbed across the last of the galleys and peered through the horizontal doorway into the ex/rec area. An emergency light glowed there as well; the exercise machines and game tables, now growing out of the wall, were wrapped in shadow.

O'Donnell hooked himself over the edge of the doorway. A hand reached out of the darkness and dragged him through. He landed on his head, stayed upright for a second, then toppled onto his back. Something flashed above him. He tried to roll over, but the edge of the tray caught him in the ribs. The pain stung.

Ramsanjawi bolted for the door. O'Donnell desperately swung out a leg to trip him. The satchel popped out of the *kurta* and sailed into the upturned equipment. Both men scrambled after it like opposing linemen vying for a loose football on a wet field. Ramsanjawi came up with it and lurched away. O'Donnell hurled himself after him.

It was a crunching tackle.

O'Donnell drove the shoulder of his hardened EMU suit into Ramsanjawi's ribs, and both men fell into the rowing machine. One of O'Donnell's legs became wedged in the mechanism. He tried to brace himself, but his weight combined with Ramsanjawi's was too much. The sound of his shinbone snapping echoed through his EMU. He roared with the sudden unbearable pain.

For a second they hung as if frozen. Then the rowing machine's mounts gave way. O'Donnell, Ramsanjawi, and the machine toppled over, splintering storage compartments along the far wall.

O'Donnell held onto Ramsanjawi's upper arm, the force multipliers of one glove digging deeply into the flabby flesh, like motor-driven pincers. The Indian gave a high-pitched scream and tried to wriggle free. O'Donnell tried to reach Ramsanjawi's air hose with his other gloved hand. He wanted to give Ramsanjawi a taste of the cabin air. But his glove tips fell short by inches and the EMU restricted him from moving any closer. Pain swirled up from his leg, choking him, purpling his vision. Ramsanjawi squirmed like a hooked fish, trying to free himself from the glove's viselike grip. If O'Donnell let go, the slithering Indian bastard would get away. Into the lifeboat. Into forever.

O'Donnell stretched his arm until he thought his

shoulder would dislocate. His free hand inched closer
to Ramsanjawi's shaking air hose. His fingers curled
around it. He pulled.

He couldn't hear the air rush out. But he felt the
change come over Ramsanjawi. The Indian stopped
squirming. O'Donnell let his hand fall from
Ramsanjawi's arm.

A moment later, there was a knock on his helmet. It
sounded polite, almost friendly. Ramsanjawi stared at
him with a benign smile on his face. His mouth
moved and O'Donnell heard, like a voice in a dream,
"Would you like some tea, sir?"

"What the hell," O'Donnell said, and let the pain
and darkness engulf him.

In the weak light of the emergency lamp, Dan pried
the transparent cover from the emergency controller
receptacle. The ACS malfunction left him with only
one option: killing the spin rate by manually firing the
thrusters. It wasn't an easy task; Trikon Station wasn't
designed to be flown like a space shuttle. It was a
fragile, delicate bird, no more capable of real maneuvering than the bonsai creatures he cherished. But it
was spinning drunkenly, tearing itself apart; Dan had
to get it back under control. And fast. Without power
from the solar panels he had only minutes.

Outside the command center, Lance slowly regained consciousness. His helmet was gone, he realized. The cabin air had a slight flowery scent that
tickled his throat for a moment, then seemed to die
away, evaporate. He tried to take a deep breath but the
knife-sharp pain in his ribs made him gasp. For long
moments he clutched at a handhold, panting painfully
as his head slowly cleared. Then he saw Commander
Tighe at the controls.

"Finally couldn't ignore me," he muttered. He
flung himself headlong toward the commander.

Dan was fitting the emergency controller into its receptacle and did not sense Lance's rush until it was too late. Lance blasted him out of his anchoring loops. The two men crashed against the bulkhead in a flurry of punches and kicks. Lance was frothing, gurgling, biting at Dan's EMU. Dan fended off the blows as best he could. He no longer felt anger. He could not be incensed with a youngster who had obviously snapped his tether. Dan felt more bemused than anything else, like a fully suited football player being physically attacked by a fan in street clothes.

But Muncie was almost fully suited too. His gloved fists were flurrying madly, and even though most of his punches were wild, enough were landing on Dan's torso to hurt.

There was no time for niceties. Dan grabbed the shoulders of Muncie's EMU and butted his helmet into the youngster's forehead. Muncie's arms stopped flailing; his jaw fell slack, stunned.

"Sorry, kid," Dan muttered as he braced his feet against the wall and landed a bone-breaking right squarely on Muncie's jaw. Muncie's eyes rolled up and he hung in midair like a balloon slowly leaking air. Slowly, slowly he sagged toward the floor under the slight but discernible gravity.

"That ought to keep you quiet for a while," Dan mumbled, realizing his ribs felt sore.

He made his way back to the control panel. The emergency controller was a joystick with a pistol grip. Once in place, it automatically overrode all other commands to the ACS. Dan positioned himself so that his right hand gripped the controller and he could see clearly out the viewport. The horizon rolled past like a roller coaster and then the window showed black space with a sprinkling of stars.

Dan squeezed off a command to the forward nadir translation-thruster assembly. The stars slowed their spin past the viewport. He wrenched the joystick to his right and ordered a blast from the aft nadir thrusters. The stars stopped for an instant, then reversed field. He moved the joystick from side to side, squeezing the pistol with each turn. When the horizon crossed the port, it was moving appreciably slower.

For a crazy instant he remembered his son playing video games. I should have spent more time with him, Dan thought grimly.

With the Earth in full view, Dan switched the joystick from translation control to attitude control. He nudged pitch, yaw, and roll; took a gross reading through the port with his eye; then repeated the firing sequence with ever finer thrusts until the station had resumed something resembling gravity gradient attitude.

"That's as good as I can get it," he muttered.

He punched up the main computer. A light on the screen flickered.

"Come on, Freddy. Come on," he said, coaxing the computer back to life. "Let's see what you've done."

Emergency options scrolled across the main screen. A smaller monitor reported structural damage: one solar panel disconnected, one radiator lost. He could see the RMS arm still hanging free of its cradle, but it was no longer waving; it stood stiffly at an odd angle, like a broken bone.

Dan keyed in the ACS program. The primary gyro system responded briefly, only to fail. The secondary system came to life. The numbers on the attitude readout edged toward stability.

He puffed out an enormous, heartfelt sigh. It's out of my hands for now, he knew. He kicked out of the anchoring loops. The sick bay contained several oxygen units. Lorraine was sorely in need of some fresh air. He cradled her in his arms and gently patted her cheek. Her lips moved slightly, but locked within his EMU he couldn't hear if she made a sound. He fit the oxygen mask over her nose and mouth. Her eyes opened, and when her gaze penetrated his visor she smiled in recognition. Dan gently patted her shoulder. They had much to discuss.

6 SEPTEMBER 1998
TRIKON STATION

Crewman Muncie confessed freely to the murders of Aaron Weiss and Carla Sue Gamble, claiming that God told him they were evil and should be killed. He further stated that God wanted him to destroy Trikon Station because it was an outpost of the devil set in God's heavens.

He was heavily tranquilized and under physical restraints when he made the confession, but no sodium pentothal or other truth serum was used. Nor was coercive force. I don't know if his confession will stand up in court, but as far as possible we did not violate his civil rights.

Personally, I believe that the psychologists who examined Muncie and passed him for duty on Trikon Station are as much responsible for the murders as he is.

—Report of Cmdr. D. Tighe, 4 September 1998

"No, I WILL not leave the station," said Fabio Bianco.

Dan Tighe grimaced. The old man hovered in the doorway of Dan's office. Beyond his slim form Dan could see the relief crew from the newly docked *Constellation* at their stations in the command module. There was a lot of work to do, and Bianco was not making it any easier.

"Sir," he said, keeping his voice even, "Trikon Station will need at least two months for repair and refurbishment. All the scientific work is stopped.

Most of your scientists are demanding to go back to Earth."

"I will remain here," Bianco said.

"The shuttle *Constellation* will remain docked with us for eleven hours more," Dan continued firmly. "You must be on it when it leaves."

"It will do you no good to frown at me," Bianco said, actually smiling as if amused with Dan. "It has taken me all my life to get here. I will not leave. Not now. Not ever."

"As commander of . . ."

Bianco's smile widened. "Oh yes, of course. As *commandante* of this station you can have me carried off and put into the *Constellation*. I assure you, that is what you will have to do to get rid of me." The smile flicked off like an electric light. Bianco's face hardened into an old man's stubborn scowl. "And I assure you, Commander Tighe, that the instant I set foot on Earth once again, where I am no longer under your orders, I will fire you from Trikon. And then return here."

Dan glowered, fuming. The old bastard means what he says, he realized.

Bianco turned on the smile again. "*Commandante*, I am a reasonable man. You be reasonable too."

"But the work we have to do now . . ."

"I will not interfere with the repair work. Perhaps even the repair crews will work a little faster with me on board to peer over their shoulders, no?"

"You could be injured. We all were damned near killed."

"Yes, and you saved us, Commander. It would be a pity to fire you after such heroism." The smile made the old man's eyes twinkle.

Dan had no response to that.

"Commander," Bianco said kindly. "Dan—may I call you that?"

"Yes, of course."

"*Bene.* Dan, look at me. You never knew me back on Earth, but observe me now." Bianco gripped the sides of the doorway and drew himself up to his full height, almost.

"A week ago I was a tired, sick old man. I was dying on Earth. Now I feel strong, I feel almost healthy! I have not taken any medication since my first day here. Weightlessness agrees with me."

Dan grudgingly admitted. "It certainly seems to."

"It does. Ask your Dr. Renoir; she is astounded at how my blood pressure has gone down."

"I know," Dan said. "So has mine."

"Do not send me back to Earth, Dan," the old man said, his voice suddenly low, almost pleading. "Do not send me back to die. Let me live up here."

Dan huffed out an exasperated sigh. "Now I know how you got to be Trikon's CEO."

Bianco beamed at him. "*Mille grazie, comman-dante.*"

The old man bobbed up and down in the doorway, happy and perky as a pup. Maybe he's right, Dan said to himself. Maybe living in micro-gee will keep him healthy. Both of us. One thing's for sure, he'd fire my ass in a hot second if I sent him back. No question about that.

Bianco had turned to leave the command module, but as Dan started to slide out of his office, the old man spun in midair.

"About Dr. Renoir," he said to Dan.

"What about her?"

"Do you love her?"

Dan felt a jolt of electricity in his gut. He froze his emotions, clamped his jaw tight.

"Ah, you do, I can see it. Good. She is in love with you, very much. I think you two should get married."

He sailed for the hatch to the connecting tunnel, leaving Dan hanging in midair. The crewmen at the command console grinned to one another, but carefully kept their commander from seeing it.

"I have failed you."

Bianco looked into the dark, unfathomable eyes of Hisashi Oyamo. The Japanese biologist had asked for a private meeting before he left the station. The two men stood close enough almost to touch noses inside Bianco's cramped sleep compartment. Bianco's slippered feet were firmly tethered in floor loops. Oyamo hovered before him. Both men hung in the slightly crouched question-mark posture of microgravity.

"Failed me?" Bianco asked softly. "In what way?"

Oyamo took in a deep hissing breath, as if a knife wound was paining him. "I have not put the interests of Trikon International foremost in my work. I have thought as a Japanese rather than as a member of the human race at large, as you have wished us to do."

"It is not merely my wish," Bianco said, his voice low but firm as bedrock. "It is necessary. For the salvation of Japan. For the salvation of all."

Oyamo bowed his head, eyes closed. "I have shamed myself."

"No, no," said Bianco. He was tempted to reach out and grasp the man's shoulder, but refrained, not knowing how a Japanese would react to an Italian gesture of friendliness.

"The whale deaths showed me the truth of it. And then what has happened here on the station proved it. By seeking individual gain we have nearly destroyed everything."

"It is not too late to change," Bianco said. "Not too late to begin anew."

Oyamo made no reply. His eyes remained shut.

"Will you be willing to return to this station once it is ready for operation again?"

His eyes snapped open. "You would want me to return?"

"If you can work for the good of all."

Oyamo bowed deeply. "Yes! That is my deepest desire."

"Your employers in Tokyo . . ."

"They could not refuse a direct request from your illustrious self?"

Bianco nodded gently. "Perhaps we truly can bring together a team of men and women who understand the realities of the world. Perhaps we can make a new beginning."

"I would be honored to have your trust," said Oyamo.

Bianco gazed deeply into his eyes once again and saw that they were no longer guarded, no longer unfathomable. Oyamo was begging for forgiveness, and a new chance to prove himself.

"You have my trust," he said. And he clasped both Oyamo's shoulders. The Japanese biologist radiated gratitude.

"It was among the pile of messages waiting for me when the comm blackout was lifted," said Lorraine Renoir.

Thora Skillen fought down the wave of bewilderment, almost giddiness, that surged through her. When the doctor had called her to the infirmary she had thought it was to tell her the results of her tests the previous week. But Lorraine's news was totally unexpected, shattering.

Keeping her voice as flat and unemotional as she could, she asked, "Human trials, you say."

"Yes," Lorraine replied, smiling happily. "Human trials."

"With what success rate?"

"Better than eighty percent." Dr. Renoir glanced at her desktop computer screen. "Eighty-two, to be precise."

Skillen took a deep breath. So much had happened

in the past few days. And now this. Her world was threatening to tumble topsy-turvy. Everything would be changed if . . .

"It's real, Thora. The Tufts University School of Medicine is one of the most respected in the world."

"It repairs the CFTR defect."

"In eighty-two percent of the patients tried so far." Another glance at the computer screen. "A total of forty-seven men, women, and children."

Skillen heard someone giggle, and realized it was herself. Lorraine was smiling broadly at her.

"They can correct the cellular defect that causes cystic fibrosis," the doctor repeated. "You can be cured, Thora."

It was impossibly ironic. "Through genetic engineering."

"Yes, healthy CFTR genes can be inserted into you to replace the defective ones that cause the disease."

Skillen laughed out loud. It was so *funny!* Dr. Renoir's expression went from happiness to amusement to troubled, doubting worry.

"Don't be afraid," Skillen said, struggling to control herself. "I'm not going to be hysterical. It's just that . . ." She stopped. What could she say? How could she tell someone who was not a sister?

"I know," Lorraine said kindly. "It's rather overwhelming. It means an entire new life for you, doesn't it?"

"More than you know," Skillen said. "Much more than you know."

She thanked Dr. Renoir and pushed out of the infirmary as quickly as she decently could. The irony of it! The wild, crazy, delicious mixed-up convoluted incongruity of it! A molecular geneticist dying of a genetic disease whose only thought for the past two years has been to punish the rest of the world finds out that other molecular geneticists have learned how to cure her.

Skillen laughed openly as she swam back toward The Bakery. Repair-crew personnel and technicians stared at her as she floated down the tunnel past them. She could not care less.

Here I've been telling myself that science and technology have been at fault, that it's *their* fault I came down with cystic fibrosis, and all the while it's my own scientific discipline that's been working to save me. Wait till my sisters hear this!

Bianco was smiling happily as he pushed along the tunnel past ELM and The Bakery, heading for Hab 2. If Oyamo could see past his nationality and work for the ultimate good, then he had no doubt that a new team of scientists and technicians could be assembled that would grasp the necessity of cooperation rather than competition. We can learn from our mistakes, he told himself. We can do better next time.

Thora Skillen swam by him, heading in the opposite direction, beaming happily. A thread of memory tickled Bianco's consciousness. But all he could remember was the sight of a waitress from a Venice café from fifty years ago. It must be the drug that was in the air, he thought. It is still playing tricks with my mind.

The lab modules he passed were chaotic messes of smashed equipment and spattered chemicals. The repair crews were working hard, but it would take time before Trikon Station was ready to function again. Bianco's face hardened. His hands clenched into fists.

A Trikon security guard hovered in the corridor of Hab 2, looking slightly green around the gills. His first time in weightlessness, Bianco understood. I wonder if he would be worth anything if it came to a fight.

The guard made a curt nod of recognition as Bianco sailed past him. No matter, the old man thought. There is no fight left in Ramsanjawi, and Muncie is safely wrapped up in the *Constellation*.

He knocked once at Ramsanjawi's door and slid it open. A little gasp of surprise puffed from his lips.

Ramsanjawi hovered up near the compartment's ceiling, hands folded placidly over his middle, his laptop computer floating in front of him, tethered by a single bungee cord.

The Indian was in a royal-blue flight suit. His dark hair, neatly tucked into a mesh net, sparkled as if freshly washed. Gone were the *kurta* and the cloying perfume.

"So you were in disguise all along," Bianco said. Pushing into the compartment, he added, "Or is this your disguise?"

Ramsanjawi pushed gently down to the floor. "I have said all that I intend to say, sir, until I have benefit of counsel."

"Yes, I know. We will respect your rights as a British subject," said Bianco.

"Of course. Not even Trikon Station is above the law." A hint of a smirk twitched at the corners of Ramsanjawi's fleshy face.

Bianco stared into his deep-brown eyes. He saw fear there: the inescapable fear of a man who knew that his fate was forever sealed.

"Before you recovered from the effects of the drug you put into the station's air system . . ."

"Lethe," said Ramsanjawi softly. "I created it myself, you know."

"Yes." Bianco nodded. "I have learned much about you in the past day and a half."

The Indian looked almost pleased with himself.

"While you were still under the drug's influence," Bianco went on, "you loudly proclaimed that you were under the protection of Sir Derek Brock-Smythe."

"Did I? How foolish."

"You deny the truth of your own statement?"

"Certainly."

Bianco rubbed his chin for a moment. "If anyone is above the law, it would be a personage as lofty as Sir Derek, would it not?"

"Perhaps." Ramsanjawi tried to keep his face expressionless, and failed. Bianco saw contempt, anger, and the barest hint of hope there.

"However, I fail to see," the Italian went on, "why a man of Sir Derek's stature would want to involve himself in protecting you. He did not protect you when you were fired from Oxford, did he?"

Ramsanjawi's nostrils flared angrily. "He could not make any money out of that fiasco."

"But out of *this* fiasco . . . ?"

"He is a major owner of several companies that would profit enormously from a toxic-waste bioremediation microbe."

"Ah. I see," said Bianco.

"I have told you nothing that you could not find out from the newspapers," Ramsanjawi said.

"I am not a legal expert," said Bianco. "Nor am I a detective. But I will use the best lawyers and detectives on Earth to determine what role Sir Derek Brock-Smythe has played in the attempted destruction of Trikon Station. I promise you that."

Ramsanjawi gave the old man a pitying smile. "What good would that do, except to satisfy your curiosity? Sir Derek will never leave enough evidence to bring him to court, let alone convict him."

"I do not need a court of law," Bianco said, his voice as thin and sharp as a stiletto.

Ramsanjawi blinked once, twice. Then he understood. And he had no reply.

17 OCTOBER 1998
CORONA DEL MAR,
CALIFORNIA

"Hello, Dad?"

"Bill? Is it really you?"

"Yeah. How are you?"

"Where are you calling from, son?"

"From school. I transferred to Wichita State."

"Oh . . . It's good to hear your voice, son."

"Are you okay? I mean, we heard about the trouble on the station. It was on all the news shows."

"Sure, everything's okay here. We're getting things patched up. Why'd you transfer? What happened . . ."

"I'm not cut out for liberal arts, Dad. They've got a good engineering school here at Wichita."

"Engineering? What kind?"

"Aerospace."

[Silence for four seconds.]

"Uh, Dad . . . I got kind of worried about you."

"I'm all right."

"Are you coming back down to Earth?"

"Not for a while. I'd sure like it if you could come up here, once we've got everything shipshape again."

"You would?"

"Sure."

"For real?"

"Certainly, Bill."

[Uncertain sound, possibly laughter.] "I told Mom you would. She claimed you didn't want to have *anything to do with me."*

"Didn't want . . . ! Hell, I wanted you to come up on the space plane two weeks ago. But I guess it's a good thing that you didn't. Things got kind of hairy up here for a while."

"But it's all okay now, isn't it?"

"Yep. Everything's fine now."

"Uh, Dad, is it okay if I call you again?"

"Sure! Certainly. I'd like to call you . . ."

"Well, Mom gets kind of upset when you call, you know. That's why I waited until I got to campus."

"I see."

"She gets all wound up."

"I do want to see you, son. Whether it's up here or back on Earth."

"I'd sure get a blast out of coming up there!"

"Okay, we'll try to work something out for you."

"Great!"

"I'll call you in a day or two."

"Okay. Make it around this time in the afternoon. I'm usually in the dorm then."

"I want you to tell your mother, Bill. It's not a good thing to keep secrets from her."

"Sure, okay. I'm learning how to handle her—I think. So long for now, Dad."

"So long for now, son."

—Transcript of telephone conversation,
   William R. Tighe (Wichita, Kansas) to Cmdr. D.
   Tighe (Trikon Station), 11 September 1998.

HUGH O'DONNELL STARED at the foaming water of the Jacuzzi. He had always had wiry, marathon runner's legs, but after six weeks in a hip cast his right leg was toothpick thin. And hairless. From the waist down he looked like two different people. That's why he enjoyed the Jacuzzi: he didn't have to see that damn leg.

The synthesized tone of the videophone sliced through the humid air. The apartment may have been equipped with this fancy bathroom/spa, but its only telephone was located in the living room. The rings mounted, five, six, seven times. No one else wanted to answer. Hugh swung out of the water, knotted his bathrobe around his waist, and hobbled into the living room on his cane.

His leg was still too stiff to bend comfortably unless it was immersed in warm water, so he leaned on the back of the sofa and shouted the phone's answering code. The faces of Dan and Lorraine appeared on the monitor; him grinning, her smiling radiantly.

"How are you, buddy?" Dan asked.

"Hobbling along. I sure miss microgravity, with this leg. How's everything up there?"

"Hobbling along," Lorraine answered.

Dan cast a disapproving glance at her. "Repairs are on schedule. We'll be open for business again in three weeks."

"Great."

"It helps to have Bianco here," Dan added. "It's funny: he doesn't push anybody, but somehow things seem to be getting done much faster with him watching."

"He's an inspirational force," said Lorraine.

"I'll bet," Hugh said.

"How is your leg?" Lorraine asked. "Is the therapy proceeding satisfactorily?"

"Yeah, I guess. Slow but steady, you know."

"You ought to come back up here," Dan said. "It would be good for you."

Hugh nodded, knowing that it was impossible. Changing the subject, he said, "I hear congratulations are in order."

Lorraine looked surprised. Dan tried to look noncommittal.

Hugh grinned at them. "Come on, the rumor's all over the tabloids. 'Space station commander and medical officer to marry.'"

Lorraine broke into a hugh smile. "Dan told me what I said under the influence of the Lethe. He asked if I wanted to retract any of it. I said no."

"Tighe, you're a true romantic," said Hugh.

"Ramsanjawi would be surprised to learn he's a matchmaker, huh?" said Dan. "Is your leg really coming along okay? Is there anything we can do?"

"I'll miss the next Olympics," said High. Out of the corner of his eye he saw clothes being tossed into a suitcase on his bed. "You guys are okay up there?"

"The lab modules are still a mess," said Dan. "Otherwise, we're operational."

He continued as if issuing a report to the Joint Chiefs of Staff. The Mars module had fared the best because it had separated early and somehow had avoided a collision as the station cartwheeled across the sky. Half of the Martians had resigned from the project. NASA and ESA were requiring the rest to recertify, including Jaeckle. Although his demented separation order had saved the multibillion-dollar module from severe damage, neither agency was treating him as a hero.

Fabio Bianco, that old coot, was busily selecting a new contingent of scientists and preaching that the entire incident was an object lesson on the need for international cooperation.

Hugh listened absently to Dan's account. His time in the station seemed part of a distant past, a dream that reverberated in the deepest chambers of his mind whenever he dropped off to sleep. And these two people, his only friends since he had ceased existing as Jack O'Neill, were now images on a screen.

But there was one memory that prodded him daily. He remembered waking up in the ex/rec area, floating among the debris and damaged equipment. His shat-

tered leg throbbing red-hot inside his EMU, sending
up blinding waves of pain. Dan and Lorraine swam
out of the shadows. They pried him out of his suit and
fashioned a splint for his leg. Later, at the sick bay,
Lorraine offered him a painkiller.

"No drugs," he had said, and slipped back into the
darkness. She had honored his request.

Dan stopped talking, and Hugh realized that they
were staring at him. He shifted his weight on the cane.
From the bedroom came the sound of heavy luggage
being slammed shut.

"Company?" Dan asked, arching his eyebrows.

Welch stepped out of the bedroom and peered at
Hugh over the tops of his sunglasses. Freddy Aviles,
walking rockily on prosthetic legs, passed behind him.
Both men carefully stayed out of range of the
videophone's lens. Welch pointed at the screen and
drew his finger across his neck.

"Sort of," said Hugh. "I've got to go now."

"Come up and see us," Lorraine said.

"Right," Dan agreed. "Whenever you can. Just let
me know and I'll set up the transportation for you."

"Thanks," said Hugh, feeling awkward, under sur-
veillance. "I'll try."

"Move your ass," said Welch as soon as Hugh cut
the phone connection. "Plane leaves in an hour."

Hugh started for the bedroom, leaning heavily on
his cane. The damned leg hurt like hellfire.

His eye caught Freddy's. He saw sympathy there. A
shared pain.

"I'm not going on the plane," Hugh heard himself
say to Welch.

"What?"

"I'm not going with you. I'm going back to Trikon
Station."

Welch's face looked like a smoldering volcano.
"What do you think . . ."

"I'll finish the job aboard Trikon," Hugh said,

feeling stronger with each word. "Otherwise no deal."

"I'll have you in the slammer so fast your god-damned ass'll be singed!"

"Hey, wait up a minute, Mr. Welch." Freddy's gold tooth glimmered in his smile.

Pointing a finger, Welch said, "You keep out of this, Aviles."

Ignoring the order, Freddy said, "You want O'Donnell to finish the cocaine project, right? O'Donnell wants to finish it. What're you arguin' about? What difference does it make where he finishes, huh?"

"It makes a difference to me," Hugh said, tapping his right thigh. "I finish the project in micro-gee or you find yourself another boy, Welch."

Welch started to reply, but Hugh added, "And Freddy comes with me."

Freddy's smile dazzled. He turned to Welch. "An' you can have these tin legs back. Give 'em to somebody who really needs 'em."

Welch growled at the two of them. But he did not say no.

BRITISH LORD MURDERED

BATH—Sir Derek Brock-Smythe, outspoken former foreign minister and well-known philanthropist, was found murdered in his Avonshire home this morning. According to police, he had been shot to death sometime Friday night, but the body was not discovered earlier because he had dismissed his servants for the weekend.

Police stated that his unclothed body was found in bed, wrists and ankles tied to the bedposts with a woman's nylon stockings. He died of a gunshot wound to the head. Apparently the pistol was held in his mouth when the trigger was pulled.

"It's a grisly sight," said Inspector Carlin Mayes. "Some sort of sexual thing gone wrong, undoubtedly."

Police are questioning the household servants and known friends of Sir Derek's.

Ms. Joanna Ames, a frequent houseguest, revealed that he had "unusual" sexual tastes. "It might have been some game he was playing with someone that simply went too far," she said.

Sir Derek had been a member of Parliament since 1976 and served as foreign minister from 1990 to 1994, when he resigned over the government's decision to quit the European Community.

After his resignation he devoted most of his time to philanthropic and scientific pursuits. He founded and financed the Sir Walter Brock Laboratory in Lancashire in the hope of attracting "the flower of British science to forge a technology worthy of the coming millennium."

Sir Derek's adoptive brother, Dr. Chakra Ramsanjawi, is currently in a Zurich prison awaiting trial on charges of criminal conspiracy and theft brought by Trikon International Corp. and Ciba-Geigy A.G. He is also fighting extradition to the United States, where he has been indicted on drug and assault charges stemming from the recent Trikon space station incident.

When asked if there might be any relationship between Dr. Ramsanjawi's arrest and Sir Derek's murder, Ms. Ames replied, "I simply don't know. That's something the police will have to consider."

Ms. Ames, who was in London for the weekend, said the news of Sir Derek's murder reached her just before she left for Italy. She is taking sabbatical leave from her faculty position at Oxford to spend a year teaching in Venice on a Trikon International fellowship.

—*The London Express,* 2 November 1998

FIRST WEDDING IN SPACE

HOUSTON (AP)—Commander Daniel Tighe and Dr. Lorraine Renoir were married yesterday aboard the space shuttle Constellation while it was docked to the Trikon Station in orbit 300 miles above the Earth. It was the first wedding ever performed in space.

N.J. Williamson, commander of Constellation, officiated. The groom is the commander and the bride is the medical officer of Trikon Station, a commercial and industrial space station owned and operated by the Trikon International consortium.

Best man was Dr. Hugh O'Donnell; the bridegroom's son, William Tighe, served as usher. Maid of honor was Dr. Thora Skillen, former head of the Trikon/North American research group aboard the station.

The station was severely damaged three months ago when a crewman suffering from a delusional illness known as Orbital Dementia seized control of the command module and fired a series of thruster bursts that sent the station into a spin.

Though the station was crippled and virtually without electrical power, Cmdr. Tighe single-handedly reoriented the station and maintained life support until help arrived.

Cmdr. Tighe and Dr. Renoir, who will retain her maiden name, intend to remain on the station to supervise the repair work.

Fabio Bianco, founder and CEO of Trikon Interna-

tional, who is now living permanently aboard the orbital station, gave the bride away.

"This day marks a new beginning for Trikon and for the human race," Bianco told reporters via videophone. "Our program to create a microorganism that will eliminate toxic wastes has restarted and I expect success within six months to a year."

Bianco added, "We will save the whales that now face extinction. And we will save the human race, as well."

—The Hartford Courant, 7 December 1998